Love. Ambition. Conflict. Success. The struggle to be her own person.

These are the exciting themes that terrific new contemporary writer Merla Zellerbach explores in

## THE WILDES OF NOB HILL

Lauren Wilde is rich beyond anyone's imagination, but she wants more. Her journey from wealthy dilettante to a woman of the world is a fascinating story that will delight readers from coast to coast.

# THE WILDES OF NOB HILL

## Merla Zellerbach

BALLANTINE BOOKS • NEW YORK

All rights reserved under International and Pan-American Copyright Con-
ventions. Published in the United States of America by Ballantine Books,
a division of Random House, Inc., New York, and simultaneously in
Canada by Random House of Canada Limited, Toronto.

Library of Congress Catalog Card Number: 86-90927

ISBN 0-345-33279-2

Printed in Canada

First Edition: October 1986

# CHAPTER
# 1

THE RAIN SHOWED NO MERCY. MARCH OF 1985 HAD COME in growling and roaring, and looked to be going out that way, too. The lion had devoured the proverbial lamb for breakfast and chewed its bones for dinner.

Out her window and across the street, Lauren could see the sprawling gray-rock structure of the Nob Hill Plaza Hotel. Like an overgrown southern plantation, it sat solidly, regally, behind an arched entrance supported by heavy stone pillars. Rain, fog, or sunshine, Everett the doorman stood watch, resplendent in his scarlet uniform with shiny gold buttons and a bronze-rimmed topper.

Gilt and luxury were no strangers to Lauren Wilde. Everything about her bespoke money, taste, elegance—well reflected in the decor of her dazzling penthouse apartment. The pictures in last month's *Architectural Digest* had hardly done it justice, for they could only capture sections—not the dramatic effect of the whole. A high front door of dark-carved mahogany and polished brass trim opened onto a vast living room where mirrored walls served as backdrop to lush Scalamandre draperies harmonizing with travertine marble floors. In one corner, sliding glass doors led to an open terrace looking out over all of San Francisco. The view was enhanced by a pair of Chinese jardinieres bearing azaleas, alternating with hundred-year-old potted bonsai trees.

Inside, pink, red, and violet arrangements of anemones sparkled in Steuben crystal vases, one on a table between the soft white leather McGuire chairs, the second on a stand beside an intricately carved Coromandel screen. A third graced the Mason & Chandler grand piano used by Luisa Tetrazzini's voice teacher. Equally historic was the six-foot tortoiseshell bird cage with jade interior, designed in China for William Randolph Hearst and bought at an auction from his San Simeon estate. The stunning effect was exactly what the decorator ordered, and Lauren loved its brazen opulence. Who wouldn't?

A flick of the remote switch darkened the television screen. She glanced at her watch; ten past eleven at the close of another in the round of empty days that comprised her life. How had she passed the hours? Where had they gone?

The nonevents replayed themselves in her mind. Shortly before eight, she had awakened, grabbed a prune Danish and cup of coffee, and phoned her mother. Edna Wilde expected the daily call and cherished a close relationship with her only daughter. Much as she enjoyed son Christopher, his nonconforming conformist wife, Zelda, and their spunky toddler, Mallory, Lauren was her emotional mainstay, her source of joy, and—because she had yet to show any interest in the marriage and "respectability" her mother craved for her—a major frustration. But Edna was both persistent and determined, and never lacked plans for Lauren's future.

The conversation had been short. Edna was giving a dinner party two weeks hence and wanted to be sure that Lauren, a lively and decorative asset, would attend. Her daughter was welcome to bring someone, providing that someone "fitted in"—a euphemism designed to exclude the unscrubbed literati she occasionally dated.

No argument. Lauren had long since given up trying to make Edna appreciate her friends. She would either drag some social-registered dullard who worked at a bank, or come alone—probably the latter, as she was increasingly disinclined to spend even a few hours with the kind of man her parents deemed acceptable.

A ten o'clock meeting at Missy Edwards's house to help plan the Cancer Society Gala had been boring and predictable, saved only by the warmth and wit of the hostess. Missy, so called because she hailed from Mississippi and hated her given name, Loretta, was the city's favorite party-giver and Lauren's good friend. Any charity event with Missy's unmistakable trademarks—invitations full of sparkles that made a mess when you opened them, a high-priced tariff, and an impressive list of patrons headed by an "Honorary Chairman," who enjoyed the glory without the work—was a preordained success. But oh, that meeting had been interminable. . . .

"The hotel is offering us three dinner menus," Missy had explained, passing out pens and notepads. "We can feast on veal for fifty-two dollars, dine on roast beef for fifty, or gobble turkey for forty-eight."

"Let's gobble," said a blonde in pink Bill Blass. "We want to raise money for cancer research, don't we?"

"My friends aren't paying two hundred and fifty bucks a head to eat turkey," growled a husky-voiced redhead, a cigarette bobbing between her lips. "With veal, at least they'll feel they're getting *something* for their money."

"Why not compromise on the beef?" asked a third voice.

"Who gives a damn?" sniped a fourth. "Once we've got their money, we can feed 'em chili dogs."

Missy smiled benignly. "I'm glad you all agree with me that we shouldn't stint on the food, so I've ordered the veal." Before anyone could protest, she announced, "Now I need one of you to take charge of decorations." Silence fell over the room, then Missy's eyes lighted on a young woman who hadn't moved an eyelash. "Sally, bless you for volunteering. Now tell me exactly whom you want on your committee. . . ."

Fortunately, Lauren had not been "volunteered" and was able to flee the meeting early, promising to fill a table for ten. Modeling at a benefit for the Pacific Presbyterian Medical Center took her through the lunch hour, and then, since the fashion show had taken place at the Nob Hill Plaza, she stopped by to see Victor.

Fine thing, she thought, smiling to herself. Here she was, twenty-nine years old, living on a generous income from a

trust fund, reasonably bright, a tall, willowy, long-haired
blonde with shapely legs, large blue eyes, and what *W* magazine called the "perfect Golden Girl face"—and the most
exciting man in her life was still Daddy.

It was hard to fault Lauren's judgment where her father was
concerned, for Victor Benedict Wilde was indeed an extraordinary man. Born in Berkshire, England, in 1918, he spent
his earliest years as an overprotected only child in a prosper-
ous working-class family. His father had started out as gardener and caretaker to a duchess; his mother repaired and
altered dresses.

When their employer died in 1929, the titled lady left one
of her country homes to Robert Wilde, who had so lovingly
tended its acreage. The Wildes lacked the means to live in the
lavish dwelling and sold it back to the duchess's family for
the equivalent of ninety-five thousand U.S. dollars—a tiny
fraction of her estate, but, to the young gardener and his wife,
an unbelievable fortune.

They crossed the Atlantic on a freighter and made their way
from east to west by train, destination California. Martha
Wilde had often dreamed of a cozy cottage by the beach; she
settled for a large white stucco mansion in San Francisco's
posh Pacific Heights. The view of the bay was clean and expansive, and Martha was ecstatic; their window in Berkshire
had looked out on two garbage cans and a patch of weeds.

A phlegmatic, hardworking woman, Martha doted on
twelve-year-old Victor and joyfully watched him blossom into
a sturdy, energetic youth with a knack for making friends.
Her sole goal was to make him "a gentleman," with manners
and mannerisms reflecting the old-world notions of gentility
that she had observed in her employers. Every aspect of his
growth and development was orchestrated as carefully as a
symphony score, with round-the-clock rehearsals for adult-
hood. Using the wrong fork at dinner, wearing black socks
with navy knickers, and muttering, "Oh, crud!" when his
goldfish died were all occasions for sound scoldings.

Taking advantage of their new riches, Martha sent Victor
to a private military academy in Marin County, across the
Golden Gate Bridge, where he boarded Monday through Fri-

day, learning toughness and discipline along with his studies. On weekends, his mother filled his free hours with French and piano lessons and Saturday-night classes in ballroom dancing.

In the early thirties, while Victor was box-stepping into his teens, his father was busily buying up Depression-priced land and property. To Martha's chagrin, he invested all their inheritance in real estate. Savings accounts had no growth potential, he insisted, and the stock market was still rocky. Dresses, jewelry, and roaming the globe, he promised, would come later.

Gradually, Robert Wilde began to become a force in the community, involving himself in worthy causes, gaining financial acumen and the first signs of sophistication. Unlike many who acquire sudden wealth, he never denied his background or lack of formal schooling, had no pretensions, and generally viewed life as an overgrown game of Monopoly. People liked the amiable Wilde. He was solid, macho without flaunting it, and often bubbled forth with unexpected wit. Snobbery was unknown to him, and it was with surprise and some embarrassment that the Wildes found themselves slowly but relentlessly being pushed up the social ladder.

About that time, and without consulting Martha, who would never have approved, Robert Wilde plunged into a business deal he could not refuse. Mortgaging all his property and taking a huge bank loan, he acquired the beautiful but ailing Nob Hill Plaza Hotel. Rising costs had caused a continual decline of business, and lackluster management had all but bankrupted its previous owners.

Determined to turn the hotel into the kind of plush, aristocratic hostelry he had seen in Europe, Wilde began a series of "daring" improvements. Hoping to enhance the quiet dignity of the lobby, he replaced its windows with stained-glass insets and, at outrageous cost, shipped two white marble pillars from Italy, topped them with gold-and-crystal candelabra, and installed them on either side of the reception desk. The center of the lobby featured a pink marble table with elaborate carved legs, and an extravagant floral centerpiece that was changed daily.

The Nob Hill Plaza began to flourish, and so did its owner. By the time Victor reached college, Robert Wilde had paid off all debts and achieved the heady nickname King of Nob Hill. Lung cancer claimed the sixty-year-old monarch in 1949; the title fell to his only son.

At age thirty-one, Victor proved to be all his father was and more. Standing six feet tall with massive arms and shoulders, he was not Cary Grant handsome, but he had a full head of curly brown hair and bright hazel eyes that sparkled with energy. His chin was strong, his manner determined, and one almost expected fire to flare from his overwide nostrils. Everything about him bespoke masculinity, vitality, intensity.

Having earned a degree in business administration, and having worked as hotel manager for ten years, he was familiar with all aspects of the operation. He and his father, however, had often clashed.

"That lobby looks like the setting for an undertakers' convention," Victor had growled in one of their last conversations. "You can't imagine the business we lose simply because people poke their heads in the door and get depressed."

"Balderdash and tommyrot! My generation appreciates our keeping the traditional understatement of the lobby, and your generation needs some reminder that there's more to the world than Frank Sinatra."

- "Foreigners already know that," Victor had argued, "and they're fifty percent of our business. All they see is a reception area that looks like a cemetery."

Robert Wilde had been just as adamant. "We've spent enough on this hotel. It's time to diversify. Money is like manure. You've got to—"

"Spread it around before it does any good." Victor sighed. "And you're right; every dollar we spend here, on our *own* soil, will come back to us tenfold in a year or two."

The Monopoly game was at an impasse, and Robert Wilde was not about to surrender his hotel to his son. No sooner did Victor come into his inheritance, however, than he began to order extensive changes. "Understatement" was not a word in his vocabulary. The Nob Hill Plaza was *not* going to be everybody's favorite secret. A high-priced advertising agency took over promotion. Dinner invitations went out to travel, society, and entertainment editors. Full-page ads began appearing in national magazines and newspapers.

Losing no time, Victor converted the stodgy old oak bar into a bright, colorful carousel with wooden horses for stools, waiters and waitresses dressed as clowns, and a nightly Happy Hour featuring free hors d'oeuvres and half-priced drinks. Another cocktail area became a lively Mexican cantina with tacos cart and strolling mariachis. An old unused swimming pool was soon surrounded by tables and tropical palms. Three musicians learned to balance their instruments on a floating raft while an ingenious shower mechanism produced hourly "rainstorms" over the water.

Giving in to a longtime dream, Victor transformed the main dining area into the Orchid Room, a lavish supper club with twenty-five-foot-high ceilings and a capacity of 450. Edith Piaf opened with a five-day run, followed by Sophie Tucker, the Mills Brothers, Nat King Cole, Ella Fitzgerald, Rosemary Clooney, and a parade of big-name entertainers.

Important people demanded important quarters. A team of architects and engineers replaced the oldest wing of the building with a modern twenty-four-story annex containing two- and three-room suites with every imaginable luxury—and rates to match. Outside, a glass-enclosed elevator resembling a giant thermometer sped leery but fascinated guests to an elaborate dining area atop The Tower, as it was soon christened. Floor-to-ceiling windows looked out over the Bay Bridge, Golden Gate Bridge, Alcatraz, and half the city. Nothing would do for Le Ciel, "San Francisco's Premier French Restaurant," but to import the master chef of Parisian cuisine, Louis Genaux, to train the staff and make media appearances before returning to his four-star kitchen.

Back in the lobby, changes were happening everywhere. Out went the drab gray rugs in the entrance hall. In their place blazed a vivid red-and-black floral print—loud but striking. Down came the dim lighting fixtures that for so many years had flickered above patrons' heads in a ghostly imitation of gaslight. Up went crystal chandeliers that branched out like jeweled crowns. Faded lavender silk curtains gave way to red velvet draperies, while cozy groupings of plush settees replaced the stiff armchairs.

Enter Edna Washington, twenty-six years wise, blond, round-faced, not beautiful but pretty and appealing. Flawless skin, perfect teeth, a ready smile, and wide brown eyes that twinkled with gaiety gave her the appearance of a teenager. Her looks at first deceived Victor; how could she work for his decorator when she obviously belonged on a football field waving pompoms? Miss Washington, he soon found out, had degrees in design and art history and was highly qualified. Her job was to seek out appropriate paintings and sculpture to enhance the new decor.

Distrustful, Victor would sometimes accompany the determined young lady to a local gallery or loft to see the works she recommended. He never liked any of them.

"That stuff's too highbrow," was his inevitable reaction. "If I don't understand it, I can't expect others to like it. I know the lobby is garish and rococo, but that's what it is. I don't want bent clocks and flying eyeballs. Get me some pink-skinned nudes dancing around a fountain, or some fat little cherubs. When it comes to art, I'd rather have whorehouse than Bauhaus."

Stung, Edna would retreat for a few days, swallow the hurt and frustration, then try again. Her job, after all, was to please him. But her good name, unknown as it was at the time, would forever be associated with the hotel, and it was not a credit she wanted to cringe about. There had to be a way to compromise.

Without thinking of it in those terms—well, not exactly— Edna decided to use her greatest asset: charm. In times when women "didn't do that sort of thing," she called Victor one morning from her temporary office at the hotel, said she had acquired theater tickets for the following night, and asked if he would care to join her. He politely declined. All his life, there had been women around when he wanted them. He had never had time for the silliness of dating and was not about to start.

Besides, he had a genuine excuse, for he was dining with his mother that evening. When he called to check with her on plans, Mrs. Wilde did something she had never done before; she asked him if he would like to bring someone. "Bring someone?" he repeated, nonplussed. "You mean—a date?"

"That's exactly what I mean," said Martha Wilde. "You're far too wrapped up in that hotel. You're a young, healthy man, and it's time you started seeing some young, healthy women.''

''You want young, healthy grandchildren?'' he asked, laughing.

''I don't give a hoot in hell about grandchildren, Victor. All I care about is you. And it's time you started to enjoy some of the things your father worked so hard to provide for you.''

''I wouldn't know where to look for a date,'' he said, honestly puzzled. ''There's a cute waitress in the Circus Bar, but she chews gum like a pregnant cow. Great legs on the hatcheck girl, but she'd probably go home with your silver. Uh-oh, wait a minute, Mom—I just may know someone. . . .''

Edna Washington was shocked to get a call from Victor on the afternoon of the same day he had so coolly declined her invitation. Certain that she had alienated him by being so forward, she was in the midst of drafting a memo to her employer asking to be put on another job.

''Look here,'' Victor said on the phone. ''I know you have theater tickets, but if you'll give them away this time, I promise to make it up to you another time.''

In the stunned silence that followed, he added, ''I'll be honest with you, Miss Washington. May I call you . . . er . . .''

''Edna. Yes.''

''I'll be honest with you, Edna. I don't go out much, and my mother worries. Even at my advanced age. So if you'd do me the honor of accompanying me to dinner at her home tomorrow night, I think you'd relieve her mind about me, and I know you'd relieve my mind.''

''Your mind, Mr. Wilde?''

''Yes, and you'd better call me Victor in front of her. I mean . . . well, call me that anyway, not just in front of her. Miss Wash—Edna—I'm frankly very nervous about calling you.''

''Don't be, Victor,'' she said, suddenly brightening. ''I'd love to give away the theater tickets and go with you. It'll be delightful to see you away from the office and be able to talk as two human beings. How dressy should I be?''

''Oh, not terribly. Thank you, Edna. You're really a lifesaver. Mother is rather proper—old school, I guess—but I think you'll enjoy her wit and sense of humor. And I know she has your kind of taste in art.''

Don't touch *that* line, Edna's instincts told her. "If you must know, Victor, I'm pretty old school myself. I'm sure we'll get along."

"Fortunately, it's only one evening," he murmured, regretting it as soon as he said it.

Edna dashed down to I. Magnin the next day and spent half a week's salary on a high-necked, long-sleeved navy-blue dress with a prim white collar and bow; the evening, she thought, called for a special look. Her demeanor at dinner matched her dress: quiet, reserved, charming, and tasteful. Gone was the bouncy cheerleader, replaced by an almost priggish schoolmarm type, who was, in fact, a much more accurate reflection of Edna's true character.

Discreet questioning provided Martha Wilde with the answers she sought. Edna's parents owned a profitable hardware store in San Rafael, California, and they had been able to send both their daughters to college. The elder girl, Amy, lasted a year at the University of California at Berkeley. She was married now, with two babies.

Edna chose Stanford and finished with honors. First prize in a nationwide contest won her a graduate scholarship to the prestigious Art Academy of Cincinnati, where she learned graphic arts and other aspects of design. Knowing she would return to the Bay Area, one of her instructors wrote a letter of recommendation to a decorating firm in San Francisco. Edna was promptly hired and had worked three years for the company when the Nob Hill Plaza contract was signed. She liked her job—most aspects of it, anyway, she said, with nary a nod to Victor—and hoped, one day, to be able to open her own design shop.

Martha Wilde was enchanted. Edna was a no-nonsense girl who came from solid, hardworking middle-class stock like her, had a good family, a career she loved, and, to all appearances, high moral values. Martha's approval was genuine and complete, a feeling she lost no time communicating to her son.

Victor was delighted to have pleased his mother but somewhat taken aback by the machinery he had set in motion. What he needed was sex, not a relationship, and he suspected the straitlaced Miss Washington would not provide the former. Nevertheless, his mother was right. He had to assume some of his father's obligations to the community, had to start attending parties and testimonials and public events, and he needed a suitable companion.

The evening at Martha Wilde's home had made a tremendous impression on Edna. Back on her own pillow that night, she made her assessment quite methodically: Victor was a loyal, loving son, unusually patient and gentle with an overly possessive mother, and a much nicer person than she had imagined. Beneath the tough façade lay layers of kindness; he seemed to embody most of the qualities she wanted in a man. Money wasn't everything, but when it came wrapped in that kind of package, it was irresistible. This was the man she must have—and have him she did.

Two years later, patience and proximity—along with the fact that she maintained her maidenhood until after the ceremony—won fair gentleman. The wedding was a gala event planned by Victor, staged by Victor, paid for by Victor, and held in the dramatic Deauville Room of the Nob Hill Plaza Hotel.

Early married life was not easy for the loving but strong-willed duo. Edna wanted more say in refurbishing the hotel. Her tasteful color schemes and dramatic redecorating proposals, however, were almost always negated by a single spousal "No." Victor's word was final, ultimate, supreme. Edna had to accept his authority or risk a tempestuous marriage. With admirable restraint, she held her anger, simmered in silence, and occasionally tried to get around her husband with wiles, soon learning that Victor hated to be manipulated. The only way to approach him was openly, honestly, and with love. Then he would be fair—if it suited his purposes.

Nine pounds of Christopher came along in 1954, followed two years later by a sister, Lauren. The children changed everything. Edna no longer worried about the garishness of the lobby, the smell of disinfectant in the ladies' room, or the fact that paintings in the suites were expensive reproductions rather than moderately priced originals. The hotel staff was well paid to tend to such matters. She had better ways to spend her hours.

The children absorbed and exhausted Edna but gave her new purpose and direction. To her delight, Victor became an adoring, attentive father, never neglecting the hotel but delegating more, trusting his employees more, and, consequently, allotting more time for his family.

Martha Wilde lived to know her grandchildren only briefly. She died of a stroke shortly after Lauren's birth, leaving Victor the family home with all its treasures and furnishings. Edna was thrilled to move. The children needed a playroom, a garden, space to run around. Victor would have his father's handsome study with its solid oak walls, grand mahogany desk, and expansive view of the bay and the towering Golden Gate Bridge. Best of all, Edna at last has an outlet for the talents that had been forced underground since her marriage.

Because Victor knew that his wife had educated taste, even though it was not his taste—or what he deemed suitable for the hotel—he gave her carte blanche in their new home. She could keep or discard whatever she liked and utilize her skills to transform the long-neglected mansion into a stunning showplace.

That was exactly what she did. To her family's pride and occasional amusement, Edna finally gave vent to her repressed creativity. Redecorating the home became her permanent and ongoing project.

"Shhh. Don't announce me." Lauren touched finger to lip, smiled at the devoted red-haired—or, more accurately, red-wigged—Dora, then tiptoed into the executive suite. Secretly, Lauren agreed with her mother. The walls, papered with gold flocking, the purple velvet draperies, and the ornate Oriental carpets made the room seem more like a high-class brothel than an office. From the doorway, she watched Victor poring over papers at his desk. Her father's curly mass of hair, bushy eyebrows, full-jowled face, and slightly jutting chin showed a strong, uncompromising will, one she both rebelled against and respected.

Friends, employees, even daughters, were allowed to disagree with the sixty-seven-year-old patriarch. Though Victor Wilde held strong views on almost every subject, he could, albeit reluctantly, accept the fact that there were other opinions besides his own. What he could not accept were lies, false excuses, or broken promises. She had learned that as a child. Whenever he felt he had been used, double-crossed, or deceived, he became angry. Then his great wrath exploded, the earth rocked, the heavens trembled, and all who knew him got out of his path as fast as they could.

She stood a moment, staring silently as her father continued his paperwork, still unaware that she had entered the room. This great six-foot bear of a man—part grizzly, party teddy—intimidated so many people. He enjoyed having wealth and power, and relished presiding over what reporters called "the Nob Hill Cabinet"—a small, elite corps of businessmen who owned vast amounts of real estate, ruled parts of city government, made and unmade national politicians with a flick of their checkbooks.

Victor's generosity was as legendary as his influence. "Philanthropy" scarcely described the man who had never known hunger or poverty yet had grown up to give millions to projects for the needy, to colleges and scholarship funds, hospitals and medical research. Not a penny, however, went to organized religion, which he blamed for most of the world's strife.

Sensing a presence, he looked up. The brows unclenched as his eyes grew soft. "I was hoping you'd come by. How was the fashion show?"

Lauren's pupils rolled upward. "Borrrring. How'd you know about it?"

"My spies told me. I hear you wore some gold knit Fernando or something—"

"Adolfo."

"And stopped the show. Was it really that pretty? Would you like it?"

"Daddy," she laughed, coming around to kiss his forehead, "you're too much. That dress cost eight thousand dollars!"

"Well, would you like a sleeve?"

"Not even a button. But thanks for the thought. Do you realize how many Milky Way bars I could buy for that kind of money? Missy and Trina have to pay those prices: they're in the public eye. Maybe they rationalize. I can think of better ways to spend money."

"That's because anything you wear looks like a million dollars, baby." His smile faded into parental concern. "But you're much too thin. Have you had lunch?" Before she could reply, he lifted the phone. Moments later, two waiters wheeled in a table with a platter of shrimp Louis and a spun-sugar basket of petits fours. Brother Chris, a handsome young man with his father's wavy hair and steely jaw, was summoned to join their afternoon "tea."

"Well, if it ain't the princess," he greeted his sister, kissing her cheek. "What brings you all the way across the street?"

She kissed him back affectionately. "I needed the exercise."

"Oh, I know. You must've been in that fashion show. You don't usually run around with purple eyes and a half inch of makeup. Why don't you wash that crap off your face?"

He left himself open to the obvious retort that she didn't care to look like his wife, Zelda, whose pseudo-artsy-intellectual life-style allowed no time for such activities as applying lipstick or visiting a beauty shop. Kindness, however, prevailed. "Wash it off! The eyes are just the beginning. Wait'll you see my new pointy punk haircut."

"Great! Mallory can play horseshoes on your head."

The waiters finished fussing with the table and motioned her into a chair. Chris and Victor joined her. "How *is* your darling grandchild, Dad? Do you think he'll be toilet-trained before he goes off to college?"

Victor struggled for a straight face. He and Lauren had discussed Zelda's permissiveness and agreed that it was absurd to run around after a three-year-old with a mop. "Cut it out, kids. You're too old to fight anymore."

"Who's fighting?" Chris shrugged good-naturedly and ignored his sister's jab. Years of normal squabbling had brought them to a deep closeness and mutual affection. He turned to Lauren. "Why don't you bring one of your thrilling escorts to our opening Tuesday night?"

"Oh, I don't know. I'm so bored with my dumb life. I'm bored with people and parties and opening nights. And I'm bored with feeling guilty about being bored."

"You're talking nonsense," said Victor. "Ninety-nine percent of the world's inhabitants would trade places with you without a thought. I suppose we've spoiled you kids—"

"It's not that, Dad. I hear what she's saying. She just wants to do more with her life—maybe do something that would help others—or that would give her a goal and a sense of achievement."

"Exactly! I *know* how lucky I am. But it's not enough to be a decorative parasite—"

Victor's ears picked up danger signals. "Now don't fill your head with foolish notions, young lady. You do more than most with your charity benefits and your committee work. Why don't you bring Missy Edwards and some of the people who work so hard for the city to the show Tuesday night?"

The thought of seeing Missy made her brighten. "Who'll be there?"

"Count Basie's orchestra," said Chris. "First time with us since the Count died. Remember the last time he was in the Orchid Room? They brought him onstage in a wheelchair, and then lifted him to his seat at the piano. It was pathetic to watch, and he could barely play, but he's such a legend they kept giving him standing ovations. I think we'll get a crowd—"

"Your brother's doing a fine job with the Orchid Room," said Victor, his eyes shining. "I'm damn proud of him. Ever since he started booking entertainers last year, our attendance has been steadily increasing."

"Hear that, Chrissy-face?" Lauren helped herself to seconds of the shrimp Louis. "You can stop comping all your friends now. Speaking of which, maybe I *will* come. Can you squeeze in a table for six? Make it eight. I'll get Missy and Al, the Blairs, the Crockersons . . . and let's see. Who'll I dredge up for myself?"

Chris groaned. "Now there's a scintillating crowd. What do you see in those snobby broads?"

"Aside from Missy, whom I adore, zero. Zilch. But I owe them for a couple of parties, and this way I don't have to sit and talk to them all night. Besides, Lutie Blair and Claire Crockerson are good copy. They'll give Sherry Peters something to write about."

Victor shook his head approvingly. "Put 'em right up front, Chris. Your sister's doing you a favor."

"Yeah, she's all heart."

The three chatted on about problems in the hotel, their mother's health, the state of the world. Lauren and Chris always found much to talk about despite the fact that their lives led in different directions. Zelda Wilde, who only recently consented to use her husband's name, devoted all her energies to sculpting nude male bodies and large jungle animals. She was addicted to such terms as "growing into my consciousness" and "needing my space," embraced only artists and other "creative souls," and felt she had little in common with her "social gadfly" sister-in-law.

Had Zelda taken the trouble to peer beneath the façade, she would have found a far different sister-in-law than she knew, or thought she knew. The beauty, glamour, trappings of wealth, the easy charm and bubbling laugh, were all that most people saw in Lauren Wilde. There was no reason to look deeper; she represented a fantasy—an image—the American dream.

It was not always thus. Christened Lauren Angelina Wilde, Daddy's "little angel" was anything but a beautiful child. At the age of two, her parents became concerned about her runny nose, lack of appetite, pale complexion, and black-shadowed eyes. A doctor diagnosed allergy, and tests proved him right. Chocolate, seafood, wheat, and citrus fruits were immediately banned from her diet. Stuffed animals and other dust-catchers were removed from her room. Despite Chris's loud wailing, even the family cat was dispatched and replaced by a dander-free aquarium of tropical fish.

As she grew, a dry, itchy allergic rash defaced her tiny hands, the backs of her knees, and parts of her neck, and later, at the Katherine Delmar Burke School for Girls, hay fever progressed to asthma. Always a sickly child, Lauren knew the loneliness of being shunned and teased, of sitting home waiting for party invitations that never came, of wanting to die when her wheezing became so pronounced that the teacher sent her home from school.

By age thirteen, she seemed to have outgrown most of her allergies, but the psychic wounds were deep. She began Miss Burke's high school as a gangling, pigtailed, withdrawn adolescent with large metal braces on her teeth. One teacher described her as "looking as if she would crumble if anyone spoke to her." For lack of companions, she took to reading and, making the happy discovery of *The Golden Notebook,* became an immediate and adoring Doris Lessing fan. How that woman could take dry subjects and inject them with life! Suddenly she, Lauren, was Anna Wulf—or even better, she was Greta Garbo playing Anna Wulf in the movie version. Both Wulf and Garbo melded into her ideal woman: talented, romantic, rebellious, beautiful—alone against the world.

Great books and English composition quickly became her favorite subjects. When she wasn't reading stories, she was writing them—either some romantic fantasy about an ugly duckling transformed into a beauty, or the tale of a young girl who grew up to be Eleanor Roosevelt or Doris Lessing. It was a happy, satisfying pastime and crystallized her determination to become a writer.

The braces came off two years later, the allergies disappeared, her schoolmates were starting to be aware of her family's wealth and prestige, and suddenly everything changed. Girls began to seek her out and were gratified to find a warm and fun-loving person who blossomed with each new friendship. For the first time, Lauren began to take passionate interest in clothes, the newest dance steps, rock music—and, of course, boys.

To her astonishment and delight, boys began to find her of interest as well. Victor insisted fifteen was too young to date, but with the help of friends whose parents were more lenient, Lauren managed to meet and get to know a variety of young men from many backgrounds.

Top grades and credits in school activities made it easy for her to enter Sarah Lawrence, where she had wanted to go ever since she had read a passage by Alice Walker crediting the college with providing a stimulating and responsive environment. Walker's gutsy, sensitive writing introduced Lauren to the pains of being a black woman in a white society, and if Sarah Lawrence could inspire Walker to that kind of creativity, why couldn't the school stimulate Lauren as well? Another advantage was that the New York campus was far enough from home so that for the first time in her life, she would be free of her parents' intrusion and scrutiny.

The beginning year, however, demanded major adjustments, both socially and academically. From her high school status as a pretty, popular, and much-sought-after senior, she was suddenly an anonymous face in a crowd of anonymous freshmen, all determined to be class president and Phi Beta Kappa. Her family name meant nothing on the East Coast; gone were the gasps of recognition and sudden obeisance to which she had become accustomed. The realization of how much she had come to depend on instant approbation spurred her into working doubly hard to make new friends and become the kind of woman who would be liked for herself.

She wasn't always successful. Several girls in her dorm decided she needed humbling and one day sneaked into her room and spilled her Christian Dior nail polish and Chloe perfume all over her Yves Saint Laurent skirts and Valentino cashmeres. When Lauren came home to the disaster, she was devastated—not so much by the loss but by the fact that her schoolmates disliked her enough to do that. She began to cry, and suddenly she desperately wanted Victor; Daddy would stroke her hair and cuddle her and tell her that those girls were mean and ugly and jealous, and he would buy her a whole new wardrobe twice as pretty as the old one. The awareness of how *much* she wanted him strengthened her determination to break free of his yoke, loving as it was, and become her own woman.

It taught her another painful lesson, too. People who were not wealthy resented people who were, particularly if they seemed to flaunt it. She mailed home the Mikimoto pearls and lavender jade ring Victor had bought for her last two birthdays, replaced her worldly goods with far less costly substitutes, learned to wear faded jeans and jogging shoes, and gradually began to feel accepted.

Once she realized—with some amazement—how protected she had been from the variety of persons and personalities who inhabit this planet, a great curiosity awakened. She wanted to know and experience all strata of society, particularly those segments to which she had never been exposed. Not that many Sarah Lawrence students lived at poverty level or that their I.Q.'s were anywhere near average, but most did indeed live quite differently from how she did, and finding out how they thought and felt about marriage, sex, men, what kind of music they liked, what books and magazines they read, even listening to their speech patterns, became her favorite leisure-time project.

Leisure time, however, was in short supply. The academic adjustment was even greater than the social. What a difference from her small, pampered high school, where good grades meant a few hours' nightly homework or private tutoring whenever she needed it. At Sarah Lawrence, no one told her to go to her room and study, but, as she quickly realized, no one had to. Competition was severe, and passing even a "cinch" course meant hours and hours of reading, memorizing data, taking notes, quizzing oneself, and often staying up gulping black coffee until dawn. Failing a test could mean failing the course—an eventuality her self-image would not permit.

Still determined to become a writer, she majored in English literature, minored in journalism—and, when both her curiosity and her libido were aroused by reading Anna Wulf's long discourse on clitoral versus vaginal orgasm, lost her virginity at nineteen to a philosophy professor twenty years older and too wise to continue an affair with a student.

She would never forget their last moments together, sitting in Albert's dusty blue Honda parked among the trees behind her dorm.

"Will I see you tomorrow night?" she had asked as she always did before they parted.

"I want to talk to you about that—about us," he replied. "Lauren, my pet, I don't think we can keep seeing each other."

"I knew it," she teased. "You're married."

"I'm divorced. I told you the truth." He took her hand in his as he had probably done, she realized later, several dozen times before. "I'm a simple professor, and not a very rich one. I need my job. If anyone found out about us, I could never work again—anywhere."

"Why didn't you think of that sooner?"

"I did," he said, squeezing her ring finger till it ached. "I loved you and wanted you so much that nothing else mattered."

"And now it matters?"

"Now I've come to my senses," he whispered. "I realize it isn't fair to you—"

"To me?" She was beginning to understand. "You're tearing us apart for my sake? Don't you know how much I love you? My family has money. We'll never have to worry—"

"Your family would never accept me. I don't fool myself, dear. When you're a ripe, desirable woman of forty, I'll be a balding old goat of sixty. I'm sorry; it just wouldn't work out."

She fought back the tears. Pride mixed with hurt, anger, confusion. "I don't care about the future, Albert. Why can't we have the present? If we're careful, nobody will catch us."

"I wish I could believe that. Alas, my naiveté flew away many years ago. I'm going to say good-bye now." He kissed her forehead tenderly. "Stay as sweet as you are. I'll never forget you."

Then he opened the car door for her, and, too stunned to argue, Lauren had climbed out and watched him drive away. Not a wave, not a glance; he never looked back, and they never went out again.

Her wounded pride eventually healed. With it came the realization that her handsome lover was a belt-notcher, and she had merely been a dalliance. He had been skilled and tender with her, however, and she would always be grateful that her introduction to sex had been a happy one.

After that, she had several suitors, but no more involvements, and no more affairs during college. Much of her senior year was devoted to creative writing, learning to spot and eliminate clichés, trim unnecessary words, and refer to E. B. White's *Elements of Style,* the writer's bible, for answers to questions about form or usage. Her ambition was the same as it had been as a child. She would write sensitive, romantic women's novels and perhaps one day play Garbo-like heroines in the movie versions.

Coming home from college to the luxurious penthouse Victor had given her for her twenty-first birthday was quite a transition. Not wanting to lose her academic discipline, she forced herself to spend several hours a day reading, reviewing old textbooks, or writing fictional biographies of famous women. It took less than a month for her to find out there were myriad things to distract her, and they were all more enjoyable than what she was doing at her desk.

Gradually, she gave in to friends' requests to serve on various boards, get involved in causes, become active in both charitable and social events. Trina enlisted her help in political campaigns, Missy counted on her to be on at least one committee a month, plus there were showers to give and weddings to attend, family obligations, and a perennial parade of men passing through her life. Only one made an impact, another older man she met while working for the American Friends Service Committee, a Quaker group dedicated to helping the needy of the world.

Religion had never been important to Lauren. Edna was a nonpracticing Methodist, Victor an agnostic tending toward atheism. Together, they had decided to let their children make their own choices when they were grown. Chris adopted his father's agnosticism; Lauren simply chose not to choose—that is, until she fell in love with George Dukayne, widower, pacifist, and deeply dedicated Quaker.

Their affair lasted two years, despite Edna's objection that he was twice her age and Victor's insistence that he had no brains, money, or future. What he did have was a selflessness of purpose, a gigantic heart that opened itself to every suffering soul, and a simple desire to devote his life to others. His salary, as executive director of the local Friends chapter, was barely enough to live on, but his two sons were grown and employed, and his own needs meager.

In the first blush of romance, Lauren embraced his religion and became a Quaker—of sorts. She soon learned that nothing she did was enough for her marvelous coworkers. If she worked six hours a day, they wanted her to work ten. If she had money to give, they asked for all she could spare and then some. *They* gave everything they had and expected no less from one of their own. Eventually, Lauren realized that George would never be happy until she renounced all materialism and took on his values. Their parting was bittersweet, yet in many ways a relief to both.

Almost as a rebellion against her rebellion, Lauren returned to the social scene she had temporarily renounced, plunging back into the swim with vigor and energy. Once again, she spread herself thin as a wood veneer, becoming more dilettante than doer, moving from selflessness to self-indulgence. The years with George had made too strong an impression to be obliterated, however, and her purposeless life caused her more guilt and anguish than most people, including her judgmental sister-in-law, would have thought her capable of feeling.

After wiping the petit four crumbs from her lips and kissing her father good-bye, Lauren darted across Sacramento Street to the handsome high-rise she called home. A waiting elevator sped her to her penthouse. There, she relaxed and undressed, repaired her nail polish, checked her Phone-Mate for messages and returned several calls, read the evening *Examiner*, watched the late news, cold-creamed her face—and, with only insignificant changes from the previous twenty-four hours, yet another day was over. Almost. Blast that telephone! No one but weirdos and wrong numbers bothered people after eleven P.M. Unwilling to be ignored, the ringing persisted seven, eight times. She answered warily.

"It's your friendly mayor," said a voice. "Am I interrupting something?"

"Trina?" She exhaled in relief. "I wish you were. Unfortunately, I'm alone and sitting on my duff, as usual. Is anything wrong?"

"No . . ." came the hesitant reply. "I'm just a bit tired.

And I need to ask a favor. What are you doing tomorrow morning?''

"Let me see." Lauren flipped pages in a large red date-book. "Nine A.M.—deciding whether to paint my toenails green or pink; eleven A.M.—trying to choose between a tuna sandwich at home or a hamburger at the hotel—"

"Seriously . . ."

"Seriously? Mom's remodeling the guest room for the eightieth time and wants my opinion on some fabrics. What can I do for you?"

"Scott's mother is coming to town. I could send the city limo for her, but I'm afraid that's too impersonal for a mother-in-law. Do you think you could pick her up at the airport?"

"Sure, I'd love to! What time is the plane?"

"Around eleven. Liz can give you all the details. I'm so swamped tomorrow with the delegation from Shanghai and—"

The voice on the phone sounded drained. Depleted. But Edna had taught her daughter never to tell anyone "You sound tired" or "You look tired." It only made them feel worse. "Don't explain. I'm happy to do it. Shall I take her to lunch?"

"Would you? I'll pay for it."

"Good, I'll send you the bill. Is mileage included? Wear and tear on my panty hose? Now go to sleep and don't worry. I'll call Liz in the morning."

"You're a good friend, Laur—"

"Shh. Get some rest."

Poor Trina, she thought, replacing the receiver. *Poor* Trina? What was poor about being the first woman mayor of San Francisco? What was poor about being capable, brilliant, a slim, stunning five-foot-ten brunette married to a charming man who adored her? What was poor about living in a spec-tacular three-story home in Presidio Terrace, an elite cul-de-sac of private mansions, or getting your picture on the cover of *Time*, or having people talk about running you for vice-president of the United States?

Being mayor was still a lousy job. Whatever you did, what-ever statement or decision you made, thousands of people would love you and thousands would hate you for it. Wherever you went, an armed bodyguard went, too. Lauren had once asked if Rudy went into the john with her, and Trina had replied, "No, but he waits outside and times me." Critics said she had no sense of humor. How little they knew her! Yet with all the negatives, running the city was a job Trina had wanted very, very much.

Lauren thought back to a day years ago, when the future mayor and Christopher Wilde had played together as children. Their large houses stood side by side on Jackson Street. The Jarman residence was a boxlike brick mansion, its front door directly facing the sidewalk. Adjoining it, a tall, palatial white stucco structure sat partially hidden behind a hedge of hydrangeas. Parting the flowers, a wrought-iron gate opened onto a small pathway, decked by camelias and roses, that led to the Wilde's front door. It often seemed that Trina Jarman, an only child, spent more time at the big white house than she did at home.

They were sharing fantasies that afternoon. Ten-year-old Chris was going to be a football coach when he grew up, eight-year-old Lauren would be a best-selling novelist, and fourteen-year-old Trina . . . well, *she* was going to marry a king and be a queen! How Chris had laughed about that, teased her mercilessly, and nicknamed her "Queena Latrina"—a title she detested. She fought back hard, calling him "Chrissy Wetpants" (after an unfortunate incident on a roller coaster), and swore that when *she* ruled the world, he would be assigned to clean the "latrinas" in her palace.

How many times Lauren had run to her mother crying because Trina and Chris had excluded her from their games. And how she had loved-hated them both. Even when her mother invited friends her own age to the house, Lauren had only wanted to be with Trina and Chris. It was infuriating to be so young!

As the children grew, the age gap narrowed. Lauren idolized her pretty sixteen-year-old neighbor as only a ten-year-old could. And the Jarmans encouraged a "big sister" relationship to the Wilde children. As long as their spirited teenager was doing homework, having dinner, or watching television at the house next door, they knew she was not getting into trouble.

Lauren had never had any doubts that Trina would marry Chris one day and become her "real" sister. It was most upsetting when Trina became engaged at nineteen to Scott Bellamy, a person she had never even heard of. It was equally distressing that Chris didn't seem to mind in the least and wished her well in a brotherly sort of way.

The pain was somewhat eased by an invitation to join the wedding party. At thirteen, she was the youngest bridesmaid, but by far the most thrilled and excited of the eight ladies so honored.

Even then, Lauren remembered, Trina showed signs of what was to come. It was the bride, not the groom, who made the toast at the reception, carefully naming her new in-laws, thanking all the friends and gift-givers, and, in a master stroke of diplomacy, inviting the caterer and the florist to take their well-earned bows. How could anyone not have foreseen her destiny?

Trina finished college after marriage, earned a degree in political science, and immediately began to involve herself in causes and campaigns. When she decided to run for supervisor a few years later, Scott was supportive. As a lawyer, he could offer advice in many areas. As a husband, he spent most of his free time plastering "Mission to Marina, San Francisco Needs Trina" signs about the city.

Scott Bellamy had hoped for a more conventional married life, but the only little footsteps that pattered about the house were those of the campaign volunteers determined to see his wife become mayor. And so they did in 1982, after an unsuccessful try in the prior election.

Trina took to the job like a lion to red meat. She consumed the office and it consumed her. There was little time for anyone or anything else, including socializing for its own sake. While Lauren missed the occasional do-nothing lunches or shopping excursions with her friend, their relationship remained close and solid.

In a way, Lauren envied Trina's obsession with politics. How wonderful, she thought after their late-night talk, and as she had thought so many times before, to have a single, important, worthy goal and to be able to devote all your time and resources to it. What a contrast to her own life—shallow, unfocused, accomplishing nothing and going nowhere. Such familiar self-flagellation only heightened her ennui and floated her off into restless sleep.

# CHAPTER
## 2

"WHY DID YOU CUT YOUR HAIR, DEAR? IT MAKES you look so ordinary, just like everyone else."

"That's the way you greet your only daughter?" Lauren found her mother watching the morning soaps and needle-pointing her three hundredth pillow in the upstairs den.

It was Edna Wilde's favorite room, full of books, pictures, knickknacks, and all the clutter her decorator abhorred. She had agreed to let him lighten the dark wood panels and replace the heavy draperies with woven blinds, but as the years passed, Edna found herself preferring her own homey touches to his predictable chic. There were two things in the house she would never try to modernize: herself and her sitting room.

Lauren brushed her mother's cheek. "I like my hair just a wee bit shorter, Mom. Then I don't have to fuss with it."

"Well, you should fuss with it. You're much too pretty to go around looking like a"—she searched for the strongest word—"a shopgirl or something."

The visitor giggled. "Who *was* my real father, anyway? Nobody else in the family has blue eyes. Come on, tell the truth, was it Daddy's old roommate, Sam? The one who had the crush on you?"

"Behave yourself," Edna scolded mildly, refusing to be baited. "Where are you going?"

"Didn't you want me to look at some fabrics?"

"Oh, I'm sorry, dear." She stopped knitting and clasped her hands apologetically. "I should've called you. They haven't gotten here yet."

"Not yet? How will you possibly get along?"

Edna smiled tolerantly. She knew her redecorating was a family joke and didn't mind a bit. It gave them something to tease her about.

"I'll survive, I suppose." The years had been kind to Edna Wilde, now a very young-looking sixty-two. She had long ago made her peace with the hotel, with Victor, with herself. The cuteness of her youth had ripened into a quiet, ladylike maturity, and she carried her five-foot-five frame erect, confident that she was still an attractive woman. Soft lines were etched around her eyes and mouth, but the rest of the skin on her face was taut and unwrinkled. Her hair was a natural silvery white, and, to her daughter's dismay, she wore it teased, poufed, sprayed, and occasionally blue-rinsed. "Your father says you look too thin, dear. Have you lost weight?"

"No, and I think I'm about to gain some. Chin promised to make me a batch of spinach crepes for the freezer. I hope he didn't forget."

"He won't forget *you*. He remembers what he wants to." Her sarcasm was more resigned than bitter. "That miserable little man will drive me to murder someday. He thinks the kitchen is his private domain."

"What else is new? After twenty-three years he has a right to be proprietary. Besides, he's a terrific cook and a—" Lauren stopped midsentence, noting her mother's appraising eye. "What now?"

"It's your bra, dear. I don't think it gives you the right kind of uplift."

"I haven't had any complaints."

"You'd better take yourself down to Miss True at Saks and get fitted in a Daisy Perfectform."

"Are you kidding? I'm not ready for a harness yet. Anyway, I've gotta run. I'm picking up Trina's mother-in-law at the airport."

Edna seemed not to hear. Her needles clicked with the speed of an Oriental's chopsticks. "Did you invite anyone to the dinner party?"

"No." Lauren waved a kiss and called as she walked out, "There's no man in my life, Mom. I'm going to be your old-maid spinster daughter forever and ever, so you might as well get used to it."

Two neatly wrapped boxes labeled "Miss L." awaited her on a bench at the foot of the spiral staircase. She grabbed them and made her way to the kitchen. "Thank you, Chin. You're wonderful to remember. I'll savor each gooey bite."

A small wizened man turned from the stove. "Okay, okay, Miss Nolly." He grinned through a large gap in his front teeth. "You want more? I make more."

"This will hold me for a while. Thanks, you're a love."

No problem getting along with Chin, she thought, hurrying across the thick carpet. You just had to stay out of the kitchen, let him cook whatever he liked, and tell him everything he did was magnificent. But Chin and her mother had been battling for over two decades and had no reason to call a truce now.

Off the spacious entrance hall was a small alcove; a telephone sat on a spindly antique table. Lauren perched on a chair and dialed Trina's private direct number. "Hi, Liz, it's Lauren's Chauffeur Service. What time is Mrs. Bellamy's plane?"

"Oh, Laurie, I've been trying to reach you. The plane is two hours late and Scott's going to get her, so you don't have to do anything. You're free as a bird. Trina said to tell you a million thanks."

"Are you sure? There's nothing I can do?"

"Not a thing. You have the whole afternoon just for yourself. What a windfall. God, how I envy you!"

"Yes, aren't I lucky," she sighed with some irony. "Thanks, Liz."

Envy indeed. Liz Meredith had an exciting job as personal secretary to the mayor. There was challenge and purpose to her life. For her, a free day was an unimaginable luxury. For Lauren, the cancellation was a sharp disappointment, forcing her once again to face hours of emptiness. Even so minor a task as picking up Trina's mother-in-law had made her feel useful; now she had to fill the time. She could call a friend for lunch, browse at the bookstore, put in some volunteer hours at the hospital gift shop, clean closets, or work on those unfinished biographies. . . .

Outside, the air was fresh, crisp, and dry—a lull between storms or the beginning of spring? A friendly greeting punctured her thoughts.

"Oh, hi, Dr. Robinson." She smiled at the portly, bespectacled man who had bought the Jarman house several years earlier. Their exchanges had always been brief and pleasant. All she knew about him was that he and his wife were both practicing psychiatrists. They had offices in their home and were said to be strict Freudians. "What are you doing out in daylight? Psychiatrists are supposed to stay in their caves all day shrinking heads and dispensing wisdom."

A hint of a smile appeared on his deceptively cherubic face. "This is my recreation break—and Plutarch's. We both need exercise." The German shepherd was straining at his leash. "Okay, Plutie, calm down. Care to stroll with us?"

"Are you sure that beast is safe?"

"Plutie's just playful."

"Good. I need exercise, too." Lauren reached for her sunglasses, then hoisted her shoulder bag as they fell into step. Jackson Street seemed virtually deserted at ten-ten in the morning, except for an occasional delivery truck or a gardener fussing over a well-tended lawn. Lauren kept pace with an easy, graceful stride, thankful that for once no eyes were following her. She was used to stares. Men undressed and caressed her in their silent fantasies; women admired, envied, or studied her with curiosity, recognizing her from her frequent appearances in the social pages.

"Were you on your way someplace?" he asked.

Yes, she would have liked to say, I'm meeting a client. Seeing a patient. I'm due in court. I have the afternoon shift. "No, I really wasn't going anywhere. Matter of fact, I found myself with a whole day stretching before me and nothing to do."

He looked over curiously. "I don't understand. You're al-

ways so busy modeling or working for some charity or other.
I see your picture in the paper all the time."

"Fools' names and fools' faces." She shrugged. "It's all
a big, phony façade—a world of showing off that you've got
nothing else to show off but your money. I guess I'm one of
the most fortunate women in the world, but it's depressing to
be so fortunate. Do I sound terribly neurotic?"

"Are you depressed?"

The air, rain-washed and seemingly free of pollutants, made
the shrubs and flowers along the way stand out like pop-ups
in a children's storybook. Drops of moisture sparkled on the
leaves, reflecting the welcome sunlight. It was too lovely a
day for problems, and Lauren felt embarrassed to be making
the doctor work on his break. She laughed self-consciously.
"Whatever feelings I have are superficial. I'm afraid everything about me is superficial, even my depression."

"You don't sound neurotic or superficial to me. It's quite
healthy to find yourself in a pattern of activity that doesn't
answer your needs, and then want to change it."

Typical psychiatrist talk! His convoluted interpretation was
making all her negatives sound positive. "That's just the problem. I—" The words stuck in her throat. "It's not fair of me
to bother you in your free time. Maybe . . . we could talk one
day in your office?"

"I don't think you need therapy, Lauren," he said kindly.

"Maybe not. But I need a friendly ear and some good advice. I really do. Mother keeps trying to marry me off, Daddy
scares away any man who looks sideways at me, and they're
both so overprotective they drive me nuts. I love them dearly,
but I feel like screaming at them—and the whole world—to
leave me alone."

His voice became semiprofessional, detached. "Why don't
you tell me about it now? If you don't mind walking."

"I love walking—"

"Then let's not waste time."

"Okay." She turned to catch his expression. It was pleasant, noncommittal. "Okay, dammit, I will." She started
slowly, gaining momentum as she spoke. "Everyone tells me
how lucky I am, and I'm sick of hearing it, even if it's true.
I know I have brains and abilities, and I'm determined to

become more than a pretty face or a name in the Social Register. . . ." Layers of protective coating began to drop away, thoughts and emotions pouring out almost faster than she could control them.

Half an hour later, they were back at his front door. Dr. Robinson had not said more than thirty words. Now he spoke quietly. "I have to go, Lauren. I hope you've found it helpful to express your feelings, but I'm not going to hide behind my psychiatric mask of silence and let you drive off thinking you've got deep neuroses."

She smoothed her wind-tossed hair, lowered her sunglasses, and peered over the rims. "Please don't say I haven't got problems or that I'm imagining everything. I don't think I could stand that diagnosis."

"I didn't say you haven't got problems. Making decisions is always difficult, and you have some big ones to make. But you're perfectly capable of making them without therapy. If I were to give you a one-sentence prescription, it would be to find a job—a paying job that gives you a sense of worth. Find a field that interests you, whether it's fashion or public relations or something altogether new to your life. When you begin to take pride in yourself and your accomplishments, you'll no longer have the guilt and the emptiness you complain about."

"What you're saying is that I should get off my butt and find a job because nothing's going to come looking for me, right?"

He answered as any well-trained Freudian would: "Did you hear what you said?"

"Sure. I guess I knew it. I just needed a push, and you've given it to me." Leaning over impulsively, she kissed him on the cheek. "How can I thank you?"

"You just did. Remember that the next time I see you, I want you to be gainfully employed—and *not* in your father's hotel. Do we understand each other?"

She nodded wordlessly. The future was suddenly very clear.

The offices of KSF-TV were located in a large modern building spanning half a city block on the outskirts of downtown. The front entrance was conspicuously closed to the public. An armed policeman stood inside the door behind bulletproof windows, motioning Lauren to a small voicebox. She pushed a button and announced her name. "I have an appointment with Rick Seely."

The guard checked a list, nodded, and pressed a buzzer to permit entrance. "Come in and have a seat, please. I'll tell him you're here."

"Thank you." Such precautions at two in the afternoon astounded her. "Are you always so locked up?"

"We've had problems, miss. We don't take chances."

Now it came back to her. Barely three months ago, a crazed junkie had shot a receptionist, gunned his way into the studio, and wounded a talk-show host whose views had upset him. No wonder security was tighter than a CIA records vault.

That question answered, her thoughts turned inward. This was her first job interview, and she was nervous. Funny how the idea had germinated last night as she was watching the late news and wondering where to start looking for work. On the screen, anchorperson Wendy Dickerson, noticeably bulging, announced she would be taking maternity leave starting that Friday. No replacement was mentioned, and Lauren rightly presumed the producer might be looking for one. Why couldn't *she* take over? Dr. Robinson had made a point of saying she should find work she enjoyed. And the glamour of being on television, coupled with the challenge of editing and reporting the news, had tremendous appeal. Impulsively, she called the studio the next morning.

A curt voice in the personnel office told her they were not hiring at the moment; if she wanted to send in her resume, they would keep it on file. Resume? It hadn't occurred to her to write one. She thanked the voice, immediately tackled her typewriter, and turned out two double-spaced pages describing her education, board affiliations, and volunteer work.

Then she called back. This time, instead of going through personnel, she used her most confident voice to ask to speak to the news director. "I'm interested in replacing Ms. Dickerson," she told the man who answered.

He was equally direct. "Are you qualified?"

"Yes. May I come in with my resume?"

Her professionalism intrigued him, and time was short. "Okay," he said cautiously, "come in at two o'clock today."

"Thank you. I'll be there."

Only after she'd hung up did she realize she had no idea of the name of the man she was seeing, nor had she left hers. It would not do to bother him again. The message operator was happy to spell out S-e-e-l-y, Rick Seely, and to pass along to him the identity of his afternoon appointment.

She had dressed carefully for the interview, in a cream-colored silk blouse and matching wool skirt, with a brown tweed jacket and low-heeled black-and-beige Chanel pumps. Clothes were both a chore and a joy to her, and while an hour of shopping was fun, two hours often became tedious. Luckily, she didn't have to run from store to store. Miss Elina at I. Magnin knew her taste and always called when a garment came in that "had her name on it." It was usually Yves Saint Laurent and expensive, and Lauren usually bought it. Edna had long ago taught her the wisdom of buying one good item rather than three mediocre ones.

She had taken pains with her hair, too, teasing it slightly off her forehead, then blow-drying it into a soft pageboy. Wisely, her makeup was light, limited to eyeliner and mascara, a touch of rouge, and a bright red lipstick. Her speech was well rehearsed but, as it proved, unnecessary.

"He'll see you now, miss. Take the steps to the top, down the hall to your right, through the double glass doors at the end."

"Thank you."

It was two thirty-five before she was finally ushered into the news director's office. A small balding man with thick glasses sat behind three desk-top television sets, all running, and an ashtray full of butts. He made the briefest motion of rising. No apology for making her wait.

"Hello, Miss Wilde. Sit down. May I see your resume?"

"Yes, of course." She handed it over quickly.

"I see you've had a good education. I'm hoping my oldest daughter makes it to Sarah Lawrence next year. What have you done in television?"

The question was not unexpected. "I've never actually worked in television. Most of my experience has been appearing before the public as a fashion model. I'm told I speak and photograph well, and I'm sure I'd catch on very quickly.''

"Catch on? Do you think television is a parlor game? Do you think that because a professional makes it look easy that there's no skill involved? Have you ever done *any* work in the media? Have you ever been on radio?''

"I've been interviewed in connection with some charities.''

"Get out of here, please.'' He stood up and thrust back her resume. "You're wasting both our time.''

"But—how can I get experience if you won't try me?''

His face reddened. "We're not running a school for starry-eyed amateurs. You told me you were qualified. I should have known better than to take your word. Well, you talked your way in here, Miss Wilde, but don't you ever let me see or hear from you again. Is that clear?''

Tears blurred her vision as she grabbed her jacket, hurried down the hall and stairs, and, too choked even to speak to the guard, fled out the door. Not since she had been teased and ridiculed as a child had anyone spoken to her so cruelly. Once inside the car, she released her hurt in a torrent of sobs.

How different the questions had been from what she'd expected: "You say your name is Wilde? That's a big name in this town. Are you related to the Wildes of Nob Hill?''

"Well, yes,'' she had planned to answer, "but I want you to hire me because you think I can do the job, and for no other reason.''

What a fantasy! What a leveling! What a stab to the jugular! Her face and fortune interested Mr. Seely about as much as a piss-ant crossing the Mohave Desert. And maybe less. She vowed the lesson and the experience would not be wasted. Wounds would heal, scars would form, and she would never again be so foolish as to think her looks and social status would open doors in the business world. As it turned out, she was wrong about that, too.

The next twenty-four hours passed slowly. Once again, Lauren pored over her books, her neglected correspondence, her half-written biographies. Several jobs advertised in the paper had sounded promising. When she called, however, they were not what they seemed. She hated the thought of selling a product or a service, being someone's "right hand" or "girl Friday," or scrapping with the piranhas in the fashion industry. Rick Seely was right; she *was* unqualified—for the kind of work she wanted to do.

She spoke to no one of her problem; it was a situation she had to tackle and conquer herself. That night, Saturday, she attended Missy's benefit dinner dance at the Museum of Modern Art with Fred Hill, a bright and witty literary agent she had met at a gallery opening. They were good friends with no romantic interest on either side. The following night was Ann and Gordon Getty's reception for the Leakey Foundation. She dragged Clary Goldsmith, an old high school flame whose fire had long ago been extinguished—and wondered why she bothered.

Monday she stayed home all day, thinking, dreaming, poring through ads and making calls, and here it was Tuesday, with still no prospect of a job. Brooding was not going to help, she decided, fastening the tiny buttons on a delicate pink-and-black rose print chiffon dress. Her taste ran to simpler clothes, but Victor had seen this full-skirted Chloe in Vogue, loved its romantic Scarlett O'Hara look, and insisted on buying it for her. He wouldn't be at the opening tonight, but the press would, and it would please him to learn she had worn it.

The thought of seeing Missy in a few hours raised her spirits, and as luck would have it, Ben Carson, Missy's newly divorced brother, whom Lauren had met several times, was visiting from Mississippi. The Edwardses were bringing him along, saving her the trouble of asking a date.

Holding her hair against the wind, Lauren crossed the street to the Nob Hill Plaza shortly before eight, greeted the grinning Everett, and hurried through the bustling lobby and down the hall to her destination. She always liked the Orchid Room. Its high ceilings and walls painted with scenes of country gardens reminded her of Renoir—not his impressionist brushwork but the colorful, luminous gardens of his more classic period. Arnold, the German-born maître d', greeted her effusively. "Your table's ready, Miss Wilde. I think you'll be pleased with the flowers."

She had been trying to coax him to use her first name for years. "Thanks, Arnold. Is my brother coming tonight?"

"Yes, but his party is having dinner in Le Ciel. You know Mrs. Wilde—she likes . . . er, unusual food."

"Tell me about it." She laughed. Their poor guests were probably dining on carrot soup and zucchini quiche. Why Zelda insisted on inflicting her vegetarianism on others, Lauren could never understand.

Her head was high and her walk confident as she followed Arnold past the other tables, through the crowded, candle-lit room. She knew that she looked exceptionally well, that her dress was elegant and dramatic, and that her appearance at an opening night added to the importance and festiveness of the occasion. A buzz rose as her name quickly spread around the room. Several friends greeted her, and members of the local press stared intently, hungry for any newsworthy detail.

"Mmm, the table looks beautiful." She smiled, admiring the sprays of tiny white orchids intertwined with baby pink roses. "Let's see, we have Beluga caviar with Stolichnaya, Chablis, Grand Cru thirty-six, Stephen Zellerbach Cabernet Sauvignon eighty, Moet and Chandon champagne—and you've ordered the Grand Marnier soufflés?"

"Yes, of course. And we'll bring menus right after the caviar so they can choose their entrées. May I take your wrap?"

"Thanks, Arnold." She slipped off her black mink jacket before he could help her out of it. "You must have a computer in your brain. You always get everything right." Quickly arranging the place cards, she seated herself at the end farthest from the dance floor. No sooner had she done so than the sound of voices made her turn.

"Hello, Miss Wildflower," beamed Missy, a tall reddish-blonde with large brown eyes and a deep throaty voice. Her slightly rounded figure was encased in a purple silk cocktail dress with football shoulders. "Couldn't you get a good table?"

Al Edwards, shorter, stocky, and unsmiling, growled, "If we were any closer, we'd be the entertainment."

"Forgive my family; they're gross." Except for the eyes and height, Ben Carson looked nothing like his younger sister.

His hair was dark and slicked-down, his suntanned features missed being handsome, his red tie and black gabardine suit seemed more appropriate for Las Vegas. He embraced his hostess warmly. "Well, there's one good thing about getting divorced; I get to escort Lauren Wilde—" He looked down at the table. "That is, I am your date tonight, aren't I? Or have you got backups?"

"You're my one and only." She laughed and linked arms with him. "You look fabulous, Ben. I've learned never to say I'm sorry when friends split up. I mean—I'm sorry for the sadness and the trauma, but I also know some divorces are made in heaven."

"Mine was absolute hell," he groaned. "I'll tell you all about it."

"If you do, I'll break your hair," said Missy, smiling between gritted teeth.

The Blairs and the Crockersons made their noisy entrance, no introductions were needed, and the party was under way. Missy was not one to waste words. She immediately leaned across her brother. "Say, Laur, do you think Victor would underwrite a dinner here for the California Historical Library?"

"Are you feeling all right?"

"Me? Why?"

Lauren glanced at Ben's watch. "It took you four minutes and twelve seconds to get around to asking that."

Missy grinned. "I guess I'm slowing down. What do you think?"

"I think you should ask Victor yourself. What's this sudden and highly out-of-character shyness?"

"I am terribly shy, aren't I? It's just that Victor's always such a doll and he's given so much. . . . I hate to keep hitting the same people all the time."

"You don't hate it at all, Missy Edwards. You'd take your mother's last nickel if you were short a balloon for a benefit. If they ever give Oscars for wheedling money out of people—"

"Hey, are we here to talk business or to have a good time?" Ben Carson grabbed Lauren's hand. "Let's dance so I can show you off."

The whole party moved to the floor and, to Ben's dismay, soon began switching partners. Before he knew it, it was show time, and he and Lauren had only had a foxtrot and a half. The lights dimmed, the waiters doused the candles on the tables, the chatter subsided, and the bandleader announced a "rising young comedian" no one had ever heard of. The man strolled to center stage, delivered the usual self-deprecating monologue, then tailored his gags to what he considered local humor. "Hey, didja hear about the two gays in church? One says to the other, 'Do you think Christ was really divine?' And the other says, 'No, just terribly attractive.' "

He paused for laughter, then continued, "I was glad to hear they caught those two gays who raped Trina Bellamy. You hadn't heard about it? One held her down while the other did her hair."

The audience howled. Trina's perfect, never-out-of-place coiffure had been fodder for comedians ever since Herb Caen, the city's best-read columnist, had teasingly referred to her "Planet of the Apes" hairdo.

Lutie Blair, who loved any excuse to call attention to herself, jumped to her feet clapping, while her embarrassed husband pretended not to notice. Missy, devoted to the mayor, leaned across her brother again. "Who writes his material? Edward Teller?"

Lauren was torn between her loyalty to Trina and not wanting to knock Chris's entertainment. Before she could answer, Ben Carson whispered, "Shush, you two. The guy's *funny*."

The comic was followed by the energetic Count Basie orchestra, leading off with "April in Paris" and inviting the audience to dance. Ben tried to keep Lauren to himself, steering her to a far corner of the floor, but every time he launched into his tale of misery, someone mercifully interrupted. "I feel like a second-class citizen tonight," Ben complained, leading her back to her chair. "Don't people ever leave you alone? Being with you is murder on a guy's self-image."

"Just wait till those Mississippi belles find out you're single again," she reassured him. "You'll have to hire a bodyguard." She felt sorry for him, but not as sorry as he felt for himself. And when Missy whispered that the divorce had occurred because his wife had taken her affections elsewhere, Lauren realized it was Ben's ego hurting more than his heart.

Two familiar faces waltzed by. Chris looked chic and dignified in a gray Brooks Brothers suit, and he mouthed a kiss. Zelda wore her chestnut hair pulled back with gift-wrap ribbon; her pudgy frame was encased in a loose gold Moroccan caftan accessorized with Mexican leather sandals. She lifted a finger in a weak imitation of a wave.

Nothing escaped Missy, who was not bitchy, or Claire Crockerson, who was. "Who dresses your sister-in-law?" she asked. "Bertha the bag lady? I hate my sister-in-law, too. It's plain old jealousy that makes her run around looking like a circus tent, Lauren. Don't let it bother you."

Fred Crockerson tried to muzzle his inebriated wife, with little luck. "You know something else?" she went on. "I've noticed that the more money a family has, the more the in-laws squabble. My Guatemalan maid has four sisters, and they share everything and never have a mean word. Now, my brother's wife . . ."

The evening dragged slowly for Lauren. Public adulation was fun but fleeting—and utterly meaningless. And the more she tried to be kind to Ben, the more resentful he became. As the party broke up, he mumbled something about "out of my league" and barely said good night. Missy rolled her eyes, Al grumbled, "Thanks, helluva shindig," everyone kissed everyone else's cheek and, to her infinite relief, went their separate ways.

Eight days later, Lauren was still in limbo. She had seen Missy for lunch and, after a quick discussion of Ben and his ego ache, which both agreed was temporary, had confided her desire to find a challenging job. Missy's prompt phone calls resulted in two offers, one to be a spokeswoman for a new perfume and the other to do jewelry promotion for Cartier. Neither felt right.

She decided to shelve her problems for the moment and try to enjoy the evening ahead. Staring into a full-length mirror, she fluffed up her sleeves and retied the waistband of the long pink taffeta gown she had chosen for her parents' formal dinner. As expected, no marvelous male had materialized, and she was going alone.

The house was lit up like a small-town airport as she parked her blue BMW on the street at a few minutes past eight. Edna even had lights tucked into the hydrangeas by the front gate, giving the blossoms an eerie, glowing iridescence. The smell of paint tickled Lauren's nostrils, and yes, the big white mansion was now a soft pearly gray with navy-trimmed windows. Edna had neglected to mention this latest whim, and with good reason. The last paint job was only six months old.

Standing urns of spring flowers decked the entrance hall, and a lace-aproned waitress smiled as she took the visitor's wrap. "Good evening, Lauren. How pretty you look!"

"Thanks, Ann, I'll return the compliment. When did Mom paint the house?"

The young woman giggled. "They just finished today, at five o'clock. Your poor mother was a wreck thinking they wouldn't be done in time."

Amused glances passed between them. "Are all the guests here?"

"Yes, I think so. Your father's waving at you."

Beaming, a glass in one hand and a stogie in the other, Victor hurried across the room to greet his daughter. Ashes clung to the lapel of his smoking jacket and drifted down his strained shirtfront. An expanding middle was not in his image, but good food and liquor were, and something had to give. It looked as if it might be his cummerbund. "You're late, baby. We were getting worried."

"Dad, that cigar stinks! I thought you were giving those things up."

"What things?" he twinkled. His way of dealing with criticism was not to hear it. Or to change the subject. "I wish you'd let me send the car for you. I don't like your driving alone at night."

"I lock the doors and I carry a hatpin." She sighed, brushed off his collar, then linked arms. Inside the spacious living room, the lights were low and flattering, mostly from tall candles in shimmering crystal candelabra. Fresh flowers were everywhere; Edna had arranged them herself with a careful eye to shape and color. Fortuny pillows were fluffed to perfection on aqua-colored velvet couches; above them, a discreet spot highlighted a Degas watercolor in muted pastels. About thirty formal-clad guests stood sipping drinks and chatting in small groups while a white-gloved butler wove in and out with trays of hors d'oeuvres.

Victor insisted on taking his daughter around and presenting her to family friends, most of whom she had known all her life. No one minded; his face shone with love and pride.

Promptly at eight-thirty, the butler announced dinner, and a slim, somewhat stooped gentleman came up and took Lauren's arm. Deep semicircles framed his mouth in parentheses, his nose was long and aquiline, his eyes flashed like polished steel. The moment he spoke, his loud, imperious voice commanded attention. "Good tidings, buttercup. Your conniving mother has seated us together tonight. Do you think she has designs on me for you?"

"What mother wouldn't?"

Edna's choice of a dinner partner for Lauren delighted her. Walter Belloc, head of Belloc Publishing and owner of the *San Francisco Herald*, the city's only morning newspaper, was a grand old curmudgeon. Unlike her father, who never denied a worthy person or cause, Walter was said to be so tight he sent his chauffeur to return twenty-cent soda bottles. He also took great glee in buying ailing businesses and trying to turn them around. At last count, his publishing empire included two national magazines, three suburban newspapers, the *Herald*, and a radio station. The conglomerate grossed millions each year.

"May I say you're looking unusually lovely this evening? Ah, my dear, if only I were fifty and frisky again." He settled her in her chair.

"If you were any friskier, Walter, I couldn't keep up with you."

"Nonsense! There's nothing you can do with us old geezers except count out our pills and spend our money."

"Well, some people need a little help with that."

A gibe at his penuriousness or a simple allusion to his wealth? It was immaterial. He turned his gleaming eyes to her. "Now, tell this aging voyeur all the exotic, erotic details of your exciting young life."

She giggled. "That's like asking a pauper to list his bank accounts. I'm afraid you'd find my supersecret, highly confidential diary about as X-rated as a Greyhound bus schedule—and equally stimulating."

"Effective use of similes, my pet, but I don't believe a word. Didn't Sherry Peters write some unctuous drivel about your dazzling opening-night party at the Plaza? And didn't you have several high-powered guests?"

"Ah, yes, the big names. The celebrities who are well known for being well known. If only someone could tell the truth—tell what some of these people are really like. Remember what Oscar Wilde said? 'Never speak disrespectfully of society, Algernon. Only people who can't get into it do that.' What a crock! You and I know it looks even worse from the inside. I call these ubiquitous 'names' the social MAFIA—Media Adulation Freaks and International . . . er—the last word is impolite."

"But quite apt, my dear, quite apt." With a start, he noticed that three dollar-size pancakes had been arranged in perfect symmetry on his plate. The butler hovered over him, bearing a large bowl of dark gray caviar set in a carved-ice swan. Walter waved him away and turned to his dinner partner. "I do hope your mother's going to serve better fare than this. If the Lord had wanted us to have fish eggs swimming around our guts, he'd have given us gills."

Across the table, Edna spotted his frown of disapproval. "What is Walter fussing about, dear?"

"I merely—"

"He says it's the best caviar he's ever eaten, Mom."

"Oh, that's nice." She smiled and turned back to her companion.

Walter glowered. "I've always said you were a very wicked child."

"And you're a food philistine." She speared her blini with obvious and noisy relish. "Ummm. Ecstasy."

"You're very cruel to an old man who's on the verge of suicide," he whispered.

"You're not going to kill yourself over the appetizer, are you? You'd at least want to exit with a decent headline."

"I'm losing Sherry Peters," he blurted. "The bitch wants to reproduce her silly self. The whole thing is too disgusting."

"Really?" Lauren leaned closer. Sherry Peters had been writing a society-gossip column for several years and was one of the *Herald*'s biggest assets. "Have you thought of paying her?"

"I have not only been *over*paying the hussy; I offered her a paid leave of absence to foal, a part-time assistant, even a new ribbon for her typewriter. What more could the ungrateful wench want?"

"I can't imagine. Maybe a kind word about her unctuous drivel."

"Rubbish. Everyone knows management never pays compliments."

"You mean because someone might ask for a raise?"

"Precisely. That's routine, my dear. If you're working steadily and no one tells you how bad you are, you must presume that your work is passable. That's the best anyone can hope for in this business."

"Thank God I'm not in it." The second course was more to Walter's liking. He helped himself to a huge portion of crab legs and avocado mold.

"Who's taking her place?"

"Oh, Lordy!" He threw up his hands in mock despair. "You have electrocuted my raw nerve. I haven't the remotest notion who'll replace her. *You* know everyone in town. Give me some names. Mind you, she can be poor as a pretzel or rich as royalty. What she *cannot* be is nouveau. I *loathe* new money."

"Does it have to be a she?"

"Yes, it does. I can push women around more."

"What about Missy?"

"Missy only writes letters asking for money."

"What about Ruthie Swan? She's written some travel articles."

"Too fat. And too ugly."

"Hmm. Deke Hunter's new wife—Tina? She's supposed to be writing a novel or something."

"Impossible. His other wives would never forgive me."

"Well, I give up. You're too fussy for me."

"I am *not* fussy. I am particular, and there's a difference. All I want is someone beautiful, brainy, sophisticated, socially secure, and so rich that she's willing to work for the glory and doesn't give a poof for the money."

"She doesn't exist. You won't find her."

"I already have." His eyes were suddenly ablaze. "She's sitting right next to me."

"Oh, no, you don't!" Lauren's self-protective hackles rose in force. "Number one, you silver-tongued serpent, my grandfather was a gardener and our money's not old enough for your lofty standards. Number two, I'm not a writer. Number three, society bores the blank out of me. And number four, I'd want an astronomical salary and you'd probably have a heart attack just thinking about it."

"How much?"

"How much what?"

"How much money do you want?"

"For what?"

"For taking the job. Tell you what: I'll start you at three hundred a week with full medical benefits, retirement pension—"

"Save your voice." She laughed. "I'm not interested in writing that gibberish."

"Well, then, don't write gibberish. Write something of substance. Or be daring. Write the truth. Expose the social MAFIA, as you so cleverly tagged it. Surely you have the brains to improve on what presently passes as a society column."

"Flattery won't do it, Walter. I'm just not interested."

"You should be, buttercup. What in God's name else are you doing with your so-called life? Is it more of a stepping-stone to immortality to deck your bones with embroidered evening gowns that cost twelve Philippine seamstresses their eyesight? Do you enjoy dating foppish young men with alcoholic mothers and fathers who dye their hair and wear girdles? Does it make—"

"Now hold on—slow down—shut up a minute!" There was sudden silence as four eyes locked in combat. Anyone telling Walter Belloc to shut up had better have a reason.

Lauren took a moment to collect her thoughts. Then she

spoke slowly and quietly, hoping the other guests would return to their conversations. "You're right about my life going nowhere, and I know it. You've found my Achilles' heel—or maybe my Achilles' whole foot. I've been looking for direction—purpose—something challenging to do. Strangely enough, I studied journalism in college and always wanted to be a writer—of fiction, actually. I guess I've never had the need or the discipline to do it."

Her listener dared not move a hair. Even the crab legs could wait as he very cautiously let out his line, dangling the bait before his wary prey. "Nothing is more challenging than writing for a newspaper, chicken, and trying to reach readers of every philosophical and economic background."

"That part appeals to me," she admitted, still unsure of her response. "It would be an enormous challenge. But I've never written nonfiction. I have no idea how to do news stories—"

"Dear God, who said anything about news stories?" At least he had her thinking seriously now. He had manipulated enough talent over the years to believe that a careful selling job and the right choice of words could reel her in. "Don't you know that the best journalists in America write fiction?"

"They do?"

"Do the names Art Buchwald, Art Hoppe, Russell Baker, Garry Trudeau, mean anything? I'm talking satire, my sweet. Looking at the world through truth-colored glasses, cutting through the manure, fielding the fertilizer, slicing through the shit, if you'll forgive my indelicacy. Why, you'd be the talk of the city—maybe the nation—if you could somehow, in your own clever way, manage to shatter the smugness of the social scene."

The butler deftly scooped up the Steuben salad plate bearing six uneaten crab legs and replaced it with a gleaming Royal Copenhagen dinner dish embossed with Edna Washington Wilde's tiny gold monogram. Walter was too intent on his catch to notice the exchange. "Well?"

"Well, what?"

"What do you say to giving it a try? Privately, I mean. Just between you and Uncle Walter. Not a syllable to your parents, mind you. They'll have my head. All I'm requesting,

cherry blossom, is that you sit down and give birth to a sample
column or two. Expose the poseurs, the pompous, the preten-
tious. Peel away façades, skewer the sanctimonious, get your
friends furious at you. Play with the idea, flirt with it, take it
to bed. Run it through your typewriter and back again.''

He paused a split second for emphasis. ''I *know* you can
do it, and what's more, you're going to savor the seeds of
your own creativity. The sense of pride and satisfaction you
enjoy will make everything else in your life seem pale and
nonessential. If you're one-tenth the talent I think you to be,
you will begin before the sun comes up on the morrow. And
no matter what *you* may think of your efforts, you will lose
no time in sending them to your dear Uncle Walter at the
*Herald*—postage paid, of course.''

Thus delivered of his final pitch, the publisher leaned back
in his chair, cursed the absent butler for removing his crab
legs, sniffed the pouilly-fuissé, and politely turned to the lady
on his right.

# CHAPTER
## 3

Two weeks after her parents' dinner party, Lauren stood outside the *San Francisco Herald* building on Market Street, her heart racing. Walter's secretary had not indicated whether or not her employer liked the three sample columns she had sent, merely that he wanted to talk to her. It wasn't as if she were auditioning for a job; he had already offered it. And yet seeing her work might have changed his mind. Perhaps he was calling her in to tell her he had spoken too hastily—that she had no future as a journalist.

Inside the brass doors, the security guard slapped a "Visitor" label on her jacket and directed her to the elevator. Up several floors, a pleasant receptionist showed her to a seat, and moments later, at ten past four, a tall, no-nonsense woman named Amelia Martin ushered her into the hallowed chambers of the publisher.

"I don't care if *Jesus Christ* is marching," Walter was bellowing to a young man, "I do not want any more save-the-environment stories this week. Is that clear?"

"Sure, Mr. B. Shall I kill the overturned truck, too?"

"No, no, *that's* news." Walter brightened at the sight of his guest. "Come in, buttercup. Don't we look ravishing! How

you manage to stretch out whatever pitiful pittance your father
doles out to you is quite a credit to your ingenuity."

"Yes, it's hard trying to look stylish in these two-thousand-
dollar Chanel suits he keeps pushing on me." She chuckled
and kissed his cheek.

Walter helped her into a straight-backed seat opposite his
grand mahogany desk, ensconced himself in a swivel armchair, and fixed her with his trademark stare. "Your efforts
show potential, my dear. You have penetrating eyes and an
agile pen. Let's take your first endeavor." He read aloud:
" '*The Debutante Cotillion; Flesh for Sale.*' Somewhat distasteful title, but a promising lead: '*Even the dictionary lies.
In* Webster's New Collegiate, *the word "debutante" is de-
fined as "a young woman making her formal entrance into
society." This is not true; the young woman entered "society" when she happened to be born to parents with money,
connections, traceable California ancestries, or the ability to
exchange "unsuitable" friends for those higher up on the social ladder.*' "

Walter furrowed his brow. "Too vague. Too many as-
sumptions and generalizations. What connections? Why unsuitable? Never attack without substance, chicken. You go on
to say, '*If Noah Webster were truthful . . .* ' The dear boy
left us a century ago, so we'll make that, '*If the* dictionary
*were truthful, it would define a debutante as "a young woman
of questionable charms whose parents deem it necessary to
fork over*'—inelegant phrase—'*deem it necessary to spend
thousands of dollars to advertise their daughter's marriage-
ability in a round of costume parades and parties.*' Do you
write from firsthand experience?"

"Not really. Mom wanted me to 'come out'; Dad said it
was nothing but a meat market and bought me a car instead.
They made the decision. I hope the article doesn't sound like
sour grapes."

"Not in your case, my dear. But it does have problems.
You should assume that the average reader is naive as a new-
born puppy in matters social; you must take him by the furry
paw and explain exactly what the debutante season is, its os-
tensible reasons for being, what it costs and why, how the
young buds are picked. . . ."

She nodded as he continued, "All three of your columns share a common failing. They lack facts—substance—texture—details. You must construct your building block by block, termite, before you gnaw away its foundations."

"Yes, I see. I can correct that."

"I have no doubts that you can." He leaned back in his seat, assuming a falsely casual attitude she spotted immediately. What was he going to spring on her now?

The voice was almost fatherly as he advised, "Permit me to point out that a columnist, unlike a reporter, need not aspire to objectivity. Controversy, in fact, is the fertilizer of good column writing. It may stink, but it gets noticed."

"How poetic! I'll remember that."

"Tell me, buttercup," he continued, sneaking up on his subject like a cat on a mouse. "In some cases, your playful pokes become jugular jabs. What makes the fairest bloom of the flower bed want to uproot the garden?"

So that was it; he wanted to know what made Lauren run. Did he think she was hiding some traumatic childhood episode that had made her a traitor to her peers? Perhaps he feared schizophrenia—or some other mental illness—or anything that might make her unreliable as an employee.

She nodded as if to say, "I understand the question," then took a moment to compose her thoughts. Finally she shrugged. "I'm no crusader, Walter. I went through my 'selfless' period, trying to renounce money and materialism, and I failed the test. I *like* money. I like having it and I like spending it. My main dispute is with contemporary heroes and heroines—so-called role models. Millions of people out there are so incredibly gullible they'll follow almost any charismatic celebrity, even if he's a Jim Jones serving up suicide punch."

A buzz broke her pause. Walter pressed a button and asked impatiently, "What is it, Amelia? . . . Who? . . . No, tell Mrs. Edwards I most assuredly *did* get her letter and I do *not* wish to purchase an ad in her opera program. Tell her—oh, tell her we'll donate fifty dollars. . . . How much? . . . Out of the question! . . . Yes, that's as final as death. . . . *Yes*, I'm still here. . . . No, I'm like a lavatory on an airplane—occupied. Have them call tomorrow."

Walter seemed more amused than angry as he turned back

to his visitor. "Now, there's fodder for a column; Missy Edwards and her velvet blackjack. You were saying?"

"I was trying to explain my motivation. I hate to see the media glorify people who are sad caricatures of what human beings should be. Take Lutie Blair, an elegant woman, ruthless in her snobbery. Her whole life is shopping, partying, being seen with the right faces, and getting her name in the right publications, including your society column." Hearing no argument, Lauren continued, "She and the once beautiful Claire Crockerson, a jaded alcoholic with a bitchy tongue, are the leaders of the pack—the 'A' crowd, if you will. Those two man-eaters, and their poor detesticled husbands are on every climber's party list. They're the social lions who piss on other people's trees to mark their territories. And the other people not only let them; they hold out their limbs and say, 'Please, oh, *please* piss on me!' "

Walter raised a wary eyebrow. Did this very intense young woman have any idea of the idols she was tempting to topple? "You entertained those felines rather recently, pussycat. Are they not your friends?"

"Even before I talked to you, Walter, I knew that that evening was the finale—paying those two women back for the invitations I've accepted over the years and signing off with a clear slate—kind of a last supper. I used them to get publicity for my brother's opening, and they used me to bask in the royal box and play queen bee. We've never pretended to do anything but use each other, so no, I wouldn't call us friends."

"Then it's fair game to knife them in the scapulae?"

"No, of course not." She shook her head firmly. "I don't want to hurt anyone. I'd just like to open people's eyes. The characters I'd poke fun at would be composites of people, not anyone you'd recognize."

"That *is* reassuring, my pet. I trust you will burn the midnight fluorescents for a few days, polish these gems to perfection, and have them ready by—when can you start?"

"Start doing what?"

"Working for me. Sherry leaves day after tomorrow. That's Friday, April twenty-sixth. Is Monday, April twenty-ninth, convenient?"

"I—don't know." Her heart began to pound again, but this

time with excitement. It almost seemed as if fate were trying to push her into the shoes of pregnant women. First it was KSF-TV's Wendy Dickerson, and now Sherry Peters. Just as these women were trading in their careers for bibs and diapers, she was getting her first job. Well, better belated than never. "What exactly do you want me to do?"

"What you do so very well, Tinkerbell. Write columns. Say, six a week? Or if that's too many, we can drop it to five."

"Impossible!" Lauren exclaimed. "It took me ten days of sweat and agony to write those three, and now I have to sweat and agonize all over again. I don't want to live with that kind of pressure."

He frowned. "Do you want to be a journalist?"

"I think so."

"Then you live with pressure. You *marry* pressure, for better or worse, till death or mortal wounds or retirement. Now—money."

"No, not now, Walter. I won't be bullied!"

His eyes narrowed. "I'm offering you your own column in a newspaper with a circulation of over half a million, a full salary with all benefits, your byline in big letters—a job ninety-four thousand writers would kill for—and you have the temerity to suggest I am bullying you?"

"You *wish* you could bully me." She laughed, beginning to enjoy the theatrics. She could well understand his powers of intimidation, how his imposing presence and forceful delivery could freeze the heart of any would-be writer or employee. The high-ceilinged office with its built-in shelves of trophies and memorabilia, its dark paneled-wood walls groaning with plaques and certificates, was an impressive backdrop—a stage from which Walter Belloc played his tyrannical role with flair and fervor.

She was also aware of the uniqueness of her position. Because of the way the job interview had come about, and because he was in a bind from which only a special type of woman—her type—could extricate him, she knew she had extraordinary advantages. Not many would-be employees could be so cavalier with their bosses, nor could many young women

with no training or experience walk into a personal byline . . .
and a prestigious job.

Walter knew it, too. Accustomed as he was to playing dic-
tator, he was wise enough to sit silently for a few moments,
letting her speak.

"I've given a lot of thought to our meeting today," she
said, uncrossing her legs and leaning forward. "I knew you
would either tell me to go back to charity work or repeat your
offer of a job, and I was ready to accept either option. Naturally, I'm pleased that you think I have potential, and I'd like
to work for you—on my terms."

It was his turn to be anxious. "And those are . . . ?"

"I was going to say two columns a week, but I'm willing
to try three—Monday, Wednesday, Friday, or any days you
wish. I don't want to be labeled a social satirist or a society
reporter or whatever, and I don't want any limitations. I want
to be free to write about whatever I please. As to salary, I
think five hundred a week would be a fair place to start."

An eyebrow lifted, a glint came into the cold eyes, and
Walter gave a grudging nod. Clearly he did not relish his
position.

"All right, you little minx. You're your father's daughter,
and I'm well aware of the Wilde mule streak. You have your
three columns, five hundred a week, and freedom of subject
matter. I'm putting you in the Today section under Rosa Cortez. She'll be your editor, your guru, your Svengali, and, I
hope, your friend." He pushed a button. "Amelia, send in
Rosa. Now—can you start Monday?"

"I don't have to punch a time clock or anything, do I? I
mean, as long as I produce three columns a week, I can come
and go as I please?"

"Precisely, my dear. You could even work entirely at home;
some columnists do. In your case, I fear that would be a
mistake. You will find the office atmosphere much more stimulating and conducive to creativity." He flipped the pages of
a desk calendar. "Your first column will appear—let us say—
four weeks hence, on Monday, May twenty-seventh. That will
give *you* time to revise and polish your gems for us, and it
will give us time to herald this momentous event." He flicked
the button again. "Get Crater in here."

"Okay, Mr. B. Rosa's here."

"Send her in."

The door opened, and a short, pretty, dark-haired woman entered. Her white blouse was starched and crisp, her beige linen skirt wrinkled in the right places, her manner cool and efficient.

"Rosa, meet Lauren Wilde. She's going to do a column for us."

"How nice." The editor's smile seemed genuine. "I had no idea—we've run your picture so many times. Will you be replacing Sherry?"

"No."

"What will you be writing about?"

"I think—"

"Whatever the hell she wants to write about!" Walter bellowed. "She'll run Monday, Wednesday, Friday, under her picture and her byline. I want sample layouts by Monday, and—"

A man knocked perfunctorily and breezed through the open door. "You rang?"

"Tom Crater, promotion director—meet Lauren Wilde. She's doing a column for us. Get some shots of her with local flavor—Coit Tower, Lombard Street, the park, the bridges. I want a citywide campaign starting yesterday. Any questions?"

Unflustered by the assignment, Crater extended a hand. Dyed blond hair fell over his forehead; his four-second glance seemed to read the labels on her clothes. "Welcome to the asylum. How's tomorrow?"

"For pictures?"

"Nine A.M. okay? I'll have the photographer pick you up and he'll drive you around. Probably need about two hours."

"Well—sure. What should I wear?"

"What you have on is smashing. Saint Laurent?"

"Uh . . . yes."

"Something like that. Cityish. Tailored. Bring a few changes—skirts, suits, sweaters, what you normally wear around town. Here—" He offered pen and paper. "Write down your phone number and address."

Lauren complied, then returned the pad. "I'll be waiting in the lobby at nine."

"And *I* want the proof sheets by noon." Walter came out from behind his desk and, to Lauren's surprise, held out a formal hand. "Good luck, young lady, and may this historic liaison bear fruit for all of us."

His change of demeanor made sense. For both their sakes, he had to be impersonal. She was a working member of his team now, hired for her brains as well as her other attributes, and not because she knew the publisher. He was back on stage; actor and director combined, trying to place his protégée in the proper setting.

"I'll do my best, Mr. Belloc," she said, resisting the urge to curtsy. "Thanks for your trust in me."


Missy Edwards was only four minutes late, double-checking her watch as she spotted her luncheon date in a booth, and hurried across the small Union Street restaurant.

"Sorry to keep you waiting." She grinned and set down a leather briefcase, then slid onto the banquette. "I just came from your father. He's going to underwrite the library benefit. What an angel—in more ways than one."

"It doesn't hurt that he happens to think you're the greatest thing since instant replay." Lauren chuckled. "You didn't tell him you were meeting me, did you?"

"No, but only because I had too much on my mind." She reached for a mirror to check her lipstick. At thirty-seven, Missy looked somewhat older than her years, perhaps because her animated facial expressions were beginning to etch into her skin. The features were imperfect; nose a bit too wide, teeth a tad too prominent, chin a little too rounded. But her eyes were warm, her smile dazzling, and her magnetism strong. She had the kind of carriage, presence, and charm that lit up any room she entered. "Secrets from Daddy?"

"Not really." Lauren motioned the waitress. "We'd better order. I know you've got a one o'clock appointment. Thanks for squeezing me in."

"You said it was important." Missy checked the menu, requested a tuna sandwich with no butter, and fixed her friend with attention. "What is it?"

"I found a job. Not the ones you so sweetly tried to help

me get, but something . . . well, something I've always wanted to do—write.''

"That's wonderful!'' Missy's face came alive. ''For whom?''

"Walter Belloc.''

Four eyes stared at each other, two squinting and disbelieving, two wide open and amused. Suddenly, both women burst into laughter. ''Laur, are you serious? Oh, merciful God, I think you are. Why? How? What?''

Lauren quickly related the details, then waited for a response.

"Well, that's super! You got the old scrooge to come begging you to work for him, dictated your terms, and now you're about to eviscerate San Francisco society. I adore it. You haven't dropped this little bomb on your folks yet, have you?''

"That's why I wanted to talk to you. You know Victor as well as anybody. How should I approach him?''

"Carefully''—Missy laughed—''very carefully. Before you do anything else, make up your mind that nothing he says or does—no screams, no laying on of guilt trips, no bribery, no threats, *nothing* is going to stop you from taking this job. Tell him that at the outset. His greatest worry, as you and I have so often discussed, is somehow losing control of you. The idea that Walter Belloc, of all people, will be playing a major role in your life—a kind of fatherly role at that—will infuriate him more than anything. It won't be easy, but you've simply got to stand up to him.''

"How?''

"Just *do* it, for Chrissake! If you don't break away now, you could spend the rest of your life molding away in that marble museum you live in. Do you want Victor still keeping you tucked away in the Taj of Sacramento Street when you're forty years old?''

"Good! Well done! That's what I needed you to tell me. Now I feel fortified. Bring on the enemy—the Soviet Union— the universe. Even my darling father. Missy the miracle worker. Is there anything I can do for *you*?''

"For me? Plenty. Our tickets aren't selling for the Cancer Society benefit. If you could work a mention in your first column somewhere. . . .''

The women chatted through their sandwiches and soon parted. Lauren felt much relieved to have confided her fears. Missy's warm and total support gave her strength and confidence, and she came home in lofty spirits, almost ready to face Victor, but not quite. First she would call her brother.

"What's up, princess?" came his cheery greeting. "Find a job yet?"

"Why, you little old mind reader. How'd you know?"

"Brotherly intuition. Let's see if I can guess. You're modeling inflatable brassieres for Brooks Brothers?"

"Nope."

"Starting a dating bureau for handsome millionaires?"

"Nope."

"Hmm. Heading the Trina Bellamy–for–President fan club?"

"Nope. What's the most unlikely thing you'd ever find me doing?"

"Taking ten three-year-olds on a camping trip."

"You've got a point." She laughed. "I'll end your suspense. I'm writing a column for the *Herald*. Walter hired me."

"Omigod." Sudden silence. "Honest?"

"Honest."

"Is he paying you in pencil stubs or old gum wrappers?"

"M-o-n-e-y. The real stuff. Genuine, legal tender."

"Yes, but how far will twelve cents go these days?"

"*Chrissst*opher—" She reserved his full name for pretended exasperation.

"What kind of column will it be? Let's see: 'Dear Laurie: When my husband comes home at night, he likes to put on a pink negligee and high heels. The children are beginning to ask questions. Do you think—' "

"*Not* Dear Abby. If you'd shush a minute . . ." Her brief recitation reassured him that Walter was not using her for slave labor, and, once informed, he began to share her enthusiasm.

"Boy, can I give you material! You wouldn't believe the conversation I had yesterday with a couple who claim to be friends of yours. They wanted to take over Le Ciel for a private party, and they wanted me to give them a fifty-percent discount because of all the publicity we'd get."

"What couple?"

"The Stuarts."

"Goodie and Pete? They could *buy* the restaurant if they wanted."

" 'Them that has . . . ' " He sighed.

"What did you tell them?"

"They were so friggin' pushy I got mad. I told them we were not an Oriental bazaar and that our menu prices were not negotiable. So then Mrs. Stuart—what's her cutesy name?"

"Goodie."

"Goodie says to me, 'You're going to hate yourself when you see the three-page color spread in *Town and Country*—at the Hilton. *They'll* probably give us the party free.'

"I said, 'Shall I drive you over, or do you have a car?' "

"You didn't—"

"I did. And then she took that pompous prick of a husband by the arm and said, 'We will *never* do business with you again.' And you'd have been proud of me. I didn't say, 'Promise?' I just showed 'em to the door, and then I called Dad. They'd be the kind who'd write him a letter about what a bastard I was."

"What did Dad say?"

"He recited the slang dictionary. You know what he's like when he gets ticked off. It turns out the magazine had already contacted us about a spread on Le Ciel. The Stuarts apparently heard about it, decided to make it *their* party, get a discount, get the prestige, the coverage, etcetera etcetera. So that was pure B.S. about going over to the Hilton. Dad said they knew *he* wouldn't deal with them, so they thought they could wave their carrots in front of me."

"Karats with a k?"

"That, too. Anyway, Dad said I was more patient than he would've been. Speaking of Victor . . ."

"Don't remind me," she groaned. "I foresee a small nuclear explosion."

"Do you want me to break the news?"

"It'd be so easy to say yes, but I can't. I'm a big girl, almost thirty, and I shouldn't be afraid to tell my father I've got an exciting job." She paused before asking, "You're on my side, aren't you?"

"Aren't I always? I'm going to have a famous—famous*er*—sister. I'll bask in reflected glory. Or are you going to be mean and nasty so I'll have to cringe in doorways?"

"Not mean, just honest. I *love* the Stuarts' story. Can't wait to get to my typewriter."

"You'll change names to protect the guilty?"

She nodded. "You won't even recognize them. Gotta run now. Hi to Zelda, kiss my nephew."

"Hi to Uncle Walter," he said, "and don't take any IOUs from the old bastard."

The white surface stared back at her brazenly, almost defiantly. Was it Sinclair Lewis who said, "Hell is a blank sheet of paper"? This was the agonizing part of writing—creating something readable out of nothing.

After several long minutes, she began to type: " *'Noblesse oblige' is a grand old term given us by the French. It refers to the obligation of 'honorable, generous, and responsible behavior' associated with persons of wealth and privilege. For some denizens"*—she crossed out "denizens" and wrote: *"people in this city, however, 'noblesse oblige' means just the opposite: the right to take advantage of situations and individuals because of their social and celebrity status."*

New paragraph: *"You may wonder how people get to be 'media darlings.' Do they start out as honest, idealistic citizens dedicated to improving the quality of life for themselves and others? Or do they spend all their days in hedonistic and narcissistic pursuits—as Cyrano de Bergerac said, 'struggling to insinuate their names in the columns of the* Mercury*'?"*

On and on she wrote, transferring her indignation to the keyboard in a four-page diatribe. Then she tore the paper from the machine, reread and corrected it briefly, and sealed it in an envelope addressed to Rosa Cortez. Anxious for feedback, she drove it down to the *Herald* and delivered it to the security guard.

To her surprise, the phone rang several hours later. "It's Rosa," said an impersonal voice. "I have your copy. We need to talk."

Lauren felt her heart quicken. "Is it that bad?"

"It needs work, and we don't have much time. Let me

see. . . ." Papers rustled, and the editor began mumbling to herself. "I don't have a minute tomorrow—not a minute."

"What about now? I could come right down—"

"No, it's too late."

"Could you stop by my apartment on your way home? It's only ten minutes from the paper."

"No, I . . ." Rosa paused. "Maybe I'd better. I've made suggestions, and I want to show you what I've done. What's your address?"

After relaying directions, Lauren brushed her hair into a neat ponytail, filled a bucket of ice, and set out a tray of dry wafers and Brie. The hour-and-a-half wait seemed interminable. Over and over she reread her carbon copy. Some spots were rough, but on the whole, the article seemed to say what she hoped it would. At six-fifty, the doorbell rang.

"Come on in," said Lauren. "You must be exhausted."

"No more so than usual." Rosa half smiled and adjusted a heavy shoulder bag. Her navy blazer, red plaid skirt, and bow-tied white blouse looked as fresh as if they'd been newly purchased. No sign of the day's hassles marred her makeup or her pleasant expression. "What a stunning apartment! Do you live here alone?"

"Yes—fortunately or otherwise. This was my dad's gift to me for my twenty-first birthday. My brother says he set me up like some flirty young mistress, right under his nose where he can keep his eye on me."

"And does he?"

Lauren laughed self-consciously and led into the living room. "Have you ever heard of a one-way umbilical cord? I keep cutting it and he keeps sewing it up. Or trying to. What may I fix you?"

"Nothing, thanks." Rosa sank into the leather couch. "On second thought—any white wine?"

"Sure. I'll join you." The hostess returned several moments later with a bottle and two goblets. She poured, and they clicked glasses.

"Here's to success in your new career. I think it was Emerson who said, 'Talent alone cannot make a writer.' A lot of eyes will be watching to see what you do with your abilities. And a lot of those eyes, I'm afraid, will be green."

"I know." Lauren set down the wine and leaned forward in her chair. "It's a fairy tale for me to walk into this job with no credentials and no experience. I realize that. And it never would've happened if I hadn't had a well-known family and all the other things I never had to work for. But that only makes me want to prove myself *more*." She paused in her intensity. "What about you? You're young and smart and pretty. Have you had to overcome a lot of jealousy?"

Rosa shook her head. "Thanks for the compliment. I'm not so young—forty-one. I came to the *Herald* twenty years ago, right out of college. There was a lot of pressure to hire minorities, and a Mexican surname helped. I went from file clerk to copygirl to secretary to reporter to editor. I've worked too hard for anyone to be jealous—except possibly my ex-husband."

"You were married?"

"For a short time. We fell in love when I was twenty-six. He—Patrick, that is—assured me he understood about my job—the incessant demands, the long hours. And he tried to adjust. The rest is almost too cliché to repeat. After a few years he decided he wanted babies and a hot dinner on the table. So we parted."

"That must have been traumatic."

"Yes, but for the best. And now to work."

Lauren slid closer and watched anxiously as Rosa extracted a clipboard from her bag. The mass of red-penciled corrections that greeted her eyes caused an involuntary swallow of air.

Rosa ignored it. "To start with, you have two different ideas here: how people get to be social 'names,' and the Gaylords' trying to haggle in the restaurant. Keep your themes separate, short, and to the point. Your columns should not run longer than two double-spaced pages.

"The lead is weak," she continued, "so I cut the first two sentences. Start right in: 'For some people in this city, "noblesse oblige" means . . . ' Then give examples, situations, tangibles."

"You mean real names?"

"No, no, your characters are all composites, aren't they?"

"Sort of. Although there *is* a couple like the Gaylords."

"Well, I'm sure there are many. Just don't make them identifiable. Cut all this sarcastic dribble. Show us what you mean by word pictures, people doing things, people in action. . . ."

It took Rosa less than half an hour to demolish Lauren's article and head for the door. "One thing more," she said, "in the nature of a friendly suggestion. The less you get involved in office gossip—politics—intrigue—the better off you'll be. I don't mean you should be aloof; that's worse. I always think of it as kind of glass wall between me and the rest of the staff. Let them see through it, but don't let them in."

"Thanks—that's good advice."

"And don't be discouraged," were her parting words. "I know it's a pain, but if I were you, I'd toss the whole thing out and start over."

Lauren was devastated. Why hadn't her old college professor—who gave her solid A's and told her she was too talented for journalism and should concentrate on writing novels—why hadn't *he* taught her to be more descriptive, and not to run her thoughts together, and not to stray from the central theme?

The ache deepened as she began to see what a long way she was from becoming what could even pass for a columnist. She barely knew the basics. Oh, the writing courses had taught her not to use clichés and to eliminate unnecessary words, but how could she know what was extraneous and what wasn't? Only an experienced eye, like Rosa's, could immediately see which paragraphs to cut, which phrases and sentences to slash.

Back to the typewriter. With Rosa's words echoing in her ears, she began anew, working and reworking the two ideas until her eyes closed in the chair and didn't open again till morning. Most of Friday and all day Saturday she spent rewriting, correcting, and polishing, and by Saturday evening, she felt—she hoped—the revisions were a big improvement.

Her date that night, a young lawyer she had met at a party several weeks previous, was disappointed to find himself in the company of a woman quite different from the lively young beauty he remembered. This new Lauren was withdrawn, distracted, seemingly off in another galaxy. When questioned, she explained about the job and pleaded exhaustion. The evening he had so happily anticipated ended in disappointment at the ridiculous hour of ten P.M.

Rereading the columns when she came home was a mistake; the time and distance she had taken made her see all sorts of problems and imperfections she hadn't seen before. Frustrated and depressed, she crumpled up two days' work and dropped it in the wastebasket. Then, too weary even to put a clean sheet in the typewriter, she fell into a deep, dream-filled sleep.

Four days had passed before Lauren acknowledged to herself that she could no longer postpone telling her parents. The photographer had phoned to say the pictures they took were excellent and promotion posters would be on the newsstands within a week.

Personal confrontation was best, she decided, and she would tackle her parents together. That way, if her father got unruly, her mother would be there to quiet him.

"I've got some good news for you," she announced as the three of them sat down to dinner. The Wildes made a point of never going out on Sunday. It was family night, and their children, always welcome to join them, did so as often as they could. Tonight only Lauren was there.

"What is it, dear?" Edna leaned down to inspect her lace placemat. "This French laundry is getting so careless. I suppose I'm going to have to get someone in to do my linens." She looked up at her daughter questioningly. "A new man in your life?"

"Not exactly new. His name is Walter Belloc."

"You stay away from that old skinflint," snapped Victor, instantly wary. "He'd sell his mother for pet food. What's he conned you into doing?"

"He hasn't conned me into anything, Dad. He offered me a job—writing. I'm going to do a column for the *Herald*."

The silence was almost audible as both heads fixed on her.

"Surely you jest?" asked Victor.

"No jest. I've always wanted to write. You know those short stories and biographies I've been working on for years. Anyway, I wrote a couple of sample columns for Walter, and he liked my work. He called me into his office and offered me three hundred a week. I said I wanted five hundred, and he said fine. Aren't you proud of me?"

"Do you need money, dear?" Edna's voice was concerned.

"Of course not. You and Daddy spoil me to death. I needed something money can't buy—excuse the cliché. I needed purpose, direction, a single place to focus my energies and whatever talents I may have. Walter thinks I can write, and I intend to prove him right."

Victor's eyes widened. To Lauren's relief, he seemed more curious than angry. "How did all this come about?"

She told the story, emphasizing that it was obviously her parents' fault for having seated them together at dinner.

"I wish you had asked me about that miserable miser," Victor muttered when she had finished. "If I'd known you were serious about wanting a job, I'd have put you in charge of my charity fund. I need someone to advise me who's to get what and how much—someone I can trust. The job's still open, baby. It wields lots of power, and I'll double what Walter's paying you."

"Dad, thank you, it's not the money. It's . . . well—I have to prove myself—prove I can make it on my own without the family's help."

"Horseshit, honey. Do you think you'd have gotten the job if your name were Lauren Smith or Lauren Snazzlefoop?"

"No, and that's my point. My name got me in the door, but it won't keep me there unless I can produce. And I'm damn well determined to do so!"

"And you'll damn well make a fool of yourself and the rest of us along with you! Where's your pride? Your dignity? Your sense of family loyalty? How can you let that aging paperweight use you and exploit you that way?"

"Now, now, dear, remember your blood pressure," soothed Edna. "Perhaps he'll hide her in the back pages somewhere or in the sports section, where nobody will see her."

"Edna, this may come as a shock, but quite a few people read the sports section. And if I know Walter, he won't hide her at all. He'll *feature* her."

Clearly this was not the time to mention the newsstand posters.

"Your father has a point." Edna looked pensive. "You know, I'll bet I could get you a job at the museum. It wouldn't pay much, I'm sure, but you'd be working in a quiet, cultural

atmosphere, and you'd be serving the community at the same
time."

"Thanks, Mom. Thanks both of you. I've already decided
that if I'm going to fall on my face or any other part of my
anatomy, I'm going to do it myself."

"She's your daughter." Edna shrugged. "She's got the
Wilde stubborn streak. Six armored tanks couldn't budge her,
so you might as well save your energy."

"I'll save my energy all right," Victor sputtered, his jaw
clenched in anger. "Just wait till the next time that loathsome
old toad of a child abuser wants a favor from me."

Both happy and unhappy that Victor had chosen Walter as
the object of his wrath instead of her, Lauren was at least
relieved to have that hurdle behind her. Her parents had been
predictably appalled, outraged, and incensed, and now she
was even more determined to show them they were wrong.
They could and would be proud of her in a very short time.

Monday morning, she reported to work at nine. No one had
told her where to go or when to be there, nor had anyone
alerted the security guard, who quite properly refused to admit
her. Amelia Martin was finally called; yes, Ms. Wilde did
work there and would be coming in regularly.

Anna, the third-floor receptionist, remembered Lauren from
Friday—her arrival had been well noted and discussed—and
pressed the button to unlock the door to the city room. "Rosa
isn't in yet, but the Today office is that last section—see, down
there?—just past the library on the right-hand side."

"Thanks, Anna. I'll go wait."

An area half the size of a football field housed the working
reporters, news desk, copy desk, mailroom, library, art, sport,
and Today sections. It seemed strangely quiet to Lauren, not
the beehive she would have expected. Only half a dozen men
and several women sat at computer terminals pressing mys-
terious buttons, watching words and figures flick across their
screens.

The Today umbrella covered fashion, society, people, home
decorating, gardening, sewing, etiquette, beauty, health and
fitness, and more. Lauren counted ten desks and a large,
horseshoe-shaped table that seated five. At least half the desks

looked as if they'd been shot through a hurricane; unsightly messes strewn with open books and magazines, paper clips, letters, press releases, pens and pencils, pads, message slips, dirty coffee mugs, and, in one case, stale-looking crackers and a half-eaten apple.

Atop a long file cabinet sat stacks of last week's newspapers, both the morning *Herald* and the rival evening *Examiner*. Beside them, open metal boxes marked with unfamiliar names bulged with the weekend mail. Curious, Lauren picked a folder from a file on the horseshoe table. It was marked "Unwritten Jits" and contained a batch of letters and releases, all announcing future events.

"You must be Lauren."

Startled, she turned to face a mass of chestnut curls on a plump young woman wearing a red turtleneck T-shirt and plaid jumper. Two deep blue eyes shone with merriment. "I'm Sara Tibbett and happy to know you. This your first day on the job?"

Lauren smiled nervously and returned the "unwritten jits" to their place. "It's the first working day of my life, and I'm scared to death I'll blow it—the job, I mean. Any other kind of work . . . well, if you make a fool of yourself, only a few people know it. This way, hundreds, maybe even thousands, of people could say to themselves, 'God, what an ass that woman is! Why on earth did the paper hire *her*?'"

"Why did they hire you?"

Lauren chuckled. "Good question. I'm not exactly sure. I think Wa—Mr. B. was so desperate to replace Sherry, he grabbed the first body that came along."

"Are you kidding? C'mere, I'll show you something." Sara pattered across the floor. "This is Rosa's desk, and these"— she lifted a folder three inches thick—"are the applicants for Sherry's job. Or *any* job. Look at the resumes. Some of these people are practically qualified to be president."

Lauren leafed through the file. " 'Twelve years on the *New York Times*,' 'society editor for the *Boston Globe*,' and here's one: this woman *owned* a newspaper—wait, three newspapers. God, these people all sound so professional and experienced. I can't imagine—"

"Why he would pick you?"

"Yes."

"Well, my guess is—if it won't hurt your feelings—"

"It won't."

"Because you're well known, socially prominent and all that, and people are curious about you. Mr. B.'s enough of a newsman to know what interests the public. If you do well, I'm sure he'll be pleased. If you don't . . . well, you were his guinea pig—or maybe his Pygmalion. *Can* a ravishingly pretty, rich, young single woman living a life of luncheons and parties and fashion shows settle down to become a working newspaperwoman?"

"I guess the time has come to find out." Lauren slipped off her jacket and draped it over a chair. "Is there a typewriter I can use?"

Forty-five minutes later, the fourteen other members of the Today staff began to straggle in. Some ignored the new arrival, some smiled, a few stopped to introduce themselves. Promptly at ten, Rosa appeared, leather purse slung over her shoulder, arms laden with envelopes and packages.

"Oh, hi, Lauren," she said breathlessly, dumping the mail on an already overburdened desk. "I'll be with you in a minute." Lifting the phone, she announced, "It's Rosa and I'm in. . . . Pardon? . . . No, I'll be here all day."

Lauren watched curiously as Rosa riffled through thirty or forty letters, dropping quite a few into the wastebasket intact. Still standing, she grabbed a pointed instrument and split open the rest, one by one. Each letter took about ten seconds to peruse; then she would either place it on a pile of papers, throw it away, or spindle it. Half a dozen Jiffy bags full of books and beauty product samples sat unopened; those she stacked on another pile of papers.

Rosa looked up to catch Lauren's eyes and walked quickly over. "Marcy Burgeson will be in at noon and she'll want her desk. We'll have to find you somewhere else to sit."

"Are all the desks taken?"

"For the moment. Oh, wait—use Glenn's, that neat one over in the corner. He's on vacation this week."

"I'll move right away. Thanks."

"Now, suppose we walk around so I can introduce you to our cast of characters."

They were a blur of names and faces. Most of the women seemed pleasant, attractive, well dressed. A few were polite but cool. Two men sat at private desks. The bearded one rose to shake hands; the balding one grunted. A pair of younger men at the horseshoe desk jumped to their feet and greeted her with smiles.

"We're copypersons. I'm Johnny and he's Dag."

"I'll speak for myself, jerko. I'm Dag—D-a-g, rhymes with fag, which I'm not."

Lauren laughed. "Okay. Nice to meet both of you."

"You'll get to know everyone very fast," said Rosa. "We're a friendly place. Anyone who isn't doesn't last very long."

A warning? It didn't matter. The new columnist could get along with people. "They all seem terrific. Would you have a moment to talk to me now?"

"Yes, let's go to my desk."

Lauren brought over the latest results of her labors and drew up a chair.

"These are better. You're making progress." Grabbing a pencil, Rosa once again began marking passages for correction or deletion, inserting question marks, scribbling notes in the margin.

"You still tend to digress," she said, returning the battle-scarred copy ten minutes later. "You bring in too much superfluous material. I've cut away everything that doesn't directly enhance your main theme. Mr. B. sent over your three sample columns. I'll try to get to them this week."

"Thanks for your patience." Lauren tried to keep the disappointment from her voice. "Shall I leave these on your desk when I finish reworking and retyping them?"

"Oh, dear." Rosa's face fell. "You've never used a VDT?"

"A what?"

"Video display terminal. A computer. It's no big problem, but you'll need a few days to get used to it."

"I'll teach her," said a cheerful voice. Sara Tibbett was standing nearby, obviously listening.

"That's fine. Sara will show you what to do. You'll have to excuse me now." Rosa reached for her daily calendar and let out a groan. She was late for a staff meeting, her phone was ringing, her assistant was waiting, and she had already spent more time than she could afford.

The morning sped by. Lauren was, by her own admission, "hopelessly unmechanical," but Sara managed to teach her the basics in two hours. The next hour she spent practicing and asking questions.

A tap on the arm broke her concentration. A large-framed woman about forty, with straight bangs and thick glasses, peered over her head at the screen. "You misspelled 'iridescent.' We only use one 'r' here."

Lauren turned to stare at the towering figure; could anyone be that gross? Her appearance matched her personality. Thick, broad shoulders sat atop overlong, muscular arms and wide, fleshy hips, one noticeably higher than the other. Nothing matched. Nothing worked about her body. She gave the impression God must have been drunk at creation time.

"Uh . . . thanks. Spelling is not my strong point. I'm Lauren Wilde."

"Yes, I know. My brother, Jerry Burgeson, took you out once."

Visions of an older man with foul-smelling breath and a rampaging libido flashed through her brain. Once had been one time too many. "Sure, I remember Jerry. Very bright man."

"He's a nuclear physicist at the university. Married now to a professor of advanced mathematics."

"Wonderful. Give him my best. Did you tell me your name?"

"Marcy Burgeson, of course. Don't you ever read the *Herald*?"

"Your byline is very familiar. I just didn't connect it with your face; I'm sorry. Today's my first day at the VDT and I'm a bit rattled."

"Then maybe you shouldn't be working here." The woman turned sharply and strode past the file cabinet, down the hall to the library. Lauren watched her disappear—a tall, lumbering moose with run-down heels and a disposition to match.

"Marcy overwhelming you with her graciousness?" The voice belonged to Lee Paige, the man who had risen to meet her earlier in the day.

Lauren shuddered. "I can still feel the ice. Is it personal or general?"

"Both. Marcy doesn't like most people, but she doesn't like pretty young female people most of all. We call her the Incredible Hulk. She got badly shortchanged in the looks department and I gather had to overcome a lot of prejudice to get where she is. But she deserves it. She's the best reporter in our section—writes rings around the rest of us."

"Why is she so hostile?"

"Like I said, she resents good-looking females—particularly ones who seemingly walk into good jobs without having had to struggle. Not to mention ones who rejected her adored brother, which I take it you did."

"It was mutual disagreement. He said yes and I said no."

"Sit down a minute." Lee drew up a chair for her, facing his desk. "Don't let the witch bother you. She's a steaming brew of snake fangs and bile, and she boils over easily. She also thinks she's the only talent around here and that she should be writing the sequel to *War and Peace* instead of fighting deadlines. Unfortunately, she still has to eat and pay the rent."

"I feel better."

"Mind if I smoke?"

"No. Thanks for asking." She watched him take four matches to light his pipe. "What kind of stories do you write?"

He puffed contentedly, exhaling in the opposite direction. "Feature, news, first-person, anything. I'm just a dull old reporter."

"Does someone tell you what to write, or do you decide?"

"All of the above. Usually I'll submit an idea to Rosa and she'll okay it. If she doesn't like it, she'll scribble me a note telling why. Or I'll submit twenty ideas and she'll pick the ten best. Or the two best. Or maybe none. Sometimes she assigns me to interview a visiting celebrity or investigate a topic that's in the news."

"It hardly sounds dull! Is that lovely woman in the picture your wife?"

Lee beamed. He looked to be in his mid-thirties, with a trim goatee and bright blue eyes that glistened as he stared at the photo on his desk. "Yes, that's Fukiko. Isn't she a doll? I found her twelve years ago in Kōbe. Couldn't speak a word of English. Now she edits my manuscript."

"You're writing a book?"

"Isn't everyone?"

"Sometimes it seems that way. Fukiko must be brilliant. Who taught her English?"

"I did. And she read magazines and went to movies and lectures and English classes. Amazing woman. I'm a lucky guy."

"She didn't do too badly." Lauren smiled and moved her chair back to its place. "I'd better let you get to work. Thanks for the word on Marcy."

"Anytime, kid," he said.

By Thursday of her first week, Lauren was beginning to feel less intimidated by the VDT and less pressured by her work. Rosa had taken her scalpel to the three sample columns, but at least she had passed on the other two, and they were now in the system, edited, approved, and awaiting publication.

For the most part, her fellow workers were cordial but guarded. Competition among them was keen; who would get to interview Jane Fonda? Who would be invited to Mayor Bellamy's dinner for Jimmy and Rosalynn Carter? Who would spend a free weekend at the new Sonoma Health Spa?

Fortunately, Lauren was removed from the jousting for assignments. Her needs, at the moment, were to know what was going on around her and to settle into a routine. The Today department put out a daily four-to-six-page section covering human interest and other nonthreatening features that were timely but lacked the frantic immediacy of wars, riots, crime, and disasters.

The input of material was enormous, and for Rosa, deciding what to include and what to ignore was a constant and demanding task. She was besieged by publicists touting new books and touring authors; pushing boutiques, beauty shops, hotels, and every possible service establishment; suggesting close-ups on movie or TV personalities, or stars of the new stage shows opening next month, or interviews with restaurateurs, gymnasts, professional birdcallers, and left-handed baton twirlers.

Along with press agent recommendations and the reporters' own ideas, stories rolled in off the wire services, piled up from magazines and other publications, and flowed into the office in the form of a thousand or more letters a week from the public. Most suggested nephew Mark's adventures on his paper route, grandmother Maude's ninetieth birthday, the opening of the neighborhood pet store, or, quite often, the writer's own self for an "in-depth" story.

Lauren enjoyed the continuing inflow, the undercurrent of excitement, the challenge of being on her own. It took only a day for her to realize that whatever she wanted done around the office she would have to do herself. Without asking anyone, she tacked her name onto one of the smaller mail shelves, then spent half a morning tracking down the only man who could assign her space on the computer. She found him and officially became the "Wilde L" file.

While enjoying the ease and convenience of writing on the VDT, she soon discovered that she surrendered all privacy. Anyone in any department on the paper could look up her file name, press a few buttons, and see exactly what she was working on, her list of possible subjects, her backlog, if any, of unpublished columns. Perhaps in the future she would confine her best ideas to paper.

Shortly past nine-thirty, Sara arrived, out of breath and bubbling. "Did you hear the good news?"

Lauren set down the instruction book she was studying. "No, what?"

"They're moving Al—you know, the bald guy? The pain in the ass? They're moving him back to cityside, where he used to be. He hated being here almost as much as we hated having him. Anyway, you're getting his desk, your very own desk. Isn't that exciting?"

"Hmm. On a scale of one to ten, about a five. No, make

it six, because it's right next to you and far away from Marcy. When did all this happen?''

"I guess it's been in the works. I saw chrome-dome start to move his stuff yesterday after you'd left. And I heard Rosa tell him to take *everything* because she was moving you in today. Maybe you should act surprised when she tells you.''

"Okay, that's easy.'' Lauren fished into her purse for a small gift-wrapped box. "Look, this is nothing. Just a tiny way to say thank you for all you've done for me.''

"Oh, no!'' Sara's face reddened. "What have I done?''

"Take it, silly. I told you it's nothing.''

Sara reached gingerly for the package and tore off the paper. Inside a velvet box sat a pink coral buddha on a thin gold chain. She drew it out slowly, ran to the closet, and held it to her face in the mirror. "It's exquisite!''

"Here, let me fasten it.'' A quick snap secured the chain, then Lauren rearranged it on her neck. "It's lovely on you. Matches your pretty complexion.''

"Thank you. You really shouldn't—''

"What have we here, the lesbian hour?'' A harsh voice made them start.

"Look what Lauren gave me, Marcy. Isn't it gorgeous?''

"Yes, it's nice.'' The new arrival donned her glasses and approached for a closer look. "Very nice. Do we all get one?''

Lauren's head moved sideways. "Nope. Only people who spend three days teaching me how to use the VDT.''

"What a pity. I like coral.''

For a quick moment, Lauren flirted with the idea of bringing Marcy a coral necklace she had at home, one she had bought in Hawaii and never worn. On second thought, the gift would not be appreciated, and Marcy would surely find a way to make her look bad for giving it. She reprimanded herself for even thinking she could buy Marcy's friendship. Nothing short of a cannonball could knock the chip off that woman's shoulder.

"Oh, I forgot.'' Marcy slapped an envelope on Lauren's desk. "I picked up your mail. From Mr. B., no less.''

"Thanks.'' Lauren felt a wave of apprehension as she tore open the seal. Inside were Xeroxed copies of two letters, one bearing the familiar logo of the Nob Hill Plaza, the other written on the formal stationery of the *San Francisco Herald*.

Grabbing the hotel letter first, she nervously read, "Walter, you miserable bastard: You dine at a man's home in friendship, and lure his only daughter into a life of notoriety and self-destruction. You have preyed on Lauren's innocence and trust, and I beg you to end this vulgar intrusion on me and my family as soon as possible. I'm sure you can devise a way to sever your alliance and save the child's feelings and self-respect. If such action is not immediately forthcoming, the Nob Hill Plaza will take steps to cancel its advertising. Sincerely, Victor."

Blood drained from her face as she read the reply. "Victor: Your letter is unspeakably rude and insulting. It is time you stopped playing outraged parent and realized that your 'child' is bright, self-willed, and more mature than you and I together. What I have offered her is a chance for a glamorous and creative career in the most exciting and respectable field there is, literary journalism. I have no intention of breaking her heart or my word. Sincerely, Walter.

"P.S. Feel free to insert your advertising wherever it seems appropriate."

"Oh, God," she whispered. "I was afraid of this." Her eyes automatically darted over to Rosa, who had just come in and quickly crossed the room to Lauren's desk.

"What is it? You're pale as a corpse."

"Look at these love letters."

Rosa suppressed a snicker as she read Victor's prose. " 'Life of notoriety and self-destruction'? What does he think we run here?"

"A white-slave ring, no doubt."

"I can't believe this letter! Would your father really pull his advertising? That could cost Mr. B. almost six figures."

"Dad's bluffing. He knows he can't run the hotel without advertising, and Mr. B. knows he knows." She shrugged. "Mr. B. holds all the cards. If he were to stop running ads for the Orchid Room or stop running stories on the entertainment, there wouldn't be any Orchid Room. Those two wily characters are trying to outfox each other, but they both need each other and they both know it. So there's an impasse, and

I guess Mr. B. is just letting me know what's going on. Damned if I know what to do.''

"Why do anything? Let them fight it out."

"That makes sense. I'm not even going to tell Dad I saw his letter. Can you *believe* him? The sweetest man in the world, but he still thinks I'm twelve years old and never been kissed. Thanks for the reassuring words. Sorry to bother you.''

"Don't mention it.'' Rosa noted Marcy's appearance down the corridor and lowered her voice. "It's actually quite entertaining—like a soap opera. I can't help feeling your father's got a lot of fight left. He's not a quitter.''

"Tell me about it.''

"You must know him better than anyone. Can't you crawl into his mind and figure out what he's going to do next?''

"If only I could!'' Lauren tucked the letters into her purse and out of sight. "Unfortunately, he's too complicated to be predictable. Stay tuned for the next episode. I can hardly wait myself.''

# CHAPTER
## 4

THE FIRST COLUMN RAN MONDAY, MAY 27. IT WAS CAP-
tioned NEWS MAKES NAMES and detailed the step-by-step route
to becoming a media personality, including instructions on
how to prepare quotable quotes and witty ad-libs.

The piece was short, farcical, and biting and lived up to
Victor's greatest fears—that she would expose the kind of
smugness and superficiality they had often discussed in private
. . . but never with anyone else. Most of his friends, not to
mention his business associates, would not be amused.

Ever since the first newsstand poster had appeared two
weeks before, he had known that Walter was going to exploit
his name, reputation, and daughter to the fullest. He had
quickly called a meeting of his top executives, promotion staff,
legal and business advisers. After three hours of exploring
alternatives, the consensus was unanimous: they could not run
the hotel without the morning newspaper.

One time several years ago, Victor had tried to trim the
advertising budget. The bar, restaurant, supper club, and even
room occupancy dropped so badly, he ended up allotting more
money for advertising than before. Clearly, and despite his
threats, "boycotting" the *Herald* was not the answer.

Nor were there grounds for a lawsuit. "Malicious brainwashing,'' as Victor called it, seemed unlikely in a bright capable twenty-nine-year-old woman who had only seen her employer twice—once socially and once in his office—in the days immediately preceding her hiring. As tactfully as possible, Victor's lawyers tried to tell him he was overreacting, that the publicity campaign was temporary and the talk around town would soon wane. Any steps he took to retaliate against Walter's actions would only arouse public interest and sell more papers. His nemesis, it was pointed out, would like nothing better than a public feud.

Wisely, but with great difficulty, Victor decided to sit back and wait. Despite her headstrong streak, Lauren had always been a reasonable child, and the negative feedback she would soon be getting from her friends and peers might knock some sense into her brain.

Meanwhile, on the third floor of the *San Francisco Herald*, the new columnist's phone was ringing nonstop, and the feedback was far from negative. Missy called to offer congratulations and gently remind her about the Cancer Society Gala; Chris informed her that Victor had gone into orbit as expected but seemed to be drifting back to earth; Liz Meredith delivered love and good luck from the mayor; even George Dukayne, her onetime lover, wished her well and expressed the hope that she would continue to expose the ills of a sick and violent society.

Hairdressers, restaurateurs, shopowners she knew, all phoned to offer congratulations and perhaps plant a seed of recognition they could cultivate later. Publicists who had always found her friendly and cooperative called to say they hoped the new relationship would be as ''mutually beneficial'' as the old one.

By now, Lauren knew everyone in the Today office, at least by name. They were a remarkably independent and competitive group and, except for the five people at the copy desk, worked more as individuals than as a team. Each writer was solely responsible for his or her assignment. They might ask one another for sources or references, but they rarely shared ideas or collaborated.

The copypeople were different. They worked closely with

the writers, checking style, punctuation, spelling, grammar, verifying facts, and, of course, deleting any statements that might be libelous. They also supplied art—whatever drawings, photos, or illustrations accompanied the copy—and worked with the printing department to produce dramatic and eye-catching layouts.

The first week, Lauren had had a minor problem with Dag and Johnny, who she knew were whispering and laughing at her expense.

"Want to let me in on the joke?" she asked one afternoon, walking over to them.

Dag looked up innocently. "What joke?"

"Why don't you tell her," urged Johnny. "Maybe she can solve the mystery."

"Well, if you insist. We were just wondering if you piss Dom Pérignon," Dag blurted, then dissolved into uncontrollable giggles.

"Ask her the rest, too."

"Forget it," said Lauren, returning to her desk. "I get the level of your humor."

To the copyboys' amazement, Lauren was neither cool nor hostile after that and treated them no differently than before. Two days later, she received a note from them that read: "We wanted to buy you some 'Dom' to apologize, but we couldn't afford it. In our minds, you are a lady—and the answer to the question will always be 'Yes!' "

The only sour note in the office was Marcy, whose tongue was as sharp as her jealousy. That Monday afternoon, however, she seemed almost cheerful as she approached Lauren's desk. "I've been hearing a lot of gossip about you and your column."

Lauren pressed the keys to save the copy she was working on and swung around. She had no desire to chat with the woman but couldn't very well avoid her. All right, she'd bite. "What kind of gossip?"

"Mainly about how your father made a deal with Mr. B. to get you this job."

Lauren didn't know whether to laugh or get angry. The latter seemed more appropriate, so she scowled. "What deal?"

Marcy nodded smugly, mistaking the object of her listener's irritation. "I thought you'd want to know about what your father did, since apparently it was all behind your back."

"What are you talking about?"

"Don't you know that Mr. B. was just made chairman of the Newspaper Publishers Association? They have a big convention coming up in eighty-six." The reporter took a bobby pin from between her teeth and fastened back a thick wad of hair. "He needed a major hotel with a central location, and your father needed a job for his daughter, who wanted to be a columnist."

"Do tell."

"So now Mr. B.'s a big man with his cronies; he's gotten them all fancy suites at cut rates at the Nob Hill Plaza. And the *Herald* has a new columnist."

Lauren was momentarily speechless. Even if Walter were heading the NPA convention, he would make a point of taking his business anywhere *but* the Nob Hill Plaza. It was a spiteful, demeaning story, and it infuriated her. "That's a damn lie! My father hates my working here. He's done everything possible to keep me from taking this job. Where did you hear that rumor? I'd like to stop it at the source."

"Sorry, I gave my word. And it wouldn't do any good, anyway, because whether *you* believe it or not, everyone around here knows it's true."

The phone was ringing insistently. "Sara," she called impatiently to the next desk, "take a message for me, please? Marcy, I don't know what more to tell you except that that's a pretty rotten story to spread and I think you know it."

"I don't know it at all. Why else would Mr. B. hire a complete novice when qualified people are lined up around the block waiting for jobs?"

"I don't have to justify myself to you."

"That's exactly what I thought." Marcy sniffed self-righteously, pursed her lips, and stalked away. Resisting the urge to call out an unprintable phrase, Lauren turned to Sara, who pretended to be busy working but had heard everything. "Thanks for getting the call. Who was it?"

"One of your admirers. What kind of crap was Marcy giving you?"

"Her usual. I'm trying to school myself to ignore it. One of my admirers? Any message?"

"No, he just said your name, I said you were busy, and he hung up."

"What'd he sound like?"

"Older. Important. Maybe your father?"

"I doubt it. My dad's an armored tank when he wants something. He would have been more insistent; had me paged or—" A ring interrupted her words. "Hello? . . . Oh, hi, Dad."

Sara slid an imaginary knife across her throat.

"No, of course you're not. How's Mom? How's everything?" Lauren rolled her eyes. "I can't tonight, but maybe Sunday. . . . No, I haven't seen him. . . . Sure, I'll be there. . . . Okay. I love you, too."

"What was that about?"

"He tickles me," said Lauren, momentarily forgetting Marcy as she set down the receiver. "Such a big baby. Didn't mention my column this morning, not a word. As if it didn't exist. Just wanted to know if I'd seen Mr. B. I think he was worried I'd be mad at him for a letter he wrote. I *should* be, but I understand him too well."

"What kind of letter?"

"Oh, trying to get Mr. B. to unhire me. You might say he's a mite overprotective."

"A mite! Christ, what's he going to do when you decide to get married and he's not the most important man in your life?"

"That," said Lauren, "is something I'd rather not think about."


Sunday-night dinner with her parents was like a preview of the Fourth of July. Three columns had run—Monday, Wednesday, and Friday—and Victor was already feeling their impact. Typically, his friends had exclaimed, "That daughter of yours is really stirring up the shit, isn't she!" Or, with genuine curiosity, "What the hell's Lauren trying to prove, Victor?"

He had no answers for them—or for himself. "She's always been a bit of a rebel," he'd reply, trying to pass it off lightly.

"She's got to get this out of her system. She doesn't mean to insult anybody." Then, furious at himself for feeling the need to defend her, he'd quickly add, "That girl of mine's got quite a talent. Old Tightbucks Belloc doesn't part with *that* kind of dough unless he's got a sure winner."

No one, of course, had any idea what kind of dough Victor was talking about, but the fact that Walter was paying her at all was impressive.

The moment the Wildes sat down at the table, the fireworks started. Victor turned to his daughter. "Where the hell did you get that stupid story you ran Friday? It sounded very familiar."

"I explained to you, Dad, my columns are all fictitious."

"Don't tell me that one was. Who told you about the Stuarts?" He glared accusingly at his son. "You the big mouth?"

"That isn't the point," Lauren snapped before Chris could answer. "A lot of people tell me things. The information goes into my brain and mixes with all the other rumors and gossip and junk in there, and whatever comes out is part fact and part fantasy."

"Friday's piece of crap was pretty damn factual. You had no business holding the Stuarts up to ridicule that way."

Denials would be useless; her father was far too sharp. "But only you and I and Chris know it was the Stuarts," she protested. "I changed their name and *all* the circumstances. I'll bet you anything they wouldn't even recognize themselves."

"You'd lose the bet. Goodie Stuart called me Friday morning with murder in her heart—and screaming lawsuits."

"She—what?" Lauren felt herself go pale. "She honestly called you? What did you say?"

"I lied my goddamn head off. I told her I didn't know what she was yelling about. Then she said Chris must've talked to you, and I said that was unlikely because Chris had been in New York all week. I finally convinced her that I knew nothing of her desire to have a party in Le Ciel, and that if she was still interested, I'd be happy to see that she was taken care of."

"You'd give that bitch a fifty-percent discount?" asked Chris, glowering.

"We didn't discuss price. She was still screaming about her lawyer, and I finally had to tell her that I thought the Gaylords in your 'article' were loathsome toads, and if she wanted the public to think that the Gaylords and the Stuarts were one and the same—well, all she had to do was institute a lawsuit."

"Oh, no." Lauren was shaking nervously, on the verge of tears. "I feel absolutely terrible! I *never* wanted to hurt them or have anyone think I was referring to them. I was sure I'd changed the story enough to make the characters unrecognizable."

"Maybe this will teach you a lesson," charged Victor, sensing his advantage and homing in. "Maybe you'll stay out of fields where you don't belong, and go back to doing what you do best."

Upset as she was, his condescension infuriated her, momentarily converting guilt to anger. "And just what is that? Modeling tits and ass to a bunch of fatuous idiots who only care about going to fashion shows and getting their names in print? What do I do best, Dad? Run around to committee meetings and engage in three-hour discussions on whether to serve champagne before or after the door prize? That kind of life is about as stimulating as a puddle of upchuck—sorry, Mother—and so are some of our so-called friends. When I hear of them trying to use their rank and social position to take advantage of honest business people—well, it stinks!"

"Yes, it stinks," snarled Victor, his nostrils flaring, "but that's the world, young lady, and who are you to come charging along on your white horse and start making judgments about the way people live their lives?"

"Someone has to—"

"Please stop this bickering instantly," cried Edna, rapping her glass. "I won't have it at my table. We see each other once a week—not even that much—and I want it to be a happy time."

"Families do have problems, Edna," Victor growled with a sidelong look to his daughter. "Better to air them in private than to drag them out in public. Or don't you think so, Miss Save-the-World?"

"Mom's right," said Chris, who hadn't spoken before. His initial anger and feeling of betrayal had subsided with the realization that Lauren really did think she had sufficiently camouflaged her subjects. "Give her a chance, Dad. Hell, the only way she'll learn is by screwing up."

"I think you showed a lot of guts." The unexpected soft-voiced praise came from Zelda, who made it almost a religion to stay out of family arguments. All heads turned to her in surprise. "I don't know the Stuarts," she continued in the same low tones, "but I read all your columns, Lauren, and I said to myself, 'Brava! She's finally pulling her head out of the sand and looking around.' I know why you're worried, Papa Victor, but I think that when the talk dies down and people realize what she's trying to say with that column— you're going to be a very proud father."

He scowled at his daughter-in-law. "All right, Miss Zelda, suppose *you* tell me what she's trying to say and then we'll both know."

"Enough!" cried Edna sharply. "I will *not* have this scene at my dinner table." Her voice had a steel-sharp edge her family knew well. Unlike Victor's wrath, Edna's almost never surfaced, but on the rare occasions when someone pushed her too far, she could be formidable.

In the silence that followed her outburst, Edna spoke calmly. "No one has asked me my opinion of my daughter's new career, and I'll have to say, frankly, that I think we'd all be better off if Lauren were not in a job where she feels it necessary to make fun of the people and the society she's been fortunate enough to grow up in. My friends have been calling all week—Lordy, they haven't left me alone a minute! 'Why is she doing it?' 'What do you think of it?' I can't answer them, because I don't know what's turned my sweet daughter into a maverick. But I will say this—Victor, Chris, Zelda— and you, too, Lauren: The Wildes are a family. Our closeness is our strength. We have always stuck together, and as long as your father and I are alive, we always will. When we get up from this table tonight, not a word of what we've discussed will leave this room. From now on, our answer to the world is that it's Lauren's life and Lauren's decision, and whatever directions her talents lead her, we're with her a thousand percent."

"Are you quite finished with your little Pollyanna speech, Edna?" asked Victor. "May I say something?"

"No, dear, you may not." She smiled and turned to her son. "Now, weren't you going to tell me about Mallory's asthma?"

Later that evening, Lauren lay awake thinking, worrying, hurting. The Stuarts had never harmed her in any way; they had always been very pleasant, in fact, and, even though they were in their mid-forties, considered themselves friends of both generations of Wildes. It was true that they had tried to trade their social cachet for monetary gain, but that didn't make them bad people. Was it any different from a reporter trading publicity for a free evening in the Orchid Room? Damn right it was! The reporter *needed* to be there to get material for his story.

Over and over the words she had written—"pushy," "scheming," "parasitic"—continued to sting her conscience. Certain passages haunted her: "The Gaylords had enough money to buy the restaurant several times over. Why is it that the wealthiest people are the first ones to try to cheat others of their honest profits?" Victor was right; who the hell was she to be judging anyone? And worse, to be criticizing people—especially people whose hospitality she had accepted and returned and who thought of themselves as her friends?

The more she began to gain some sense of the enormous power she wielded, the more she began to fear it. Her motivation was right; she had no doubts that her ultimate goal was to benefit civilization and that even in her small way she might succeed in opening some eyes. But she had already hurt her brother and her parents; she had made lifelong enemies of the Stuarts and probably some of their friends; she had detractors at the paper who were spreading vicious rumors—and all of this for what? So she could lie in bed and feel miserable?

Using a meditation technique she had learned from Albert, her old lover-professor, she started repeating the word "nothing" over and over in her mind, forcing out all other thoughts and ideas that tried to creep in, until finally, at several hours past midnight, her eyes grew heavy with sleep.

At work the next morning, Lauren was happy to find a message that Rosa wanted to talk to her. She had been anxiously awaiting editorial feedback, someone to tell her that what she was doing was wonderful or mediocre or even terrible. So far, no one at the paper had said a word, not even Walter.

Rosa arrived at ten, looking neat and crisp as always, in a peach silk blouse and cocoa wool skirt. Her dark eyes were direct and honest, her lipstick too red, her makeup a shade too pale. Out of the office she had been warm and friendly with Lauren; her work persona, however, was different. Face and body gave the same message to everyone: "I'm management. I'm the boss. We respect each other. We work together. But remember the glass wall."

Dropping her mail on the desk, she scanned the letters, then pulled up a chair and motioned to Lauren to join her. "I want to talk to you about Friday's column."

The Gaylords again? Lauren sat on the edge of her seat, amazed at the intensity of her reaction. Why did she suddenly feel on the verge of passing out—clammy hands, spinning head, nausea in the pit of her stomach? The answer was easy; she had worked harder than she had ever worked in her life this last month, and she had publicly committed to doing a job. It was too late to back away; the Wildes had a reputation for finishing whatever they tackled. Even though she had made a colossal blunder, one that she could never undo, she must not give up. First, though, she would have to suffer the consequences.

"The Stuarts paid a call on Mr. B.," said Rosa with a sigh. "They want your scalp. Suppose you tell me exactly how that column was born."

Lauren's words came haltingly at first as she repeated the conversation with Chris and how careful she had been to alter the facts. Her closing argument was weak, however, and she knew it. "I don't understand why the Stuarts are so convinced it was a personal attack. People try to make deals like that all the time."

"Yes, but this *was* a personal attack. Apparently the Stuarts hadn't taken your brother's answer as final. They were trying to make arrangements through a friend of theirs at *Town and Country*. A lot of people knew that party was in the works. Your timing was very unfortunate." Rosa seemed both vexed and curious. "Didn't it ever occur to you that you were out to crucify them? That you were taking a privileged conversation with your brother and turning it into a cause célèbre?"

"No, I honestly thought my allusions were too general." She paused to let the guilt sink in. "I feel so devastated by this. My family's mad at me—I've let everyone down, including myself. What can I do?"

Rosa tried to sound casual. "Mr. B. suggests you shift emphasis."

"To what?"

"To safer, less controversial areas, for the time being. Maybe trends or social events you attend. What's happening in fashion or music or art—whatever. You might ask your friends who's giving parties or what's going on—"

"He's trying to turn me into a Sherry?"

"No, not at all." Rosa plainly disliked her role. She saw herself as Lauren's friend and mentor, but she also represented authority. "You still have your freedom. And you can still do social commentary now and then. Mr. B. just feels that since you know so many people in the community, perhaps you ought to be writing more about them, using real names, real happenings, getting real quotes from people."

"What about the four columns I've already written?"

"They'll keep. We'll spread them out so they don't lose their impact by repetition. Do you think you could write a new one by two this afternoon for tomorrow?"

A long sigh. "Oh, God, I don't know. This thing's got me so terribly shaken—so unsure of myself. And there's that whole stack of letters to answer—"

"They'll keep, too." For a moment, the glass doors slid open. "Don't be too crushed, Lauren. This is a business like any other. You get inflated and you get deflated. You made a bad mistake and you're hurting. That's natural. You didn't expect to launch a career without any setbacks, did you?"

"I didn't expect to make so many enemies so soon."

"That goes with the territory. Unless you write cotton-candy stuff like Sherry did, you're going to step on toes—and ankles and knees and a few bodies."

"So I'm learning. I'm sorry to start off giving you problems—"

"Forget it. Oh, one last thing. Mr. B. wants to look over your columns before they run, so be sure to give us at least a week on them. He may want to make a suggestion or two."

"Now he doesn't even trust me," Lauren groaned. "Christ, have I screwed up!"

Rosa frowned. "Stop feeling sorry for yourself. You did screw up—royally—and so did Mr. B. He had no business throwing you into that kind of job with no training, but he did it and it's done. Now it's up to you to get right back to work and show everyone that you can take it as well as dish it out."

"Thanks for the pep talk." Lauren managed half a smile. "I needed that."

No one, except possibly the whole fashion industry, could take offense at the column Lauren turned out for Wednesday. She had always hated being told to shorten or lengthen hems, wear loud clashing colors, ugly styles, and unflattering shapes simply because they were "in." High heels were another pet hate; unhealthy, uncomfortable, and unsafe—a definite hazard on San Francisco's steep hills. Even though she could afford whatever clothes she wanted, it annoyed her that the expensive jacket she bought last year was too long for the shorter styles now being promoted. She poured her feelings into good, strong, opinionated prose, full of generalities, not personalities. Since deadline was imminent, Rosa assured her it would run with minimal changes.

As soon as Lauren had finished the piece, signed off her VDT, and taken a few moments to reflect on the day's developments, she realized that the morning's wounds had begun to heal and her fight was returning. Thinking about Walter, a slow burn set in. He had blatantly gone back on his word, seduced her with promises of editorial freedom, and now he was setting all sorts of limits and restrictions. What was going on? Did one mistake—bad as it was—negate everything they had discussed and agreed on? Was Walter really as unscru pulous as her father claimed? Was Victor putting on new pressures she didn't know about?

Impulsively, she dialed the publisher's extension. "Miss Martin? It's Lauren Wilde. I wonder if I could have about ten minutes of Mr. B's time."

"Why, of course," came the cool reply. "It will have to be next week—possibly late Tuesday afternoon?"

"Next week? Wouldn't he have . . . well, just five minutes today?"

"I'm afraid not. He's booked solid this afternoon, and the rest of the week, too."

The burn was turning to broil. "What time Tuesday?"

"Four-thirty."

"All right, Miss Martin, I'll be there."

The city room was deserted Saturday morning when Lauren arrived at nine, determined to get a day's work done, with no phones, no people, no noises to distract her. After an hour or so at the VDT, her back began to ache and she looked around for relief. Wandering into the newsroom, she saw exactly what she wanted: a tall, straight, nonswivel chair with firm back and padded seat. Dragging it over to her desk, she settled in and returned to work.

Barely ten minutes later, a loud voice shattered her concentration. "Who's been sitting in *my* chair?"

Turning with a start, she faced two glaring eyes and a tight-lipped, unsmiling mouth. Its owner wore earphones and horn-rimmed glasses. Brown-gray hair spilled over the collar of a frayed shirt. His jeans were faded and wrinkled. Yet all the pieces fitted together, forming a singularly attractive man.

"Would you believe Cinderella?" she asked.

"Try Goldilocks."

"Okay, would you believe Goldilocks?"

"No, I don't believe in fairy tales."

"Then I'd better give you your chair." She rose and started to drag it across the floor.

"Don't be ridiculous!" He grabbed the chair and returned it to her desk. "I don't need it yet. I'm watching the game in there. My damn TV at home's on the blink. I'll let you know when I need it."

MERLA ZELLERBACH89

"Thanks, whoever you are."

"Ken Ferriday, political editor. And you're Lauren Wilde."

"How did you know?"

"Because you're spoiled, bitchy, and beautiful, just as I expected."

"How can you say that? I didn't know it was your chair—"

"No offense. I can really only vouch for the third adjective. I just guessed at the other two."

The man was strange. Intense. Intriguing. "Why?"

"Who knows? Who cares? Good-bye." As suddenly as he had materialized, he turned and disappeared down the hall. She stared after him a moment, shook her head, then resumed writing. Much to her frustration, however, she couldn't stop wondering about him. Nor could she shake her sense of a compelling presence just a few dozen feet away.

Ken Ferriday stood about five feet ten, she guessed, and looked to be in his early forties. Obviously some sort of athlete, he had a thickly muscled neck and well-formed shoulders that seemed almost too broad for his lean, taut frame. Yet with all the body bravado, he reminded her of a half-finished sculpture: rough, flawed, unpolished.

His facial features were equally rough-hewn and not attractive in the usual sense; eyes too harsh, nose too long, chin too square—and his expression definitely lacked warmth. Then why was she wasting so much time analyzing him? What kind of perverse magnetism did he wield? How, in only two or three sentences, had he managed to give the impression of wired dynamite waiting to explode? All her instincts told her this was a man to avoid.

It was almost noon when Ken reappeared at her desk, minus earphones. The game was over, he reported, the wrong team had won, and he wished to reclaim his property. "Could the princess get her royal ass off the throne?"

"It's your chair," she said, tempted to suggest what anatomical impossibility he might perform with it.

"May I bring you another to replace it?"

"No, you may crawl back under the rocks and leave me alone."

"As you like." He started to walk away, then stopped and

turned around. "One question first. Why are you working here?"

"Why are you?"

"I need the money, I know a fair amount about politics, and I'm a good writer. Next?"

"It's none of your business." She wished he would disappear.

"It's my business to speak up when I see something that's wrong. And you're taking a perfectly good job away from someone who needs it."

"Who, for instance?"

"Any number of better-qualified people."

He sounded as if he'd been talking to Marcy. "That's vague and abstract."

"Aren't your columns?"

"Apparently not, from some of the complaints that have come in."

"That's all you can say in your favor?"

"Look, I don't think I care to continue this discussion, Mr. Ferriday. You are rude and pompous and I have work to do."

"Very well, Miss Wilde. Fuck you." He saluted her with a mock bow, then with one hand lifted the chair over his head as if it were weightless and strode across the floor.

Mustering all her willpower, she dismissed his boorish behavior and faced the screen. The half-written article almost defied her to finish it. Her goal had been to write two columns or at least a first draft of them, but over three hours had passed and she hadn't finished even one. Determined to regain her concentration, she began moving the cursor when suddenly, without warning, the screen went blank. "Oh, no," she gasped, "it can't be!"

But it was. Frantically, she pushed buttons, numbers, codes. Nothing. She had forgotten to "save" her work as she went along; could the hungry machine have gobbled it up forever?

"Hello?" She almost shouted into the receiver. "This is Lauren. Could you give me VDT repair?"

"No one's there today, honey," said the operator. "They'll be in on Sunday."

"No one? No one at all?"

"Not until tomorrow."

"Ayyy." She banged a fist against her head. "Okay,
thanks." Once again, she pressed the "command" button to
instruct the computer. Once again, nothing happened. Grabbing the instruction sheet, she ran down the hall till she spotted a lone figure, puffing a cigarette by the vending machine.

"Mr. Ferriday, I'm desperate! Can you help me with the
VDT? It's swallowed my copy."

Smoke issued from one side of his mouth. "There's nothing
I can do. The system's down."

"But we usually get a warning—"

"No one's supposed to be working on Saturday."

"Please? I'm really in trouble—"

"Okay, I'll have a look." Squashing his cigarette on a paper plate, he strolled toward her. "No use to hurry. It's either
there or it isn't."

"Thank you."

Following several steps behind, he was not unaware of
gently rounded hips and shapely, suntanned legs beneath the
loose-fitting skirt. Her blond hair, tied back with a blue ribbon, looked casual and soft. A quick try at the machine, then
he turned to her. "The system's still down. All we can do is
wait."

"How long?"

He shrugged. "It could be five minutes or five hours. We
seem to be reluctant shipmates on this desert island. If you
don't mind slumming, I'll buy you a beer and a sandwich
across the street."

Instinct told her to decline. The man was hostile and arrogant. But he was also the only one who could help her rescue
three hours of hard work. "Sure. Thank you. In my panic, I
guess I forget all about eating."

Lunch in a dark booth in the Hofbrau Restaurant was more
enjoyable than she would have expected. Three beers had their
relaxing effect, and Lauren soon learned that her companion
was thirty-nine years old, twelve years divorced, and the father
of two teenagers who lived in the east with their mother.

"Do you ever see them?" she asked.

"My ex left me for an art professor," he replied. "I wasn't
cultured enough for her. Friends tell me he's been a good

stepfather to my kids. I still support them, but no, I never see them. What about you? Any ex-husbands? Fiancés?''

"No." She smiled. "Just a father."

"Sounds incestuous."

"Oops! I didn't mean to include him with my love interests. It's just that he's kind of a dominating force—overpossessive, if you will. Anyway, he's the only man in my life at the moment. I love him, but trying to keep him *out* of my life is the real challenge."

"Does he approve of your new job?"

"No, he hates it. He'd do anything to get me out of here and back to my charity committees."

"He must be a fascinating guy. I've always wanted to meet Victor B. Wilde."

She let the hint slip by and changed topics. "Politics isn't my favorite subject, but I have to admit you make dry stories very readable. I've often thought that you write brilliantly."

"You mean that?" He beamed with pleasure. "I suppose it's because I don't find politics dry at all. The hot-air speeches, the predictable press conferences, the well-rehearsed interviews, yes. But what a challenge to try to understand the individual—to analyze the rise of an unknown to power, the use and abuse of that power, the psychology of winning votes and public confidence, the facets that go into the making of a Ronald Reagan or a Henry Kissinger or even a Richard Nixon—these are the stories that intrigue me, not whether or not Trina Bellamy vetoes the newest gay rights bill."

"You know the mayor?"

"We've met. When she doesn't like a story or feels she's been misquoted, she doesn't call the guy who wrote it or the City Hall reporter, she calls me."

"And what do you do?"

"If she *was* misquoted, we'll retract. If she's just pissed because she got bad ink, I tell her she probably deserved it. Drives her press secretary right up the wall, poor schmuck, because *he's* supposed to be dealing with the press. But she's a typical female—bull-headed, aggressive, a real ball-breaker."

Lauren speared an olive with some hostility. "I won't even bother to oink at you. But it happens not to be true."

"How would you know?"

"Because we're friends. We grew up together. I was a bridesmaid at her wedding."

"Oh?" He looked at her with sudden interest.

"For your information, Scott Bellamy is very much his own man. Trina is a doer and a leader, and she does a terrific job running the city, but I assure you it's quite different at home. No one pushes Scott around."

"You're loyal; I'll say that."

"It's the truth." She finished the last of her ham on rye and wondered if she should reach for the check.

"You could be right," he said unconvincingly. "I really don't know the lady. I'd like to sit down and chat with her sometime, away from the office, maybe at dinner."

"Maybe you will—sometime."

"Can you arrange dinner for the four of us?"

She ignored the assumption that she would be willing to be his date for the evening. "No, I'm sorry. A lot of people know we're friends and ask me to arrange a meeting or want some favor from her. I have a stock answer: 'Write her a letter. You're welcome to mention my name. But I never mix politics with friendship.' "

He motioned for the check. "Then don't."

"Errr . . ." She fumbled with her purse. "Would you be insulted if I offered to share that with you?"

"I'd rather you took me to lunch next week."

And she would rather take the check and be done with it. He wasn't going to extort a promise of a date, but neither could she risk offending him. "Anything's possible," she murmured, slipping on her jacket.

The system was back up when they returned to the office, and Ken's expert manipulations succeeded. To Lauren's joy and relief, the morning's labors were retrieved and restored to her file intact. She thanked him profusely, packed up her notes, and drove home. What a curious, complicated man he was. And what a masochist she must be—already planning where she would take him to lunch next week.

* * *

As usual, Lauren was first to arrive in the office Monday morning. Somehow, she had managed to relegate the Stuarts to a back corner of her mind, where they remained, simmering and taunting, like an unsolved puzzle. Her greatest hope was that time would cool their anger and fade the incident into history. In the interim, life had to go on. Her typical work day started at eight-thirty or nine, Sara showed up at nine-thirty, and the others appeared at ten or thereabouts and stayed until six—or thereabouts. The schedule was flexible and varied with the work load.

The small mail slot Lauren had allotted herself had been changed for a bigger one to accommodate the several dozen letters she received each day. Having to write a new set of columns meant stopping everything else, and she had fallen behind in answering—a chore she took seriously. Every reader was a potential fan or foe, and every letter meant that someone felt moved enough to write, be it to express pleasure or scorn. The latter was usually vented by way of a sarcastic attack on her wealth, supposed materialism, and other superficial values or lack of experience. But even some of the hate missives, if signed, were worthy of a reply.

Covering a yawn, she collected the weekend's accumulation and began to leaf through them. One immediately caught her eye. The name and address were spelled out in colored letters cut from magazines. "Someone's been watching too many movies," she muttered, opening it. Inside, a note in the same script ominously warned: "You are being watched."

"Not very funny." She laid the envelope aside, trying to dismiss it as a sick joke, and tackled the remaining pile. But something—or maybe everything—about the letter bothered her. It wasn't the usual type of hate mail that insulted, demeaned, or attempted to shock her with foul language. Someone had spent a good hour cutting and piecing those words together; not a casual undertaking.

Sara's reaction was even stronger. "This isn't your everyday kook," she said, viewing the note with alarm. "He sounds like a psycho. You'd better show Rosa."

"What's she going to do about it?"

"I don't know. Maybe she'll recognize the handwriting."

"Is that like a joke?"

"No, I'm serious. We have lots of regulars. Anything really hostile goes into the crank file. Could be the guy—or gal— just likes to cut up magazines and has done this before."

The letter, however, proved unfamiliar to Rosa, who assured Lauren that all columnists got threats, then sent her directly to Dave Helms, the chief security officer. A husky black man in a well-worn uniform, he examined the note and asked Lauren into his office, just off the main-floor lobby. Six television screens sat on his desk; they covered all entrances to the *Herald* building as well as the executive quarters. Another officer sat in a corner monitoring the sets; they were watched twenty-four hours a day.

"We take all threats very seriously," said Helms, helping her into a chair. "Have you ever had anything like this happen before?"

"No, never. Oh, I'd get hate letters sometimes when my name or my picture was in the paper. But nothing like this."

"No obscene or threatening phone calls?"

"Not since I got an unlisted number five years ago."

"Do you know of anyone who might be angry at you or want to harm you?"

Now *he* was sounding like a B movie. "No, I don't have any enemies that I know of."

"Nevertheless, we must take every precaution. Where do you park your car?"

"Across the street in the garage."

"Do you go out for lunch?"

"Sometimes. Not today, though, I've got too much to do."

"I want you to let us know every time you leave the building. One of us will escort you to your car. Do you live alone?"

"Yes."

"What kind of security do you have?"

Was that his worry, too? His credibility might suffer if anything happened to her at work—but at home? "I live at the top of a twelve-story building," She replied. "The entrances have deadbolt locks, and we've got twenty-four-hour doormen."

"Is there a garage?"

"Yes, under the building. I take the elevator right up to my door."

"I want you to pick up the doorman in the evening before you park," he said gravely. "Have him drive with you to the basement, stay with you in the elevator, and see you safely inside your front door."

"Do you really think that's necessary?"

Helms frowned. "I don't want to alarm you, Miss Wilde, but please do as I say."

"All right."

"One more thing. Vary your schedule. Don't come here and leave at the same time every day. Don't make regular appointments at the beauty shop or anywhere. The chances are ninety-nine-point-nine percent that we're dealing with a prankster or possibly a jealousy factor, but it's the point-one percent that concerns me."

"I understand."

"And of course, be sure to tell me right away if you get another letter or if anything—anything at all—out of the ordinary happens. Be careful and be alert."

"You forgot 'Have a nice day.'"

He stared coldly. "I'm afraid these are violent times."

Instantly, she regretted her sarcasm. "I'm sorry. You're right, and I do appreciate your concern. I'll follow your orders and I'll stay in touch."


The phone, Lauren thought, had a way of knowing exactly when she climbed into the tub for a nice, soothing bath. Monday night was no different, and as she soaked in the warm bubbles, the instrument rang insistently. About the tenth ring, she succumbed.

"I knew you were home," said a deep voice. "I won't make you guess which of your admirers this is. It's Ken Ferriday. The *Herald* operator gave me your number."

"Oh, hi," she said with relief. At least it was someone she knew. "Sorry, I was in the tub."

"I was going to give it an even dozen rings. How was your day?"

"Fine." She wrapped the towel tighter and curled into a chair. "Thanks to your rescue operation, I finished that column."

"Are you pleased with it?"

"Not terribly. Are you ever pleased with what you write?"

"I'm always pleased," he said. "When something doesn't read well, I figure it's the material, not the writer."

"Sure wish I had your confidence." She stretched the towel across her shivering shoulders. "How was *your* day?"

"Uneventful. I looked for you about ten-thirty, but some fat woman was sitting at your desk."

"Oh, that must have been Sara answering my phone. She's not fat; she's 'full-figured.' "

"Yeah, so's the battleship I was on during the war."

"That's unkind," she said. "Anyway, I was down seeing Mr. Helms."

"The Gestapo?"

"He *is* a bit of a stickler, isn't he."

"Stickler! If that guy had turned to crime instead of becoming a copy, he'd be the Godfather. What were you seeing Helms for?"

She hesitated, wondering if it was wise to confide. But it was too late to be coy, and it would do her good to talk to someone. "I got a letter—words all cut out and pasted together from magazines. Some creep said he was 'watching' me. Helms decided I needed a bodyguard to walk me to my car."

"Sounds like a put-on. Are you worried?"

"Not really. I agree with you—it's too much like a bad script."

A thoughtful pause; then his voice lowered. "If you're scared, little girl, I could come over and spend the night with you."

"Old silver tongue strikes again." She laughed.

"No hanky-pank. I'll sleep in your nice warm bed and you can have the couch."

"Thanks anyway."

"Well, if I can't protect you, I can at least let you buy me lunch. Tomorrow?"

The man could give lessons in chutzpah. "Who could resist your charm?"

"Shall we start rumors, or shall I meet you in the lobby?"

"My bodyguard and I will meet you in the lobby at noon."

"I'll take care of your bodyguard," he said. "Bring lots of money."

Ken Ferriday was very much on her mind as she lay awake that night, regretting her plans for tomorrow and vowing it would be their first and last date. Maybe she would think up a story, pretend she was engaged or going with someone— except that she had already told him she wasn't. Perhaps an old beau could materialize—no, the tangled web wasn't worth the deceit. Her Quaker friend George used to quote Mark Twain's line "When in doubt, tell the truth." It was still good advice.

The truth, however, would have to be softened. She could hardly inform Ken that she thought him hostile, crude, and aggressive. Nor could she tell him that he lacked polish and finesse, and would never be comfortable with her friends or her family. Least of all would she be inclined to mention what alarmed her most about him: that he reminded her of how she felt as a child when she was told about the third rail—curious and scared, yet dying to touch to see if she really would get electrocuted.

His arrogant stature, determined walk, almost a swagger, and taut, athletic body packed a strong physical message—one that he would have no trouble delivering, she was sure. Yet the feelings he aroused were strangely foreign to her. The two affairs she had had, both with older men, had started with love, admiration, and kindness and later ripened into desire. With Ken, there were no thoughts of love or tenderness, only stirrings of—she hated the bluntness of the phrase, but it fit— animal attraction. That brilliant, cynical mind was housed in a stallion's body, and much as she might have liked to know the two sides of him separately, she had strong intimations that that would never be possible.

Why was she overthinking the situation, anyway? How could a mere luncheon date have lasting consequences? She was expert at controlling her emotions, and she would simply have to explain to Ken that involvement was out of the question. She had worked too hard to win her fellow workers' respect and friendship, and she wasn't about to jeopardize her reputation for the sake of an office romance. They could be friends, she would assure him, but nothing more.

# CHAPTER
## 5

KEN WAS WAITING WHEN LAUREN ARRIVED IN THE LOBBY at noon the following day. He wore a tweed sport coat with leather elbows, a bow tie that almost matched, and wool slacks that needed pressing. Yet somehow it all worked and even suited his journalist image. He stood erect and appeared taller than his height.

"You look so nice," were her first words. "I hadn't expected you to dress."

"Shall I undress?" He took her arm, waved to the security officer who was watching, and guided her to the door. "In order to dispatch your bodyguard, I had to promise I wouldn't let you out of my sight for the next twenty-four hours."

"Twenty-four hours?"

"Or until we come back to the building, which *could* be twenty-four hours."

She laughed, not displeased. "What is it with you? Don't you think of anything else?"

"Yes, I do," he answered seriously, "but I also happen to be with a beautiful woman about whom I have very mixed feelings. Part of me says she belongs to a society scene full of snobbery and pretensions that I loathe, and part of me—a much stronger part of me—wants to take her in my arms and see if she's the woman I think she is.''

Avoiding the question in his eyes, she looked across the street. "Your car or mine?"

"Mine," he said, "unless you're afraid to ride in a dirty old Honda. You might soil that nice blue dress. Is it silk?"

"Yes." And if you knew what the nice blue dress cost, she thought, you'd join the Communists. She had modeled the pretty Galanos in a fashion show several years ago. Victor had been there and surprised her by buying it ($1,445 plus tax) for her birthday. Now, several seasons and a dozen dry cleanings later, she deemed it fit for the office. "I'm not worried about the dress. Where are we going?"

He opened the car door, switched some papers to the backseat, and helped her inside. "What about the Nob Hill Plaza? You'd probably get a discount, and I'd enjoy walking in with the boss's daughter."

"No thanks." A flood of excuses rushed to mind, but none of them worked. She would be as truthful as she dared. "Dad would know I was there in four seconds. He'd probably insist we have lunch with him."

"I hear he's quite a guy. I'm anxious to meet him."

"Forget it. I'm not in the mood for parental guidance." Nor was she prepared to explain Ken Ferriday to Victor. She could even write his dialogue: "You disgrace the family by going to work for a newspaper, and that's not enough? Now you're running around with reporters?"

"Papa probably wouldn't approve of the company you're keeping, right?" he asked, starting the motor.

He was more perceptive than she thought. "Papa never approves of the company I keep. Male company, that is."

"Why not? Is he afraid everyone's after your money?"

"Not really. Whatever I have he's got tied up in trusts that he controls. I think it's more personal. I'm still his little girl. I still need to be protected from the big bad world."

"Why are you sitting that way?"

She looked at him curiously. "What way?"

"As if you've got one foot out the door. I don't bite—at least not while I'm driving. Move over."

She moved.

"More."

"That's enough. Where are we going?"

"Do you like seafood?"

"Love it."

The sun blazed warmly, the sky was clear, the air blowing in was cool and invigorating. He drove up several hills to California Street, turned left, then turned again at Taylor and followed it to Fisherman's Wharf. Putting his "Working Press—Official Business" sign on the windshield, he left the car in an alley, then led her down the street to a small restaurant, where the owner seemed less than overjoyed to see him and showed them to a corner table.

Time dissolved in a medley of rex sole and chatter. The latter he peppered with strong likes and dislikes, and brief bios of some of the office characters. She was fascinated to learn that Marcy Burgeson had been raped several years ago ("The guy must've been blind"), had followed the horrifying experience with a six-part series on the subject, and had won a national award. The other tales concerned people she knew by name or not at all. Much of it was hearsay, he admitted, including the rumor that Walter Belloc had a cash register in his bar and always gave no-host cocktail parties.

The restaurant owner had been astounded to hear Lauren ask for the check. Mr. Ferriday had been coming there for years and—as an influential journalist who occasionally favored them with a mention—had never yet been charged for a meal.

Ken admitted he had known that would be the case and insisted she still owed him lunch. After giving him fifteen minutes of reasons why she could not possibly see him again, they made a date for the following week.

Later that same Tuesday afternoon, Lauren strode down the hall to keep her four-thirty appointment with the publisher. The ever-efficient Ms. Martin showed her in immediately.

Walter was waiting by the door, kissed her cheek, and stood back to admire. "Ah, my dear child, your beauty lights up these drab and dismal quarters. I'm overjoyed to see you."

They were alone, of course, and he had reverted to his "old family friend" persona. "Dear Uncle Walter," she said sweetly. "You *are* a chameleon. What kind of monster have you created?"

His eyes gleamed with the challenge. "Could you possibly be referring to yourself?"

"Yes, you scoundrel. You take a poor innocent girl, hook her on the heroin of instant celebrity, and then tie her down with all sorts of laws and limitations."

"Brava, my dear." He leaned back and clapped appreciatively. "I can see the muse is with you even if you do sound a twiddle like your father. Do I detect a note of unhappiness?"

"Walter, *you* suggested satire. *You* promised artistic freedom. Now I have to write about real people and real places, and I have to get your approval on everything first."

"Heavens no," he growled. "Messages get so distorted around this place. You did absolutely right by coming to me directly. I merely told Rosa, my cherry pie, that I did not want you to type yourself as a satirist. These first few weeks are crucial. Our readers are deciding whether or not you're worth reading. You have to keep them off balance. Give them a variety of styles and subjects, something for everyone."

He paused for impact, dropping chin to chest and peering over his spectacles. "You simply can't afford to lose all the readers who hate satire. Keep them baffled. Social commentary is superb on Monday, but follow it with perhaps a fashion critique on Wednesday, then on Friday a review of a party or a play, or even a sparkling interview. Don't you see, peach blossom, that far from limiting you, I'm setting you free? I'm encouraging you *not* to associate yourself with a single style or point of view, not to get labeled, and not to get yourself into a journalistic bind."

Her mind clicked like a computer, checking every word. He was double-talking her again, but he made sense, too.

"As to the other snarl, petunia, I merely hoped you might share the fruits of my wisdom and experience. If I can point out an error *before* it sees print rather than after, I suspect that would be to all our advantage."

"I suspect so." She sighed guiltily. "I have the strongest feeling there's something you're not telling me. Whatever happened with the Stuarts? I'm so embarrassed about that. I hear they called on you."

"I was about to broach that delicate matter, rosebud. They not only called on me; they sent their thieving attorney to call on my thieving attorney. After much legal hugger-mugger and several rather incendiary debates, the Stuarts magnanimously agreed to drop their alleged lawsuit—"

"Thank God!"

"For a cash settlement of thirty thousand dollars, which would not be an admission of guilt on our part, merely a goodwill gesture—plus all their legal expenses."

"Oh, no." Lauren's voice was barely audible as she asked, "What's the total?"

"Thirty-nine thousand. Small compensation for being publicly humiliated, if indeed they were, but adequate under the circumstances. It will be a sterling lesson to you, my dear, albeit a costly one."

Costly? Her first inclination had been to offer to pay the bill herself. Money had never been a concern, and that amount would hardly dent the family coffers. But all riches flowed from the paternal source, and while a new BMW or a dozen Rosenthal china place settings would barely raise an eyebrow, this kind of expenditure would not inspire Victor's largesse. "Costly to whom?"

"Ahhh." Walter emitted a low grunt. "Much as it pains me to offer you the right to terminate our brief alliance, whipped cream, brutal circumstances force me to do so. In such an instance, you would quietly slip into the stratosphere and direct your formidable talents to other literary pursuits. My twenty-five-thousand-dollar-deductible libel insurance would pay fourteen thousand of the due bill, I would be forced to part with certain valuable assets to produce the remaining twenty-five thousand dollars, and my policy rate would bloom like a pustule on a proboscis."

"Does that mean you're firing me?"

"I am aware that I am not known for my philanthropy, hollyhock. Nevertheless, my genuine and long-standing fondness for you and your family"—his thin lips widened as his eyes glazed benignly—"stir my highest and most noble instincts. I have an alternative proposition. Would you care to consider it?"

He had her over the proverbial barrel, clearly relishing his regained supremacy. Now she was worried. "Yes."

"Very well. I am willing to offer you the opportunity to continue producing your fine columns in the mode we discussed earlier and, at the same time, allow you to pay off this very unfortunate debt with minimal deductions from your salary—let us say three hundred a week—until the balance reaches zero."

Was she hearing right? "Walter—you want to take three hundred a week from my salary—let's see, three hundred times fifty-two is over fifteen thousand dollars a year—for two or three years or until the whole thirty-nine thousand is paid off?"

"That is precisely the nature of my munificent offer. Along with your other talents, I see you have a fine head for finances. If you choose this option over the previous one, I would not be forced to liquidate my assets to provide the needed cash flow, because you, in effect, would be borrowing it from the bank. My lawyer would formalize the arrangements."

"Wait, you're going too fast for me." She felt as if she were being sucked into a pool of quicksand. "In other words, your lawyer arranges for me to take out a thirty-nine-thousand-dollar bank loan, which I pay back at the rate of three hundred a week—with interest?"

"It is my understanding that banks usually require it."

"With interest, then, until I've paid off the principal. What if I leave your employ before then?"

"The debt accompanies you, grapenuts. You would still be responsible for the loan. If you do decide to accept my generous proposal, I daresay it would be to everyone's advantage to keep these details absolutely and irrevocably confidential." He stared at her unsmilingly. "Would I have your word on that?"

"I certainly wouldn't race for the phone to call Victor," she replied, her humor starting to come back with the relief of knowing that she could still have her job if she accepted his terms. "I don't know what to say. You've got my arms so twisted, they're pretzels. I can't even call my lawyer for advice because he'd feel obliged to tell the family."

Walter bristled at the suggestion. "Dear girl, do you imply that I am in any way attempting to take advantage of you or to capitalize on our longtime and, I trust, mutual affection for each other?''

"Heaven forfend! I've never been offered two such wonderful choices: I can either leave my job and admit to my family and friends that I'm a slanderer, a failure, and a quitter, or I can stay on the job and pay you a mere thirty-nine thousand dollars with interest. Who wouldn't be thrilled with those options?''

"Pay the *bank*, buttercup. There's an ocean of difference. I have no desire to seek personal gain from the misfortune of others. Do we have an agreement?''

"Don't rush me.''

"While you are cogitating, pray tell me if you've received any more of those despicable cut-up letters?''

"No, just the one I got yesterday.''

"Some silly child playing a game, no doubt. If any other incident of this nature occurs in the future, I hope you will come to me at once.''

"Yes—at once.'' She flirted with the idea of telling him his watchdog secretary had made her wait almost a week to see him, then decided to remain silent. It would be foolish to make an enemy of Ms. Martin. "Well, I guess you've still got yourself a columnist if you want me—poorer but wiser. Where do I sign?''

"Capital, my dear! No pun intended.'' His pleasure seemed as genuine as his relief at having unloaded the debt. "The firm of Truman and Jones will contact you shortly. In the meantime, we had best corroborate our fairy tale. My suggestion is that we tell anyone impertinent enough to ask that 'the Stuart matter has been forgotten.' No more, no less.''

"Will Rosa buy it?''

"Not for an instant; she is far too astute. She is also far too astute to pursue it.'' He blinked with self-satisfaction, then, with uncharacteristic warmth, came around the desk and took her hands. "Here's to a fruitful partnership, tangerine. Long may it ripen and blossom.''

"Walter,'' she said, "why do I have the strongest feeling I've just been screwed?''

"A matter of semantics, my dear,'' he corrected. "I prefer to think you've been wooed and won.''

* * *

Despite the one-sided financial arrangement, her third week at the paper was starting auspiciously, Lauren decided. After the visit with Walter, Rosa had become even friendlier than before and was taking her to lunch that Monday. The publisher had apparently sent word that Lauren was to have all the editorial guidance and help she needed, and Rosa—with Sara's approval—had assigned Sara to work as Lauren's part-time assistant. Her job would be to help for a few hours every day, answering mail and calls, phoning for quotes and information, and doing whatever she could to give Lauren more time to write.

Rosa had wisely suggested that they leave the office separately and meet in the small delicatessen down the block. She hadn't needed to explain to Lauren that it wouldn't do to have the others in the office think they were getting chummy.

Lauren was nursing a Tab at a corner table when her editor arrived.

"I felt like I was sneaking off to meet a lover." Rosa smiled, pulling up a chair. "But you can't be too careful with Marcy around. I sometimes wonder why we put up with all her garbage."

"Why do you?"

"Because she's a fine reporter—excellent, in fact. And because she's been at the paper almost as long as I have. And mainly, I suppose, because she belongs to the guild, and her severance pay, if we fired her, would be up into five figures."

"Mightn't it be worth paying her off just to get rid of her? She stirs up so much dissension."

"Mr. B. doesn't think so." Rosa unfolded her napkin and spread it on her lap. "He told me you two had a chat."

"Yes. He seems to feel I shouldn't limit myself to skewering the smart set. I suppose he's right. I've been thinking of doing several pieces, including one on—well, I know three couples who were childhood sweethearts, married others, became divorced or widowed, then found each other again in their fifties. What do you think?"

"Frankly, not much—unless you can get some lively quotes. Any other ideas?"

"Well, what about a picture story on slob clothes—what

some of our local clotheshorses wear around the house or in the garden or whenever they're not dressing up for *Women's Wear*."

"Assuming they'd be willing to be photographed as slobs, which I doubt, that has possibilities. Sounds as if you're getting rather conservative in your subject matter. Did something happen with the Stuarts?"

Lauren felt herself flushing. She and Rosa were just beginning to trust and confide in each other, and she hated to withhold information. "Yes—something did. But Walter swore me to secrecy. I wish I could tell you—"

"You don't have to. Knowing Mr. B., I have a pretty good idea. There won't be a lawsuit?"

"No."

"Good." She motioned to a blackboard on the wall. "There's the menu. If you like corned beef, I recommend it."

"Sounds great."

"Two number fours, please," she called to the waitress. "Now—what else is happening? Your father still on your back?"

"Like a mink stole on a prom queen. What about you? Do you have any family around here?"

"My parents live in San Diego. They're always after me to get married again, but they don't realize the pathetic male situation in this city. It's not even that the men are all married or gay. The worst part is that the eligible ones are so sought after and spoiled, they'd be impossible to live with."

"I agree—especially some of the ones who work at the *Herald*."

Rosa's eyes twinkled with amusement. "Speaking of that, did you see the notice on the bulletin board about the big *Herald* picnic a week from Saturday?"

"Yes. Annual event, I take it. Sounds dreadful. How many people go?"

"We usually get about two hundred fifty adults, screaming kids, and hungry dogs. It's a mob scene, but sometimes it's kind of fun. Might be good PR for you to show up."

"So the others don't think I'm too snooty, huh? All right. Can I drive you over?"

Rosa nodded. "Thanks, but we'd better show up by ourselves. No reason we can't sit together, though—that is, unless you have plans."

"Why would I—" She read her companion's questioning look. "Oho! You wouldn't mean Ken Ferriday?"

"That possibility did cross my mind."

Lauren burst into laughter. "Good Lord, is *nothing* sacred in that office? I had lunch with him—twice. And we're supposed to have lunch tomorrow, if you want to make an item out of that. Even if we did have a relationship, which we don't, I doubt I'd care to announce it at the company picnic."

"What do you think of him?"

Lauren blew a strand of hair from her forehead. "The truth? I think he's obnoxious. Bright. Ballsy. And sexy as hell."

Rosa's shoulders heaved in resignation. "I was afraid of that."

"Why?"

"Do we both agree that it's none of my business?" Lauren nodded, and the editor continued, "There's lots of talk about him around the office, because, as you say, he is attractive and single. He also has a vicious tongue and a horrible temper. And I hear he gets pretty nasty when he drinks."

"Is that all?"

"Let me change that. Nasty bordering on violent. I've even seen him nasty when he's sober. Personally, I can't stand the man. He gives me bad vibes."

"Me, too," said Lauren. "But then he starts slinging the bull and charms me right out of them."

"Oh, he can sling it all right when he wants to. Just don't be bamboozled. He'd like nothing better than to have a Wilde in his pocket."

The insinuation hurt. Did he really see her as a conquest or a trophy rather than a woman? Was it possible that Rosa's strong, almost bitter reaction was based on personal experience—perhaps a rejection? She was too tactful to suggest it. "Well, I'm glad you told me. The unfortunate thing, human nature being what it is, is that the more I'm warned about this ogre, the more I'm intrigued."

"In that case, you're hopeless." Rosa turned her attentions to sawing through two inches of corned beef. "No wonder your poor father worries."

* * *

Later that afternoon, Sara carried the contents of the mailbox to her desk and dropped twenty or thirty letters onto the blotter. Her intake of air was audible as she suddenly fastened on one envelope. "Uggh."

"What is it?" Lauren looked over and felt the color drain from her face. "Another love letter?"

"I'm afraid so. Want me to open it? Maybe we should wear gloves."

"Let's let Mr. Helms open it." She grabbed the missive with its now familiar script and hurried downstairs to the security officer, who did put on gloves, then pulled out the contents with tweezers. Inside was the same white bond paper, the same cut-out letters, and another melodramatic threat: "I am coming for you."

"I've done everything you suggested," said Lauren weakly.

"The words—a sexual twist," muttered Helms, still staring. "We can't take chances. I'm calling the police right away."

"Do you need me?"

"Has anything—anything at *all* happened in your life that's unusual? Any phone calls with no one there?"

"No, I would've told you. Nothing's happened."

"Then continue all precautions," he ordered. "I'll call when we need you."

The rest of the day was uneventful, with no further word from Helms or the police. Perhaps they were less concerned than he. She drove home wondering if Ken was still planning to meet her at noon tomorrow. Strange man—so aggressive, so brash, yet not a word from him since their lunch a week ago. Had she said or done something to alienate him? She almost found herself missing him.

The suspense ended that evening about eight. "Did I get you out of the bath?"

His deep voice on the phone was unmistakable.

"Oh, hi, Ken. No, I'm dressed and dry. Where've you been all week?"

"Busier'n a cat covering shit. And you?"

"Working." She was anxious to tell him about the second letter but decided to wait.

"Look, I'm sorry for the late notice, but I can't make lunch tomorrow. Two congressmen are coming to town, and the conference is at noon. What about dinner?"

Going out at night changed friendship to romance. She specifically did not want to start dating him. "Ummm . . . I'm afraid that's bad for me."

"You busy or just unwilling?"

"Why do you always have to ask questions? It's both. I *am* busy, and I explained to you last week why I wanted us 'purely platonic.' "

"Purely platonic is fine," he said, his voice perking up. "Can't we be platonic at dinner as well as lunch?"

"It's harder by candlelight," she replied, smiling to herself. It all did sound rather foolish.

"Look here, I may be a boor and a beast and a male chauvinist and all the things you think I am, but one thing I don't do is break my word. And I give you my word. I swear to you by God and my mother and the fourteen buddhas of Sringalaka that I will never, ever, lay a finger on your pretty skin unless I have your consent and permission in writing. Will you accept that?"

"In writing?" She laughed merrily. "I don't believe you. In writing?"

"You have my word. Are you still busy tomorrow night?"

"Do you want to know where I live?"

"I already know. I'll see you at seven," he said, and clicked off.

The anticipation of seeing him was diluted by a sudden feeling of uneasiness. Where had he gotten her address?

At four minutes past seven Tuesday evening, the doorman rang to announce that Mr. Ferriday was on his way up. It was Lauren's first night out in over a week. Pleading exhaustion, she had turned down all invitations except dinner with the family. The new job demanded every ounce of energy she had.

With some sense of anticipation, she had washed her hair, brushed it soft and shiny, and slipped into a pale green wool suit with a matching silk print blouse. She greeted him at the door, hand outstretched.

He shook it formally. "You look lovely."

"Thank you. I'll return the compliment." Clothes looked good on him, but he seemed to care so little about them. "New suit?"

"Nope, *only* suit. I wear it at least once a year. The tie's new. I bought it in your honor."

Black and white daisies stood out against a shocking-pink background. Fortunately, his suit was charcoal gray and handled it. "I'm flattered. May I fix you a drink?"

"Thanks, but we don't have time. Are you ready?"

"Almost. By the way, who'd you bribe to get my address?"

"I don't go around bribing people. A little computer told me."

"You got into the personnel file?"

"Yeah. It's like a slot machine. If you play it long enough, you get lucky and hit the jackpot."

"Don't they arrest people for doing things like that?"

"Sometimes. But who's going to know unless you tell them? And you're too young to die, so go fetch your purse and your mad money. We've got a seven-thirty reservation."

Mario's was a small spaghetti house in the Marina district that served, according to Ken, the best pasta in town. Faded grapevines hung down from the ceiling, red-checkered plastic covered the tables, and the smell of garlic almost overwhelmed the senses. In one corner, an old jukebox was playing Glenn Miller's "Moonlight Serenade." The lights were dim and flattering and the atmosphere warm and friendly.

"How's the cannelloni?" he asked. "On a scale of one to ten?"

"Superb. At least a nine." An appreciative "Mmmm" underscored the compliment. "I had the best corned-beef sandwich of my life yesterday, and now this. Ever been to that little deli down the block from the paper?"

"Sure, did you have lunch there? Alone?"

"With Rosa, my editor. I suspect she's one of your old flames."

He looked honestly surprised. "Rosa Cortez? Are you out of your skull?"

"Why? She's an attractive lady."

"She doesn't exist for me. I see her at staff meetings every morning, but I *don't* see her, if you know what I mean. I look right through her."

What a cruel appraisal. No wonder Rosa disliked him. "What kind of woman does appeal to you?"

"You taking a survey?"

"Just curious. You never talk about your old lovers or your deep, dark past. You're quite a mystery to me."

His brow furrowed and his tone was irritable. "My deep, dark past will stay deep and dark. What's over is over."

Such a strong response to a half-teasing question. She changed to a more current subject. "Did I tell you I got another of those ghastly letters yesterday?"

"I know," he said, pleasant again, and twirling his fork in the spaghetti. "I want to talk to you about it."

"Helms told you?"

He nodded. "I saw him this afternoon, convinced him I was your closest friend and worried as hell about you. It took all my persuasive powers, but he finally showed me the report from the police lab."

Her hand stopped in midair. "What report?"

"Nothing significant. I'll tell you in a minute. First, I'd like to ask you a question or two, okay?"

"All right." Her tone spoke otherwise. "I haven't a thing to tell, though. No one's followed me; no one's bothered me—"

"Lauren . . ." It was unusual for him to use her name. "Please think carefully. Has anyone you know—have any of your friends—tried to stop you from writing your column?"

"No, they've all been wonderfully encouraging—except for one couple I inadvertently insulted the first week. And they've been appeased."

"Any old boyfriends or rejected suitors who might want to get back at you for something?"

"No, not a soul." Why was he so interested? Why was he acting as if it were *his* problem—or up to him to be her protector?

"Anyone in your circle of friends who might be jealous and possibly have a screw loose?"

"Lots of jealousy, I suppose. Lots of loose screws, too—oops! I didn't mean it that way. I can't think of anyone who'd be sick enough to sit down and spend all that time." She was getting exasperated. "Why do you keep insisting it's someone I know? Or someone who's jealous? What did the police find out?"

His voice dropped. "I'll answer all three questions at once. The police collected the letter yesterday morning and brought back the report late this afternoon, just as I was leaving. Helms, as I said, showed it to me, and I told him I'd talk to you."

Her heart was racing. Why didn't he get to the point?

"The person who sent it is right-handed, a male, and probably has money," he explained. "They could tell the right-handedness from the way he cut out the letters; the sex they got from chromosomes or some damn thing in the saliva under the stamp, and the scissors were very sharp and probably an expensive German blade."

"Incredible!"

"They also picked up a vestige of fancy fragrance, probably male, and the magazines, the sources of the letters, were new and fairly costly."

"They could tell all that?"

"Sure. The average person would use newspapers or find some old magazines lying around the basement. This guy went out and bought half a dozen two- and three-dollar magazines to cut up."

"Wow. Anything else?"

"From his dexterity, they estimate his age to be over forty. He could be a mental case, or he could be someone deliberately trying to scare the shit out of you."

She set down her fork and stared in disbelief. "Could someone really hate me that much?"

"It's not necessarily hate. Tell me, who didn't want you to write the column?"

"Ken, for God's sake, I told you ten times, no one. No one! Outside of my parents I didn't even discuss it with anyone."

"And your parents?"

"Well, Dad, of cour— Oh no!" Slowly, she lifted her head

to meet his eyes, anger mounting like volcanic lava. "You can't . . . ?"

"What about your father?"

"That does it." She spoke quietly, still in control, folded her napkin on the seat, and rose. "I'm getting a cab."

"Don't be ridiculous."

"Buzz off."

He jumped up, grabbing tight hold of her arm. "I'm not letting you go," he whispered. "Either come back or cause a scene."

"You're hurting me!"

A man at the next table stood up. "Can I help?"

"Thanks, fella," said Ken with a wink. "Just having a spat with the wife. Now come back and sit down, honey, and we'll talk it all over." His grip on her arm tightened.

"Okay." She smiled weakly. A public scene would not be in anyone's interest. Pale and shaking, she returned to the table.

"Would you just listen to me for a minute?" he said, regaining his seat beside her. "I'm not accusing your father of anything. I'm trying to help you. Much as it hurts, we have to suppose that everyone's suspicious until proven innocent."

"Surely you can eliminate—"

"I can't for a minute believe that your father would do such a thing. Okay? But we simply can't eliminate anybody until we've checked everyone out. Don't you agree?"

"No."

"Is he right-handed?"

"Oh, that's a bright question. If he's right-handed, he's a suspect?"

"If he weren't, we could eliminate him right away."

"You *can* eliminate him right away."

"Goddamn you!" This time Ken slammed down his napkin. "Why am I busting my ass to help you? You're a stubborn, spoiled, pig-headed bitch. Go get yourself raped or kidnapped or murdered. I don't give a damn."

The silence between them lasted several minutes. Lauren finally broke it with a slow, hurt voice. "I'm sorry. I'll try to be logical and not emotional. My father didn't want me to go to work; you're right. He thinks Mr. B. is exploiting me, making a fool of me, disgracing the family and all that. He tried everything possible to dissuade me; offered me twice as much money, threatened Wal—Mr. B. with pulling out his advertising—''

"How could he do that?"

"He can't. He knows he needs the *Herald* and so does Mr. B.''

Ken seemed to have spent his anger. Quietly he asked, "Was your father mad at you?"

"Strangely not. He blamed Mr. B. for taking advantage of my supposed innocence and gullibility. They were friendly adversaries for years. Now they don't speak."

"This is the hard part. Can you bear with me?"

"I'll try."

"Your father, by reputation, likes to get his own way. While no one has ever questioned his honesty, it's no secret that he has a penchant for making and breaking people—pulling strings behind the scene.''

"That's true. But he only 'breaks' people who are crooks— who deserve it."

"Is it within his character to admit defeat? To give up easily?"

"No, definitely not."

"Then let's try to be objective. Victor B. Wilde finds himself in a situation where he's powerless. Money won't buy him out of it; pulling strings does no good. His hands, in effect, are tied. Would he be likely to sit back and do nothing, or would he try to think of some other means to get his way?"

"It would depend how important it was—" The waiter interrupted with an offer of cheesecake. They both declined. "I hate this conversation," she said emotionally, "but no, it is *not* like him to sit back and do nothing. In fact, I found it strange that he was off my case so suddenly, that he stopped nagging me and didn't mention it again. It never occurred to me he might be dreaming up something."

"Does it occur to you now?" He refilled her glass with house wine.

"I still can't believe he would try to scare me off the job."

"But *is* there a possibility?"

The sigh she heaved was mountainous. "I suppose so—very, very remote."

"Okay." He sat erect. "Here's what you have to do to find out. . . ."

His instructions were simple to follow but tore away at her heart. The idea of testing her father's loyalty was unthinkable, yet Ken's explanation made sense. If Victor *were* guilty—and she was 100 percent positive he wasn't—he would have convinced himself beyond any trickle of a doubt that what he was doing was in the name of love—and his daughter's best interest.

Late the next morning, Lauren left her office for the Nob Hill Plaza. Up on the mezzanine, she crossed the hall to the executive suite and greeted her father's secretary.

"Is Dad busy?" she asked.

"He has some people with him," said the smiling Dora, buzzing open the door, "but you can go in. He'd shoot me dead if I let you get away without seeing him."

Two men in dark suits stood respectfully as she entered. She recognized them as hotel employees, names and occupations unknown.

Victor's face lit up as she entered. "Well, well . . . gentlemen, you know my beautiful daughter—"

"Don't want to bother you," she said in a semiwhisper. "I'll just give you a kiss, Dad, and then run—"

"I haven't seen you in days," Victor scolded. "Can't you sit down a minute?"

The visitors took the hint, promised to return later, and departed.

She sank into a chair, trying hard to act casual. "How's everything? Mom okay?"

"Your mother's fine—worried about you. You never call anymore."

"That's idiocy, Dad, and I won't let you lay a guilt trip on me. I explained why I couldn't call her every single morning. Besides, I've got worries of my own."

"What worries?"

"Oh, you know—people, personalities, getting used to a

new job. Lots of pressure, which I don't always handle too well. Maybe I should see a psychiatrist."

"A what?" His bushy eyebrows formed a *V* at the bridge of his nose. "Those quacks don't know a goddamn thing about anything. What do you want to throw money away for?"

"Well . . ." Her old drama coach would have been proud of her. "I wasn't going to burden you with this, but I've been getting threatening letters. Anonymous, of course. And they're making me very nervous."

His eyes widened. "What kind of threats?"

"Some psycho, I guess. Letters cut out of magazines. Says he's coming to get me. It's a bit scary—"

His voice was stern. "Why didn't you tell me all this?"

"What could *you* do? Besides, I didn't want to worry you."

"Well, I am worried." Victor got up from his chair and came around to face her. "This is nothing to take lightly. I'm hiring you a bodyguard. Twenty-four hours a day."

"No, you're not."

"You're going to go on this way? Worrying yourself to a skeleton? You'll end up in the hospital!"

"I'll be okay, Dad," she said, bowing her head dejectedly.

"I can't let you do this to yourself. Baby," he said gently, "I know you want to write—want to prove to the world that you're not just a pretty face or a—a socialite. Isn't it possible you're going about it the wrong way?"

It was all she could do to keep her voice from breaking as she asked, "What do you mean?"

"I mean, exposing yourself to sick, perverted minds, like whoever's sending those letters. Putting yourself in front of the public—you're just setting yourself up as a target, don't you see?"

"So?"

He spoke with compassion. "It could be that you're in the wrong profession, honey. Maybe you should be home where it's safe, working on those romantic novels you were always talking about. Can whatever rewards you get from writing that—that column—be worth the hell you're going through now?"

She fought to control her mounting anger. Everything he had said was what Ken had predicted he would say if he were the culprit. One more test to go. How she hoped he would fail it.

"I'm sure the police will catch the guy," she said, pretending optimism. "It's just a matter of time."

His eyes flashed. "The police? Are they involved?"

"The police, the FBI, the *Herald*'s whole security force. Their labs have been working full-time on this. They already know it's a right-handed male over forty who uses expensive German shears. They know the kind of cologne he wears, and that he can afford to buy and cut up new magazines. Apparently they have a suspect in mind. They say they're ninety-five percent sure. They just need one more letter to clinch it."

"What suspect? Who?"

"I haven't the vaguest idea. They won't tell me yet."

"Well, they're sure as hell going to tell me!"

She sat up with a start. "What did you say?"

"I said I'm going to pay a call on our local police chief. He owes me a favor or three. I want this criminal caught and I want him caught now!"

Tears flooded her eyes as she realized, with a bursting heart, that her father had completely flunked the last test. If he had been guilty, as Ken suspected, he would have wanted no part of the police and would, in fact, have shied away from any action that would link him with the investigation. Yet here he was, willing to call in his markers and stir up the whole department.

"Dad," she said emotionally, "I know you're trying to help, but honestly, the paper's security men are doing all they can. Please don't embarrass me by interfering."

"Embarrass you? Would it do that?" He seemed to have run out of resources. "All right, if that's what you want, I'll stay out of it. I won't even tell your mother. But you know how I worry, baby. Will you call me as soon as you have any news?"

"Of course I will."

For a brief second their eyes met and they communicated silently—intimately.

"You're the greatest father in the world," she whispered. And the wave of relief that engulfed her was formidable.

* * *

Lauren stayed home from work that afternoon, trying to sort out the flood of feelings washing over her. Guilt was prime among them. It appalled her that she had let Ken talk her into testing her father that way. What business was it of his? And what right did that bossy Dave Helms have to give Ken the information? Impulsively, she called the security officer.

"Yes, Miss Wilde?" he said anxiously. "Has anything happened?"

"No, nothing. But I wonder why you gave the results of the police report to Ken Ferriday instead of to me."

A stunned silence followed. "Why—Mr. Ferriday said you were close friends—that you had told him all about the letters. He said you were very busy and asked him to check with me to see what progress we were making. Isn't that true?"

"That isn't true. We are friends, but I didn't ask him to talk to you."

"I'm exceedingly sorry, Miss Wilde. That was unprofessional of me not to have checked with you first. But a man of Mr. Ferriday's reputation, I had no—"

"It's okay. I understand. You were both trying to help. In the future, just talk to me, please. Could you recap the police report?"

"Yes, certainly. It appears our suspect is male, middle-aged or older, right-handed, used German-made scissors on new magazines, and wears Aramis cologne."

"Aramis?" she asked, startled. "You know the brand?"

"Yes, it has a distinctive odor that the lab was able to identify."

Damnation! If only Ken had told her that, instead of calling it a "fancy fragrance," she could have eliminated her father right away. Victor used Givenchy's Gentleman exclusively. He ordered it directly from Paris, because American colognes were "too sweet" for his taste.

"Is something wrong?"

"No—no, that's great news, actually. It confirms something I already knew. Thanks for your efforts, and please don't worry about the other. Just poor communication."

"My sincere apologies, Miss Wilde."

\* \* \*

The hours drifted by, and Lauren fell into a deep, dream-filled sleep, only to be jolted awake by the phone. She sat up with a start. It was five o'clock, and she had forgotten her promise to call Ken. Her inclination was to ignore the ring, but she knew she had to talk to him.

"Dammit, where've you been?" came his angry voice. "I've been waiting for you to come back all day. What happened?"

"I'm sorry. The emotion and the letdown—I just felt drained. I came home."

"What letdown? Were we right?"

"No, *you* were wrong. That's the good news. The bad news is that we still have to find the creep."

"That is good and bad news." He paused to digest it. "Well, I'm glad for your sake it wasn't your father. Did you ask all the questions we discussed?"

"Yes." She nodded sleepily to the phone. "I fed him all your lines, including the one about having a definite suspect. He exploded—wanted to run right down to his friend the police chief and demand action. I finally convinced him to stay out of it, but it took some doing."

"Must've been a rough time for you."

"It was awful. But at least it had a happy ending." A poor choice of words; she regretted them instantly. "Until we find the sicko, anyway. Thanks for your help."

"Yeah . . ." He sounded thoughtful. "Coming in tomorrow?"

"Bright and early."

"What about that lunch you owe me?"

She chuckled. "Can't we put that line to rest? I tried to take you to dinner last night—"

"That was dinner. You don't owe me dinner. You owe me lunch."

Despite all her misgivings, he was making it hard for her not to like him. Perhaps "like" was the wrong word. She felt more and more drawn to him. He had kept his promise not to make a pass; so much so, in fact, that she was almost regretting it. His arms were strong and solid, and she had begun to imagine them pulling her close to him . . . to wonder whether he would smell of sweat or cologne—how his lips would feel— if he opened them when he kissed . . .

"Do you like lamb curry?" she asked impulsively.

"Lamb curry?" he repeated. "Sure."

"I'm a lousy cook, but my curry's great. I've got some in the freezer."

"Is that an invitation?"

"Not much of one, I admit. If you'd like—"

"I'd like," he said. "What time tomorrow?"

"Around eight. Don't dress up."

"May I bring something?"

"Hmm . . . no, just your appetite. I mean—a reasonable appetite. I've only got enough for two helpings. We may have to fill up on steamed rice."

A short silence. Then he asked, "Didn't your mother ever tell you the way to a man's heart is not through steamed rice?"

"Yeah, I guess she did. She never taught me how to cook, though. Chin—that's our cook—showed me how to make perfect steamed rice. My rice is poetry. Every kernel is separate and dry, not soggy or mushy. Wait'll you taste it."

"I'll bring dessert," he said, "in case I get hungry."

The rain drizzled gently past the wide bay window. It was unusual weather for a June night in San Francisco, but weather was not known for its predictability.

She had debated lighting a fire in the fireplace, setting out candles, playing her favorite Chopin tapes, and then decided against all of them. No sense setting up a stereotype seduction scene. If it happened, it would happen, and the more she considered the possibility, the less she resisted it.

They had a unique, unsettling relationship. So much about him displeased her: his coldness, his aggressiveness, his shrewd, calculating mind. Well as she was beginning to know him, she felt no warmth or love emanating from him, only a solidness of purpose and the drive to do whatever he set out to do. In this way, he and Victor were not dissimilar. But Victor could be a familiar old teddy bear at times, and Ken was always the big, growling grizzly. You didn't want to curl up and snuggle with him. If anything, you wanted to be crushed in his arms and feel the force of his libido.

What about her own libido? He was Machiavellian, she decided, the way he had sworn not to touch her. They had

had four dates so far, spent hours talking and being together, and he had not so much as held her hand. She wasn't even sure she wanted him to. But she was getting sure.

In all fairness, he did have his good points—namely, a keen, incisive mind with a phenomenal grasp of history and the workings of government. His general knowledge was equally impressive. Name a topic; he could expound—and would, sometimes ad infinitum. Along with a warehouse of facts, he had strong opinions on just about every subject and expressed them in an articulate, compelling manner. As dates went, he was excellent company.

She particularly admired the respect he had for his body, keeping it lean and well exercised, limiting himself to one cigarette a day, preferring beer and wine to Scotch and martinis. Health was a gift, he liked to say, and one he cherished above all others. Damn! There she was, thinking about his body again. . . .

"That carrot cake was delicious," he said, wiping the crumbs from his mouth. "One of the best I've eaten."

"That's all you can say about my dinner?" she asked, her head resting on her hands as she pretended to scowl across the table. "You liked the carrot cake you brought."

"Yes, I did. I liked the sample of your curry, too. When do we get the meal?"

"I froze those portions for me," she apologized. "I didn't realize they were less than man-sized. You seemed to like the rice."

"I hate steamed rice. It tastes like starch. But I was hungry. And it wasn't bad starch. The salad was okay. Good dressing. Where'd you buy it?"

"Maybe I made it."

"Yeah, and maybe whales can fly."

His sarcasm no longer fazed her. "I can offer you four after-dinner choices," she said, rising. "We can do the dishes, we can sit and talk, we can watch TV, or you can go home."

"What would *you* like to do?" he asked uncharacteristically. He came around the table and stood facing her, arms folded. "Isn't there a fifth choice?"

"Scrabble?"

"I hate games." He remained in the same position, his eyes intense, riveted to hers. A white long-sleeved shirt open at the collar showed the top of his chest. It was smooth and suntanned, not hairy. "You have a lovely body," he said, his glance moving from head to ankles, then back up to her breasts. "Lean in spots, but good proportions."

It was awkward just standing there. She knew he wanted to take her in his arms. She read it in his face, his stance, his gestures. Her nonverbal messages told him to go ahead. Surely he didn't expect a spoken invitation. What kind of game was he playing?

"I guess that's a compliment," she said. "Shall we sit down?"

He walked behind her, ears attuned to the rustle of her silk blouse, watching the sway of her hips in a wool challis skirt, the curves of her bare legs in flat leather sandals. Then he joined her on the couch, leaving several feet between them. "Read any good books?"

"Yes," she replied, "but I hate having to shout."

"Well, move over—as long as we don't touch. I never break a promise."

So that was it. "You can touch," she said. "It's okay."

"I need written permission."

Grabbing pen and pencil from a drawer by the couch, she scribbled, "Okay to touch," and handed him the paper.

"Good," he said, folding it in his breast pocket. "Now come here."

She slid toward him and felt his arms enclose her, pulling her tight against him. His heart was beating fast.

"Need any more written permission?" she asked softly.

"I don't know. It depends how you interpret the word 'touch.' "

"Mmm. Let's call it kind of a blanket word."

"In that case . . ." He found her lips and pressed hard, his tongue thrusting hungrily. She felt herself relax to him, letting her head drop back as he kissed her neck, then unbuttoned her blouse and moved to her breasts. She was aroused now; there was no thought of resisting.

"I like to be comfortable," he whispered, sliding an arm under her legs and picking her up. Hearing no objection, he carried her down the hall and into the bedroom, still kissing her breast as he slipped off the rest of her clothes.

The seven A.M. alarm woke Lauren with a start. Blinking and rubbing her eyes, she looked around for Ken, then remembered he had gone home earlier—sometime during the night. A soreness where she wasn't usually sore reminded her of their intense and unbelievable lovemaking.

Not that she needed a reminder. The man was unlike any other she had ever known—or heard of. He had wanted to continue—prolong the act—but after a frenetic hour, she was both satisfied and spent. The second time, only half an hour later, he had seemed even hungrier and had taken her with a passion bordering on fury. He'd seemed almost out of control as he'd plunged into her again and again, alternately whispering and shouting obscenities. His potency, his endurance, his ability to look her in the eyes as he spoke the most offensive and intimate of words, excited her as she had never been excited. It also frightened her. Just before he'd climaxed, he'd again seemed on the brink of losing control. His cries of release had electrified the walls and brought reassuring exhaustion. Ken was all the lover he had promised to be—and more. Maybe too much more.

He'd made no claim to being tender or loving, and Lauren had neither wanted nor expected it. Was she growing up sexually or just growing cynical? If anyone had told her a year ago that she would give herself to a man she didn't love, she would have wagered her soul against it.

Perhaps she could place the blame on Ken. He was a master of seduction, with an exquisite sense of timing. Every move he made had heightened the sexual tension between them. In a way, it was a relief not to love him; it was also a worry. What would happen to a relationship that was destined from the beginning—never to have a future?

A glance at the clock told her she had no time for reflection. Bouncing out of bed, she stopped with a groan. It hurt to move. Too bad. She had to go to work, and she had to move naturally no matter how it hurt. It would not do to duck-waddle into the office and have everyone ask questions. Or maybe they wouldn't ask; one look and they would know exactly what she had been doing.

Soaking in the tub seemed to help, and by the time she was dressed and driving, she felt confident that she could steal into the office unnoticed. No one even looked up as she ambled past the city room. A sealed envelope lay waiting on her desk; the paper inside read, "You owe me one lunch." How could Ken have gotten to work before she did? She rang his extension; no answer. Easing into a chair, she corrected copy on the VDT for half an hour, then, momentarily forgetting her sore spots, reached across her machine for a notepad.

An involuntary "Ouch!" escaped, and she quickly moaned, "Oh, my poor back. I must've pulled a muscle."

"Want some Ben-Gay?" Lee Paige had just come in and was hanging up his sport coat. "I've got aspirin, too, if you need some."

Lauren smiled weakly. "Thanks, doctor, but I think it's fine now. How's the manuscript going?"

"Ah, just what I want to talk to you about . . . um, in private. Come with me a minute?"

"Well, yes—sure." She followed him down the hall to the conference room, a bare-walled chamber with a single maple table and half a dozen hard wooden chairs. Obviously, no one was expected to stay very long.

The reporter seemed ill at ease as he lit his pipe and sat down opposite her. "I got you here on a ruse, Lauren. It has nothing to do with my manuscript. I'm sorry. I didn't want to talk to you in the office."

"Is something wrong?"

"No . . . well, I'll make this brief. Fukiko knows how much I like you, and she said it was my obligation to tell you. It's about Ken Ferriday."

"It is?" Lauren felt a chill. "Did he murder someone?"

"Not that I know of." Lee strained to smile, glad for a hint of humor to break the tension. "I've known Ken over fourteen years, through both wives—"

"*Both* wives?"

"Yeah, the second one was only two years ago—a nice gal,

Ronda. She was a nurse—still is, I suppose. That lasted five minutes . . . well, actually, five months.''

"What happened?"

"That's what I want to tell you, even though it's none of my blooming affair.'' Lee set down his pipe and rested his hands in his lap. "Look, I know you're seeing Ken. Anyone's business is everyone's business in this office, as you've probably gathered. He's a dynamic writer, a brilliant guy, and an attractive guy. I don't know what he's got—maybe it's that peacock swagger—but even Fukiko calls him sexy.''

"Go on." Lauren sat spellbound.

"This is hard to say. With all your background and your money and your sophistication, you still strike me as a good person and a trusting one, and . . . well, I don't want you to be hurt.''

Damn it, she thought, get specific.

Sensing her impatience, he blurted. "Both of Ken's wives left him for the same reason; he beat them up—badly.''

"Wow." A wave of nausea made her close her eyes and sit very still. After a moment, she asked quietly, "How do you know that?''

"I'm sorry as hell to have to tell you this,'' he said, squirming in his seat. "I think you know I'm not making it up. I *saw* Ronda—she came into the office one evening and we all saw her. She looked as if she'd collided with a cement truck. I was working with Ken in those days, and she told me she was leaving him, going to Idaho or Iowa or wherever her parents lived. She was scared to death of him and wasn't even going to pack her things. So I drove her to the bus station, bloody face and all, and that was the last I saw of her. A few days later, Ken told me she'd left him and they were getting a divorce.''

"What about the first wife?"

"Oh, I forgot. Ronda told me she'd heard from a number of people that the same thing happened with Carrie. She asked him, he denied it, and she believed him until it happened to her. She said he was a troubled, violent man, and he needed psychiatric help. So . . .'' Lee stood up, eyeing the glass-topped door as if expecting Ken to burst through at any moment. "That's my story. Now, are you ready for the good news?"

"Good news?"

"Yeah," he said. "At least you're not married to the guy."

# CHAPTER
## 6

Lee Paige's revelation that Ken had two ex-wives, both of whom he reportedly beat up, startled and frightened Lauren. It wasn't the sort of rumor one spread casually, nor was Lee given to invention. She had little doubt of its veracity, however, and even though she knew there was no possible excuse for such behavior, she wanted to hear Ken's version. She owed him that much.

When he phoned about lunch that Friday noon, she suggested dinner instead and, suddenly reluctant to be alone with him, gave some excuse for wanting to meet at the restaurant.

The food and decor were Chinese, the ambiance informal. Ken was waiting in a booth. He wore a red shirt open at the collar, a navy turtleneck sweater with frayed elbows, and greeted her with a winning smile. Could this attractive man really be a wife beater?

"Hi," she said, squeezing in. "Been waiting long?"

"No, I came early so I could surprise you and order some special dishes. Hope you like garlic."

"Yes."

"So do I, especially secondhand." He leaned toward her lips.

"Ken, wait—we have to talk."

He recoiled instantly. "Uh-oh, trouble. I thought you seemed rather cool. Are you sorry that we're not platonic anymore? Is that it? I kept my word, you know."

"No, that's not it." She hated to spoil his mood, but she had no choice. "You don't know me too well. When something's bothering me I usually keep it to myself—"

"This time you're not going to, correct?"

"Correct. If I tell you something, will you promise not to ask where I heard it?"

"I promise nothing."

"Hmm."

"You don't need my promise. A good journalist has a right to protect his sources. Or her sources. It's more than a right; it's an obligation."

"Fair enough. I heard that you've been married twice—"

"I never said I hadn't."

"And that both your wives left you because you—beat them up."

To her amazement and immeasurable relief, he looked into her eyes with amusement, then threw back his head and laughed. "Good Lord, you don't have to protect Lee Paige. He's been spreading that ridiculous lie for two years."

"He has?"

"Yes, he has. I shouldn't have to defend myself against a fourteen-karat asshole, but since he took the trouble to warn you about me, I have no choice." He spoke almost mechanically, as if he were bored hearing himself repeat the story. "Fact number one: Carrie, my first wife, left me because she fell in love with someone else. I had every reason to be furious, but the truth is, I was hurt—not because I loved her but because she wounded my ego. I admit I called her every name I could think of, but I never laid a hand on her. Not a finger! If you don't believe me, you can phone her in New Jersey. Would you like the number?"

"No." She wanted to believe him; she also knew that if he had harmed her, he would not be likely to admit it.

"Fact number two: Ronda, my second mistake, was so jealous she used to smell my clothes for perfume. She never found any, but that didn't matter. She was sure I was boffing the receptionist, the phone operator, the cooking editor, and everything else of female gender, including all ships at sea.

"One day," he continued, "she found lipstick on my handkerchief—I'd been kissed by a lady politician who looked like a combination Betty Friedan and Bella Abzug—and Ronda went crazy. She started screaming and swearing, picked up a kitchen knife, and came at me. She was a strong woman, and she meant business. I grabbed her arm and we wrestled. I finally made her drop the knife, then I slapped her face to calm her hysteria. Her glasses broke and cut her cheek."

"Good grief, how awful!"

"Yeah, it was soap opera time. I insisted she see a doctor, packed her in the car—against her will—and drove her to the emergency entrance at the hospital. She was working the night shift, so I just left her there and didn't expect her back until morning. Later I learned she didn't even go into the hospital. She took a cab down to the newspaper, walked into the city room with blood streaming down her face, and showed everyone what I had done to her. My good friend Lee Paige agreed that I was a vicious monster, told her her life was in danger, gave her some bandages and some money, and put her on a Greyhound bus to Idaho, where her parents lived."

"And you never heard from her?"

"I heard from her. She wanted me to pack up all her things and send them to her. She wanted me to explain why she hadn't shown up at the hospital and collect her back pay. She wanted me to do this, do that, and I refused. I told her to come home, that we would see a marriage counselor and try to work things out. That was a big concession for me—offering to see a marriage counselor. She wouldn't come back. She was already 'home,' she said, and I guess her parents put a lot of pressure on her to stay."

Lauren nodded in sympathy. "Didn't you ever explain to Lee what happened?"

"I tried to." His palms opened in a gesture of helplessness. "He wouldn't listen. All he knew was that pretty little Ronda staggered in with her face cut open and said I'd done it. He told me there was no excuse, no possible explanation. I called Ronda that night and asked her again to come back—even though it was hard for me to do. I told her I had never been unfaithful, which was true. Her answer . . . well, I won't repeat it. So that was that. My next call was to the Salvation Army, to take away all her stuff, and then to my lawyer. She had, in effect, 'deserted' me, and we got a quickie divorce.''

"What a story." She wanted to believe him; she wanted to trust him. He admitted slapping his second wife, but with major provocation and in self-defense. Lee Paige had reported what he'd seen, in all good faith, and Ken had confirmed the story, but from a very different point of view. Yet still she had doubts. His recital was almost too pat—too perfect—too self-serving, and his boyish, good-natured, do-what-you-will-to-me-I'll-rise-above-it attitude a little too snake-oil smooth. Such charm was *meant* to be irresistible. Even his delivery, spiced with a mere touch of indignation instead of the deep anger and bitterness she knew he harbored, lacked verisimilitude. Or was she being overly critical?

"Thanks for the explanation. You didn't need to tell me all that, but I'm glad you did."

"Thanks for asking." His voice was unusually subdued. "I hate to be judged without a trial. Now—will you come here?"

Feeling guilty for having interrogated him, she moved closer. "Did I happen to mention that last night was wonderful? I've been glowing all day."

"You were rather impressive for a sweet, innocent-looking and very proper young lady. Did anyone ever tell you you were a sex fiend?"

"No, am I?"

"You have great promise," he murmured, tilting her head to his, "but you need practice."

She pulled back gently. "Not tonight, dear. The ache's a bit lower than my head. I didn't even think I could walk this morning."

"Really?" He seemed proud of himself. "You shouldn't be sore after that tiny bit of loving. You *do* need practice. . . ."

"No, you don't," she said, removing his hands. "Honestly, you put me out of action for at least a week."

"A week? I can't stay away from you a whole week. Can't we go to bed and just snuggle?"

"No," she said, "that's masochism."

"You're right. In that case, I suppose we should eat our food. I'm going on an overnight hike tomorrow, but I'll be back Sunday about four. Can we have dinner?"

"Thanks, but I promised I'd go to my folks."

"Great!" he said, filling her plate with lobster in black bean sauce. "I'm dying to meet your father."

"I don't remember inviting you—"

"I invited me. Please?"

"Well, I don't know—it's really family night. . . ."

"Tell you what. I'll be at your place at five, and you can check my wardrobe and brief me on how to behave. I promise not to ask a lot of questions, and I won't even let on that their daughter is the greatest thing in the sack since Perma-Prest sheets. Okay?"

"I'm such a pigeon." She sighed.

"You're a lovely pigeon," he whispered. "And you'd better heal fast. Seven days of abstinence is out of the question."

The doorman phoned promptly at five; Ken's punctuality was promising. Now if only she could count on him not to wear the shocking-pink tie with the daisies. No matter how "respectable" he looked, however, the prospect of introducing him to her father was not a happy one. She had stressed to her mother that Ken was simply a good friend, a man who had been helpful and kind, and not a romance. He was "an admirer of Daddy's," she'd explained, "and a bit aggressive, but a brilliant writer and a fascinating conversationalist."

The bell interrupted her thoughts, and her date appeared—without a tie. "Hello, sexpot," he said, closing the door behind him. "Still sore?"

"That's your first question to me? That's all you care about?"

"For the moment . . . yes." He drew her toward him and sought her lips. "Mmm—do we have time?"

"No. Yes. I mean no, we don't have time, and yes, I'm still out of commission. Ken, you are a crazy man! We're due at the house in half an hour; dinner's at six. Where's your tie?"

"Not to worry." He reached into his pocket and brought

out five striped polyesters, all bright-colored except one that was gray, white, and black. "Which do you like?"

"Guess."

"I already know." He held up the drab one and returned the others to his pocket. "The undertaker's special, right?"

"It's not morbid at all. It's very handsome. And—so are you."

"Flattery will get you everywhere, young lady." He grabbed her waist. "Would cortisone cream help?"

"*No!* Rest is the only thing that will help. Subject closed."

"Is that a pun?"

"How was your hike?"

He grinned and released her. "Wonderful! I belong to a club of outdoor freaks. Fifteen of us. We each take turns scouting new locations within a hundred-mile radius, and every third week we go camping. Last night we slept on a moonlit white-sand beach along the coast. I kept wishing you were with me."

"Nothing personal, but I'm glad I wasn't." She headed down the hall, raising her voice as she walked. "I'm not fond of roughing it. I like the great outdoors from the window of a car."

"Why are you going in the bedroom?" he called. "Is that a hint?"

"No," she called back. "I'm repairing the lipstick you damaged. I'll be right there."

"I'll just smear it again. Do you ever fantasize about my nude body?"

"No!" She reappeared, fresh and sunny, wearing a beige cashmere dress with a camel hair coat. She took his arm. "You did promise you'd behave, remember?"

"Why are you so nervous?"

"Let's go," she said, sighing, "and get it over with."

The Wilde mansion looked strange to Lauren with its new coat of somber gray and navy trim. She took consolation in the knowledge her mother would undoubtedly paint it again before too long and would also, she hoped, restore it to its pristine white.

Lights blazed inside the three-story house. Ann, the down-stairs maid, opened the door with a smile.

"Ann, this is Ken," said Lauren, who hated the idea of calling employees by their first names and having them call you "Miss" or "Mister." She answered to "Miss Lauren" only when her parents were around. "You've probably seen his byline: Ken Ferriday. He covers the political scene for the *Herald*."

"He's not bad-looking, either," she teased. Ann was in her early thirties, studying computer technology, and working nights and weekends until she could earn a living in her field. "I love men in horn-rimmed glasses. They look so intellectual."

"You're a very astute young lady," he said.

Lauren grabbed his hand. "Come on, intellectual. Mom and Dad are upstairs in the den."

Victor Wilde stood waiting in the hallway, still a handsome and imposing presence at sixty-seven, his unruly hair streaked with gray, a protruding waistline neatly camouflaged by a black velvet smoking jacket. He hugged and kissed his daughter with obvious joy.

"Dad," she said, breaking away nervously, "this is Ken Ferriday. He's one of your fans."

"Ferriday, eh?" Victor saw his guest for the first time and extended a hand. "I read your stuff, but I don't always agree with you."

"That's your privilege, sir. I told your daughter I've been wanting to meet you for a long time. You and your family have done so many outstanding things for this city."

"Well, this city's been good to us. What do you drink?"

"Scotch, if you have it, please. On the rocks." He winked to Lauren and followed Victor into the den. "Hello, Mrs. Wilde, I'm Ken Ferriday. You're very gracious to let me join you this evening."

Edna looked up over her glasses and offered a hand. "Hello, young man. Sit down and be comfortable. This is just family tonight, so we're very informal."

"Thank you." He joined her on the couch. "Is that a pillow you're knitting?"

"Knitting! Shame on you." She giggled in delight. "Don't

you know the difference between knitting and needlepointing? Didn't your mother ever knit?''

''No, I'm afraid she didn't. She—'' His eyes caught Lauren's and read their message. No need to announce that his mother taught high school, reared three children, and had never had time to learn to knit. ''She . . . wasn't very good with her hands.''

''Too bad. I've made Lauren some pretty things. Have you seen her apartment?''

''Well . . . er, yes, I picked her up there tonight. It's quite a place.'' This time it was Victor staring at him, holding his drink, and obviously trying to decide just what he was doing with his precious daughter. What the hell did he *think* he was doing? He had promised Lauren to behave, however, and would take the man's attitude in stride.

Cocktails were blessedly brief, and at dinner, Ken found himself on the answering end of questions, mostly about the newspaper—and its publisher.

''I've known Walter Belloc for forty years,'' said Victor, helping himself to a serving of shrimps and tomato mousse. ''He's in a position to do so much good for the city, but he's the tightest son-of-a-bitch that ever walked. How do you get along with him?''

Ken considered inventing a relationship, then decided to opt for honesty. It would be foolish to underestimate his host. ''I don't, Mr. Wilde. I never have much to do with him. I was hired by the managing editor, and he's the one I answer to. If Mr. Belloc doesn't like something I write, I get it second- or third-hand. I would prefer to hear it directly, of course, but those aren't his rules. He tries to avoid being personally involved with any of his staff except those directly under him—and I can't say I blame him.''

''He got personally involved with my daughter.''

''I don't know too much about that,'' Ken lied, ''but I would guess that once Lauren became a working journalist, she would neither see nor hear much of Mr. B.—er, Belloc.''

Victor turned to Lauren. ''Is that true, baby?''

''Yes, I never see him. I had a complaint once, and his secretary made me make an appointment a week in advance.''

Instant belligerence. ''What kind of complaint?''

"Well"—she shrugged—"he had told me I could write whatever I wanted. Then suddenly my editor started telling me what I could and couldn't write. So I wanted to get things straight."

"And did you?"

"Yes. We got it settled. He told me his suggestions had been misinterpreted and I was still free to write what I wanted. Some of his friends, apparently, felt I was making too much fun of the social scene."

"Weren't you?"

"Perhaps. But if they can't laugh at themselves, that's their problem." Lauren could hardly believe the conversation. It was the first time Victor was discussing her work without open rancor. Maybe it was a good omen. "Dad . . . I know how you feel about Walter, my job, all of this. But I also know you want me to be happy, and I must tell you that I've never been happier. I love the writing, the feedback, the feeling of doing something creative . . . and I like being in an office and getting to know the people. I've made a lot of goofs and some enemies, but it's still a much more satisfying life than what I was doing before."

"What you were doing before," he replied, unmoved by her admission, "was serving the community, using your position, your charm, and your beauty to help the less fortunate of the world. What you're doing now is serving your own ego. Have you gotten any more of that fan mail we talked about?"

"No, nothing."

"You will. You'll be the target of all sorts of lunatics and kidnappers—"

"May I respectfully disagree?" asked Ken.

"No, you may not," snapped Victor. "You're a good journalist, you know your subject, and you do your job. You're a man in a man's job. Lauren has lived a very sheltered life, and she has no idea what the world is like. She trusts people like Walter Belloc; she trusts people she hardly knows . . ."

"Like me, sir?"

"Yes, like you, sir. I don't know anything about you, and you're here in my house for dinner."

"Victor, you're making our guest very uncomfortable,"

scolded Edna. "Let's change the subject. Do you ever go to the symphony, Mr. Ferriday?"

"I enjoy classical music, but I'm not a symphony-goer. And I assure you, Mrs. Wilde, I'm not uncomfortable. Your husband has a reputation for being direct, and I would expect nothing less when it concerns his daughter. If it puts your minds at ease, we're good friends and we respect each other professionally. I asked Lauren to bring me here tonight because I've been reading about Victor B. Wilde for many years and I wanted to meet the great legend. If I may so, Mr. Wilde, your brilliance and your integrity are quite extraordinary."

Victor speared his shrimps without comment. Edna looked apprehensive, and Lauren broke the awkward silence with a question to her mother about pillow fabrics. Having expressed his displeasure at Ken's presence, Victor remained quiet for the rest of the meal, then rose directly after dessert, announced he had heartburn, and left with no good-byes. Edna made some excuse about his hiatal hernia, Lauren suddenly remembered a long-distance call she was expecting, and by eight o'clock, Ken and Lauren were standing outside the door to her apartment.

"I won't ask you in," she said. "I apologize again for Dad's behavior, but I warned you he might be hostile. It has absolutely nothing to do with you personally; he just automatically dislikes any man I date."

"Is that what I am—a date?"

"Ken, please. I'm tired, I'm upset, I'm frustrated, and tomorrow's Monday. I'm steeling myself in case I hear from that letter-writing creep again."

His eyes hardened as he turned to the elevator. "Who're you trying to bullshit? We both know who that 'letter-writing creep' is because we just had dinner with him. The only thing your daddy *didn't* teach you was how to be a good liar!"

Rosa, her editor, Sara, her assistant, and security chief Dave Helms were all relieved to learn that Monday's mail brought no further word from the magazine-clipper. Helms suggested that the added security may have scared him off but warned that Lauren might still be in danger and should continue the vigil for several weeks. Later that morning, her mother surprised her with a call. She said nothing about the previous evening's debacle, merely that she and Dad had "something exciting" they wanted to discuss with her.

"Can it wait till Sunday, Mom?" she asked.

"Yes, dear, but be sure to come alone."

Would she ever! Her father had behaved even more rudely than expected. Or perhaps it was Ken's obsequiousness—a quality she had never seen in him before—that had turned Victor off. Whatever it was, it was her own fault. She should have listened to her instincts and never brought the two men together. Her sympathies had been with Ken all evening, until they'd parted and he'd made it clear he still refused to accept Victor's innocence. Or perhaps he didn't want to accept it. He seemed deliberately out to make Victor look bad to her. Nevertheless, she knew Ken's pride was hurt and that swallowing humiliation was not easy for him. Impulsively, she rang his extension.

"Ferriday," he announced wearily.

"Hi, it's me. I mean it's I."

"Good morning," he said, his voice picking up. "What's on for tonight—the rack? The wheel? The Chinese water torture?"

"Funny," she said, not about to offer further apologies. "Tonight is hot bath and television time. But tomorrow—if you're free—I know a great steak place. I'd like to take you to dinner."

"What time?"

"Want me to pick you up?" she asked.

"No thanks, I'd have to clean my room. And you shouldn't be driving alone at night anyway. I have an interview in Sacramento. . . . Let's see, I'll be back about six. Is seven too late?"

"No, perfect. I'll see you then, and you can wear the tie with the daisies."

"That was just a joke," he mumbled. "I know it's bad taste."

Tuesday morning, the office seemed particularly hectic. Marcy's story, "Power People in the Bay Area," had the phones ringing nonstop; readers kept calling in with corrections, complaints, and suggestions of names that should have been included. The V.I.P. calls went to Rosa; most of the others went to Sara, who sounded like a stuck record repeating, "Yes, thank you, I'll tell Ms. Burgeson." It amazed Lauren how many people called with additions for an article *after* it appeared. Didn't they realize the story would probably never run again?

"I purposely didn't use your father."

"Pardon?" Lauren looked up to find Marcy pulling over a chair. It was not a pleasant sight.

"I wanted to tell you why I didn't use your father in my power story," said Marcy, momentarily relishing her own power. "He's been overdone."

"It was your story. You can name or leave out anyone you please. I doubt it ruined my father's breakfast." Lauren was tempted to add that he rarely read the Today section, including his daughter's column.

"Well, I'm sure he was pissed. He runs the Nob Hill Cabinet; everyone knows that. So I omitted him along with the mayor and police chief. He was in good company."

"That was probably wise. The story was well written and researched, Marcy. I thought it was excellent. Congratulations."

"I busted my butt interviewing people and nosing around to ferret out some of those characters, like the man who names the streets. That was a stroke of genius."

What did she want—sainthood? "Yes, that was great. If you'll excuse me now, I've got to finish—"

"You don't like me much, do you?"

The blunt question caught Lauren unprepared. "I don't know you very well. I think—" Suddenly she caught Rosa's eye across the room. Sensing trouble, the editor beckoned. "Oops, excuse me a minute. Rosa wants something."

The uninvited guest made no effort to remove herself as Lauren crossed the floor. Nor did she budge ten minutes later, when Rosa walked Lauren back, presumably to spirit Marcy away.

"What happened to my screen?" asked Lauren, sudden panic in her voice.

"The system's down," said Marcy.

"Did you save my copy?"

"Why should I save your copy?"

Lauren swallowed hard and tried for control. "I've been working two hours on that column. You came over and started talking to me—"

"Was there any warning?" asked Rosa. "Did the system stop for maintenance, or did it just break down?"

"There was warning," offered Sara from the next desk. "Five minutes' warning to save whatever you were working on. I wish I'd realized—"

Rosa stared at Marcy incredulously. "You just sat there looking at Lauren's work, knowing the system was going down, and you couldn't call over to us or press two keys to save her copy?"

"What am I—her royal nursemaid?" Marcy slammed down a clipboard with obvious contempt, rose, and strode noisily back to her desk.

"Excuse me," said Lauren, shaken. "I'd better try to re-write that column—what I still remember of it."

"Yes, go ahead," mumbled Rosa, her mind elsewhere. "There's something I have to take care of right away, too."

Twenty minutes later, Rosa called Marcy over. "I've just seen Kirk Denebaum. He's losing one of his top reporters."

"What's that got to do with me?"

"Quite a bit. He wanted to know who our best reporter was, and I said you. He wants you—so I'm reassigning you to cityside."

Marcy's eyes narrowed. "You can't do that to me. You can't send me over there. I'm a human-interest writer—a storyteller—not a hard-news reporter."

"You're whatever I say you are."

"The hell I am. I'll get the union—the guild—"

"Get the president." Rosa shrugged. "Get anyone you please. You've been around long enough to know that we have the right to reassign you."

"You won't get away with this." She turned to glare at Lauren. "It's all her fault, isn't it? Miss Rich Bitch who thinks her shit smells like Shalimar. Everything's changed since she came along. Everyone's so busy sucking up to her, they don't see what a whore she is. I'd *kill* myself if my father had to buy me a job.''

"She has nothing to do with—"

"She has *everything* to do with it, and you know it," hissed Marcy, getting up and storming across the room to where Lauren sat typing. "You goddamn little priss, someone ought to take that silver spoon you were born with and ram it down your throat. I'll have your ass for this!"

Lauren's eyes stared dumbly as Lee Paige came running over. "Shut up, Marcy," he said, grabbing her arm. "Shut up and get the hell back to work."

"Let go of me, Jap lover!" Marcy jerked away from his grasp and straightened up her huge frame. "You have to be the big macho hero, don't you? Gotta protect little Miss Moneybags. What does it matter that Marcy Burgeson has won more awards for this section than anyone else? What does it matter that Marcy Burgeson has integrity and guts and twenty years' experience—that she's recognized across the country as a top feature writer? She's not rich or pretty or social, is she? So let's put the brilliant award-winning journalist out to pasture and make her eat cow dung. Score one for the Today section. Hooray, we got rid of Marcy! And so you did—for now, you bunch of phony no-talent hacks!"

Having spilled her venom, Marcy turned abruptly, stopped by her desk to sling a woven bag over one shoulder, and, as the rest of the office watched in shocked silence, clumped angrily down the hall.

Feeling somewhat calmer after half a Valium and a nap, Lauren was determined to forget the day's unpleasantness and make the evening enjoyable for Ken. She insisted on playing hostess at the intimate French restaurant she had chosen for dinner and ordered Caesar salad, filet mignons, and champagne.

"Do you want to tell me what happened today?" he asked as they settled into chairs. "I've heard three different versions already."

"I'll tell you briefly and then let's forget it, please? Marcy exploded, called me a lot of names, and made a big scene. Rosa reassigned her to cityside, and she's furious."

"Did she threaten you?"

"She threatened everyone. The woman loves to be melodramatic. What a relief it'll be not to have her lurking around the office."

Ken paused thoughtfully. "I know you're convinced your father didn't write those letters. What about Marcy? Could she be the culprit?

"That thought did occur to me." Lauren stirred her screwdriver. "But she's not rich and she's not a man."

"The 'rich' doesn't mean anything; it was an assumption. She could easily have spent twelve bucks for new magazines; she could have borrowed the German scissors, too. And she's done enough police lab stories to know how they operate. All she had to do was get some guy to lick and attach the stamps before she addressed the envelopes."

"Good Lord, I never thought of that!"

"Think about it. I'd say she's your prime suspect."

It pleased her that he seemed to have given up on Victor. "But if it *was* Marcy, why did she stop? Why didn't I get a letter yesterday?"

"Standard operating procedure if you're trying to psych someone. Never be predictable. Do the unexpected. Keep your target nervous and off guard."

"How insidious." She was silent a moment, hoping to catch her own target off guard. "Ken . . . tell me about the *Herald* picnic Saturday. Are you planning to go?"

"Are you kidding? It's nothing but a big noisy, messy gangbang."

That was good news. At least he wouldn't want to be taking her. "It sounds awful."

"I hate those damn things. Besides, I'm leaving tomorrow for a week in Washington. Will you miss me?"

"Just your body," she teased.

"That," he said, "is a remarkable coincidence."

The food was excellent, the early evening passed pleasantly, and later, he proved to be as demanding a lover as the first time—frantic and seemingly insatiable. Against her wiser judgment, she let him stay the night, finally sending him home at six A.M. His assignment in Washington was well timed; she was due for a rest.

* * *

The parking lot was crammed with cars, mostly Volkswagens and Japanese imports. Lauren found an empty space in a far corner shaded by redwoods and was grateful her shiny BMW would not be too conspicuous. The balmy Marin weather was ideal for the company picnic, and the drive across the Golden Gate Bridge—from thick fog into glowing sunshine—had been exhilarating.

She felt quite properly attired in her striped T-shirt and jeans as she trod the dirt road to the picnic grounds. Rosa had explained that although Kentland was a public park, a large section of it was reserved every year for the *Herald* party. Signs, balloons, screaming children, and the smell of hotdogs told her she had arrived. People were everywhere—sprawled on the grass, lined up by the barbecue, tossing balls, chasing kids and dogs, drinking beer. No one seemed to notice her arrival, and after several minutes of searching, she finally found Rosa, sitting cross-legged on a blanket with Dag, from the copy desk, and Fukiko Paige, who was deep into a book on photography.

Rosa introduced the women, then smiled. "Welcome to the social event of the year. I was afraid they might run out of hotdogs before you got here."

"Is that all they have to eat?" asked Lauren, squatting on the grass. "I'm starved."

"Yup," said Dag. "Every year Mr. Bountiful empties his small-change jar and tells his generals to buy food and drink for the peasants. They count out the pennies so there's just enough for one beer and one hotdog per person. That's why we always bring sandwiches." He passed her a large wooden basket brimming with food. "Help yourself."

"Mmm . . . there *is* a God," said Lauren, extracting a cheese on rye. "If I'd known, I would've brought something. Whom do I thank?"

"Rosa," said Dag. "There's a saying at the paper that no one ever leaves Mr. B.'s parties hungry. That's because you either eat beforehand or bring your own food."

"Some reputation." Lauren laughed and bit into her sandwich. "Thanks, Rosa, it's good. Where's Lee?"

"Playing softball over by the bubble-gum-blowing contest. They're very big on games here."

She had barely finished the sentence when a tall man appeared, carrying a large burlap bag. "Hey, Rosa, wanna get in the sack with me?"

"Thanks, Roy. Try me next picnic." She turned to Lauren. "He waits all year just to run around, ask the women that question, and watch their reaction. If they ever canceled the sack race, he'd be devastated."

The hours passed quickly until three-thirty. When the Paiges decided to leave before the mass exodus, Lauren joined them. She walked them to their car near the entrance to the parking lot, waved good-bye as they drove off, then headed for the back. As she searched her shoulder bag for keys, a low voice called her name. "Psst, Lauren. Over here!"

Startled, she spun around toward the rear, where the lot ended and the trees began. Seeing no one, she shouted, "Who's there?"

"I'm here," came the muffled cry. "I need help."

Help or not, she was not about to venture into the woods after an unknown voice. She moved cautiously to the edge and stared into the shrubbery. "Who are you?"

"It's Marcy." The voice sounded closer. "I was chasing a ball. I think I broke my leg."

Marcy! All her senses went on red alert. "Stay where you are. I'll get help."

No sooner had she spoken than a large arm shot out and pulled her into the brush. Before she could scream, a gag was stuffed in her mouth and her wrists were bound together with a rough cord.

"Well, now, that's better." In the flickers of light that crept through the thickness, Marcy's towering form loomed ominous; hate-filled eyes fixed on her terrified captive. "Ready for a new face, Miss Lauren? Ready to find out what it's like to be ugly and scarred and have people turn away from you in disgust? Ready to have me make hamburger of those dainty little features you flaunt around so proudly?"

A knife blade caught a speck of sunlight and flashed menacingly. Lauren's knees gave away beneath her, and she dropped to the ground.

"Prefer to take it lying down? That's okay, sweets. We have a score to settle, you know. A lot of scores. One cut for my brother, two for turning Rosa against me, and all the rest for getting me kicked out of my job. Let's see how we'll do this—wish I had more light. I'll just have to work by feel."

Two big hands grabbed Lauren's head and jerked it upward. She opened her eyes to catch the glint of steel. "Want to watch, do you? All the better. Now, let's see—no hurry, is there? I think I'll begin at the side and work in. Ready?"

The blade tore into Lauren's skin with a slashing sound and sharp, stinging pain as the warm blood coursed down her neck. Marcy's hand poised to strike again—when a sound in the brush made her start. "Who's that? Someone there?"

The noise grew louder and closer, and suddenly the keen eyes of a black male Doberman peered through the bushes. The large dog barked.

"Go away! Shut up, mutt! Want me to carve up your face, too?" Brandishing her knife, Marcy lunged for the animal. Snarling and aroused, he leaped upon her with tremendous force. The knife went flying as she kicked and struggled and pounded her thick fists on the dog's back, momentarily pushing him off. The enraged animal bounded back, ripping into her shoulder before she threw him off again. "You'll die for that, mutt!"

Furious, she grabbed for the dog's neck, at the same time delivering a fierce kick to his underbelly. The animal uttered a cry and backed away, but only long enough to take aim and propel his carcass full force onto her chest, knocking her to the ground. His teeth were bared for the kill when a voice shouted, "Stop, Sam!"

A figure came running over to where the dog stood panting, his drooling mouth only inches from Marcy's throat. "Good boy. Hold her there." He rushed over to Lauren, pulled off the gag, and pressed a handkerchief to her bleeding wound. "It's all right," he said quietly. "It's okay, Lauren. The nightmare's over."

She half opened her eyes long enough to recognize the worried features of Dave Helms. And then she fainted.

* * *

The room was dark, quiet, and unfamiliar. Lauren blinked as the memories slowly began to come back. Her hand instinctively shot up to her cheek, encountering a thick bandage.

"Are you awake?"

A face came into focus, and Rosa smiled down at her. "Good news. You're going to be one hundred percent. The plastic surgeon says you won't even have a visible scar—just a tiny one in the hairline. How do you feel?"

Lauren cleared her throat and answered weakly. "Okay—at least, it doesn't hurt anymore. What time is it?"

"Almost eight. You've been out for four hours."

"What happened?"

"Marcy went crazy—completely psychotic. She's in the hospital—locked away. Apparently she drove into the parking lot earlier in the day, spotted your car, and hid out in the brush waiting for you. Dave Helms and a couple of plainclothesmen were on duty at the picnic—it's a *Herald* party even when it's on public property. Helms saw you leave with the Paiges, saw them drive out of the park, but no Lauren. So he took his dog Sam and went back to the parking lot looking for you. That's when Sam found you."

The terror came home to her in a vivid flashback, and she began to tremble. "Oh, God, Rosa, it was—it was—"

"Yes, I know." Rosa took her hand and held it. "I know what you've been through, and I know how you must feel now. But you've got to be calm and you've got to be strong. Don't think about what happened. Just listen to me."

Lauren nodded silently.

"The doctor wanted to keep you here overnight, even though the surgery was minor—not even half a face lift. You lost some blood, but not a lot. I wouldn't let him sedate you anymore. I told him I would be responsible, and that it was imperative he *not* phone your parents. I'm sorry—I had to explain why."

"What did you tell him?"

"That you were thirty years old—that your parents were hyperprotective, didn't want you to work, and would probably send you to a convent in Siberia if they found out what happened. I had to sign some papers, but he was understanding and said okay, he wouldn't have to notify them, since the injury was superficial. I'm the only one Helms talked to besides the ambulance drivers and Mr. B.—who came to see you, by the way, while you were sleeping."

"What did he say?"

"We all agreed that if you feel up to it, I'll take you home and stay with you tonight. Of course, if you *want* to call your parents—"

"Good Lord, no!" Lauren pulled up to a sitting position. "What do I look like? Where's a mirror?"

Rosa helped her out of bed and over to the bathroom. She stared at her reflection. "Hmmm . . . not *too* bad. The bandage isn't as big as it feels. The doctor really said there wouldn't be a scar?"

"He said a tiny scar, yes, but not visible. He thought at first he might have to do the other side of your face to make it even, but then he said the pull was so small it wouldn't be noticeable. He wants to see you at his office tomorrow at ten. He's coming in on a Sunday especially for you."

"Sunday?" Lauren frowned. "I'm supposed to have dinner with my folks tomorrow night."

"Maybe you'd better be sick or something. How do you feel now? I've got you released from the hospital if you're up to going home."

"Yes—sure." She placed a hand on Rosa's arm. "I'm so grateful you didn't call them. It'd be the quickest career in newspaper history. How can I thank you for all you've done?"

"By getting well fast. Shall we exit the premises?"

Lauren reached behind her neck and untied her gown. "Yes! If there's one thing I hate more than picnics—it's hospitals."

Sunday morning, Rosa awakened Lauren gently. "Time to get up—it's nine o'clock. I'd have cooked breakfast, but all you have is canned junk and stale bread. What do you live on?"

"Canned junk and stale bread." Lauren stretched out her arms. "I must've slept ten hours. How's my face—swollen?"

"I can't tell under the bandages. Looks about the same."

"How did *you* sleep? I really appreciate your staying—"

"Will you please stop thanking me? I love that guest room. By the way, you've already had a call from Mr. B."

"Well, isn't he the thoughtful one. What does he want, besides my viscera?"

Rosa chuckled. "You're right; he wants something. We're to meet him in his office this morning, after the doctor's."

"On Sunday?"

"Yes, I imagine it has something to do with . . . yesterday. Can you handle it?"

Lauren gave an involuntary shudder. "Not really. Will you come with me?"

"Of course."

"In that case, let's get it over with."

Lauren's relief was enormous as she and Rosa knocked on the door of the publisher's office. The doctor had allowed her to look at her face and had pointed out the stitches—well hidden in her hair. It would take several weeks for the swelling to disappear, but disappear it would, leaving no noticeable scars. He had changed the large bandage for a smaller one and would remove the stitches in several days. In the meantime, a scarf tied under the chin covered most of it.

Walter opened the door immediately. "Come in, come in, my macaroons. You've seen the medicine man?"

"Yes, the doctor thinks she'll heal completely in two weeks," said Rosa. "She'll be as pretty as ever."

"That *is* excellent news." He helped them into chairs. "I believe both of you know Edwin Truman the Third, my noted barrister. His time is more expensive than God's, so with the ladies' kind indulgence, we'll tend to this decidedly distasteful business, then perhaps we can chat."

Business? Lauren looked up at the lawyer suspiciously. What now? She had signed the bank note over two weeks ago, and her weekly salary checks already reflected the unwelcome deductions.

Walter fixed his visitors sternly. "Do we all agree, chickens, that the details of yesterday's unspeakable horror must be kept as sub rosa as a senator in a brothel?"

Lauren strove to control her emotions. The mere allusion triggered a wave of nausea. Rosa nodded assent.

"Excellent. I know this is difficult for you, sweet pea, but it must be dealt with. We must lose no time agreeing on our prevarication, as I am informed that rumors already abound. Fact one: The ambulance was clearly visible. Lauren, my pet, it is our considered suggestion that you claim to have been struck in the face by a flying Frisbee. Fact two: Marcy did not attend the picnic, nor did anyone see the wretched lunatic, since she remained concealed all day in the lot. Dave Helms had the incredible foresight to bind the creature down and out of sight in the back of Lauren's car, even before the ambulance arrived. Conclusion: Marcy was *not* at the picnic or anywhere in its proximity. Are you with me, turtledoves?''

Again, Rosa nodded.

''When the cautious Mr. Helms called me, we decided he should deliver the malignancy to a private mental hospital. I hardly need remind either of you astute ladies what kind of scandal and ugliness would have erupted had we taken her to the local gendarmerie and the details of her attack become public.''

Lauren spoke for the first time, her tone anxious. ''How long will they keep her there?''

''Precisely where this tedious monologue is leading me, pigeon. My esteemed attorney has already called the beast's family, her brother, to be exact. We have agreed—pending your approval—that this primordial ooze will be committed for a period of no less than twelve months or one year—if you, peach blossom, will sign a document agreeing that no charges will be pressed.''

Lauren's voice rose in alarm. ''What's to stop her from getting out in a year and coming after me again?''

This time the lawyer spoke. ''Miss Wilde, may I remind you of the many loopholes of our judicial system? If Miss Burgeson had been taken to jail, you would risk the chance of some clever attorney getting her out on bail immediately. Since there were no witnesses to the actual attack, she might also have initiated a countersuit claiming you provoked her—''

''What?'' Lauren's eyes stared in new horror.

''Those are only two of numerous possibilities. The lady is crazy, but she's not stupid. That's why we urge you to sign this agreement. The family agrees to keep Marcy institutionalized for a year or longer, if necessary, and you agree not to

divulge details or press charges, which you probably weren't
going to do anyway."

"I never even thought about it."

Rosa turned to the lawyer. "Who pays for Marcy's hospital?"

"We do, through the *Herald*'s medical insurance. Just as
we take care of all of Miss Wilde's medical bills. For the
record, Miss Burgeson will be taking 'medical retirement.'
Would you like to see the documents?"

"Plural?" asked Rosa.

"One agreement protects you, Miss Wilde, by making sure
Marcy remains incarcerated. The second agreement protects
the *Herald* from any possible damage suits by you or members
of your family."

Suddenly all the legal mumbo-jumbo was starting to make
sense. Lauren took the documents and scanned them quickly.
"I'd like to show these to my own lawyer before I sign them."

To her surprise, Walter offered no resistance. "A wise precaution, buttercup. But do so at your own risk. I had hoped
to keep your estimable parents out of this."

Damn it, the sly old fox had her again! She could always
hire a new lawyer who had no connections with her family,
but could anyone be trusted to keep a secret from Victor B.
Wilde? Could any lawyer resist the temptation to run to him
with the sordid facts and thus incur the debt and gratitude of
the most powerful man in town? What if some junior clerk
saw the files and decided to blackmail her? "Could I have a
few moments to read these over?"

"By all means, petit four." Walter flashed a victory smile.
"Pass her a ballpoint, Mr. Truman."

"You did the right thing," Rosa assured her moments later
as they walked down the hall. "For once, I think it was a fair
deal. You're guaranteed Marcy will get treatment for a year,
which should help her sickness, and Mr. B. is guaranteed you
won't sue the paper, which you weren't going to do anyway."

"That's what he'd like us to think," said Lauren with a
resigned sigh. "There's only one reason for that whole cha-
rade we just played out, and that's Victor. Can you imagine
what my father would do if he knew what happened?"

"He'd probably build you a dungeon—"

"No, he'd put Walter away—or try to. He'd place the entire blame on Mr. B., call out his legal troops, claim I'd been traumatized for life, and declare all-out war. I know my father; he'd use every weapon possible to get even with Mr. B. for the dastardly deed of putting me to work."

Rosa stared at her. "You think that's why Mr. B. was so anxious to get your signature?"

"No doubt of it. For a moment, I was tempted to call his bluff—to insist on bringing my lawyer—and my dad—into it. But that would've been disastrous for everyone. I really had no choice, and actually, I'm glad I signed. The sooner all this is behind us, the better."

"Agreed." They stood in silence several seconds before Rosa said, "I doubt you'll be getting any more of those cut-up letters with Marcy put away. What do you think?"

Lauren nodded. "I'm convinced it was she. Ken explained to me that she'd probably gotten some guy to lick the stamps so the police would think a man was sending them."

"Ken figured that out?"

"Yes. In fact, do we have a minute? I'd like to leave a note on his desk."

"Sure. I have to get something from the library. I'll meet you by the elevator."

Lauren hurried back to the city room, where Ken shared a small alcove with the education writer. His desk was orderly: magazines, newspapers, and several days' mail were stacked in neat piles, awaiting his return Tuesday morning.

She scribbled a quick note telling him that Marcy had suffered a "psychotic episode" and congratulating him for fingering her as the letter writer. Realizing it was not the sort of memo to leave lying around, she opened his top drawer, searching for an envelope. Nothing but papers. Surely he had a supply of *Herald* stationery somewhere. A second drawer held various books, pamphlets, typewriter ribbons, and a can opener. Just as she was closing it, a rattling sound made her reach to the back and draw out a small bottle. The sight of it caused her to gasp aloud: Aramis!

Ken's words flashed across her brain like neon. "I use an electric razor and Ivory soap. Period. Any guy who'd pay ten

or twenty bucks to smell like a gigolo is insane.'' Grabbing
the nearest chair, she slumped into it and dropped her head to
her knees, letting the blood rush back to her skull. She stayed
in that position several minutes, her mind whirling like a hurricane. Then, biting her lip and composing herself, she tore
up the note, returned the cologne to the drawer, and went to
meet Rosa by the elevator.

The mirror reflection was reassuring. Despite the swelling,
the small, neat bandage gave no sign of anything more than a
minor injury. Lauren had already decided that if she could
possibly pull herself together, she would go to dinner that
evening. Better her parents heard about the "accident" from
her than from a third party. Too many people tried to curry
favor with Victor by bringing him the latest gossip about his
daughter.

Would the shocks never end? Just as her psychic wounds
were beginning to heal from Marcy, she had to face the shattering truth about Ken. The discovery of the Aramis revealed
that the man was more than angry and hostile; he was twisted
and sick, maybe as sick as Marcy. No longer could she deny
what she had refused even to consider before—that it was Ken
who had conceived and executed the "psycho" letters; it was
he who had scented them with Aramis, not knowing Victor
scorned American colognes; it was he who so cleverly manipulated her he almost had her believing her father was the path-
ological one—and why? Why had he done it?

The only possible answer was that he wanted to cause a
break with Victor. As long as Lauren remained under her family's influence, what chance would a twice-divorced "ink-
stained Irishman"—as he'd once described himself—have with
an heiress to millions? It had to be money he was after; he
professed no interest in love, and he scorned social position—
or was that all a pose, too?

Now she was faced with ending their relationship. Their
first and last night together had been hot and intense, and they
had parted, still warm from each other's bodies. He would
come home expecting to resume where they had left off. For
a brief second, she thought of turning to Victor—telling him
of her scary discovery and letting him dispose of Ken. He

could do it—and he would, willingly. But a thirty-year-old woman did not run crying to Daddy. Or to Rosa or Missy or Chris or anyone else. Ken was her problem and hers alone.

Much as she wanted to crawl in bed and think the situation through, the clock told her it was time to dress. How she hated having to put on a smile and behave as if nothing had happened. Her nerves were tense—raw. The slightest strain, she feared, would rupture the delicate threads holding mind and body together, and she would fizzle like a punctured balloon.

"What's that son-of-a-bitch done to you now?" thundered Victor as Lauren walked into the den, where her parents were having cocktails.

"Can't blame Walter for this one, Dad. I was playing Frisbee with some friends in the park and forgot to duck. Just a superficial injury—looks worse than it is."

"You're quite swollen, dear," said Edna, assuming her glasses for a closer look. "Have you seen the doctor?"

"I even saw a plastic surgeon to be sure there wouldn't be any scars. He says I'll be good as new; you'll never know what hit me."

"I'm more interested in *who* hit you," Victor said. "Your wonderful Mr. Ferriday?"

"Nope. He's in Washington, so you can't blame him, either. Chris and Zelda coming tonight?"

Edna shook her head. "Mallory's got chicken pox. When did the accident happen, dear?"

"Yesterday. Now will you please stop acting as if I'd been struck down by a bus?" A touch of anger usually calmed them. "Time for a new subject."

"Any more fan letters?" asked Victor, handing her a Bloody Mary.

She wondered how the vodka would mix with the aspirin she had taken. "Not a one, thank goodness."

"Fan letters?" Edna's needles clicked away noiselessly. "Someone who likes your column?"

"No, some weirdo who was threatening her."

"Really?" Edna looked up in alarm. "Did you call the police?"

"Hey, will you two please get off my back? I came here for a pleasant evening, and all you've done so far is nag me."

"My, aren't we touchy tonight." Victor took his daughter's arm. "Bring your drink and we'll go in to dinner. I think you need some food."

By the time the blueberry cheesecake came around, Lauren was beginning to feel more relaxed. There was something familiar and reassuring in Victor's recital of personnel problems and employee theft and in Edna's ongoing wars with Chin and her decorator. Or perhaps, close as they were, her parents unconsciously sensed that she needed some kind of family small talk—some indication that life was as it had always been.

"You have a birthday coming up in August, baby," Victor said as Ann cleared the dessert plates. "A big birthday."

"Don't remind me. I'd like to ignore it."

"Nonsense. Your mother and I have been racking our brains to think of what we could do for you. Somehow we felt you didn't want a big party—"

"You felt right."

"Or a new car. Or jewelry. Or a fur coat."

"Now you're talking sense. How about a quiet family dinner, and Chin can make me spinach crepes?"

"You can have that, too. We thought . . ." He cleared his throat self-consciously. He had to present the idea exactly as he had rehearsed it, or she would reject it before he could finish the sentence. "We thought you might like to take your vacation—whatever time you get off from your job—to cruise the fjords of Norway with one of your girlfriends."

Was she hearing right? Her parents had always resented her being away from home and discouraged her desire to travel—unless, of course, she was traveling with them. "Say that again?"

"An ocean cruise to the North Cape of Norway, and then to Europe and Russia. We've got the information—" He reached into his pocket for a brightly colored brochure. "Here, look it over. You'll be on a Norwegian ship, the *Sea Viking*, deluxe suite, all expenses paid for you and your girlfriend. You can take the two-week cruise or stay on for the whole trip, whichever you want."

"Are you serious?" She took the brochure and studied its

seductive photos of a sleek, beautiful ship gliding alongside stately cliffs and giant glaciers. The idea of leaving her new job after less than two months would have been unthinkable Friday. But after Saturday's horror and Sunday's painful discovery about Ken, the restful vacation her parents dangled before her was exceedingly tempting. Getting away would allow her nerves time to heal and give her the perfect excuse to break away from Ken. It might be an answer to her most pressing problem.

"It looks fabulous, Mom and Dad." She forced excitement into her voice. "I think I'd *love* to take that trip. When does it start?"

"She sails from Copenhagen Friday, August second, comes back to Copenhagen August sixteenth, then goes to Russia, Finland, Sweden, Holland, England, and across the Atlantic to New York. Thirty-four days altogether."

"Whew, that's a long time."

"Well, you can just do two weeks, as I said, but then you miss Leningrad, Helsinki . . . You'd be in Helsinki, in fact, the day of your birthday."

"Then I'll do it—all thirty-four days! I'd hate to miss Russia. I'll have to talk to Rosa—she's my editor—but I'm sure I can get some vacation time. . . ." Yes, she was sure. Rosa had even suggested she take a leave and get away from the office for a few weeks. Lauren had felt she shouldn't, but this offer was so unexpected—so extraordinary. She had been to Europe only once before, when she was twelve, and even as a child had fallen in love with Paris and Rome. Every time she had talked of traveling after that, her parents had found a way to keep her home. Now she could hardly believe it; they were even sending her away! She would accept fast and emphatically, before they changed their minds—or she changed hers.

Later that night, she lay in bed studying the brochure, her brain churning. How would she tell Ken? What would happen to her column? Whom would she take along? She had dozens of acquaintances, but few close friends except for Trina and Missy, and they were both married. She thought of Sara, then realized that her assistant would have to handle calls and mail while she was gone. Rosa could never get away that long. Her father would probably send Chris and Zelda, but her sister-in-law would insist on bringing the monster, and she had no desire to spend her vacation chasing a three-year-old. Finding a traveling companion, however, was the least of her worries. She would speak to Rosa first thing in the morning.

Going into the office with a bandaged face was less difficult than she feared. There was much talk of Marcy's taking "sick leave" and rumors that she had had a complete breakdown. Rosa confirmed that yes, Marcy was in a mental hospital and might not be back for a long time. No one seemed to connect Marcy's problem with the much less interesting news that Lauren had been hit by a Frisbee.

Rosa explained the vacation situation to Lauren; she was allowed four weeks a year after having worked at the paper eight months. In light of what had happened, however, Mr. B. would certainly approve her taking time off. Rosa suggested the possibility of getting guest columnists to fill in for her or writing her own columns five weeks in advance. The last idea made sense; if Lauren worked very hard for the next month, she could turn out seven columns a week, enough for now and the time she would be gone. It meant a strict regime: writing days, nights, and weekends—but with any luck, the work would keep her too busy to think about what she so determinedly wanted to forget.

Shortly before noon, Lauren phoned Trina's house to leave a message. They hadn't talked in several weeks, and she felt a need to make contact. No sooner had the housekeeper said, "I'll tell her you called, Miss Wilde," than Scott grabbed the phone.

"Lauren?" he said. "What a coincidence. Trina wanted me to get in touch with you today."

"Uh-oh. Anything wrong?"

"Not seriously. I took her to the hospital last night. She's okay, but she was having some trouble breathing, and the doctor wants to do tests. She'll be there overnight and possibly tomorrow."

"Oh, dear. Is she in pain?" Lauren asked anxiously.

"No, not physical, anyway. Of course she's got to cancel sixteen appointments, and she's sure the board will try to pass that meal-allowance-for-city-employees bill while she's in the hospital, and she worries her head off about the smallest details. The doctor's been reassuring everyone; he just read me the statement he's giving to the media. He plays it way down, says she's overworked and exhausted, which is true."

"I'm so sorry, Scott. What can I do?"

"I think she just wanted some sympathy. To tell you the truth, we both forgot you're a working woman now. You probably don't have the time."

"Are you serious? When can I come by?"

"Late this afternoon, say around five? She's in room nine nineteen at St. Francis Hospital. I'll be there," he added, "and make sure they let you in."

"I'll be there, too. Give her my love."

Later that morning, Sara expressed relief that another Monday had arrived with no word from the crazy cut-up. Lauren found it "amazing" that he stopped just as suddenly as he had started. She had already decided that no one, not even Rosa, would ever know the truth. Better that Rosa and Lee Paige simply think she'd decided to take their warnings about Ken.

The day passed quickly and productively. With Sara answering her phone, she was free to concentrate and write, and finished a column by four-thirty. Twenty minutes later, she was standing outside the mayor's hospital suite, knocking gingerly.

Scott opened the door a sliver and peered through. "Oh, it's you. Come on in."

The patient sat propped up in bed reading a lengthy document, her blue lace bed jacket pressed and unruffled. Wavy dark hair framed her pretty features; her makeup was perfect.

"I don't believe you!" exclaimed Lauren. "You look like an ad for *Harper's Bazaar*, not a woman on the verge of collapse."

"Who said anything about collapse? Hi, funny-face. Who hit you?"

"A flying Frisbee. I'll survive. . . . What's your prognosis?"

"Terrible," she groaned. "The doctor says I need R and

R. How can I get rest and relaxation when I'm supposed to be running a city?''

"Is that the only thing that's wrong? No heart problems, no high blood pressure, no social diseases?"

"None that I know of. I'll tell you tomorrow when the tests come back." Trina took off her glasses and set down her folder. "What's the gossip, Laur? You've gotta keep me informed. I'm out of things."

"So am I." She plopped into a green vinyl chair. "I'm not used to working all day."

"Oh, your columns are terrific. I've been meaning to tell you. You're doing great. I hear there's someone new in your life, too."

Lauren tried to sound unemotional. "You do? From whom?"

"One of my aides saw you having dinner with a *very* attractive man."

"That's all over."

"Who was he?"

Lauren frowned; she was trapped. "Ken Ferriday."

"Oho!" The mayor's face lit up. "You rascal! Two months at the *Herald* and you snag the paper's most eligible bachelor. Every time he walks into my office, the women swoon. Frankly, I can't see it. He's Mr. Macho and a sharp reporter, but there's something awfully phony about him. I'd trust him about as far as I can throw the Opera House."

"He's worse; a depraved, despicable person. Let's talk about something else." Lauren reached into her purse and drew out the folder. "You know how Mom and Dad always want me to stay home under their noses? Well, I can't believe it—they're actually sending me on a five-week cruise for my birthday. Look at this."

Trina retrieved her glasses from the bed table and stared at the brochure. "How wonderful! When are you going?"

"I leave August second. Want to come along?"

"I wish we could."

"Maybe we can." It was Scott's turn to reach for the brochure; he scanned it quickly. "You do the North Cape to Copenhagen, then stay on for Russia?"

"Yes."

"It goes to Russia?" said Trina. "I didn't see that."

Scott tilted his head quizzically. "Could I keep this for a day or two? The doctor told me the one thing my darling wife needs desperately is to get away from the city—someplace where she can't get to a phone and can turn off completely for a few weeks and regain her strength. The combination of you and Russia might be the answer to my prayers."

"Wait a minute, honey," Trina put in. "We don't know if she was kidding or if she really wants us. Maybe we'd cramp her style."

"Are you serious? Oh, my God!" Lauren jumped up. "I'd give *anything* to have you come along—absolutely anything. Do you really think you might? If there's even the slightest possibility, I'll nag you day and night. I'll—"

The door opened and a doctor entered, looking displeased to find such an enthusiastic visitor.

"Whoops." Lauren threw a kiss and hurried to the door. "Talk to the doctor about it. Sea air and all that. I'll call you tomorrow. Scott, *work* on her. 'Bye."

The moment she left the hospital, Lauren felt her joy of life beginning to return. The possibility that the one friend she admired and loved above all others might go along on the cruise gave her a tremendous lift and took her mind temporarily off Ken. Since the day Trina had become involved in politics, their time together had been rationed. Sometimes Liz Meredith would call around ten-thirty in the morning, announce that the mayor's luncheon date had been canceled, and ask if Lauren was free. She would drop everything to join Trina, but even then their moments together were rushed and rare. What a luxury it would be to have the gift of time—to be able to talk and share adventures and renew their warmth and friendship. . . . She turned off her daydream and forced herself to be realistic. At the moment, having Trina and Scott as sailing companions was no more than a far-off fantasy.

Lauren decided to stay home from work the next day. Facing Ken in the office and trying to pretend she was glad to see him would have been impossible, and once he sensed her coolness, he could easily have turned ugly. Besides, the doctor had removed both her bandage and her stitches that morning, and her badly discolored face was much more noticeable. She might even stay home the rest of the week, until the bruising faded.

How she dreaded seeing Ken! Hard as she had tried to think of alternatives—breaking off by phone or letter—she knew that those methods would never satisfy him. He would probably reject her weak excuse as well, but she dared not tell him the truth. Letting him know she had information that could possibly cost him his job and his reputation was not wise.

Controlling her anxiety, she lifted the phone and reached him at his desk.

"I just tried your extension and got Sara," he said. "What are you doing at home?"

"Working," she answered. "Your trip okay?"

"Yeah, I'll tell you all about it." He sounded busy. "You cooking dinner?"

"No. Meet me in the lobby of the Nob Hill Plaza at—what time is good—six?"

"I'll be there," he said, and clicked off.

At first she had thought of confronting him on neutral territory, but that wasn't good enough. It had to be *her* territory, and in a place where they were constantly under scrutiny. What better venue than the hotel? Everyone knew her there, or at least most of them knew who she was. As long as the hotel personnel were around, she would feel safe. She wouldn't be driving, so Ken couldn't make a scene by the car. And as soon as she could get rid of him, Everett would walk her home and see her safely inside the door.

Ken was ever punctual as Lauren awaited him in the lobby, her stomach doing calisthenics.

"Christ!" he exclaimed. "What happened to your face? Wait, don't tell me. One of your other lovers found out about me?"

His insinuation was right in character. "No, sorry. Nothing so dramatic. I went to that dumb *Herald* picnic and left early. Some kids were playing Frisbee in the parking lot. I should've ducked."

"Yeah, you should've. The rest of you better be okay."

She ignored the comment and said, "We're just going to have a drink. Come with me."

"What do you mean, just a drink? No dinner? No after dinner?"

"I'll explain."

"It better be good," he growled, following her into the cocktail lounge. The room was dark and plush, and dominated by a long, semicircular bar with polished brass railings. Only a few tables were occupied, probably because most of the hotel's conventioneers were taking their liquid refreshment at private parties. A waiter in a black tuxedo greeted her by name and showed them to a corner booth.

"What's going on?" he asked, sliding in beside her.

"Well, I went to my folks for dinner Sunday night—"

"How *is* the marquis de Sade? Your mother seems like a nice lady. How does she stand him?"

"Ken . . ." The words came out as she had rehearsed them. "My folks gave me a birthday present. I'm going to be thirty in August, and they've given me a trip—a five-week cruise to Norway and Europe."

"Five weeks! You just started your job—"

"I know. That's why I can't go out or see you or do anything but work like mad for the next month and get fifteen columns ahead."

He was startled. "I thought you cared so much about your work. . . ."

"I *do* care. But if I write columns in advance for the time I'm gone, it won't make any difference. And I'm dying to take this trip. I've always wanted to travel, and my folks always said it was too dangerous—that I might be kidnapped or something. That's why it surprised me so much."

"Well, it sure as hell doesn't surprise me." Deep bitterness edged his tone. "Doesn't it occur to that naive little brain of yours what's going on? Can't you see it's just a ploy to get you as far away from me as possible? And so far away that I can't even call you or fly to join you for a weekend?"

She pretended amazement. "Why do you think that?"

"Why do you think that?" He mimicked her high voice. "I don't think it; I know it. Jesus Christ, you're going to be thirty. You're too old to be called 'baby' and to call your father 'Daddy' and to overlook his infernal meddling. The man is sick where you're concerned; it's an obsession. He's not happy unless he's running your life—make that *ruining* your life. Look what he did to you at work; he tried everything to get you to leave your job. Now he's worried about me. So he's concocted a new little scheme that puts half the globe between us—"

"I thought you might be pleased for me."

"Pleased that you can't see me for four weeks because you're going away for five weeks? Pleased that you'll be off on some luxury ship that I couldn't afford for five minutes? Pleased that you'll be wining and dining with officers and guys panting after you every step you take? Would you really expect all that to please me?" He crushed his cocktail napkin into a ball, rose to his feet, and slammed it to the floor. "I wish that were your goddamn scheming head, Victor Wilde!"

"Don't, Ken—" She reached for his arm; he wheeled around and glared at her, clutching her shoulders. "Why are you so bloody blind about your father? Why do you shut your eyes to what's staring you in the face? You told me yourself he never wanted you to travel. Now, a few days after meeting me, for the first time in your life, he's sending you out of the country for more than a month and you don't see any connection?"

"You're hurting me." She kept her voice low—purposely. The bartender glanced over discreetly, as if to say he had no intention of intruding but was there if needed.

"Me, me, always me! Does it ever occur to you to think of anyone else?"

"Shh—everyone's looking—"

"Did you ever think of *not* taking the goddamn cruise?"

His anger frightened her. She sensed he was using all his willpower to keep himself in control. "I don't know. . . . I—"

"If it's vacation you want," he snarled, his eyes flaring, "I'll rent a camper and drive us around the state. I've thought about that—or maybe Daddy Victor wouldn't approve. He'd pay off the cops and get my license taken away. Or hire someone to chop me up in an alley. Yes, don't look at me that way. Daddy dearest wouldn't think twice about killing someone who came between him and his baby daughter. Want the bottle, honey? Or would you rather suck your daddy's cock? You both belong in a fucking Tennessee Williams play. I better leave before I break your goddamn neck.''

With his last words drawing alarmed stares, he raised his clenched fist at her and stormed out of the lounge. Too mortified to move, she shrank back in embarrassed silence.

# C H A P T E R
# 7

$T$HE MONTH HAD PASSED QUICKLY. LAUREN'S PHYSICAL recovery was complete, but her psychic wounds were slow in healing. The specter of Marcy's menacing figure remained indelibly engraved on her brain. What if she escaped from the hospital? What would happen when the year was over? Would Lauren have to live the rest of her life in fear?

There was Ken, too, who still considered her to be unfinished business and called at least once a day to shout obscenities, curse Victor, or slam down the phone when she answered. Ten days after his outburst at the hotel, he suddenly turned on the charm, repeating his offer to rent a camper and tour the state. She told him she was taking the cruise as planned and begged him to stop bothering her. His answer was a string of profanities before he hung up. That was their last contact.

The unpleasantness was canceled by another call later the same day. Liz Meredith announced that the Bellamys' travel agent had confirmed their reservation aboard the *Sea Viking*; they would be in the cabin adjoining Lauren's on the Promenade Deck. Although she had known they were considering the cruise, she had never let herself believe that Trina would take the time from her job. Now she almost whooped with excitement.

Victor had been so pleased with the news, he'd even offered to pay the Bellamys' way until Lauren reminded him that politicians didn't accept extravagant gifts. Honest politicians, that is, and Trina was scrupulously so. Besides, they could well afford their own fare. So many thoughts raced through her mind as she strapped on her seat belt and settled back for the flight to New York.

A fast four hours later, she disembarked at Kennedy and boarded the SAS jet to Copenhagen. The Bellamys were already there; they had come a day early to be feted by the Danish government. She had hoped to go with them but ended up needing the time to finish the last of her fifteen columns.

The seven-hour flight was smooth and uneventful. A waiting bus transported her and a dozen other passengers directly to the ship, where a young man who introduced himself as a "piccolo," the equivalent of a bellboy, carried her luggage up the gangplank and into the cabin.

Her first impression of the ship was glowing; it was large, immaculate, elegantly appointed, and the staff seemed cheerful despite the confusion of boarding six hundred new passengers. She tipped the piccolo, who had marked the arrival of a beautiful woman traveling alone with more than perfunctory interest, closed the door behind him, and glanced about her new quarters.

The room was surprisingly spacious. Twin beds sat at right angles, one serving as a couch, flanked with two matching chairs and a coffee table. A mirrored dresser took several feet of wall space, and a large window looked out on the Promenade Deck, where several people were walking or already relaxing on deck chairs. She examined the closets, the drawers, the bathroom; everything was neat and accommodating. Half mechanically, she opened her large suitcase and hung up the clothes that were already on hangers. Then she slipped off her shoes, plopped on the bed, and fell into instant sleep.

Several hours later, a gentle shaking awakened her. "Rise and shine, Sleeping Beauty, or you'll miss our sailing."

Lauren rubbed her eyes and blinked at the unfamiliar surroundings. Seeing Trina stirred her memory, and she sat up with a start. "Is it really you? Are we really here? Where are we?"

Trina laughed and walked to the window. "We're still in port. But we sail at five. That's ten minutes from now. And dinner's at seven-thirty, so you'll have time to put your face on. How do you like the cabin?"

"I adore it!" Lauren smoothed back her hair. "The truth is I think I'd like it even if it had padded walls and big black spiders. Make that little black spiders."

"There better *not* be any crawling things up here in the high-rent district." Trina headed for the door. "Put yourself together and come find us outside. And hurry, or you'll miss the fanfare."

"Okay, I'll see you out on deck."

A Polish band played "Dixieland," a crowd of passengers took pictures of one another and shouted to friends on the shore, Lauren and Scott tossed strings of confetti, Trina waved to the reporter who had just interviewed her, and the *Sea Viking* set sail for the fjords.

The three decided to forgo cocktails in order to finish unpacking. Promptly at seven-thirty, they found their way to the dining room. The delicate-featured blonde, the striking brunette with regal bearing, and their lanky, impeccably groomed escort commanded immediate stares and murmurs. A maître d' in white showed them to a window table.

"It's just us," Scott apologized, pushing in Lauren's chair while the officer helped Trina. "I insisted on a table for three. Hope you don't mind."

"I couldn't be happier," Lauren said, looking about the room. "I didn't realize the crowd would be so . . . um . . ."

" 'Old' is the word you're looking for," said Trina under her breath. "We've got to be the youngest passengers on the ship, except for two kids I saw running around. That's good—maybe nobody will bother us."

She had hardly spoken when a smiling sommelier appeared with champagne in an ice bucket. "Compliments of Captain Johannsen," he said. "Welcome aboard."

"Your fame is everywhere," Lauren said with a sigh.

"I don't think fame has anything to do with it," whispered Scott. "The captain's table is right in the middle of the room—

see over there? The old goat hasn't stopped staring at you since we came in.''

"Where is he?'' Lauren had no trouble finding the captain's steady gaze. She held up her glass of champagne and mouthed, "Thank you.'' He, in turn, lifted his glass slowly and imparted a look with unmistakable meaning. "Oh, no,'' she whispered. "What do I do now?''

Trina started to giggle. "I knew we'd have to muzzle you. You go around with that face of yours hanging out, and every man on the ship's going to be tailing us.''

"Tri, have you *seen* the captain? He's sixty if he's a day. My travel agent told me that all the ship's officers are good-looking Norwegians, all married with kids, and that they prefer to cohabit with attractive women, but their main requirement is that she be breathing.''

"Cohabit?'' Scott repeated.

Trina turned her head casually. "The captain's not bad-looking. Why can't you be friendly? This is good champagne.'' She smiled and gave him the two-digit "perfect'' sign. "You can't stay in your cabin doing crosswords every night. An affair would be good for you—take your mind off that awful Ken Ferriday.''

"Don't spoil my dinner. Anyway, I didn't come on this trip to perform humanitarian services for the officers. I need a rest almost as much as you do. These last few months have been crazy—''

"Tell it to the captain,'' said Scott. "He's still staring.''

"Bleep the captain,'' Lauren mumbled.

"I don't think I'm his type.''

"Just for the record,'' said Trina, "you are absolutely free to make out with the captain, the chief purser, the deck steward, or anyone else you fancy, because we—''

"Don't want to cramp my style,'' Lauren interrupted. "For God's sake, you already told me that five times. Now will you please stop worrying about my sex life and order dinner? I could eat the whole menu.''

Sleep came quickly for Lauren, but her inner timetable was confused and she awoke at midnight, read for several hours, then slept till midmorning. The dining room had already closed for breakfast, so she helped herself to the fresh fruit the cabin stewardess had brought the night before. The passengers outside her window were dressed for cold. Following their example, she slipped on a blue turtleneck and gray flannel slacks.

At that moment, a familiar figure walked by the window, and Lauren rapped on the glass. Trina turned her head—seemed to look directly into the cabin—but gave no sign of recognition. Lauren grabbed her jacket and caught up with her friend as she was approaching the ship's stern.

"Didn't you see me?" she panted.

"Was that you knocking?" The cold air turned Trina's breath to vapor. "There's one-way glass on those windows. You can see out, but I can't see in."

Lauren laughed. "That's good. I thought you were ignoring me."

"N-n-no." Trina was shivering and rubbing her hands together briskly. "God, it's freezing! Scott was smart to stay in. Let's walk faster." No sooner had she quickened her pace than she suddenly skidded forward on the deck, missed the handrail, and fell hard on her buttocks.

"Are you all right?" Lauren gripped her arm and tried to help her up.

"Yeah—ooh, wait—it hurts! My ankle—I think it's twisted."

"How bad is it? Can you walk to the chair?"

"Ooh . . . I don't know. Better call Scott. He's in the cabin."

"Okay, don't move." Lauren rushed inside and down the passageway, then pounded on Scott's door. Getting no answer, she turned the knob; the room was empty. She grabbed the phone and dialed. "Operator? Get me the doctor. It's an emergency."

What seemed like minutes but was only seconds later, a calm voice answered, "Dr. Marsten."

"Doctor, my friend slipped on the deck and hurt herself. Can you come right away?"

"Where is she?"

"Promenade Deck."

"Port or starboard?"

"I don't know. Down by the end."

"Which end? Aft or forward?"

"I don't know. Please hurry!"

"Tell her not to move. I'll be right there."

"Thank you." She ran outside and found Trina sitting on the edge of a wooden deck chair, her left leg stretched out in the air. "Scott wasn't there, but the doctor's coming right up. How are you?"

"It hurts like hell. Damnation! Wouldn't you know the very first day I'd fall on my blooming butt."

"You've fallen on it before and always recovered." Lauren stood by anxiously, trying to relax Trina with her banter. She shivered under her short jacket, her nerves growing increasingly tense. Moments later, a tall figure in white appeared down the deck. She waved and he came running.

"Are you the one who called me?"

"Yes."

He looked down at Trina and asked, "What happened?"

"I guess—I just slid on the deck. Very slippery . . . I think I sprained something."

Kneeling, he examined her outstretched leg and touched it lightly. "Where does it hurt?"

"Ouch! Right there."

"Anywhere else?"

"All along—right in there. And my . . . uh, tailbone hurts where I fell on it."

"All right. Miss?" He turned to Lauren. "Call my nurse—nine-nine-one—tell her to get right up with a stretcher. Be sure to tell her: port side, aft." He reached into a small brown pouch. "I don't think you're hurt seriously, Miss . . . ."

"Bellamy. Trina Bellamy. Could you—call my husband?"

"Yes, but first I'm going to give you something for the pain. Are you allergic to any medication?" She shook her head, and he drew out a hypodermic, then noticed that a small crowd of passengers had gathered around them.

"Please—you'll have to move on," he said loudly. "The lady's going to be fine; it's a minor spill. We have a stretcher coming, and we'll need the room."

Reluctantly, the crowd dispersed, gabbing among themselves. One woman's voice rose above the murmurs: "You'd think the mayor of a big city would know enough not to wear leather shoes on deck. . . ."

Peter Marsten unzipped Trina's skirt, pulled up her slip, and injected her. "The stretcher will be here in a few minutes, and I'll take you down for X rays. Then I'll know if there's any damage or if you've just pulled a muscle. I'm quite sure there's nothing broken."

"Thank you, you're very kind." Trina seemed to relax and looked up at the doctor for the first time. Could the drug be giving her hallucinations, or was she gazing at one of the most incredibly handsome men she had ever seen?

He stood about six feet two in his "working whites"— short-sleeved shirt and starched cotton slacks. His face bore strong, classic features: unwrinkled forehead, large brown eyes framed by barely visible crow's feet, a nose and mouth that belonged on a Greek statue. Wavy black hair lay smoothly back on his head, except for a few strands that danced in the breeze. His olive skin was clean-shaven with a healthy glow. The expression in his eyes showed kindness and concern, and total absorption in her well-being. He seemed unaware of her thoughts as he reached for a blanket from a deck chair.

Trina smiled thinly. Even in her pain, she was already claiming him for Lauren.

"You must be cold," he said, wrapping the blanket around her shoulders.

"Yes—thank you. I don't know your name."

"Peter Marsten. You mustn't talk. Try to relax and think pleasant thoughts. Let yourself go limp. Ah—I see your friend."

Lauren came running over, her hair flying in the wind, her face drawn and worried. "The stretcher's on its way. Scott was in the sauna; he'll be right up. How're you doing?"

"Fine." Trina managed a chuckle. "You don't get rid of me this easily. This is Dr. Marsten. Lauren Wilde."

"Hello," he said with a perfunctory nod. "Please tell Mrs. Bellamy to relax and let the drug work. I can see she's still in pain."

"Dammitall!" Lauren fought to restrain her anger. "Why do they have to water the decks at ten in the morning? If it hadn't been so slippery out here, she wouldn't have hurt herself."

"We rarely have this type of accident," he answered, his tone becoming defensive. "For one thing, all varnish was removed from the decks several years ago, and they were sanded down completely. For another, we water the decks between three and four A.M., and they dry in an hour. Whatever made Mrs. Bellamy slip, it can't be blamed on hosing the deck. The third point is not to blame your friend but merely to suggest that high leather heels aren't the best for shipboard wear."

"High heels? Those are two inches thick!"

The doctor turned his head a fraction and met her accusing eyes. To him, they were fashion-model eyes, tinged with mascara at eleven in the morning, strikingly beautiful on a picture-perfect face.

Lauren Wilde seemed the epitome of the kind of spoiled, petulant, narcissistic society do-gooder he detested. He was sure he knew her type well. Twelve years on the board of the Finch-Larrimore Hospital in New York had given him first-hand knowledge of the Women's Auxiliaries and their operation. How they loved to spend thousands on big fancy parties, ostensibly to raise money for cancer research, but in reality for the tax write-offs and the opportunity to wear French evening gowns, eat pheasant under glass, and get their pictures in the paper. Ninety-nine percent of the money went to pay their party expenses; whatever dribbled into the hospital coffers might buy new lights for the operating room or a fresh coat of paint for the pediatric wing.

His thoughts were broken by the arrival of his nurse, accompanied by two piccolos. They held the litter while he gently lifted Trina onto it. She seemed relaxed, almost dreamy.

"What kind of drug did you give her?" Lauren demanded as they followed the stretcher down the stairs.

The woman was getting on his nerves. "I'll talk to Mr. Bellamy," he said curtly.

"Mr. Bellamy isn't here, and I'm in charge until he is."

"As you wish. But please keep out of my hair. I'm treating my patient the best way I know how, and if I have anything to discuss with you, I'll tell you."

Lauren held her tongue. The man was rude and impossible.

A very nervous Scott stood pacing the corridor as they arrived in the ship's "hospital," a small four-bed ward. Trina smiled weakly, murmured that she felt "wonderful," and told him not to worry.

"Mr. Bellamy, I'm Dr. Marsten. I'm sure there's nothing to be concerned about. I'd like your permission to take your wife in for X rays right away."

"Yes, of course. Do whatever's necessary. What happened?"

"Her friend will fill you in."

Twenty minutes later, the doctor emerged with the hint of a smile. He spoke directly to Scott. "Your wife is fine; no sprain, no torn ligaments, no fracture. I don't think she did any more than give her ankle a good twist and give us a good scare."

"Where is she now?" he asked. "May I see her?"

"She's sleeping in the ward, and I think it's best to let her be. She should stay off her feet for at least two days. That means no walking, not even to the bathroom. With your permission, I'd prefer to keep her here, where she can get 'round-the-clock care."

"Scott and I can take care of her," protested Lauren. "One of us can be with her at all times."

"I really think she's better off in the hospital," Scott said. "I'd feel happier—in case she needs pain medication or anything."

"That's wise, Mr. Bellamy."

"Call me Scott. And this is Lauren. You probably haven't met each other officially."

"My name is Peter. And I've had the pleasure of meeting Lauren," he said with a nod in her direction.

She returned the nod. "Peter has already overwhelmed me with his warmth and graciousness. I suppose you have visiting hours—like a prison?"

"Mrs. Bellamy is the only one in the hospital," he answered, unruffled. "Come see her whenever you like."

The following day, Sunday, August fourth, the *Sea Viking* entered the Geirangerfjord, a narrow inlet known for its dramatic scenery. On either side of the ship, superb waterfalls coursed down steep cliffs and came crashing into the sea. Snow-peaked mountains towered majestically, forming a spectacular backdrop. The passengers stood muffled and bundled on deck, cameras clicking.

Lauren circled the deck six times, the equivalent of a mile, exchanged smiles with some of the faces that were becoming familiar, and was amazed to find that so many people knew about Trina and stopped to ask how she was. News was scarce on a ship, and daily gossip consisted of about one part truth to ten parts fiction. No, the mayor had not broken her leg or even sprained her ankle; she was not in a cast, and not planning to fly home. On the contrary, Trina felt so much better she had asked to move back to her cabin that morning and was probably already there.

The door was half-open; Lauren knocked and walked inside. "Anyone home?"

"C'mon in." Trina sat in her chair, fully dressed, her face bright with animation. "What a view! I saw you making your rounds. Is it as cold as it seems?"

"Freezing—and unbelievably beautiful. You look fantastic. Everyone's been asking about you. How's the ankle?"

"Much better. I'm going to try walking on it today. Peter said it should be okay. He'll take the tape off tomorrow."

"Peter? Getting pretty familiar, aren't you?"

"Laur—" She lowered her voice. "Have you ever seen such a gorgeous hunk in your life? I love my husband, but— what's the old line? 'I'm married; I'm not dead.' That man makes Paul Newman look like Quasimodo. He's also the most charming, fascinating, brilliant man I've met in years. And I'm determined *you're* going to get him."

"Good Lord, what was in that drug he gave you?" Lauren stared in disbelief. "Look, I'm fairly easygoing, and I get along with most people if they've got even a semblance of good manners. Your doctor friend was rude and arrogant the first minute I talked to him. What an egomaniac! He must think all women look at him and swoon and he can be as nasty as he wants to be and get away with it."

Trina set down her glasses and sat up excitedly. "You've got him all wrong. Totally wrong. He's not an egomaniac.

He knows he's handsome, of course, but he has no idea how absolutely devastating—''

"Yecch . . .''

"Laur, listen to me. We've had some time to talk, and Peter's not a me-boy at all. He's a dermatologist, been in private practice in New York for the last fifteen years, and he's coming out to live in L.A. and start a clinic or something. L.A. isn't far from San Francisco. You could see each other on weekends.''

"I know you mean well," Lauren said impatiently, "and I admit I haven't exactly picked winners in the past. But this Peter—what's his name?''

"Marsten. Norwegian father, Italian mother.''

"Peter Marsten is my idea of the all-time flat-out loser. His looks have made him mean and arrogant—let me finish—and completely self-absorbed. He has the charm of a bedpan and the personality of a spoiled, self-indulgent, male sexist pig. I know that pretty-boy type all too well, and I know how miserable they make the women who love them.'' Pausing for emphasis, she added, "He is absolutely the last man on earth I'd *ever* be attracted to, so cease, desist, and forget it. Do we understand each other?''

"You'll be sorry.''

"Just because you've got a nesting instinct that won't stop doesn't mean I share your compulsion. The right guy will come along someday, and I'll hear harps and violins, and maybe bells in my ears. I know it. How this jerk bamboozled you, I have no idea. You're usually so good at reading people.''

"I'm still good at it," came the indignant response. "By the way, why didn't you go with Scott to the captain's Welcome Aboard party last night?''

"Because the captain gives me a royal pain. Besides, I was tired. New subject: Do you need anything? A good mystery to read? I thought you weren't going to bring all that work with you.''

Trina reached for her clipboard and leaned back resignedly. "It relaxes me to catch up on my work. I just read the background of a bill I had tentatively approved and learned something I didn't know. I had to telex home to veto it. Sometimes

I wish I could turn off the city and my responsibilities, but I can't.''

"That's why you're such a good mayor." Lauren kissed her friend's forehead. "But you're a rotten matchmaker."

At nine A.M. Monday, the ship docked at Trondheim, third-largest city in Norway. Neither Lauren nor the Bellamys had signed up for any tours, preferring to take cabs and go on their own. It was Trina's first day on her feet, however, and she and Scott decided to stay on board, so Lauren went exploring alone. Six hours later, cold, tired, and weary of seeing sights, she caught the last shuttle back to the ship.

A message in the cabin informed her that Trina was giving herself an "unveiling party" in honor of her untaped ankle and expected Lauren for cocktails in the lounge at seven. Knowing that Peter Marsten would undoubtedly be there, and too tired to argue, she scribbled a note pleading exhaustion and slipped it under her neighbor's door. Then she unplugged the phone, hung out a "Do Not Disturb" sign, and crawled into a steamy, hot tub.

Lauren was already seated in the dining room when her tablemates arrived from the cocktail party. Because both women were independent and strong-willed, they knew better than to make demands or put pressures on each other. It was the only way their friendship could survive. When Trina told Lauren she had been missed, it was a statement of fact, not an accusation.

The Bellamys reconvened their guests for the ship's nightly after-dinner entertainment, and since Lauren had mentioned how revived she felt, she had no excuse to retire early. With careful planning, she maneuvered a seat next to a lively rancher Scott had met in the sauna, who told her more about Smack-over, Arkansas, than she wanted to know. At least she was nowhere near Peter Marsten. He never even acknowledged her presence at the party, nor she his. The evening, she felt, was a success.

Trina was up and walking with only a hint of a limp two days later as the ship plowed through the icy straits en route to Honningsvag, a large fishing village an hour's drive from the North Cape, the northernmost point of Europe. The chilly, forty-seven-degree weather was not conducive to sight-seeing, and Lauren and Trina quickly agreed that the only reason to go ashore would be to say they had been there. Their decision to stay on board was clinched by the cruise director's announcement that the temperature at the promontory was at least thirty degrees colder. Scott bundled up and departed.

After seeing him off, Trina returned to her cabin and her papers. Lauren stood alone on the foggy deck, reflecting on the paucity of boats anchored nearby and the scattering of tiny Monopoly-game houses dotting the shoreline with their red and gray rooftops. She tried to imagine what life on these barren hillsides would be like; how could people exist in such isolation? Yet nothing she had seen or heard suggested that they were any less happy with their lives than most of the people she knew, including herself.

An anxious voice broke into her thoughts. "Pardon me. Do you know where we are?"

The speaker was short, not over five feet two, incongruously dressed in spiked heels, a street-length mink, an evening gown, and a slightly askew pillbox with a black lace veil. She wore dainty white gloves and carried a black alligator purse.

"We're at the North Cape," said Lauren with a pleasant smile. The lady was either eccentric or pixilated.

"No, I mean the taxi stand. I've got some shopping to do in town."

"Oh, dear, that's a problem. I'm afraid there is no taxi stand here. There's no 'town,' either. It's just a tiny remote village. Uh . . . my name's Lauren Wilde. What's yours?"

"Alice," she said. "Alice Pendergast. Forbes Pendergast—that was my husband. I mean my last husband. He was a dear man. . . ." Her voice trailed off in memories.

"Mrs. Pendergast—"

"Alice. Everyone calls me Alice."

"Are you traveling alone?

"Oh, my, no." She lifted her veil to reveal a lovely oval face with wide blue eyes that twinkled like a friendly spaniel's. Traces of beauty shone through the lines of her skin; short gray curls completed the cameo. For no apparent reason, she suddenly grew pale, and her small hands started to tremble. "Please don't tell Mrs. Bock about me. Please? Do you swear?"

"I swear," said Lauren hastily. "Of course I won't tell. Perhaps—since there's no shopping to be done—you might want to return to your cabin?"

"Yes, I do." She stood still, looking about her, dazed and confused.

"Maybe I could walk you there," Lauren offered. "Where is your cabin?"

"I don't know. I can't remember. Please don't tell Mrs. Bock."

Lauren took the lady's arm and guided her cautiously across the deck to the door. "We won't tell her anything. We'll just stop by the desk and find out your cabin number."

"Thank you. That's sweet of you."

There was no need for questions when the pair approached the desk. "Hello, Mrs. Pendergast," said the receptionist with a wink to Lauren. "I'll bet you're on your way to one seventy-eight."

"As a matter of fact, we are," said Lauren, nodding her thanks and turning in the opposite direction. They reached the door, and Alice fumbled in her purse, finally retrieving a large brass key marked 178. She inserted it in the keyhole and was struggling to twist it when the door opened from the inside.

A heavyset woman in a white nurse's uniform folded her arms across her chest and glared angrily. "I *told* you not to leave the cabin by yourself. I was just coming to look for you. Now you get right in here, Mrs. Pendergast, and take off those ridiculous clothes."

"Yes, Mrs. Bock." Without a word, Alice bowed her head and disappeared in the cabin.

The nurse turned to Lauren, still standing in the doorway. "I suppose she was lost again?"

"Just a little confused. She seems like such a nice woman—"

"Nice, my eye. You wouldn't think she was so nice if you had to watch her twenty-four hours a day. I lie down for a ten-minute nap, wake up, and she's gone." Her voice dropped to a whisper. "I'm going to start doubling her tranquilizers. I can't have her bothering everyone on the ship."

"She was no bother. Is she . . . senile?"

"Do you have to ask?"

"How very sad. Is there anything I can do? I hate to have you load her up on drugs."

The nurse regarded her challenger with obvious dislike. "I don't see where that's your concern. I'm sure you mean well, and I thank you for returning her. Now I shall do whatever I judge is necessary."

Poor Alice, thought Lauren as the door shut in her face. All alone and at the mercy of that harridan who wanted to immobilize her with medication. Someone loved Alice enough to hire a nurse to take care of her, not to drug her into a stupor so the nurse could take her nap.

The Bellamys' cabin posted a "Do Not Disturb" sign, but Lauren was upset and wanted to talk. She turned the knob quietly, then peeked inside; Trina was asleep in her chair, her glasses balanced on the end of her nose. "Damn," the intruder whispered, and returned to her cabin.

Still disturbed by what she had seen, Lauren dialed the operator and asked for the cruise director, then the chief purser. Neither was available. Reluctantly, and with no other choice, she requested the doctor. Learning it was not an emergency, the operator explained that he was not on call when the ship was in port and suggested she phone the next morning during office hours.

Replacing the receiver, Lauren hurried out the door and down the stairway to the hospital. A large sign by the doctor's office listed his hours of consultation.

"Doctor," she called, rapping on the door. "Are you in there?"

"What is it?" came a voice from inside.

"Could I please talk to you? It's important!"

"I'm coming." Seconds later, the door opened and Peter Marsten came out. "What's wrong? Is someone hurt?"

"No, no, I'm so sorry. I didn't mean to alarm you." The blood rushed to her cheeks as she realized her presumption. "I'm—I'm—it's not me—I . . . ."

"It's okay," he said, sensing her discomfort. "Everything's okay. Now suppose you calm down and come inside. You're sure there's no emergency?''

"Not exactly. Well, sort of. . . ." She took a seat opposite his desk. The walls were lined with books, cabinets, shelves of bottles and instruments, and, in one corner of the room, an examination table and a porcelain sink. Nothing distinguished it from any other doctor's office, except its occupant, who wore a heavy woolen parka over a navy sweater and dark slacks and was indeed, as Trina kept insisting, unconscionably handsome.

"Were you on your way out?'' she asked apologetically.

"In a moment, yes. It can wait. What's bothering you?''

The words poured out in a flurry of indignation and compassion. She omitted no details of her encounter with Alice and the nurse. By the time she had finished, she felt even more upset than before.

He listened intently, then asked, "You said there was some sort of emergency. Do you fear for Alice's safety?''

"I fear that any second now that horrible woman is going to give her a shot or pills or something that will make her so drugged and so weak she won't be able to leave the cabin. I— I guess I could understand if you told me it was none of my business. I just can't—''

"Hold on. I didn't say that.'' He rapped his knuckles together as he pondered what to do. "It definitely is your business. You did the right thing to come to me, and I'm glad you did. It's a very touchy situation—''

"Yes, I realize.''

"Look,'' he said, "I have to go ashore. The people here are expecting me and my supplies. So I can't help you right now. But you can do something. Find out exactly who Alice Pendergast is, where she lives, what family she has. Get someone in the purser's office to show you her passenger registration form, and Xerox it for me. We'll have to contact her nearest relative before we take any action.''

"Of course I'll do that. You don't mind?''

"No. Let's see—find out if she eats in the dining room, if they have a table for two or four or what. Find out how long she's staying on the ship; get me all the information you can. Will you do that?''

"Yes—certainly."

"Then don't worry. Even if the nurse doubles her medication, you don't develop a dependency overnight. It takes a long time."

Lauren rose to her feet and swallowed nervously. "I don't know how to say this—we haven't exactly been friends—I really appreciate your understanding."

"We definitely haven't been friends," he replied, making no effort to soften the statement. "I thought you were only interested in getting your own way. I may have to change my opinion."

"Thanks. Me too." She offered a hand and he shook it, then opened the door for her.

"Call me," he said, "as soon as you get the data."

# C H A P T E R
## 8

Friday marked a week since sailing day. A heavy rainstorm at the North Cape had not kept Scott from setting foot on the icy terrain, and now he was paying for it with a cold. He lay on his bed, miserable to be sick but watching in awe as the impressive panorama passed his window. Clear skies shone down on huge glaciers, floating by like islands of meringue. Shortly before noon, even the blasé cruise director took to the loudspeaker to point out a dramatic gray-white avalanche of water, frozen solid in its descent between two mountains.

After bringing Scott several books from the library, Lauren headed for the hospital. It had taken more than a day and a half for her to collect the information. The hardest chore had been convincing the purser to let her make a photocopy of Alice's passenger registration form. With Trina's help, she had finally succeeded.

A thin, short-haired nurse answered her knock and informed her the doctor was not seeing anyone until his office opened at four.

"It's personal," Lauren said.

"I'm sorry. You'll have to come back."

182

"Please tell him it's Lauren Wilde and I have the data he requested."

The nurse scowled and disappeared behind the door. She returned a moment later, still hostile. "You may go in."

The doctor was all business as he stood to greet Lauren, motioned her to a chair, then sat down behind his desk. His freshly starched whites, she noted, were not unbecoming.

"Any luck?" he asked.

"Yes. I borrowed the purser's Smith-Corona and typed it out for you. And here's the photocopy you wanted. That took a bit of doing."

"I'll bet." He glanced at the sheet, then at her. "So neat and well organized. Have you had secretarial experience?"

"No, I work for a newspaper." It still felt strange to announce, "I write a column."

"You do?" He stared in surprise. "What kind of column?"

"About anything and everything. People, places, satire, trends, fashions, whatever. I only started a few months ago."

"I think that's wonderful. I always wanted to write, but I never had the time—or the discipline or the talent."

"At least you were doing something productive with your life." She smiled, and he returned it. "Do you know," she said, "that's the first time I've seen you smile?"

"Why would I have smiled? You were a pain in the gluteus the first time we met."

"And you were rude, pompous, and obnoxious."

He threw back his head and laughed, filling the room with rich, sonorous tones. "Well, so much for the mutual admiration society. Now tell me what you've learned about our mystery lady."

Lauren reached for her notes and scanned them. "At first, no one seemed to know much. All I could find out was that she'd had three or four husbands, was very rich, traveled a lot with the line, and had a daughter. Then I cornered her stewardess one day. She hates Mrs. Bock with a passion and told me everything."

"Everything? I only have an hour."

"I'll condense. All you really need to know is that Alice always used to travel with her daughter, but got to be too much for the daughter to handle, so this is the first trip she's made with a nurse. Alice's second husband was somebody Du Pont, died ten years after they were married and left her millions. They had one daughter, an only child. She's about fifty, has a grown family, lives in Delaware, and I have her phone number."

"Good work. What about Alice's health?"

"I'm getting to that. Everyone always liked Alice, and she apparently is—or was—very generous. The stewardess told me that Mrs. Bock handles her money now, and is incredibly tight. Probably steals it all for herself. Anyway, I gather the tips haven't been flowing this year, so the staff was more than happy to sound off. They say Mrs. Bock is a real bully—that Alice was quiet and happy when she first got on the ship, but now she cries a lot and seems terribly nervous. So whatever medication that ogre's been giving her, it sure hasn't helped."

"Does anyone know what's wrong with her?"

Lauren shrugged. "Everyone thinks it's Alzheimer's. What do you think?"

"I couldn't say without examining her. Senility can be due to anything from anemia or hypothyroidism to Parkinson's, Huntington's, a brain tumor, multiinfarct dementia—that's a series of small strokes—there are dozens of possible causes. I'd have to find some way to examine her, and even then I don't have the diagnostic tools to make more than an educated guess." After a five-second pause, he asked, "What about the dining room?"

"The maître d' was terrific. He said they sit by themselves at table twenty-eight, starboard side, aft." An embarrassed glance to the ceiling accompanied her admission: "I finally learned my nautical terms. He also said, confidentially, that Mrs. Bock eats everything in sight and pays no attention to Alice—that the waiter has to read her the menu and explain each dish, and the nurse couldn't care less."

"Poor lady," he said, nodding in sympathy. "One wonders how the daughter could have picked someone like that. You're a good detective, Lauren. I'll make it a point to stop by her table tonight. I'll find a reason to talk to her, and we'll take it from there."

She exhaled almost audibly. "Thanks so much. That's a big relief."

"By the way, how's Trina doing?"

"Fabulous. She's walking all over the place and not even limping. It's Scott now. He's in bed with a cold."

Peter frowned. "I'm sorry to hear that. Does he have medication?"

"I think so. All three of us are pretty much antimedicine, though. He's very leery of pills."

"He's right to be." Her words touched a nerve. The doctor uncrossed his legs and leaned forward. "I'm very antipill myself, unless it's a necessity. These days we see so much frivolous, unnecessary, and excessive medication that it's appalling—a disgrace to the medical profession."

"What can you do about it?"

"On a cruise ship, nothing. It's a different situation. Passengers get very unhappy paying five or six hundred dollars a day to stay in bed and feel terrible, so our job is to get them up and about as soon as possible. I even hesitated giving Trina that shot of Demerol when she fell, but she was wincing in pain, and that's when medicine *should* be used."

"I agree."

"What it means," he went on, "is that we don't have time to discuss the passengers' life-style or ask about diet and exercise and vitamins and stress reduction. We're not supposed to concern ourselves with prevention, only with treatment. So we have to give medicine—whatever drugs it takes to make the patient well—as fast as we can."

"You've been on ships a long time?"

He shook his head vehemently. "This is my first trip and my last trip. It goes against all my principles to practice instant medicine. I'd get off tomorrow if I could. But obviously I can't. I'll fulfill my obligation and stick it out until New York. Maybe I can do some good along the way."

"I wish you luck." She reached in her bag for a pencil and scribbled her cabin number across the top of her notes. "Let me know what happens with Alice?"

"I will," he said. "Give me two or three days to work on it."

It was sunny, crisp, and clear the following morning when the *Sea Viking* docked at Molde, Norway, only a block from the center of town. Scott felt well enough to join the ladies for a stroll along the spotlessly clean streets. Sheltered by mountains from the heavy winds, the "Town of Roses" sparkled with colorful flowers and lush, grassy parks. Potted plants bloomed in windows and on balconies, and gardens blossomed everywhere—even on the roof of the new Town Hall. Almost all the buildings were new, in fact. The Germans had bombed mercilessly before they left in 1940, and the Norwegians had rebuilt the entire city.

Their walk ended with lunch at a one-room seafood restaurant, and they were back on the ship by early afternoon. A note under the door informed Trina she had a radiogram at the front desk. Lauren ran to get it.

"Hope nothing's wrong," she said, handing over the envelope. "I wish people wouldn't send wires. It's too nerve-racking."

Trina tore it open and read quickly, her frown deepening into a scowl. "No one's sick or hurt," she announced, handing it to an anxious Scott. "We've got other problems."

He read aloud, dwelling on each word: "Major scandal breaking. Police officers paid prostitute to perform oral sex on unwilling rookie cop. Everyone lying, cover-up about to explode. Will advise. Love, Liz." He crumpled the paper in his fist and shot it into the wastebasket. "Christ, I know what this means."

"What does it mean?" asked Lauren.

Trina was already on the phone, badgering the operator. "How can you tell me there's no one in the radio room? There *has* to be!" Her fingers strummed the table as she listened impatiently. "Forty minutes? All right, I'll call back."

"I could've told you that," said Scott wearily. "The radio room's always closed in port."

"Then I'm going ashore to call. I have to know what's going on."

"Honey, for God's sake, calm down—and *sit* down," he said, taking hold of her arm and pressing her into a chair. "We sail at three o'clock. That's only forty minutes from now. The radio room will be open and you can make your call. There's no way we can go ashore, find a phone, get through to someone halfway around the world, where it's

probably two A.M., and get back on the ship in time to sail.
Am I reaching you?''

"I suppose," she conceded with a sigh. "Of all things—a
sex scandal. I wonder where it happened—how many were
involved. Do you think—"

"Hey, this is your vacation, remember?" Lauren perched
on the edge of the bed and eyed her friend sternly. "You're
here because your doctor wanted you to get away from all
this. Darn that Liz, she—"

"Don't blame Liz," Scott interrupted. "If I know my wife,
she gave orders to wire her if anything important happened."

"Of course I gave orders," snapped Trina, jumping up angrily. "I'm still the mayor, in case you both forgot. I appointed the police chief and the police commissioners, and it's
*my* head in the guillotine. I've *got* to know what's going on,
and I've got to be able to send home a statement."

"I'll see you later," murmured Lauren, departing the cabin.
Back in her room, she had the strongest feeling her dream
cruise could be coming to an early end. It spurred her to perform a chore she had been putting off for weeks. Grabbing
pen and paper, she wrote a long, descriptive letter. Edna and
Victor would read that she was having the most wonderful,
exciting trip of her life and that she had the dearest and most
generous parents a daughter could have.

The following day the *Sea Viking* had two stops on its itin-
erary, first at Flaam, then three hours later in Gudvangen; both
tiny scenic villages nestled among frosted mountains. Scott
and Trina were remaining on board, he still sniffling, she determined to reach the police chief between one and four, while
the ship crossed from port to port.

Early that morning, Lauren descended the gangplank at
Flaam, enjoying the invigorating air and the chance to be alone
with her thoughts. Walls between cabins were thin, and the
voices of her neighbors had kept her awake for several hours
during the night. Staring out the window into bright sunshine
at eleven P.M., she had been tempted to get dressed and walk
the deck. As promised in the folder, the "Land of the Midnight Sun" provided twenty-four hours of daylight. It seemed
too much effort, however, and she had closed the shades,

crawled back to bed, and tried to block out the Bellamys' voices.

The discussion had started with Scott reminding Trina that her two twenty-minute satellite calls to Liz Meredith had cost $11 a minute, for a whopping total of $440. The argument escalated with Scott challenging her priorities and Trina responding that the needs of a city were greater than his personal vacation plans. Scott assured her she was not indispensable, she assured him likewise, at which point Lauren put a pillow over her head and finally went to sleep.

She needed no crystal ball to see into the future. Trina would want to fly home early, she and Scott would try to change her mind with no success, and the three of them would leave the ship in Copenhagen. Or maybe even sooner. But for the present, she would do her best to enjoy the morning ashore; it might be among her last.

A voice from behind made her stop. She turned to see Peter Marsten running toward her in his heavy parka and a knitted stocking cap, struggling under a large backpack.

"Hi," he said breathlessly. "Where are you going?"

"For a walk." She smiled. "I like your hat."

He fell into step alongside her. "It keeps my ears warm. I never know where my temporary office is going to be. Sometimes it's outdoors."

"Temporary office?"

"Yes, I think I told you—I bring medical supplies and give free examinations whenever we dock at a small village. Today we're meeting in someone's house."

"Are you hired by the ship or the Norwegian government?"

"Hired?" He chuckled loudly. "I'm hired by no one. But people in these areas rarely get to see a modern doctor. When I found out I was coming here, I wrote to the ship's representative in each town and asked if the residents wanted free consultations and supplies. They all said yes."

"I would think so. Do you speak Norwegian?"

"My father taught me enough to get by." He shifted the weight of his backpack. "I wanted to tell you about Alice. When I stopped at the table last night, Mrs. Bock asked me for some Haldol, and I told her I couldn't dispense medication without seeing the patient. So I was able to examine Alice briefly.''

Lauren's eyes lit up with interest. "Yes?"

"It's complicated. She—" Their dialogue was interrupted by a ruddy-faced man in a plastic fishing coat and jeans.

"Dr. Marsten?" His semitoothless smile was warm and welcoming. "I am Kjell Gulbrandsen and very happy to greet you. I will take you and your nurse to my house."

"She's not—"

"Thank you," said Lauren, linking her arm in the doctor's. "Let's go."

Peter looked down at her. "You'll miss seeing the town, you'll be bored standing around, and you'll be frustrated because you can't speak the language. I strongly urge you not to come."

"Nonsense. I always go with you."

No sense trying to dissuade her; Peter helped her into their host's car, and ten minutes later they were inside a small and very crowded dining room. The fisherman's house enchanted her. What it lacked in furnishings and comforts it made up in homey touches—pictures, ceramic doodads, quilts, embroideries, and potted flowers. Peter stationed himself in the bedroom while Lauren, enjoying her new role, talked to the waiting patients—or tried to, in gestures and sign language.

Four hours passed quickly. By the time Peter had seen a dozen families, it was noon. Lauren helped pack up his supplies and instruments, and a grateful Kjell Gulbrandsen drove them back to the ship.

"I have to hand it to you, Lauren," Peter said at the top of the gangplank. "You were quite a help."

"Thanks for letting me tag along. I loved getting a taste of the local life instead of just being a tourist. Was I really a help?"

"Definitely. I usually have trouble reassuring the people that there's enough time for me to see all of them. Sometimes they start arguing over whose wife or whose kid is going to be next. You seemed able to keep everyone happy."

"Thanks to Kjell," she said. "When my gestures didn't work, he translated. Are you going to do the same thing this afternoon in Gudvangen?"

"No, we're only there two hours and it's not enough time. That was my last mission. Our next stops are all big cities where there's no shortage of medical care. So . . . thanks again, I'll see you later."

He disappeared down the companionway, and she headed for the elevator. Back in her cabin, she realized that they had been so absorbed in the morning's activities, they had forgotten to finish their conversation about Alice.

At dinner that night, Trina reported she had talked to the San Francisco police chief, who assured her the situation was under control and that there was no need for her to fly home. She trusted him, but she trusted her deputy mayor more and assigned him the task of finding out just how broad the scandal would be. The only good thing, Lauren thought, was that Trina had too much on her mind to keep pushing a romance with Peter.

Knowing this might be one of their last nights on board, the three travelers were reluctant to retire to their cabins after dinner as they usually did. It was also a formal night, and the women had taken pains to dress in their long gowns. A Texas couple was hosting a dance in the nightclub, and though they had declined all previous invitations, they decided to make an exception.

The hostess was thrilled that the ship's most glamorous celebrity had chosen to grace her gathering and left the receiving line to escort the mayor and her companions to a private table. She and her husband would join them shortly.

"I guess you're exhibit A," said Lauren, noting the stares around the room. "No wonder we don't go to these parties."

"I'm sorry already," Trina murmured. "And you're going to be even sorrier."

Lauren's eyes widened. "I am?"

"The table's for six. I think you'll have the captain on your left."

"Oh, no. Don't you think he got the message when we changed places in the dining room so I'd have my back to him?"

"Do you want to make that assumption," asked Scott, "or do you want to play it safe and sit between us?"

"You can't get up now," Trina protested. "That's too obvious."

"Who cares," said Lauren, switching seats with Scott. "I'm not entering a popularity contest and you're not running for reelection till next year, so thank you, Scott, you're a gentleman and a savior—which is more than I can say for some people, who just throw their friends to the wolves."

"Speaking of wolves . . ." Trina looked up pleasantly and nodded at the gym instructor, a lean, muscled, suntanned blond wearing a custom silk shirt and his trademark tight slacks. "I hear that man alone is responsible for keeping smiles on the faces of half the widows on Promenade Deck."

"Who told you that?" Scott asked.

"Oh, just gossip."

"Don't look now," said Lauren, "but I think he pads his pants."

Trina suppressed a laugh. "You're right. Either that, or he's awfully glad to see that waiter."

"I never should've seated you women together." Scott sighed. "Laur, would you mind if my wife and I had a dance?"

"Of course not." The three-piece band played swing, the room was becoming more and more crowded, the noise and smoke levels were growing uncomfortably high. Lauren was wondering how she could sneak away before the captain materialized, when a hand tapped her shoulder.

She looked up with dread, then relaxed into a smile. "Oh, hi, Peter."

"May I sit down?"

"Yes, please do." It was the first time she had seen him in his dress uniform. No one, she thought, should look like that and live. "What are you doing here?"

"Well, if you mean here," he said, sweeping his arm across the room, "I'm here because the captain issued orders for all officers to attend this gala event. If you mean here at this table, I'd say it was your beauty and charm if I thought I could get away with it. I must confess it was because Trina felt guilty leaving you alone and asked me to come over."

"I liked the first reason better." She laughed. "That woman never stops promoting."

"Oh, really? Has she been promoting me to you as much as she's been promoting you to me? She spent a whole morning in the hospital telling me I had the wrong impression of you and how much I'd like you if I got to know you."

"She's a frustrated matchmaker, I'm afraid." Lauren smoothed back her hair and wished she had checked her lipstick in a mirror. "She refuses to believe that anyone can be happy and unmarried at the same time."

"That's—oops." He dropped to a whisper. "We have to make a decision. I can leave you to the mercies of our libidinous captain, who's rapidly heading this way, or I can subject you to the mercies of my three left feet."

"I'd *love* to dance," she said aloud, rising. Her white strapless gown, sleek and simple, stood out in elegant contrast to the roomful of beads, sequins, and bright-colored prints; half the eyes in the nightclub took in her contours.

Peter circled his partner's waist and drew her to him. "Don't you ever eat?"

"All the time. I walk a lot, though, and I never take elevators. Do you know what they're playing?"

"No. Tell me."

" 'Just in Time,' " she hummed. "You saved me from the captain just in time."

"You may wish I hadn't. I never went to dancing school." His hand felt strong and warm on her back, and as the other couples bumped and jostled them on the crowded floor, he pulled her protectively closer. "What an obstacle course," he murmured. "I *had* to come here tonight. What's your excuse?"

"Well . . . we usually go to our cabins and read after dinner," she answered. "I guess we all felt we might as well see what these parties are like, since we may be getting off soon."

He stopped dancing and looked at her. "Trina said you were staying on till New York. Is anything wrong?"

"Not with us. City problems at home. I should've known she couldn't stay away for five weeks."

"That's too bad," he said. His hand instinctively moved up her back to bare skin.

She wanted to be held closer but reminded herself that ships often had sneaky effects on people—made them feel lonely and vulnerable and romantic. "Yes—it's too bad."

"Perhaps I should return you to your table. Everyone's there but you."

She shook her head. "I'm not going back. It's hot, noisy, and smoky in here, and I've managed to avoid the captain for ten lovely days. I'm not about to spoil my record."

"I see what you mean."

"Perhaps—if you don't mind—you could dance me over to the door. I'll send word with a waiter that I'm not feeling well."

"But you are feeling well, aren't you?" he asked, edging toward the exit.

"I will be as soon as I get out of here."

"I'll walk you to your cabin."

"Don't you have to stay?"

"No one's going to fire me," he replied, "and if they did, I'd love it."

Out in the hall, she borrowed his pen to scribble a note to Trina, who would make her apologies. The hosts wouldn't care—they had their celebrity—and the captain was on the dance floor nuzzling a pretty widow. Her presence would not be missed.

"What a relief!" she exclaimed, kicking a silver sandal into the air and almost catching it. "That place was getting to me."

"Why don't you put on some comfortable shoes and we'll breathe some fresh air?"

Moments later, they were strolling the deck in bright daylight, enjoying the drama of an unusually narrow fjord. At one spot, the shore seemed within easy swimming distance.

"I kind of like putting on sunglasses at ten-thirty at night," she mused. "I wish we had twenty-four-hour daylight at home. Think of all the crime that wouldn't be committed."

"Mmm . . . perhaps. But what would they do with all those songs about moonlight and June nights?"

"You've got a point." They moved in silence for a few minutes before she asked, "How old are you, Peter?"

"Thirty-nine going on eighty," he replied. "The gray hairs are coming fast."

"I'm going to be thirty next week. I think I'll like it."

"Next week? Happy birthday."

"Thanks. May I ask another personal question?"

"You're very good at that," he said with a sidelong glance. "I keep forgetting I'm with a reporter."

"Is that a no?"

"Yes, it's a no. I'm uncomfortable answering questions about myself. I can tell you everything you need to know about me in a few sentences."

"Really?" She stopped to secure her scarf. The wind was getting stronger. "I'm all ears—cold ones."

"Let's go inside, then." He pushed open the heavy door and she hurried ahead of him, grateful for the warmth of the corridor. "I'll tell you quickly," he said with mild resignation in his voice. "I was born in New York to a Norwegian father and an Italian mother; both, unfortunately, are gone. My father was a brilliant cardiologist; he performed some of the first transplant operations. I inherited many of his drives, including the need to make a significant contribution to medicine. I've saved enough money to build my own research and treatment clinic now—a very small one to start. I'm hoping to get a grant once we get under way."

She listened attentively, sensing how difficult it was for him to talk about himself. "What kind of research?"

"Dermatology. I'll take on the most difficult and 'hopeless' skin diseases, not only life-threatening ones, but common conditions, such as acne, psoriasis, eczema. There are so many new treatments and medications that haven't been adequately studied or tested. My sister, Margit, lives in L.A.; I've never seen my two nephews and they're already four and six years old. I thought—since I'm making the big move of my life—I might as well be near my only family. Now you know everything."

"You've only told me your professional background," she persisted. "What about your love life?"

"Have you got seventeen hours?"

"Come on, be serious." She smiled, stopping outside her cabin. "I'd ask you to come in, but that would be improper. So tell me quick."

"Quick? All right. One woman—that's all. We lived together for the last ten years. She's a lawyer, very successful, very busy. Neither of us ever stopped working long enough to enjoy our relationship. And now it's over. It died of attrition. We still care for each other, but we're going our own ways. That's why I felt free to move away from New York. A colleague talked me into taking this trip—supposedly a vacation—before I get buried in work again. That's all there is, and it's time we both got some sleep.''

"Fair enough.'' She held out her hand. "Thanks for the walk—and the talk—and the dance.''

He shook it impersonally. "My pleasure. Good night.''

Sleep came slowly as Lauren lay in bed thinking, trying to convince herself there was no future to a romance with Peter. His life was all planned; medicine came first, his sister's family came second, and he had all but admitted he had neither the time nor the energy to get involved.

Her life was equally structured; the job, for now, was her main focus. Mentally, she'd been hashing over all sorts of ideas and ways to lure new readers, including a weekly feature on the best places in town to meet singles. Her column *had* to be a success; failure was not an option. Such determination left little time for the demands and vicissitudes of a love affair.

Perhaps the best reason for waiving all fantasies was the simplest: she wouldn't be around to live them out. Trina had already broached the subject of leaving the ship when it docked in Copenhagen, and Lauren felt sure that no matter how encouraging the news about the scandal at home, Her Honor would insist on being right there—where it was all happening.

The large harbor bustled with water traffic as the *Sea Viking* pulled into dock the next morning at nine. The ship's shuttle took a load of passengers to the center of Bergen—a charming old city full of well-kept parks and steep-roofed, medieval stone structures.

The bus stopped at Torgalmenning, Bergen's extra-wide shopping street, where Lauren and the Bellamys hired a cab. An English-speaking driver amused them with tales of legendary sea serpents while showing them the city's many monuments, churches, and museums. They lunched at an overpriced restaurant near Troldhaugen, the site of Edvard Grieg's historic home, then drove back to the shopping district, where they bought twenty-four dollars' worth of prawns and crab legs at an outdoor fish market.

A wire awaiting Trina back at the ship clinched her plans to fly home in four days, as soon as they reached Copenhagen. As expected, she tried to convince Lauren to stay on board and, when reason failed, used Peter as bait by inviting him to join them for a fresh seafood dinner in the cabin. The chef provided Louis dressing, a tossed green salad, and garlic bread, the wine steward brought chilled Chablis, and the feast was a success. Peter had a stroke patient in the hospital, however, seemed worried and preoccupied, and left early. The party was over by eight-fifteen, and Lauren had not changed her mind.

The three spent the next day packing and the following afternoon went ashore at Oslo for a last excursion. At first, the capital of Norway disappointed them; it was big, sophisticated, and very much like any major European or American city. A downtown park served as repository for hundreds of discarded soft-drink cans and the scattered debris of various punk rockers, hippies, and drunks. "Norway," Scott pronounced, "has lost her virginity." It seemed sad that this would be one of the last impressions they would take away from their trip.

Driving around, however, they saw the city's famous Akershus Castle, the Viking Ship Museum with its authentic, well-preserved wooden vessels, and an unusual outdoor park containing more than 150 stone and bronze statues. A day's touring revealed Oslo's drama and history, and they happily amended their first impression. Unfortunately, this made the thought of aborting the cruise all the harder.

Back in her cabin by late afternoon, Lauren stood at the window and wished she weren't leaving. Now she would never get to visit Russia or Finland or . . . Who was she fooling? All she would really miss was Peter. Knowing she would probably never see him again, she felt a strong urge to talk to him, if only to hear his voice.

Before she could think about it and stop herself, she dialed the hospital. No answer. "Operator," she said, "it's very important that I speak to Dr. Marsten right away."

"Hold on. I'll try to reach him for you."

Miraculously, he was suddenly on the other end of the line. She thought of hanging up, but the operator would know. "Peter . . ." She hesitated. "It's Lauren. I—"

"Where the hell have you been?" His voice was almost angry. "I've been trying to reach you all day."

"We were in town—just got back."

"Are you still leaving in Copenhagen?"

"Yes. I—I wanted to find out about Alice—"

"Can you have dinner with me tonight?"

Her throat tightened with emotion. "Yes—I'd like that."

"I'll meet you at the gangway in half an hour. We're going ashore, so dress warmly," he said, and clicked off.

The restaurant was small and dimly lit and, judging by its clientele, catered mainly to locals. The chief electrician on the ship had recommended it, Peter explained, for its sumptuous smorgasbord.

"I'm glad you could join me tonight," Peter said, hanging her white wool coat on a rack by the door. "Tomorrow's the Captain's farewell party. I knew this would be our only chance."

"Yes." Being coy was not in her nature, but neither could she express the strong emotions she was feeling. "I called you because I felt something unresolved between us. I wanted to say a more personal thank-you before I left." She paused a few seconds. "I know Alice is all right because she's in your hands. But I do want to hear what's happening."

"Let's get some food and I'll tell you."

The long, candle-lit buffet table offered trays of ham, roast beef, shrimp, salmon, fried cod roe with bacon, sliced egg with anchovies, herring salad, marinated beans and mushrooms, all kinds of smoked fish, fresh-baked breads, and cheeses. Lauren and Peter served themselves modestly, too distracted by each other's presence to be concerned with food. Yet it seemed a convenient subject for conversation as they cautiously skirted more personal topics.

"This looks marvelous—and very authentic." She smiled

as he moved her chair to the table. "I'm so glad we came here. I hate the fancy tourist traps."

"Me too."

His steady gaze brought a flush to her cheeks, and she shifted her glance. Something in his expression made her feel light-headed, almost dizzy. It took an effort of will to speak. "You were going to tell me about Alice."

"So I was." Her words snapped him back. He signaled the waiter for more wine, then assumed his professional persona. "The situation was exactly as you described it and worse. Mrs. Pendergast does seem to have Alzheimer's disease. The first stage, as you know, is forgetfulness. Then comes phase two, the confused stage; and the final phase is dementia or senility. It begins at the point where a patient can't survive if he or she is left alone. I'd place Alice in early phase three."

"I'm so sorry. There's no cure, is there?"

He shook his head. "Unfortunately, the disease is progressive and irreversible. If that's what it is."

"You're not sure?"

"I'd say there's a good chance of it. No one's ever one hundred percent sure. The only way to confirm a diagnosis of Alzheimer's is to examine a sample of brain tissue, and since we don't cut up people's brains to find out if they have a terminal illness, it waits for an autopsy. Most diagnoses of Alzheimer's are made on the basis of neurological tests that tell you what it isn't."

He speared a radish, popped it into his mouth, and continued. "That night, though, I did talk to her and examine her, and I found a high aluminum count in her urine sample—probably an indication. I also talked to Mrs. Bock, who said she had seen no medical reports on Mrs. Pendergast—Alice—and had never spoken to her doctor."

"Alice's own nurse doesn't know what's wrong with her? What did you do?"

"I called her daughter in Delaware. Lovely woman, and she was appalled. Gave me full authorization to take charge. She said her mother's doctor does think she has Alzheimer's and that he was supposed to have sent along her complete history."

"Why didn't he?"

He shrugged. "I don't know. I told her that the ship requires written notification prior to sailing of any medical problems that may need attention; otherwise we can't be responsible. She was very upset, blamed Mrs. Bock for not getting the records, asked me to keep watch for the rest of the cruise. She's making arrangements to hospitalize her as soon as they get off."

Lauren poked a potato without enthusiasm. "What a shame. But it's probably the right decision, don't you think?"

"Yes. Since money is no problem, Alice should be in a medical unit where she can get proper treatment."

"How do you treat an incurable disease?"

He nodded sadly. "Any way you can. She should be taking lecithin, which contains choline and may help clear her thinking processes, and several other supplements, including vasopressin, a pituitary hormone that could improve her memory. Her diet should be closely supervised so that she's not getting foods or medication high in aluminum. And most important, she should be someplace where there's a staff trained to give therapy. There's no reason in the world she can't be kept mentally active and busy."

"Have you stopped that awful woman from feeding her tranquilizers?"

"Absolutely. I examine Alice every morning, and I've made it clear to Mrs. Bock that if I find the slightest evidence she's given her one of those chemical straitjackets, I'll make a full report of cruelty and mistreatment to her employers. Haldol, the drug she wanted, is a powerful antipsychotic. High doses can produce severe side effects: shaking, drooling, wide, staring eyes. Poor Alice would have been shuffling around the ship like a zombie. Have you seen her lately?"

"No," answered Lauren, her voice dropping in sympathy. "Is she any better?"

"You wouldn't recognize her. She's calm, unemotional, not frightened and crying all the time like she was when I first saw her." He covered his wineglass before the waiter could refill it. "No more, thanks. Maybe the lady will have some."

"None for me, thank you."

His eyes shone with admiration. "You did a nice thing, Lauren. You had the sensitivity to see what was going on and the guts to swallow your dislike for me and report it. If you hadn't, Mrs. Bock could easily have gotten some kind of pills from a pharmacy. By the time we got to New York, Alice would have been getting off on a stretcher.''

She smiled across the table. "I'm glad I did it, too. Or I'd still be disliking you—and vice versa.''

"That's ancient history.'' He lifted his wineglass. "I'd rather look to the future. Skoal—to your health.''

"Skoal,'' she repeated, momentarily self-conscious under his beaming gaze. "What are you thinking?''

"That you know all about me and I know nothing about you.'' His dinner plate sat before him, barely touched. "It's your turn now. How did you get into the writing business?''

She wanted to tell him all about herself. There were dreams and fantasies and hopes for the future she wanted very much to share with him. But there was so little time. As concisely as she could, she told of her schooling, her modeling and charity work, how dissatisfied she had been until she began working at the newspaper, how important it was for her to succeed there.

He listened closely, without comment. Then, as casually as he could, he said, "You don't mention any boyfriends or ex-husbands—''

"Fair enough.'' She laughed. "I'm afraid my romantic past is pretty dull. I've never been married, engaged, or—well, once I got pinned until my father found out about it. My dad's a terror.''

"In general or just about you?''

"Both. He's impossible when he thinks I'm the least bit interested in a man. I mean—really impossible. It's more than parental love; it's an obsession.''

The revelation seemed to fascinate him. "Your mother—is she that way, too?''

"No, she's just the opposite. Scared to death I'll be an old maid.''

He pursued the subject. "Maybe your father hasn't liked any of the men you've brought home.''

"He wouldn't like anyone,'' she insisted. "Not anyone. He's a dear and I adore him, but he can't seem to let go of me. I think—correction: I *know* he'd do almost anything to discourage someone he thought was seriously interested in me.''

"He sounds pretty neurotic," Peter murmured. "I'd say, however, that that's a very minor concern. If you love a man and he loves you, why do you need your father's approval? Can't you live your own life?"

"Yes, of course. That's what I'll have to do. I—" She stopped, hearing what she was about to say. "I know it sounds funny, but we've always been so close—too close, in fact. It's partly my fault for being such a patsy. I've never been able to do anything that would hurt him."

"That's your nature. Sometimes you have to hurt other people when your own happiness is at stake." His tone was sounding more personal than he had a right to sound. Better to change the subject. "Was your dinner all right? How about some Norwegian blotkake?"

"Not a thing. Thank you. It was delicious." She glanced down at her plate self-consciously. Neither of them had been able to finish.

They rode home in silence, boarded the gangplank, and walked down the passageway like self-propelled robots, still unable to communicate their thoughts. Outside her cabin, she stopped and looked up at him. "It was a lovely evening. I hate to have it end."

"Yes." He almost seemed frozen as he tried to sound matter-of-fact. "Have a safe trip home, Lauren. Good night."

She nodded and disappeared behind the door.

Sleep was impossible. Over and over in her mind, she reviewed the evening—his words, his gestures, the caring she had seen in his eyes. She understood his reluctance to touch her, even to hold her hand. If he felt any of what she was beginning to feel, it would have made their parting so much more difficult.

What was she feeling? No matter what the romance novels said, you didn't get tremors in your gut simply because a man was handsome and looked good in a uniform. Her life had been full of beautiful faces; why was he so confoundedly different? She knew part of the answer: he cared about people. Not about their money or their social position but about how they felt and how they treated others, and what they did with their lives. His values were the ones she wanted for her own.

Material goods were lovely and fun to have, she reflected. They pleased the ego and the senses. Yet how completely involved she and her whole family had always been with money—making it, spending it, giving it away to an impersonal art museum or a charity that gave tax benefits. How much better to be able to give of yourself to someone like Alice—and to see and feel and hear the results. . . . She was grateful to Peter for reviving her gentler instincts.

It was nearly midnight when the shrillness of the phone broke her reverie. She reached for it anxiously. "Hello?"

"Did I wake you?" Peter's voice was tense.

"No, I haven't been able to sleep."

"I'm just down the hallway. I've been walking the deck for the last two hours—thinking. May I come by and see you? I promise I won't stay more than a minute."

"Yes. Of course."

She was barely into her robe when the knock came. He stepped inside and closed the door behind him.

"You're cold—freezing," she said, reaching up and touching his cheek.

He took her hand from his face and held it. "Lauren, I've rehearsed this damn speech so much I don't know what I'm saying anymore. It boils down to this: If you leave Friday, you'll be taking something away from us—something we'll never have again. You'll go home to your demanding career, I'll get so embedded in my work I won't see daylight for months, and we'll never know what we might have found in each other."

He paused, then continued slowly—cautiously. "What I'm about to blurt out is: I want you to stay. I don't want you to go home. Give us the next few weeks to be together, to get to know each other without clocks ticking in our ears or deadlines hanging over our heads. The chance will never come again, and I don't want to let it slip away. Maybe we'll hate each other when the cruise is over, but we'll never know unless we try."

Before she could answer, he reached out and drew her toward him. He lingered uncertainly, fearing she might pull

away, until her arms crept about his neck and gave him the
message he wanted. He kissed her with infinite tenderness,
then clasped her head to his racing heart. "Will you stay,
Lauren?"

She clung tightly, not wanting to let go even to answer. He
felt her affirmative nod, and he murmured, "Promise? You
won't change your mind?"

"I promise." Her eyes widened as she looked up at him.
"I couldn't go home without seeing Russia, could I?"

He burst into laughter, full of joy and relief. "Then you'd
better get some sleep," he said, reluctantly releasing her.
"You've got a lot of unpacking to do."

The *Sea Viking* sailed from Oslo at twelve noon the next
day; last stop Copenhagen. Lauren had respected her neighbors' "Do Not Disturb" sign all morning but finally knocked
to see if they were going to lunch.

"What have you two been doing?" she asked as the door
opened. "That sign's been up for hours. I didn't dare call
you."

"Sorry," said Trina, pushing aside a large suitcase. 'Come
on in if you can find something to sit on. Scott's down getting
his last massage. I should've called you. I just needed the
morning to concentrate and prepare a statement to meet the
press at the airport."

Lauren shifted a shopping bag full of purchases to the floor,
then flopped on the bed in the space she had created. "Too
bad I won't be there for the excitement."

"Of course you'll be there. What do you mean you won't
be there?" The realization suddenly hit, and Trina's voice
jumped in pitch. "You're not going home with us? Are you
staying on board? I almost forgot—how was your dinner with
Peter? Is that why you're staying?"

"You're some matchmaker." Lauren feigned annoyance.
"Go to all that trouble to get us together and then forget all
about us."

"No, no, tell me quick! Tell me everything. Where did you
go?"

"We went to a cute little Norwegian restaurant with soft

music and candlelight. After dinner, we came home to the ship, shook hands, and retired to our respective cabins.''

"Oh." Trina's face fell. "Then why are you staying?"

"Because my date came back at midnight and delivered the most eloquent speech about how we could have the next three weeks to get to know each other and that we'd never have the chance again, and please, pretty please, would I stay.''

"And you said?"

"I said yes and he left. No pass, no errors. I have to admit he's a most unusual man. And if you say, 'I told you so—' ''

"Well, I *did* tell you so, dummy, but you wouldn't listen. I'm so happy for you, I really am." Trina held out her arms and Lauren embraced her tightly.

"I'm kind of scared, Tri," she whispered. "It's sounds corny, but I've never known a man who was so kind and caring about other people. I didn't think anyone like that existed.''

"Okay, then listen to me," said Trina, pulling back and eyeing her firmly. "I've got something to say to you while we're alone.''

"Yes, Mother?"

"*Listen* to me. Just five—" She counted her fingers. "No, six little words, probably the most important words anyone will ever say to you. Are you ready?''

"Yup."

"Don't let Victor screw it up.''

"You're so right!" Lauren shook her head, amazed, as always, at her friend's perceptiveness. "I honestly don't know what will happen with Peter. We haven't spent any time together, we don't know if we share the same goals or interests, we don't know anything about each other except that we're attracted. And I know exactly what you mean. Whether it's Peter, or someone else five years from now, won't make any difference. Dad will say he's wrong for me, or he's a gold digger or whatever, and try to break it off. I teased him about it once, and threatened to elope. Then poor Mom started to cry and made me promise I wouldn't get married without her. So I'm—"

Her speech was interrupted by Scott's noisy return. "Hey, everyone," he announced, spinning a towel in the air and tossing it on the bed. "I could eat a horse and a half right now. Are you beautiful ladies ready to take me to lunch?"

"Absolutely." Trina smiled and gave Lauren a sidelong wink. "Let's go celebrate the end of a perfect cruise."

# CHAPTER
# 9

THE *Sea Viking* WAS A FLURRY OF ACTIVITY AS THE STEWardesses scrubbed down the walls, exchanged towels and bedding, sprayed mirrors and windows, and rushed frantically through their chores so that the new passengers, boarding at three in the afternoon, would find their cabins sparkling clean.

The weather was cool and sunny in Copenhagen, and Lauren slipped into a flowered cotton dress, folded a cardigan over her arm, and strolled down the gangway to meet Peter. He had called earlier to invite her to lunch, explaining that he needed the morning to take his stroke patient to the hospital.

At a few minutes past noon, Peter pulled up in a cab, jumped out to help her inside, and off they drove.

"How did it go this morning?" she asked, glad to see him dressed casually in a navy-blue blazer and gray flannel slacks.

"Fine," he replied. "The hospital is well equipped, the doctor speaks perfect English, and I'm sure the patient will recover." He took her hand. "You look fresh as a . . . hmm, I can't use clichés around a writer—daffodil? Morning glory? What I'm trying to say in my halting fashion is that you look beautiful. Your skin has an especially luminous quality in Denmark. Do people tell you that?"

"Every time I come here." She laughed. "I'm glad you didn't know me in my teens. Zit city."

"I wish I had known you in your teens. Zits and all. I bet you had those poor little boys running in circles."

"They ran the other way. I was scrawny and ugly. Honest. Not to mention thick metal bands on my teeth, and an allergic nose that never stopped dripping. One boy, the class nerd, finally came around and asked me to a movie—I guess I was fifteen—and my dad said I was too young to date and scared him off."

He looked thoughtful a moment, then suddenly sat upright. "Is your dad by any chance named Victor?"

"Yes, he is." She turned to him in surprise. "How did you know?"

He sighed. "I'm a rotten liar. Ask a direct question and you'll get a direct answer. Trina called this morning to say good-bye. Just before she hung up, she said, 'Don't tell Lauren, but whatever you do, get her away from Victor.' I thought it was one of your boyfriends."

"Good old Trina. Matchmaking even as she flies off to save the city from a sex scandal." Lauren chuckled. "You should've heard her last words to me."

"I'm afraid to ask."

"Actually, she was so wonderful she almost had us both in tears. I don't remember exactly. She just thinks the world of you and wants us to have a happy time together."

"I'll second that. They're great people. You're lucky to have such friends." His fingers tightened on her hand. "I'm glad you decided to stay. You won't be sorry."

"I'd be sorry if I didn't." There it was—that tumbling in her stomach whenever he looked at her with a certain expression. She pretended to stare out the window. "Where are we going?"

"Are you hungry?"

Food was the last thing on her mind. "Ummm . . . not awfully. Are you?"

"I was until I saw you. You take away my appetite."

They broke into laughter at the obvious double meaning; the mirth dissolved into embarrassed silence.

"I'll have the driver show us some sights," he finally said. "What do you want to see?"

You, she thought. I don't give a fig for sights. If I *never* see another church . . . "Oh, I—anything's fine."

"Yes—okay," he murmured distractedly, and called out a request in Danish. The driver nodded and answered.

"You speak Danish, too?"

"A few words. It's close enough to Norwegian that I can get by. He'll drive us around for an hour, then maybe we'll be hungry for lunch."

She doubted it. Food was nowhere in her thoughts. "Yes—that would be nice."

They peered out their respective windows in feigned fascination as the cabbie drove them up and down the main shopping streets, then stopped at the famous statue of the Little Mermaid. As they sat, supposedly mesmerized by the sight, Peter realized how tightly he had been holding her hand and relaxed his grip. "Do you want to get out and have a look?"

"It's charming." She had no desire to move; he might let go of her hand altogether. "Do *you* want to get out?"

"I don't know. Do you?"

"We could go on like this all day." She giggled.

"Driver," he said, "let's see some more of the city, please."

Yes, let's, she thought. Why not? She only hoped no one would ask her later where she had been. Her eyes were open, but nothing was registering. Could he be having a similar problem?

"Lovely town," he remarked. "Isn't it lovely?"

"Yes, it's lovely." Now her hand was going to sleep, and she didn't know how to tell him. "I . . . uh . . . think my fingers—"

"Oh, I'm sorry." He released her quickly. "Here—shake it out. Get the circulation going."

"No, no, it's okay." She wiggled her fingers in the air. "There—it's coming back. Thank you."

"You're welcome."

What in God's name were they doing? Two supposedly adult human beings grappling with such strong feelings for each other that they could hardly talk—running up the meter driving around a strange city so they could pretend they were enjoying the sights?

"I'm starting to feel hungry," she lied a few minutes later. "What about you?"

"Yes." He nodded gratefully. "Let's go eat."

The Kong Frederick was a stately old hotel, known for its service and its seafood. The maître d' obviously liked their looks and seated them at a table by the entrance. Ordinarily, Peter would have asked for a less conspicuous location, but today his mind was functioning no better than hers.

Desperate to make some kind of small talk, she tossed out a question. "Do you like fish?"

"My Norwegian half does," he said. "My Italian half likes pasta."

"You're split evenly? Right down the middle?" Oh, help! The vision was painful.

"I lean to one side," he remarked awkwardly. His tongue was sabotaging him. "What I mean is—the pasta half is stronger."

"I suppose you could have both together, couldn't you? Seafood *with* pasta?" She wanted to scream at herself; it was the dumbest conversation she had ever had. Fortunately, the waiter appeared and poured some wine from a carafe.

"Skoal," she offered.

"Skoal." Their glasses clinked and their gazes locked. She saw his eyes drop lower, then move back up. Unconsciously, her lips parted.

"I had a patient once," he said. "Whenever he ate seafood he'd break out in terrible hives all over his lips."

"How awful," she murmured.

"Did I say lips? I meant legs. His thighs and his legs."

"That's what you said. The poor man. Did he die?"

"You mean from the hives?"

"No, just generally—"

"Not that I know of. That was a long time ago. He was fine as long as he didn't eat seafood. What the hell are we talking about him for?"

"I don't know." Their laughter brought momentary relief.

"You must be a strange combination," she went on, trying

to keep the words flowing. "Italians are so expansive and volatile; the Scandinavians are so cool and reserved. Which heritage do you take after?"

"My father used to say I was Italian outside and Norwegian inside. My mother said it was the reverse. Damned if I know. What do you think?"

"My Finnish roommate in college had a terrible temper." She winced at the non sequitur, grateful that the waiter was setting down their plates.

An hour later, they had forced down most of their lunch and were once again back in the cab. "Ready to see the old section of town?" he asked.

"Yes, that would be wonderful." He seemed to read her mind, or maybe she was reading his as he leaned toward her and held out his open hand.

She took it instantly. "Thanks for everything, Peter. I've enjoyed today. I don't want to see it end."

"It hasn't—yet," he answered.

Back on the ship two hours before the five o'clock sailing, they returned to a crowd of unfamiliar faces, passageways overrun with visitors and families of departing passengers, stewardesses dashing back and forth with glasses and trays of hors d'oeuvres, piccolos delivering welcome-aboard flower arrangements, and the usual frenzy of starting a new cruise. Only about forty "holdovers" were staying on from the last segment.

Sensing that Peter was anxious to get to a phone to check on his stroke patient, Lauren insisted he not bother seeing her to the cabin. He had asked her to join his table at dinner, but she had declined, fearing they would monopolize each other and ignore the passengers who had the honor of sitting with an officer and whom he was supposedly "hosting." They agreed to meet in the nightclub at nine.

The Opal Room was dark and near deserted, with most of the passengers down in the main lounge for the "Welcome Aboard" talk and activities staff introductions. Three officers sat in deep conversation with two of the women receptionists; a noisy foursome from the last cruise occupied their regular table, and Peter motioned to her from a corner booth.

"Hi." She smiled, sidling in. "How was dinner?"

"I wish you had been there. You know how clumsy I am at small talk. I listened to six medical histories from the first burp to the last backache and escaped as fast as I could. One good thing about my profession: I can always be needed elsewhere."

He fixed her with that look: a combination of intensity and admiration that left her almost unable to speak. She managed to ask, "Have you—been here long?"

"Half an hour," he said. "Listening to the trio and wishing you were in my arms. Dance?"

In a moment they were on the floor, their cheeks touching, their bodies swaying to the sleepy jazz.

"There ought to be a law against anyone feeling so desirable," he whispered in her ear. "Why do you have this effect on me?"

"What effect?" Her arm tightened around his neck.

Twenty minutes later, the trio broke for a recess, the bartender played a tape of Sinatra ballads, and the few couples waiting on the floor resumed dancing.

Peter brushed back her hair. "What's that damnable perfume you're wearing? 'Drive-a-Man-Crazy'?"

"I hope so." She laughed. "Otherwise I want my money back."

"Let's get out of here," he said, leading her to the door. "Like some fresh air?"

"Yes."

It was chilly on deck, and he put his arm across her shoulders. They walked several times around, then stopped and peered over the railing. Lights on the bow illuminated the frothy, silver-white wake as the ship plowed noiselessly through the water. The horizon was solid darkness, barely lit by a crescent moon.

"You're shivering," he said. "I'd better take you inside."

They were only a few steps from her cabin. She unlocked the door and he followed her in, closing it behind him. His lips found hers within seconds; she felt his hunger as strongly as she felt her own. There was no need for words. He tossed his coat over a chair, then unbuttoned her dress and let it slide to the floor.

She looked delicate and fragile in her lace slip. He kissed her neck, her shoulders, slipped off her straps and marveled at the perfection of her breasts. There was no holding back, no denying the emotions that possessed them. She murmured his name and felt herself go limp in his arms.

"Are you awake?" he whispered several hours later.

"Mmm, yes. Just wallowing." She snuggled to his chest and kissed the hollow of his neck. "Did anyone ever tell you you're a magnificent lover?"

"Only when I'm inspired." He held her tightly. "I knew it would be like this. I never used to believe in instant chemistry, but I do now. I wanted to make love to you since the day you told me about Alice."

"God bless Alice." She giggled. "By the way, I've decided your parents were both wrong. You don't look Norwegian, and you're definitely not cool and reserved in your ardor—you must be mostly Italian."

"But they're notorious womanizers. I only want to pinch one bottom."

"That's what you say today. What about tomorrow?"

"When you've got the best you don't look around."

"I'll eat to that. Mmm . . ." She nibbled at his ear. "You taste better than lunch. Confidentially, I can't even remember what we ate—or what we did."

"Neither can I—except that we wasted a lot of time. Listen, if you keep doing that, you're going to be in trouble." His hands brushed her slim, naked body as he felt himself growing newly aroused. "You know what happens to girls who tease, don't you?"

"Sure. They get attacked by Italian-Norwegian doctors. I learned that in Psychology One."

"Let's see what else you learned," he whispered, then shut her lips before she could speak.

It was almost four A.M. when Peter next looked down at his watch. She felt him move and murmured drowsily, "Anything wrong?"

"All's well."

"You going somewhere?"

"I have to go to my cabin and check in with the operator. In case someone needs me—no one knows where to reach me."

She sat up, holding the blanket to her chin, suddenly awake. "You can call from here. I have no reason to hide our relationship."

He looked at her gratefully. "That's right in character. I don't want to hide anything, either. But I'm afraid that if the operator knows, so will the whole ship."

"Do we care? Of course, all the women will be madly jealous. Maybe I should pin a sign on you: 'Hands off. This hunk taken.' Uh, for the moment, anyway."

"For the moment?" he asked with a touch of resentment. "Two weeks of a happy, carefree, wonderful shipboard romance, then you go home to your newspaper and I go to my practice; is that how it's going to be?" He didn't wait for an answer. "I got a letter from my sister, Margit, today. She's in real estate, and she's found me exactly what I wanted—a three-story building near a shopping center with room for both my office and a clinic. There's even a studio apartment in the basement, so I can live there. Apparently she had to make a fast decision, because some dentists wanted the place. She tried to call me, couldn't get through—I guess we were in port—so she bought the building with a fifty-thousand-dollar down payment."

"That's good news for you, isn't it?"

"Last week it would've been. Today it's another bloody wedge between us." He reached across her shoulders for the phone. "Operator? This is Dr. Marsten. I'll be in my cabin in ten minutes if you need me. Yes, I'm on my way—you're welcome."

"Peter," she said softly, "if we start to worry about all the problems in our lives, we'll spoil our time together."

He strained to smile. "Okay. Let's be sensualists and live for the moment."

"Promise me not to talk about going home, not even to think about it?"

"If it's important to you, I won't talk about it. But I can't vouch for my thinking processes."

She watched him dress quickly and efficiently, his face set

and determined. She had been right to extract a promise; the mere mention of the future had been a dampener—one that took several minutes to pass.

He checked himself in the mirror, then came back and perched on the edge of the bed. "I can't remember a damn thing we saw today," he said, taking her hands in his. "But I'll never forget Copenhagen."

The next two days at sea, Lauren's life evolved into a routine. Peter had regular office hours, and with a shipful of septuagenarians, not to mention some 350 staff and crew members, his time was well filled. Lauren kept busy working out in the gym, reading, chatting with the other passengers, and attending the enrichment lectures.

At noon, she and Peter met by the pool, enjoyed a Bloody Mary, helped themselves to the outdoor buffet, sat or walked on deck for an hour, then parted until evening. Directly after dinner, he went to her cabin. They talked and held each other and made love, then fell asleep until early morning, when he returned to his quarters.

At seven A.M. on the third day of the new cruise, the *Sea Viking* sailed into Leningrad. It was a port Lauren had been looking forward to; they had signed up for an eight-hour tour of the Hermitage, one of the most famous art museums in the world, and she had been reading and preparing for it.

The phone rang early, as she was zipping up her slacks.

"I have terrible news," came Peter's frustrated voice. "One of the crew members broke his leg; I'm taking him to the hospital to have it set. You go on, and maybe I can join you later."

"Poor man. Is he in terrible pain?"

"Pretty bad. Did you hear what I said?"

"Yes, but I'm not going without you. I'll be in the cabin. Call me when you get back?"

"Lauren, please," he protested. "I don't have time to argue. This may be your only chance to see the museum. You'd be crazy to miss it."

"Then I'm crazy, darling. Besides, I can use the rest."

"You're trying to tell me something?"

"Yes. Take care of your patient and then get your butt back

here as fast as you can. I don't want any of those female doctors getting ideas.''

"I'm a one-woman man. The— Whoops! Stretcher's here. Talk to you later.''

Strange, Lauren thought, replacing the receiver. Seeing the Hermitage had been one of the main reasons she'd wanted to come to Russia. For years, she had heard about the fabulous Gold Room, with its priceless antiques, the magnificent columns of malachite and tables of lapis, the masterpieces of Picasso, Rembrandt, Matisse . . . Yet all she felt was relief. What luxury to have a day to relax, write letters, and be alone with her thoughts. She knew she would probably never come back or have another chance to see the fabled museum. She also knew that she was tired and emotionally drained.

Everything was happening so fast. She could hardly believe her own behavior. Lauren Wilde, always so proper and circumspect and closemouthed about her love life, was openly living with a man she hadn't even known three weeks. Everyone on the ship saw them as a pair; they were much too handsome a couple to go unnoticed. At first they had been properly discreet, but little by little they became more open about their relationship—not from a desire to flaunt it but simply because they couldn't hide it. What was she supposed to say when people saw the way she clung to him walking along the deck or that dreamy expression in his eyes when he looked at her?

Nothing was sacred on shipboard; it was wall-to-wall soap opera from morning to morning. With little to do but sit around eating and drinking most of the time, the passengers became uncommonly interested in other people's lives. One woman, unable to contain her curiosity, even cornered Lauren in the gym and asked, ''Why aren't you sitting at Dr. Marsten's table?''

''I'm afraid we'd monopolize each other and it wouldn't be fair to the passengers,'' she had replied, smiling sweetly. What the hell. Everyone loved lovers, and it gave them something to gab about.

Six or seven couples from San Francisco had come on board. She wasn't being immodest to think they probably knew who she was; the paper had plastered her name and face all over the city and promoted her every way they could. Some had already come up, introduced themselves, and made kind remarks about her column. Anyone interested in her marital status could check the passenger list; it only showed her maiden name. Not that that proved anything. What concerned her was that some of the passengers said they knew Victor; what if they wrote to him about Peter? Well, what if they did? Nothing in her acceptance of the cruise included a promise not to fall in love.

Love. That word. There it was. She had told Peter it was a word they couldn't use. This was their fantasy time—their time to be together and enjoy the present. Love meant commitment and a future, and they weren't ready for that. They hardly knew each other, even though it seemed as if they had always known each other.

He had laughed at her directive, kissed the nape of her neck, and said, "Okay, darling. As long as I can make love to you, I don't need to talk about it."

And make love he did. Comparisons were odious, but how could she help comparing him to Ken? Where the latter was a snorting stallion poised on the brink of violence, Peter was tender and skilled, praising her beauty and her sexiness, teasing, playing, building excitement, gradually working her up to peaks so intense that she would cry out and dig her fingers into his back until they almost drew blood.

Such thoughts led her to feel the need of a cool stroll around the deck. She stared perfunctorily at the drab gray-stone buildings, too full of her feelings to think much about the Russians or even to miss seeing the Hermitage. The Hermitage! She suddenly remembered how disappointed her dinner companions had been when they'd learned the museum tour was filled and they couldn't get tickets. She phoned to offer hers; they accepted joyfully and insisted on reimbursing her. That, she said, was out of the question.

After making the delivery, Lauren returned to her cabin, hung out the "Do Not Disturb" sign, wrote a batch of postcards and a letter to Rosa, and lay on her bed for a quick nap. When next she looked at the clock, it was two in the afternoon.

Shortly before sailing time that evening, Peter brought back his patient, hobbling on crutches, his leg expertly set and sealed in a cast. There had been difficulties and interminable delays, but all had worked out.

Feeling renewed after a day of rest, Lauren asked Peter if he was too tired to stay up for the evening entertainment. He was exhausted but, hating to disappoint her and feeling guilty that they had missed the museum, agreed to escort her to the show. It was almost eleven when the magician pulled the last dove out of his sleeve, the audience applauded mechanically, the cruise director announced that the band would continue playing, and Peter stifled a yawn. "Ready to hit it?" he asked.

"Sure. You must be awfully—"

"So you're Victor's beautiful daughter," came a practiced voice.

Lauren looked up to see a suntanned, gray-haired man of about forty-five, wearing a brown polo shirt tucked into tight white slacks and beaming down at her. "I'm Kevin Vincent," he announced, laying his card on the table. "We sell your father all his kitchen equipment. I know your whole family. How about once around the floor?"

"Thanks, I—"

"Come on, the doctor won't mind if I borrow you for one dance. . . ."

"It's up to Lauren," Peter said coldly.

"Well, all right, just one, Mr. Vincent. We were about to leave—"

"Kevin's the name." He smiled and took her arm, steering her to the floor. It was almost twelve minutes later when he brought her back to the table, kissed her hand, said he hoped he would have the pleasure again, and ignored her fuming companion.

"You call that one dance?" Peter almost shouted as they left the lounge.

"Shhh. I'm sorry. He insisted on taking me over to meet his tablemates, then he started telling me how he met my brother and my father, and I couldn't very well be rude in the middle of his story."

"Why not? He was rude."

"What are you getting so upset about?" Her voice dropped to a whisper as she realized two elderly ladies were following close behind them. "I told you I was sorry. What more do you want?"

"Not a damn thing. Keys?"

They stood outside her cabin as she fumbled in her purse. "Here they are. Thank you."

"You're welcome." He opened the door. "And good night."

"You're not coming in?"

"I've had a long day, and I didn't need to watch you cozying up to that greasy gigolo."

"Cozying up? Are you crazy?"

"No, and I'm not blind, either."

"In that case—good night!" She would have liked to slam the door, but she didn't want to wake the neighbors. Damn him, anyway. She hadn't done anything wrong. She hadn't even wanted to dance with the jerk, but he had been so insistent. And he *did* know her family. . . .

A folded message under the door caught her eye. Anger changed to anxiety as she read that a radiogram awaited her at the desk. "Now what?" she said aloud, suddenly worried about her parents. Could one of them be ill? Who else would be sending her a wire?

"I'm afraid this may be bad news," said the receptionist, handing her the telex. The ship's policy was to deliver all radiograms in person; if a passenger was getting bad news, at least it could be softened with a warning.

"Thank you." Lauren felt herself go pale as she read the small slip of paper: "Marcy took her life today. I pray you let her guilt and her shame die with her. Jerry Burgeson."

"Oh, God," she said numbly.

"Are you all right, Miss Wilde?"

"Yes—thanks. I'll be fine." She didn't feel fine. Recollections of the trauma came back with frightening clarity. The whole terrifying scene began to replay itself, flashing on and off in her brain like colored slides on a screen. Trembling, she made her way to the cabin and reached for the phone.

"Dr. Marsten," snapped a still angry voice.

"I just—got a telex."

His tone changed instantly. "What is it? What's wrong? Are you in your cabin?"

"Yes."

"I'll be right there." Almost within seconds he was holding her tightly as he read the wire. "I'm here, darling," he soothed. "It's okay. Calm down." After several moments, he asked, "Who's Marcy and what's this all about?"

In a frightened voice and disjointed sentences, she related the incident in detail, feeling his body muscles tense as he reacted with horror.

"Why didn't you tell me any of this?" His protective instincts momentarily overcame all other emotions. They had exchanged so many intimacies about themselves and their lives, but she had never mentioned Marcy. "That's the kind of mental baggage you share with someone you love. You don't drag it around by yourself."

She nodded silently in his arms.

"And I did say 'love,' " he repeated, stroking her hair. "Isn't it time we stopped playing 'no-no' games and putting things out of our minds? Marcy was real. She existed. You'll have to deal with the scars for the rest of your life. But she's gone now and that's good news. It's the best news you could have. We're real, too. We exist—and I've fallen very deeply in love with you." He pulled back slightly to see her eyes. "I'm too tired to struggle not to say it, darling. I need you. I want you. I love you so very much."

"I love you—and I need you terribly," she whispered. "I'm so sorry about . . . earlier. It was selfish and inconsiderate of me."

"My fault for getting mad over such a stupid thing. It's been a long day. Let's stash all the bad memories and go to bed."

"Yes—we can both use the sleep."

He reached up to touch her breasts; the nipples felt taut and firm under her delicate silk blouse. "Who," he asked quietly, "said anything about sleep?"

The *Sea Viking*'s arrival in Finland two mornings later brought whoops and cheers from the passengers, who made no secret of being thrilled to be out of the Soviet Union. Feeling rested and energetic after spending their second day in Russia on a bus tour of the outskirts, Lauren and Peter set off to explore Helsinki on foot. The city, a wild contrast to the dismal Leningrad, was colorful, lively, and buzzing with attractive, well-dressed, happy-looking people who gave directions with a smile. The center of town was crowded with department stores and boutiques selling goods from all over the world.

Around noontime, they came to a sidewalk cafe, and Lauren slowed her step. "I hate to be a pooper," she said, "but I think my feet are going on strike."

"Can't blame them." He helped her into a chair. "We've been walking for over three hours. Of course, age has a way of sneaking up on people. Have you noticed?"

She caught the gleam in his eyes. "Here I've been patting myself on the back all morning for keeping my birthday a secret. How did you know?"

"How did I know? Your birthday was about as secret as Pearl Harbor—*after* the bombing. You told me a week ago, the purser told me yesterday, the maître d' told me to be sure to come over when they bring your cake at dinner, and Trina left a present for you. Did you really expect it to be a secret?"

"I just didn't want any fuss."

"Not even from me?" He reached into his pocket for a small box. "Happy birthday, sweetheart. I didn't have time to get it wrapped."

She took the gift gingerly and opened the lid. Inside, a heart-shaped pendant of diamonds and rubies lay sparkling on a velvet backing. "Oh, Peter, it's—breathtaking!" She shut the box quickly and handed it back. "It's . . . too much. I couldn't accept a gift like that."

"Why not?" he asked, stung by her reaction. "Don't I mean enough to you?"

"Oh, darling, no! Of course you do. You mean everything to me. I—I just feel embarrassed. It's too extravagant."

"Shut that beautiful mouth and lean over," he ordered. "I'll decide what's extravagant." With deft fingers, he fastened the narrow chain around her neck, then sat back and grinned. "You do a lot for it."

She stared at her reflection in a purse mirror and moved it

slightly to the center. "I think you've convinced me. I don't know what to say—"

"Don't say anything. If I want to buy a trinket for the woman I'm out of my mind in love with, that's my privilege. You can exchange it in the ship's gift shop if you'd rather have something else."

"Exchange it! They'll have to rip it off my torn and mutilated corpse," she exclaimed, clutching her neck. "It's the most elegant piece of jewelry I've ever seen! Now that I have your heart—"

"You have my mind and body, too. You want my soul? That's all that's left."

Laughing, she opened her arms and hugged him. "Spendthrift or not, I love you. And thank you—this is the happiest birthday I've ever had."

The following days passed as swiftly as sequences in a dream. They toured Stockholm by cab and subway, ferried through the canals of Amsterdam, and laughed their way across London, walking till there were blisters on their feet, gaping at the sights from the top of a double-decker bus, making friends of strangers, and relishing the dry British humor.

At five P.M., August 28, the *Sea Viking* sailed from the English port of Southampton and headed for the Atlantic Ocean on her last lap home. The captain chose the warm-weather route, carefully skirting all areas of turbulence so that the seven-day crossing would be smooth and untroubled. Returning to reality was something that Peter and Lauren, along with the majority of passengers, hated to think about.

A letter from Sara gave her the good news that reader response was getting more and more favorable, and the bad news that Ken had been asking when she was coming back. Rosa wrote that she hoped Jerry Burgeson's wire hadn't been too upsetting. Marcy had somehow gotten hold of a bottle of Nembutal, swallowed its contents, gone to sleep, and never awakened. No funeral or memorial services had been held, only a brief cremation ceremony. The obit was short and praiseworthy.

A cheerful note from Victor assured her that everyone was well and missed her, and that Trina had called to give him a full report on the trip. Lauren suspected that "full" was the wrong word, since Trina's narrative would surely have omitted any mention of Peter.

Even Missy had dropped her a line; she had met Lord Something-or-other at a museum benefit, found him "terribly snobby but charming," and had tentatively arranged for him to take Lauren to the symphony's Black and White Ball. Not a chance. The idea of dating again was so abhorrent it almost made her ill.

The immediate problem she faced was going home without Peter. He had showed her the excited letters from Margit, relating the difficulties she had had closing the deal for the medical building. She had fought hard and won, and was already talking to contractors. Phones had been installed, and she had had to pull strings to get him into the fall phone book, but he would be listed—for sure. A well-known dermatologist was anxious to discuss taking Peter in as a partner; it would be a great financial advantage, Margit suggested, to have a ready-made practice.

In happy detail, she wrote how she and her young sons had run around to garage and estate sales, buying furnishings and assorted doodads for his apartment. A friend of her husband's who worked for Sears had been able to get kitchen appliances at 10 percent above cost, and now she was interviewing part-time maids to cook and clean for him. Her letters glowed with pride and adoration for the big brother who was "finally going to make them a family again." Hand-painted drawings assured him that his nephews were equally anxious to lay claim to their "new" uncle.

Peter had to work long hours the last week of the trip. With the prospect of facing their same old problems and dull routines, many of the passengers' chronic symptoms resurfaced. He called it the "reality syndrome," and one of the best ways to treat it, he found, was to suggest they think about another cruise. Going home was much easier when you knew you were going away again.

Shortly after eight o'clock Tuesday morning, two days from New York, Peter called Lauren from his office. "Sorry to wake you, darling, but we've got a problem. It seems Alice has wandered off."

Lauren rubbed her eyes and propped herself up on an elbow. "You mean 'off' like off the ship?"

"That was a bad choice of words. She's disappeared. Mrs. Bock woke up a few minutes ago and found her missing from her bed."

"Couldn't she have gone for a walk? Or breakfast?"

"They always have breakfast in the cabin. Then Mrs. Bock helps her dress and brings her down to see me. Every morning."

"Including yesterday?"

"Yes, I checked her over thoroughly. She seemed no more confused than usual, and there was no sign she'd taken any medication."

"I'll get going right away." Lauren was already out of bed. "Maybe I can find her. She can't have wandered too far."

"Thanks, sweetheart."

An exhaustive three-hour search by Lauren, the housekeeper, and the crew steward failed to turn up any sign of the missing passenger. The receptionist even tried paging her: "Would Mrs. Alice Pendergast of cabin one seventy-eight please call reception? This is a personal message for Mrs. Alice Pendergast. Please call the reception desk. Thank you."

The captain issued orders not to involve the passengers, but it was impossible to keep the matter quiet as the search continued and spread to the hold, the galley, the provision rooms, the lifeboats, every recess of the large vessel.

By evening, Alice still hadn't been found, and the whole ship was talking. Peter knocked on cabin 178 half an hour before dinner.

"Any news?" asked Mrs. Bock, opening the door.

"No. May I come in?"

"If you want, but you won't find any clues here. I'd say the poor old dearie couldn't stand being sick any longer and jumped overboard."

Peter sank into a chair. "She gave no indication of being depressed. Why would she do that?"

"How do I know?"

He looked at her wearily. "Mrs. Bock, are you sure you can't even tell us what she might have been wearing? You have no idea what clothes are missing?"

"I don't keep an inventory of her wardrobe."

"Any possessions missing? Photographs of her family? Anything she particularly treasured?"

The nurse shook her head vigorously.

"Let's go over last night again. You both went to bed around eleven. What did you do before then?"

"We ate dinner, came back to the cabin, and watched a movie on television."

"That's all?"

"That's all. Then we went to bed."

"The stewardess said you called for some aspirin about eleven."

Mrs. Bock's right eye twitched. "Oh, yeah, I had a headache."

"*You* had a headache?"

"We both had headaches."

He sighed. "You gave her aspirin, didn't you."

"Are you trying to say this is *my* fault?"

"You knew she wasn't supposed to have medication. Why did you disobey my orders?"

"You have such busy days, doctor." The nurse raised an eyebrow. "*And* nights. I hated to disturb you."

He ignored the insinuation and reached to press a button. In a moment, the stewardess appeared. "Yes? Oh, hello, doctor."

"Ingrid," he said, "how many aspirin tablets did you give Mrs. Bock last night?"

"I gave her four packets. I believe they each contain two tablets. Would you like to see one?"

"Yes—please." He turned back to his increasingly hostile companion. "An honest answer is vital, Mrs. Bock. How many pills did you give Mrs. Pendergast?"

"I gave her two packets and I kept two for myself. That's the God-help-me truth."

"Did you also open the packets, hand her a glass of water, and force her to swallow them?"

The nurse stared insolently. "Well, now, isn't that too bad? I can't seem to remember."

"You damn well better remember!" Furious, Peter jumped

up and grabbed her by the shoulders. "*How many pills*, Mrs. Bock? Was it four or six, or was it all eight?"

"Let go of me!" she cried, pushing him off. "It was only four, I swear to God. I swear it was only four!"

"Only four?" He glared. "Nice work."

The stewardess appeared with a small cellophane envelope. "Here's what I gave her, Dr. Marsten."

"I thought you said aspirin. This is Anacin." He swung to the nurse. "You gave her this?"

For the first time, the large woman seemed frightened. "It was for her own good—to make her sleep."

"Sleep? Don't you know that Anacin has caffeine? You gave her a jolt of stimulant. A big jolt. No wonder she couldn't stay in bed!" His fist tightened around the yellow packet. "If anything's happened to Mrs. Pendergast, I'm holding *you* personally responsible. You haven't made one move to help us find her. I suggest you start giving it some thought."

He strode off down the corridor, only to hear Mrs. Bock's heavy footsteps come running after him. "I just thought of something," she said breathlessly. "Mrs. Murty in cabin three eleven. They played Bingo together. She might know something."

"I'll look into it." Digesting this new information, he hurried past the front desk, almost not hearing the receptionist call out his name. "I was about to page you, doctor. Can you talk to Miss Wilde?"

"What? Oh, yes, certainly." He lifted the phone. "Lauren?"

"We've been waiting thirty-five minutes for you. What's happening?"

"Where are you?"

"In the Skyview Bar with Jane and George Sidney. Remember our cocktail date?"

"No, I forgot. I'm sorry."

"Any word on Alice?"

"That's what I've been working on. One possible lead. I'm tracking it down now."

"I'll make excuses, then. Join us if you can?"

"I can't. I'm determined to find her if I have to search every inch of the ship myself."

"How can I help?"

"Look around. Listen. Stay alert. Meet me on the port side of the lounge at nine-thirty."

"Okay, sweetheart, good luck. And don't be discouraged. Remember how long it took Stanley to find Livingstone."

For a quick moment, she jarred him out of his intensity. "That helps," he said, laughing. And then he remembered where he was heading.


The first knock went unanswered. The second time, a high-pitched voice called out, "Who's there?"

"Dr. Marsten. May I have a word with you, Mrs. Murty?"

The door opened partway, and a cheerful, wrinkled face peered around. "It's the handsome doctor, is it? Come to spirit me off? You'll have to wait till I put on me bloomers."

"I'll wait." He smiled.

"Arrrrh, I was hopin' you'd say, 'Don't bother.' " A moment later, a short, tubby woman opened the door. Her grin was wide and warming. "Come in, come in, doctor. If it's not me perfect young body you're after, what is it?"

"I'm looking for Alice Pendergast. I was told you might be able to help."

"Now who'd be tellin' you that? I haven't seen the dear thing since last night's Bingo."

"Did she say or do anything unusual when you were with her?"

"Not a wee word, doctor. I can't imagine where she'd be hidin'."

Peter stared hard at the woman. "What makes you think she's hiding?"

"It's as good a guess as any." She blinked innocently. "Where else might she be?"

"That's what I came to ask you."

"You've come for naught, then. Me dear mother'd crawl out of her grave if she saw what I was turnin' away, but me poor stomach's hollerin' out for dinner."

"After all that fruit?"

She followed his eyes to the dresser; on it sat a plate with two banana peels and an apple core. "Just a wee snack, now. Out you go."

Peter walked to the door and turned around. "Your friend's in trouble, Mrs. Murty. She's confused, she's ill, and she shouldn't be left alone. If you have any idea where she is, you could be saving her life by telling me."

The woman smiled kindly. "She's a lucky lass to have you carin' for her, doctor. If I see her strollin' on the deck, I'll sure be callin' you."

It was nine-twenty when Lauren made her way through the crowded lounge to a small table for two on the port side. She hadn't seen Peter all day. Every minute of free time he had spent searching for clues or following leads. She hoped the last one had proved useful.

The room was mostly dark, save for the spotlit floor where several couples were practicing the cha-cha steps they'd learned in the morning dance class. As her eyes became accustomed to the dimness, she looked around at the faces; many belonged to elderly couples—tired, resigned, numbly awaiting whatever fate would serve up for their evening entertainment. Others were laughing, chatting, swapping stories, summoning the red-coated waiters to bring more of their favorite stimulant. Enough booze was consumed on the ship, she mused, to float away the Statue of Liberty.

Her idle glance drifted across the room and stopped curiously at the sight of a small, birdlike woman sitting by herself in the darkest corner of the lounge. She wore thick glasses and pale lipstick, and her head of straight, brownish hair almost disappeared into the cocoa-colored upholstery behind her. Something in the woman's manner—the way she cocked her neck, the way her hand fluttered slightly as she toyed with her purse—reminded Lauren—yes—of Alice Pendergast! *Could* it be? She stared in frozen silence. If it was Alice, what a perfect place to hide, disguised and inconspicuous in the middle of a crowd while half the crew was searching the hold for her.

Lauren exited the room, then entered by a second entrance and casually sat down a few feet away from the woman, who looked over, instantly wary. It was Alice—without a doubt. The spectacles half hid her tiny eyes, but the frightened, shrinking gesture was unmistakable. As Lauren sat wondering what to do, the object of her scrutiny rose and headed for the exit. From the rear, she looked exactly like any number of ladies on the ship: green polyester pantsuit, white shoulder bag, flat white espadrilles.

Glancing across the room, Lauren could find no sign of Peter, and Alice was about to vanish again. Instinctively, she got up and followed her out, down the stairs, and down another long corridor. Alice's steps picked up as she realized she was being shadowed; her head darted around nervously, and she broke into an awkward run.

"Alice, please don't be afraid. I'm your friend. I want to help you."

The sound of her name seemed to send her into more of a panic, and she dashed for the nearest door, marked "Crew Only," which opened onto the dimly lit forward deck. Lauren followed close behind as her frightened prey darted between the tall cranes and heavy anchor winches and made her way toward a small, crescent-shaped sundeck at the foremost bow of the ship.

"Don't go up there, Alice!"

Ignoring the warning, Alice clambered up the ladder to the platform. A thin iron railing was all that separated her from the crashing waves below. It wasn't the water that terrified Lauren so much as the fact that if Alice were to fall off the bow, she would instantly be plowed under by the huge vessel and diced into bits by its six-foot propellers.

Spotting a lone figure on the wing of the bridge, Lauren motioned frantically. "Help—get the doctor!" The figure disappeared, and she turned back to her problem, gasping at what she saw. Alice had one leg over the railing and was trying to straddle it, toppling precariously to one side, then the other.

"Alice," she cried, "please come down. Dr. Marsten is on his way. He wants to talk to you."

"Don't come any closer or I'll jump!"

"I'm not moving—honest. Don't you want to talk to Dr. Marsten?"

"He'll send me back to Mrs. Bock. I know he will."

"No, he won't. I promise you. You can stay with me in my cabin until we get to New York."

The invitation puzzled her. She stared for a long minute

and tried to focus her thoughts. Then she craned her neck to see better. "Who are you?"

"I'm Lauren—your friend. I'm the one who told Dr. Marsten about you."

"Dr. Marsten?" She repeated the name curiously. "Is that him?"

Lauren turned and exhaled with relief. Peter was hurrying toward them, followed by two officers.

"Hi, Alice." He waved. "How's the view up there?"

"Oh, it's too dark to see much," she answered.

He approached the first rung of the ladder. "Then what are you doing up there?"

"Don't get close or I'll jump."

"Do you remember me, Alice? I'm Dr. Marsten."

"I don't know," she said, puzzled. "Do I know you?"

"You come to see me every morning, and I check to make sure you're all right and you haven't taken any pills."

"Pills!" The word jarred her. "Mrs. Bock makes me take pills—" Her voice broke emotionally. "My doctor says I'm not supposed to take any."

"I know that. I'm your doctor." His voice lowered. "Keep her talking, Lauren." Peter looked down at his watch. One of the officers had approached and was standing beside him. "How much time?. . ."

"I gave the order eighty seconds ago," the officer said under his breath. "At a speed of nineteen point eight knots, it'll take three minutes and twenty seconds for her to stop dead in the water—about two minutes more."

Lauren's cracking voice made Peter look up. Alice had lifted her other leg over the barrier and sat perched on the edge, feet dangling over the surf, grasping the railing with her frail hands.

"What are you doing, Alice?" He tried to keep the urgency from his voice. "You're disobeying my orders."

"I'm a burden to you—to everyone. It's best this way."

"Now don't make me angry! I promised your daughter"— if only he could remember her name—"I promised her I'd take good care of you until we got to New York."

"Are we going to New York?" Her head cocked happily. "Will we see some plays?"

"One minute, doctor," whispered the officer.

One minute to go. If he could keep her talking sixty seconds longer, the ship would be stopped and she would have a chance. . . . "Yes—plays. The best of Broadway. Your daughter's already bought the tickets. Orchestra seats. You don't want to disappoint her, do you?"

"My daughter? Is she on the ship?" His answer made no impression. Alice had sunk back into nothingness, mesmerized by the roar of the ocean, staring blankly into the darkness.

The thrust of the propellers reversing direction told him the ship was grinding to a halt; he felt no movement, but the blades would be whirling for another thirty seconds.

"Don't be mad at me, doctor," she called, waving. One hand separated her from disaster.

"Wait, Alice! Before you go—" He had her attention. "Mrs. Murty—Mrs. Murty gave me a message for you."

The name jarred her recognition. "Oh, my, she's been a wonderful friend. Tell her I'm sorry I'll miss Bingo."

"She wants her wig back. She paid a lot of money for that wig. It's her best one. She wants you to be sure to return it. Shall I help you take it off?"

"The wig? Oh, dear, I almost forgot. Don't you come near me! I can do it myself." Alice reached up with one hand and began pulling out hairpins and bobby pins, shaking her head back and forth like a wet poodle. As the hairpiece finally came loose and sailed to the deck, she cried, "Give Mrs. Murty my Bingo card!" then fell forward and dropped into the blackness.

Lauren screamed, the officers ran for life preservers, Peter leaped up the ladder and dived in, reaching the icy water only seconds after Alice. Thrashing around like a shark in a net, he groped helplessly, desperately, unable to see—when suddenly a spotlight from above lit up the water, shining on a few strands of gray curls several feet away. He swam over just as the tip of her head was disappearing, plunged down, and brought Alice to the surface, water streaming from her mouth.

"Hang on," came a voice from the deck. "We're lowering a boat."

"Hurry!" he yelled, grabbing a life preserver. His frail

charge was instinctively fighting for life, choking and cough-
ing up water as he struggled to keep her afloat with one had
and himself with the other.

Six minutes seemed like hours before the soaked figures
were pulled onto the lifeboat and wrapped in blankets as the
davits once again hoisted the dinghy into its place on the side
of the ship. A physician, one of the passengers, had been
summoned to stand by. "I'm Dr. Haven," he called. "We're
ready for you."

Peter was chattering too hard to speak. He could only nod
and help the sailors hand down Alice's limp but still breathing
body. The doctor and an officer placed her on a waiting
stretcher. "I'll take care of her. Don't worry."

Peter nodded again, a silent thank-you, and tucked the blanket tight around him as he climbed out of the lifeboat and the
deep puddle made by his dripping clothes. Almost as soon as
he touched the deck, Lauren came running over, followed by
the captain.

"Peter," she said, panting, "are you all right?"

"Y-y-yes." His speech was returning. "J-just c-c-cold."

"Thank God!" She stared up at him, her face ashen. "Let's
go in and get you dry."

"One minute, Dr. Marsten." The captain's expression was
austere. "I must tell you that what you did tonight was stupid
and foolhardy. There was no way of knowing whether or not
the ship had stopped. Ten seconds sooner, and you both would
have been fish food." He paused to let the reprimand register,
then lowered his voice. "But I am also very proud of you. I
like to think I would have done the same thing myself."

Peter seemed relieved. "Th-thank you, sir. I'm s-sure you
would have."


"Warming up?"

"You might even say 'heating up.' " Peter's arms enfolded
Lauren as she climbed into bed with him several hours later.
"If I weren't so damn tired—"

"But you *are* tired, and so am I. You were fantastic tonight, darling. You saved Alice's life. You took a terrible
chance, though."

"That makes me either a hero or a jackass." He smiled.

"And the odds are on the latter. What about Alice? What did you find out?"

"Well, Dr. Havens thought she should be in the hospital overnight, but Mrs. Murty offered to take care of her, and Alice needed plenty of TLC—so he agreed to that. When I peeked into Mrs. Murty's cabin, they were both snoring soundly."

"Ah, that's good. And you warned everyone about the Dragon Lady?"

"I told the doctor, and Mrs. Murty already knew. She said she'd—let's see if I can get the exact words—'wr-r-rop 'er teeth around 'er eyeballs' if Mrs. Bock tried to take Alice back to cabin one seventy-eight. Mrs. Murty insists on taking care of her till we get to New York—a real earth mother. Had she been hiding Alice all day?"

"Yes, from what I can piece together. It looks like Alice became hyperstimulated by the pills, waited till Bock fell asleep, then went down to her friend's cabin. Mrs. Murty decided to keep Alice with her, went up and sneaked out her clothes, and, by various ruses, managed to hide her in the cabin until evening. She must have been in the closet or the bathroom when I was there."

"What about the stewardess?"

"That was the problem. Mrs. Murty knew the stewardess would be in soon to turn down the bed, so she got Alice dressed, including wig and glasses, then probably took her out on deck or to some inconspicuous place till about eight-thirty, when she had to leave her alone in the lounge and go in to dinner. You came along and spotted Alice—and you know the rest."

"Three cheers for Mrs. Murty. What a gutsy woman!"

"You're not too bad yourself," he said, drawing her closer, "except for your cold feet."

"I didn't think you'd noticed. You must be feeling better."

"Yes, things are starting to look up again."

"Oh, no, you don't!" She pulled back, trying to look stern. "You're in no condition—"

"Tomorrow's our last night together," he purred in his Bela Lugosi voice, "and I *vant* your body."

"Hmmm—fangs for the memory?"

"That is beyond reproach." He winced. "For a line like that, you must pay the price. . . ." His lips found the softness of her neck.

"I surrender." She sighed. "You vampires are all alike."

The last hours of the trip went fast. Packing kept Lauren occupied, and Peter was swamped with patients. He wrote a long letter, which Mrs. Murty promised to deliver, along with Alice, to Alice's daughter. In it, he made sure that Mrs. Bock would be reported to the Nurses' Association and whatever misguided persons had recommended her.

Peter kept his promise not to pressure Lauren with talk of the future, teased her that shipboard romances never lasted, and tried to make light of their parting. She played the game bravely, promising to call him when she "got settled." He was staying over a day in New York, so they said good-bye at dawn, as the ship pulled into the crowded harbor. He whispered, "Don't forget—you have my heart," and walked out the door without looking back.

# CHAPTER
## 10

COMING HOME WAS A LETDOWN, AS EXPECTED, BUT THE pressures of resuming her routine, reporting in to her parents, answering mail and phone calls, and having to write three columns for the following week kept Lauren too busy to dwell on her loneliness for Peter. It was always there—a slow-burning fire that smoldered painfully inside of her; not an hour of the day passed that she didn't have to keep herself from calling him. For the moment, however, his life was there and hers was here.

Sunday morning marked only three days since she had left the ship in New York. The hours dragged heavily as she struggled to unpack, every scarf, every sweater, every garment, she unfolded brought back memories of where she had been and what they had done together. His jeweled heart she tucked away in a drawer with her lingerie. That seemed appropriately intimate.

The sound of the phone made her leap up, spilling the contents of a cosmetics case. It was not the voice she wanted to hear. "Welcome home."

"Ken?" she asked, instantly wary. So much had happened, he almost seemed like a bad dream. "We have nothing to say to each other."

"Sure we do. How come you didn't come back with Trina?"

"What I do is none of your business. *Please* don't call me again—ever!"

To her relief, there was no outburst. "Why don't you be straight with me for a change? What the hell happened to us? Why didn't we give ourselves a chance? You can't blame a guy for not wanting his old lady to take off for five weeks."

His "old lady"? Was he crazy? "Look, Ken, you want me to be straight with you? I don't want to see or talk to you again as long as I live. Is that straight enough? Now goodbye!"

"Not even tomorrow night?"

She hung up the phone quietly, restraining the impulse to slam it in his ear. It rang a moment later, and she turned on her answering machine. The caller clicked off at the sound of the recording.

She returned to her suitcase, dreading the thought of dining with her parents that evening. Victor would ask all sorts of questions about what she did and where she went, and she would have to either invent a girlfriend or mention Peter. Edna would be pleased and happy for her. But the realization that telling the truth to her father was bound to bring on a scene made her both sad and resentful; she had done nothing wrong. Why should she have to lie about her life?

Dinner went much as expected. As soon as she began talking about Russia, Victor wanted to know if she had gone on the bus tour alone.

"No," she said casually. "I went with a friend—the ship's doctor."

Edna's ears perked. "Oh? Tell us about him, dear."

"Nothing to tell, Mom. We had a lot of good times together. He's a dermatologist, has family in L.A., and is starting a clinic there as soon as he gets back. Or got back, I guess."

"You mean he has a wife?" asked Victor, sniffing trouble.

"No wife. No kids. Not even an ex-wife. Just a sister and brother-in-law and some nephews."

After a moment to digest the news, Edna asked, "What's his name?"

"Peter Marsten. His father was Norwegian—a famous cardiologist. His mother was Italian. He speaks all the Scandinavian languages, so it made the ports a lot more fun. What else can I tell you? He's thirty-nine years old, brilliant, charming, and handsome."

It was Victor's turn. "You mean you met him on the first leg of the trip?"

"That's right."

"Are you going to see him again?"

"I certainly hope so, Dad. But commuting between San Francisco and L.A. makes it difficult. Plus the fact that he's a workaholic and completely dedicated to his medicine. His career is there and mine is in San Francisco, so that's that for the moment."

"You know what they say about distance," piped Edna, her eyes twinkling.

Victor exploded. "For Christ's sake, Edna, why do you encourage the child? We don't know the first thing about this—this doctor—"

"Relax, Dad," she soothed. "I understand your wanting to protect me, but I'm not a child anymore. I turned thirty last month, remember? Now, if we can change the subject, I'd like to tell you about this couple I met. . . ."

Later that evening, Lauren stood in her garage, waiting for the elevator to take her up to the penthouse. While everyone made such a fuss about her father, it was her mother, she thought, who held the family together. Victor would have alienated both his children years ago if Edna hadn't been around to assure them that he was simply a big, overgrown lion who liked to hear himself roar. Behind Edna's seeming naiveté and occasional absentmindedness, there was a woman smart enough to know when to play dumb.

She had managed to get her daughter alone for a moment to ask if the romance was serious. Lauren nodded happily and fell into her arms. "Well, that's wonderful, dear," Edna had said, "but let's not tell Daddy yet. We'll break it to him gently."

"There's nothing to break yet," Lauren had said with a sigh. "I don't even know when I'll see Peter again."

"Soon, dear. I'm sure it will be soon."

The arrival of the elevator interrupted Lauren's reflections. As she started to enter, the sound of footsteps made her whirl around. A dark figure came running from the shadows.

"Don't be scared," he called. "It's me, Ken. I have to talk to you."

She stepped back and pressed the button to close the elevator doors, but not in time. He grabbed them, held them apart, then squeezed through.

"I said I have to talk to you, Lauren. Can't you be civil?"

The whiskey on his breath smelled strong and foul. If only she could reach the alarm button . . . No, that would infuriate him, and there was no telling what he would do before help arrived.

"What is it you want?" she asked, her voice barely audible.

"I want you to be civil," he repeated, swaying slightly. Drunk as he was, his speech was clear and unslurred. "I want to talk to you. I need to talk to you. It's important."

"Important?"

He pressed the buzzer to the top floor. "I just want us to sit down like two human beings and talk," he said. "Can't you do that for me?"

Better to placate him. "Yes, yes, of course. It's just that— you scared me down there. I didn't know who you were."

"Don't give me that shit. You and your father and all your snooty friends. You think I'm not good enough for you, right? Well, I can piss all over you, understand?" He grabbed her shoulders and shook roughly. "Do you understand?"

"Yes, yes!" She was deadly pale as they reached the penthouse and the elevator opened. How could she keep him from entering?

"Give me that," he said, snatching her purse. He handed her the keys and commanded, "Open Sesame!"

With shaking fingers, she jabbed the key into the lock and turned. He followed her inside, closed the door, and went straight to the bar. "Fix you something, baby?" he asked. "That's what Daddy calls you, isn't it, baby? Goo-goo poo-poo?"

"What do you want?" she asked weakly.

"What do you think?" He was opening all her cabinets, found the whiskey, and poured himself a tall glass. "No ice? I'll have to drink it like the British. You know the British— teddibly stuffy, dontcha know? Like some other people I won't mention. Or will I?"

She sat in petrified silence, waiting for his move. "What I want from you," he said, coming toward her, "is *not* your money, not even your beautiful body, although I wouldn't mind a little of that—" He reached for her breast and she recoiled, full of fear and loathing. "Not to worry, luv, I don't think I could make it at the moment. Although I'm willing to try. . . ."

Her words came fast. "You don't want me and you don't want money. What do you want?"

"I want to talk. I want us to have a nice long talk. About you. About me. About our future."

"Please," she begged, "we can talk tomorrow, Ken. I promise. I'm really tired—"

"Tired, are you? In that case, let's go to bed." He made a move to grab her, and she sprang back, knocking over a lamp. A loud shriek escaped her lungs as the glass spattered the floor.

"Damn you, you'll bring the neighbors!" He caught her arm and twisted it behind her back. "One more sound out of you and I'll wring this delicate limb from its socket. Why are you running away from me? Don't you want my farewell gift? I know what you like, and we don't even have to go to the bedroom."

Forcing her down on the rug, he pinned her shoulders to the floor. "I warn you—I'll bash your bloody face in if you scream. I took care of Carrie—Ronda—you're as putrid as they were! I had to let them know I can't be discarded like a piece of garbage—and you've got a lesson coming, too. . . ."

"I—I won't scream," she whispered as he pulled up her dress and tugged at her panty hose.

"It all makes sense now, doesn't it? Your good friend Lee Paige was right about me. My ex-wives deserved a beating and they got it. You know something else? Those crazy 'psycho' letters you were so worried about? I'm your psycho. Yes, Ken Ferriday—admired, honored, respected by everyone in

the city except Miss Ritzypants. You'll never be able to prove
it, though, will you? That's what you and your stinking father
forced me to stoop to. Goddamn these—'' The ring of the
phone gave him a start. ''Who the hell is that?''

She thought fast. ''Probably the neighbors or the doorman.
He knows I'm home. If I don't answer . . .''

Her words made sense. Someone could easily have heard
that piercing scream and reported it. The liquor hadn't made
him insensitive to danger. ''I've wasted enough time here,''
he sputtered, glaring down at her. Then, with sudden force,
he opened his fist and smacked her upper arm, sending her
sprawling. ''A little something to remember me by, slut. And
don't complain to the doorman; he's seen me here at *your*
invitation.''

The arm stung painfully, but she didn't dare move until he
was out the door and she heard the descent of the elevator.
Then she sprang up and bolted the lock, leaning back against
the wall to gasp for breath. Her heart was pounding as if it
would leap out of her chest. And still—that insistent telephone. She staggered to the table and grabbed the receiver.
''H-hello . . .''

''Darling! Are you all right?''

The sound of Peter's voice shattered her last reserve of
strength and she burst into tears, unable to speak.

''Good God, Lauren, what's wrong? Talk to me. Please
talk to me!''

''I'm okay,'' she sobbed. ''I'm okay, Peter. Oh, God, I
need you, I need you so much. . . .''

''Is someone there? Are you in trouble?''

''No.'' She sniffed, trying to stop herself from trembling.
''Someone was here, but he's gone. I locked the door and he
can't come back.''

''Did he attack you?''

''He didn't succeed. He just scared me.''

''A stranger? Someone you know?''

''Someone I know. A sick man. He was waiting for me
tonight when I came back from my parents. He forced his
way in. . . .''

The voice in her ear sounded anguished. ''I'm catching the
next plane, sweetheart. Wait there. Don't go anywhere. Don't

talk to anyone except the police. I'll be there as soon as I can.''

She wanted to tell him it wasn't necessary, but it was; she had to see him. ''I'll be waiting for you. Hurry!''

''I'm on my way.''

Nothing, not even the imminent arrival of Peter, could still her fears. Ken had gotten past the doorman once; he could do it again—at any time. Would she ever feel safe again?

She desperately wanted to talk to someone—to hear a reassuring voice telling her it was over—but whose? Peter's words came to mind: ''Don't talk to anyone except the police.'' Reaching for the phone, she dialed the operator.

''I want to report an attempted rape,'' she said nervously.

''Is anyone hurt?''

''No. It's all over. I thought I should report it so it doesn't happen again.''

''Is there any emergency?''

''Not anymore.''

''Hold on,'' the operator said. ''I'll switch you to the precinct.''

A man's voice came on, took her story, and promised to send someone over within the hour.

Too nervous to sit and wait, she decided to take off her clothes and try to relax. The smell of liquor lingered on her skin and made her feel unclean. A bath was the answer, and she soaked in the steamy tub, keeping her bruised arm dry and out of the heat. Then, feeling fresh again, she slipped into her nightgown and a robe and lay down to clear her brain.

Shortly before eleven, the doorman called to say two policemen were on their way up. She waited by the elevator, introduced herself, and led them inside.

Joe Kaminsky was the older partner, ruggedly handsome, leather-skinned, and close to fifty, she guessed; Tom Murphy was young and fresh-faced. They wasted no time with small talk.

''Where did the rape take place?'' asked Joe, pencil poised over his clipboard.

''Attempted rape,'' she corrected. ''Right here, in my living room.''

"Was there penetration?" he asked wearily.

"No." She flushed.

"Do you know the suspect?"

"Yes. But I'd rather not give his name."

He sighed. "You don't want to give us his name? How can I make a report?"

"I don't want to press charges," she said, "Please forgive me. I'm still very upset and I'm not thinking clearly. I thought I could just make a report so you'd have it on file in case he ever came back."

"You don't want to press charges? You don't want to give his name?" The officers exchanged glances.

"Tell you what," said Tom, heading for the door. "I've got some paperwork to do in the car. You finish up here and come down when you're ready."

As soon as the door closed, Joe set down his clipboard and slunk into a chair, resting one leg on the arm.

"What is it?" asked Lauren, wondering at his sudden change of attitude.

"We might as well be friends, honey." He smiled.

"What do you mean?"

He rose and slowly stretched his arms to the side. "You don't have to be ashamed. I think I know what you want. We get calls like this all the time."

Lauren looked at him, incredulous. Was he serious? Did he really think that was why she had called the police? She felt herself trembling again, this time with rage. "If you take one step toward me, I'll scream my head off and the doorman will be here in four seconds."

"Hold on, lady, don't get excited," he said, backing away. "All I did was ask if you wanted to talk about your so-called rape. If not, that's your business. But the next time you want some attention, don't get your kicks by putting on your little pink nightie and calling the police department."

He slapped on his cap, picked up his clipboard, and made a hasty exit.

The ice pack was cold and uncomfortable on her arm, but doing its job; the swelling had subsided, leaving only an aching soreness. Much as Ken's behavior had disgusted and terrified her, it was neither surprising nor out of character. Along with all his other problems, he was a con artist supreme, and she was a first-class dumbbell to have believed his lies. Lee and Rosa had been right all along, just as Peter was right about her gullibility. When would she learn?''

The policeman's overture, however, was completely unexpected. Because she was a woman living alone, and because she called about an attempted rape and wouldn't name the suspect, the officer assumed she'd invented the story to get someone to crawl in bed with her. Worse yet, the two men had a code. On a certain signal, one disappeared and waited in the car. How, she wondered, did they decide who would stay and who would leave? Did they take turns? How many times had they done this in the past?

She pondered what to do. If accused, the officers would take their grievances to a committee; there would have to be a hearing with lawyers involved and a whole big hullaballoo with her word against theirs, as well as lots of nasty, humiliating press. (Wouldn't the *Herald* just love the scandal? Especially with two of their columnists involved?)

There was Trina to consider, too. She had her hands full with the last sex caper, and public outrage was just beginning to subside. Something like this could start the whole cycle over again and make it doubly hard to convince the public that most law enforcement officers were honest, decent human beings who risked their lives routinely to make the city safe to live in. There was no way to win in this situation, Lauren reluctantly concluded; she could do nothing but hold her anger and her tongue. Someday, when she and Trina were alone, she would have her say.

The doorman sounded concerned when she called to alert him about Peter. He had seen Ken stalk out in a drunken fury, followed by a visit from two policemen, who came down in the elevator separately, and now another man was showing up at two or three in the morning? She explained she had had a problem with Ken, the police had arrived to take her complaint, a friend was coming over to be with her, and that something had to be done about security, especially in the garage. He promised he would look into it.

It was almost four A.M. when Peter walked into her waiting

arms. They embraced in a silence heavy with emotion, then sat on the couch and talked. She told him everything that happened that night, leaving out only the details of her previous involvement with Ken. Had he asked, she would not have lied; he never asked.

His first reaction was rage, followed by a look at her arm to assure himself it wasn't serious, then an overwhelming need to protect her. "I knew I shouldn't have let you come back alone," he said, furious at himself. "I should never have listened to your protestations that we had to sort out our professional lives before we planned our future. You know there's only one thing that matters, don't you?"

"Yes." The words poured out of her. "I love you so completely, Peter. I can't imagine a life apart from you—whatever changes or sacrifices it means."

His eyes flashed. "I told you once you had everything but my soul. I take it back. You've got that, too." He drew her close to him. "I fell in love with you the day you told me about Alice and I saw who you were behind that bewitching exterior. You showed me your heart that morning, and I knew I wanted it." He hesitated a moment, then he could contain himself no longer. "Shall we send Alice a wedding announcement?"

She backed away just far enough to see the question in his eyes. "Oh, darling, yes, yes!" she exclaimed, tightening her arms around him. "A thousand times yes. Let's have five weddings, so no one can ever keep us apart again!"

"I'm only getting married once," he declared, "and so are you." Before she could answer, his lips were on hers and he was untying the sash of her robe. The softness of her body under the silky nightgown excited him almost uncontrollably.

"I love you, my bride-to-be," he whispered. "Let me show you how much."

Hours later, Lauren gently broke from Peter's arms to tiptoe into the other room and leave word for Sara that she would not be at work that Monday. Then she crawled back under the covers and slept several hours more. They awoke to the noon whistle, and his worried voice asked, "Don't you have to be at your office?"

"No." She smiled. "Not when I've got a hunk like this in my bed. I called in already."

"You told them you had a hunk in your bed?"

"Not exactly." She snuggled up to his warm, bare chest. "But I do. And I'm not letting him get away."

"You're my woman," he said, clasping her to him. "The hell with all that nonsense about people not belonging to each other. You're the only thing I own, just as surely as you own me. A few material goods may come our way momentarily, until we die and they pass on to someone else. But you're mine for as long as we live, and God help anyone who tries to take you from me."

"And vice versa," she said happily. "Do you believe in God?"

"Yes. Not a gray-haired old man with a beard. I believe in a life force that's good and honest and manifests itself through love. I couldn't be mystical and romantic and awed by the depth of my feelings for you if I didn't believe in a stronger power. What about you?"

She raised up on an elbow. "I was a practicing Quaker for a few years. It's a beautiful religion, and sometimes I'm sorry I was too spoiled and selfish to stick with it. When I gave it up, I went through a period of doubts and cynicism. Every time I read of a brutal murder or tortures in Central America or any of the horrors of the so-called civilized world, I got angry and asked myself how a merciful God could allow such things."

"What was your answer?"

"That there is no merciful God, just as there is no justice. Anyone with two eyes knows that we're not born equal and we don't live equal lives."

"You're an atheist?" he asked.

"No," she said, kissing the tip of his nose. "I'm not even an agnostic. You've made me a believer again. But like you, I don't believe in a personal God who's looking out for us. I know there's something—some source of limitless energy and love that keeps us going. I just don't think it does much good to pray for things. Maybe it helps the person who's praying, but I doubt anyone's up there listening."

"I guess we won't be married in church, then." He smiled.

"Oh, yes, I want a church wedding! Don't you?"

"I want *you*. I don't give a pickled pig's foot how we formalize it or what rituals we go through. You make the plans and I'll be there." He looked puzzled a moment. "Where will I be?"

She had already decided. "We'll have the ceremony here in San Francisco, if that's okay. Then we'll move to Los Angeles right afterward. I'm sure I can find work there. If not, I can always—"

"Hold on," he interrupted. "You're not giving up your job and you're not moving anywhere. You're the one who's established. You have your column, your family, and all your ties here. I can't let you make that sacrifice for me."

"But I want to," she protested.

"No, sweetheart. I'm the one who's starting fresh—putting down roots. I can plant them here just as easily as there."

"You mean that? What about Margit? And the new building?"

"I had an hour at the airport before my plane. I called her and we talked. She's a good-hearted person, I know you two will get along. Naturally she was disappointed that I'd be moving away. But she was thrilled to hear I was getting married—"

"You told her before you asked me?"

He grinned. "I hoped the thought might have crossed your mind. She said she was positive she could sell the building with my newly furnished apartment for a lot more than she paid for it."

"I can't believe it! She wasn't hurt or angry after all that work?"

"No, just disappointed. She knew I was miserable when I arrived; now she knows why."

Lauren kissed his ear. "You're uncanny; you've thought of everything. If you're really willing to do that, I accept joyfully. That leaves us only one more hurdle."

"Victor?"

Her expression became pained. "I'm afraid so."

"Don't you think I can handle him?"

"You don't know him. No one can handle him. I love him, but he's impossible."

"Hmm. I've got it. We'll tell him we *have* to get married."

"And nine months from now?"

"We'll produce a baby." His arms crept around her slim body and drew her to him. "Let's get to work on it, shall we?"

Lauren felt herself grow taut with tension as she and Peter drove up to her parents' house early that evening. Edna had been thrilled to get their phone call and was anxious to meet her future son-in-law. The two women had discussed how to tell Victor; her mother had advised her to be strong and honest and face up to him. She was 100 percent supportive and promised to do what she could to keep him under control.

Lauren could see that neither Victor nor Edna was prepared for Peter's startling good looks. Along with his quiet dignity and air of easy confidence, he showed none of the "worried suitor" signs that characterized most of Lauren's admirers.

"Good evening, young man," said Victor, offering a hand. His inner alarms were ringing wildly; this was not the wimp he expected. "My daughter tells me you've been very nice to her."

"Your daughter's very easy to be nice to," he replied. His handshake was solid enough to convey self-assurance but not so solid as to be arrogant. "Lauren's told me a great deal about you both. I've been looking forward to our meeting."

Edna greeted her guest with a beaming smile and a wink. "My, you're handsome," she said. "Ann's fixing us some nibbles, then she'll get your drinks. Come in and sit down."

"How did you happen to be on the *Sea Viking*?" asked Victor, leading the way into the living room. He watched closely as Peter pulled up a chair for his hostess—a gesture that seemed natural rather than forced—and sat on the couch by Lauren.

"I was in private practice in New York for fifteen years, Mr. Wilde. It was time for a change, and I felt ready to open the clinic for skin treatment and research that I'd been thinking about for a number of years. A colleague told me the *Sea Viking* was looking for a doctor who spoke Norwegian to take this cruise—a 'working vacation,' he called it—"

"It wasn't much of a vacation," Lauren put in. "Peter worked eight to ten hours a day."

"Let him finish, dear."

"That's about it," said Peter. "I had never taken time off before, and I knew that once I got settled and established in my new location, I probably never would again. It was my only chance to see Norway and Europe." He paused and looked directly at Victor. "Of course, I'm very glad I went."

The message was getting through. "And now?" he asked. "What are your plans?"

"Dad," said Lauren quietly. "Peter and I love each other. Very much. We've had a lot of time together. We're both adults; we're not impulsive adolescents. We want to get married, and we want your blessing."

The silence was tense, but only momentary. Victor showed no reaction as he asked, "Don't you think that's a little impractical, living in two different cities?"

"We won't be," she answered. "Peter's going to start his clinic here instead of in L.A. He's changed all his plans so we can be together and you won't have to fly south to see your grandchildren."

Edna's eyes lit up. "Grandchildren?"

"Not at the moment, Mrs. Wilde." Peter laughed, amused at her eagerness.

Victor was not amused. "Lauren said you had family living in Los Angeles. How do they feel about having you move so far away?"

"My parents, unfortunately, are dead," Peter replied. "It's only my sister and her family. They realize San Francisco is a lot closer than New York, so at least we can visit each other. They understand the reasons for my decision."

"Decision?" Victor showed his first emotion. "You call it a decision when you've only known my daughter three or four weeks on some romantic cruise on a—a loveboat? Real life is quite different, Dr. Martian—"

"Marsten, Dad. But you can call him Peter."

"Please do." Victor's challenge was not unexpected. "I understand your concern, Mr. Wilde. If my daughter came home with a man she had known only a short time under such circumstances, I'm sure I'd have the same reaction. I can only try to make you understand that Lauren and I have both met a lot of people in our lives, and we've found qualities in each other that neither of us has known before. I realize this is sudden—and I would think it strange if you weren't apprehensive about me. I only ask that you get to know me and the kind of person I am—and that you give me a chance to show you I can make your daughter happy.''

"Those are lovely words," growled Victor. "You have a nice, smooth way of talking—"

"Victor!" Edna said sharply.

"Wait a minute, Edna. I'm not insulting anybody. You heard his piece; let me say mine.''

"Go ahead, Dad," said Lauren resignedly.

"Thank you." He bowed to her in mock gratitude, then directed his words to Peter. "There's something you should know about this family, and that is we don't believe in divorce. There's never been one in the Wilde clan, and as long as I have anything to say, there never will be. We consider marriage a serious, permanent contract.''

Lauren reached for Peter's hand and held it tightly.

"If you two kids think you really love each other," Victor continued, "that's fine. That's wonderful. I'm not against love. Your mother and I have been happily married for . . . how many years?''

"Thirty-four, dear.''

"That's right. Next year will be our thirty-fifth anniversary. And in all those years we've never had a harsh word or a fight.''

Lauren cleared her throat noisily.

"Well, maybe when we were younger," he conceded. "They weren't serious fights, were they, Edna?" No confirmation was forthcoming. His wife could think of innumerable times when she wished she had been capable of murder. "The point is, I'm not against you. I want Lauren to be settled and happy and have a family. She ought to have five or six children and forget this nonsense about trying to be a newspaper writer. She'll come to her senses someday. In the meantime, if this is what you both want, fine. Edna and I will give you our approval. All we want is that you take your time. Do it right. Don't rush into anything.''

"What does that mean?" asked Lauren. There had to be a catch.

"You're not even engaged, are you? Let us plan your engagement. Your mother and I will throw a big party at the hotel, and we'll introduce Dr. Martian to our friends. I'm sure they'll all want to entertain for you. That will give you time to get to know each other in a different setting. And it will give us six months or a year to plan the wedding."

"Dad, that's very generous of you. But we both have busy professions, and we don't want a lot of entertaining and parties. We just want a wedding as soon as possible, so we can settle down and get on with our lives."

Victor's eyes formed a menacing scowl. "In that case," he snapped, "my approval is out of the question."

The room fell suddenly silent. It was a tone even Edna knew better than to challenge.

Peter was the first to rise. He took Lauren's hand and led her toward the door. "Thanks for your hospitality, Mrs. Wilde. Yours, too, sir. I hope you'll reconsider. Your daughter loves you very much. It would make both of us very unhappy not to have your approval."

"Get out of my house," hissed Victor, unable to contain his anger any longer. "Get out of my sight and get out of my life, you goddamn quack!"

The front door slammed behind them as Peter and Lauren strode down the pathway to the car.

"I was afraid he might throw a tantrum," she said, taking his arm. "Please don't be too upset."

"I'm only mildly upset," he answered. "It's a good thing you warned me. I'm mainly worried about you. I know how close you two have been. You must be hurting terribly."

"It hurts," she admitted, "but you know, I can't even cry. I guess I'm kind of numb inside where Dad's concerned. He's done so many things like this to me—all in the name of love. It would have been foolish to think he'd behave like a normal father—or that he might be happy for us."

"He's not that abnormal, darling. He's obviously crazy about you, and along comes some character you picked up on a ship. He doesn't know the first thing about this guy, and the same day you bring him home, you announce you want to get married. That would be a shock to any parent.''

He helped her into the car, then hurried around to the driver's seat. ''I guarantee your dad will be on the phone to New York first thing tomorrow morning, and that's fine. He should check up on me. He wants to be sure I'm not some child molester or drug pusher or gold digger after his money—or your money, if you have any.'' A worried look crossed his forehead. ''Does he pay the rent for your penthouse?''

''Well, I own it. He gave it to me for my twenty-first birthday. But I have to pay fifteen hundred a month upkeep, and that comes from a trust which he controls.''

''I see.'' The light turned green, and the driver behind honked impatiently. ''Would you be very unhappy if we had to live in a less expensive place?''

She slid over next to him. ''I can't wait to move out of that fishbowl. It was great for a single girl who liked to give parties and show off and impress people. Luckily, my needs and my life have changed. When we sell it, we'll have enough to buy our own house somewhere—maybe in Marin or down the peninsula, not too close to my parents. Wouldn't you like that?''

''I'd like us to have a house,'' he said, still reflecting. ''Not with your money, though. You put that away in a bank. We don't need it. I have enough for a down payment.''

''It's *our* money, darling. Whatever I have is yours. Please don't think that way.''

''We'll see. It won't be a problem. I've always hated dealing with the stuff, and you don't seem to mind. Would you be in charge of the family finances?''

''Gladly.'' She looked out the window. ''Better go right next block, unless you want to stop for a hamburger or something.''

''Do you have any cans in the kitchen?''

''Does Ford have cars? Does Colonel Sanders have chicken? I have enough canned goods to stock a grocery. I also happen to make the greatest Campbell's tomato-rice soup you've ever tasted. Do you mind terribly that I can't cook?''

"Yes," he said, braking for the turn, "but I know a way you can make it up to me.''

# CHAPTER
# 11

THE PHONE RANG IN LAUREN'S APARTMENT AT NINE-
thirty Tuesday morning, after she had left for work. Peter was
getting ready to fly to Los Angeles and ignored it at first; then
he realized it might be Margit.

"Dr. Martian?" said an unexpected voice. "This is Victor
Wilde. I owe you an apology for my outburst last night."

"I can understand your feelings, Mr. Wilde. Let's forget it
ever happened."

"Well, I can't forget it that easily. I'd like to show you a
different side of me. Could you drop by my office this morning?"

"I'm catching the eleven o'clock plane."

"It's important, and I'm just across the street. I'll have my
driver take you to the airport."

Peter glanced at his watch. "Could I come right away?"

"I'll be waiting for you."

He thought of calling Lauren at work, then decided against
it. She would only worry, and whatever Victor wanted, he
could tell her about later.

Packing his immediate belongings in a briefcase, he scribbled "I love you" on the telephone pad, locked the door behind him, and hurried over to the hotel.

Dora's eyes widened as Peter introduced himself. "Go right in, doctor," she said, patting her hairpiece. "He's expecting you."

The garish office was a surprising contrast to the perfect taste and quiet elegance of the Wildes' home. Victor rose and came around his desk to shake hands. "Good of you to come. Have a seat. Cigar?"

"No, thanks."

"Don't smoke, eh? Smart boy." Victor resumed his chair, folded his arms, and sat back. "We don't have much time, so I'll get to the point."

Peter nodded assent.

"I like you. You strike me as a solid young man with a lot more going for him than most of the meatheads Lauren used to bring around. My wife likes you, too. Our only feeling is that you're rushing ahead too fast."

He paused to let his words sink in, then continued, "Before you change all your plans and move to San Francisco, I'd like to make you a proposal. I'll help you start that clinic in Los Angeles; it's only an hour away from here, as you know, and you and Lauren could see each other every weekend. All I ask in return is that you hold off your marriage plans for a year. Take your time, get to know each other in the real world, where people aren't waiting on you and serving you cocktails every five minutes."

Raising his hand to forestall the answer he saw coming, Victor hastened to his clincher: "Before you say anything, hear me out. I'm prepared to back up my suggestion with a cash gift to you of—one million dollars to build your clinic: 'Dr. Martian's Skin Clinic,' or whatever you want to call it. One *million* dollars, Dr. Martian, with no strings attached."

"That's very generous of you—"

"You're damn right it is."

"But I'm afraid I can't accept it."

Victor's brows came together menacingly. "Of course you can accept it. What do you mean?"

"Just what I said. There's no price on my love for Lauren. I couldn't bear living apart from her for a year."

"I see." The copper blotter rattled noisily under his thumping fingers. "Do you realize what you're turning down?"

"Yes, I do. As I said, I'm grateful to you. I feel sorry for all the suffering people that money would have helped. However, I can't accept it under those terms."

"Hmm." Victor looked thoughtful a moment, then his eyes came alive. "All right, if that's your decision, I'll make you a counteroffer—one I don't think you'll want to refuse."

Peter checked his wristwatch; the man was wasting both their time, but he had to hear him out. "Yes?"

"Don't build your clinic in Los Angeles, build it here. Right here in San Francisco—your name on it in big letters—'The Peter Martian Skin Clinic'—the same million dollars with no strings attached."

"My name is Marsten."

"Well, whatever. What do you think?"

"I think you have something more to tell me about your offer."

"You're no fool, Martian. I like that." Victor attempted a smile. "You're right; there is one little thing I would ask. Spend as much time as you like with Lauren. Get engaged, go out everywhere—you can even live together. I never thought I'd hear myself say that, but that's the way things are today, and I have to accept it."

"You mean live together without being married?"

"Only for a year. One year. Give yourselves a chance. If you still want to get married one year from today, I will give you the biggest, most beautiful, most lavish wedding the world has ever seen."

"You are amazing," Peter murmured, shaking his head in wonder. "All the things Lauren told me about you are true."

"Then we have a deal?"

"No deal." He stood up, placed his hands on the desk, leaned forward, and fixed its occupant firmly in his gaze: "Your daughter is thirty years old, and I'm almost forty. We want to settle down, have a family before we're too much older, and live like a normal married couple. We have no doubts of our love and our total commitment, and we see no reason to wait. We prefer to get married with your approval, but either way, our decision is not negotiable."

"Don't be stupid, Martian. Who's going to make you an offer of a million dollars *and* the girl, too?"

"I'm not shopping around for offers. Lauren is everything I want, our future is together, and nothing will keep us apart. Now, if you'll excuse me, I have to catch a plane. I hope to see you at the wedding."

"Wait!" The command was loud and threatening. Peter whirled around.

"If you don't take my offer, you will *not* see me at your wedding or at any time thereafter. You will have my complete and absolute disapproval, you and my daughter will not be welcome under my roof again—ever—and I will take immediate steps to dissolve her trusts and disinherit her completely."

An obscenity danced on the end of his tongue, but Peter maintained control, held his silence, and strode out the door.

"The driver's waiting for you in the lobby, Dr. Martian," chirped Dora, freshly perfumed.

"Thanks," he said. "Tell Mr. Wilde I'm taking a cab."

Twenty minutes before takeoff, Peter stopped at an airport phone. "I just saw your father," he told Lauren breathlessly.

"Oh, no!" Her voice was almost panicked. "Peter, for God's sake, don't let him—"

"I'm not letting him do anything, sweetheart, so relax. I was tempted to trade you in for a million dollars, but I decided against it."

"He offered you a million dollars? To do what—never see me again?"

"No, he's not that foolish." The ride to the airport had given Peter time to regain perspective. Even his sense of humor was returning. "A cool million for the Peter Martian Skin Clinic—"

"He still doesn't know your name?"

"He knows. It's part of his act. A million for the clinic with no strings attached. As long as I work in L.A. and you stay in S.F. When I turned that down I got a counteroffer. A million for the clinic and I can build it in San Francisco as long as we live in sin for a year and don't get married."

Her voice was frightened. "What did you tell him?"

"What do you think I told him? No deal. So he threatened

to dissolve your trusts and cut you out of his will. Can you stand living on a doctor's salary?"

"Oh, thank God." Her sigh was loud and relieved. "You did make it clear that we're getting married and there's nothing he can do to stop us?"

"I let him know he can't buy Peter Martian. Not for a sleezy million. Now two million—"

"Oh, quit joking. I told you he would stop at nothing. What will he do next?"

"Darling, there is only one other thing your father can do, and that's hire a hit man to bump me off. And by the time the fellow gets to L.A. I'll be back in San Francisco."

"You're too much." She sighed. "Will you call me tonight?"

"Yes." He blew a kiss into the phone. "We're going house-hunting this weekend, so save the want ads. The sooner I can get you out of that glass menagerie, the better."

When Peter returned to San Francisco on Friday, he brought the good news that Margit had sold the medical building for a 20 percent profit, which he insisted she keep. He had packed up all his books and personal effects for her to send as soon he had an address, so he had no further reason to go back. Lauren had been equally busy. Her penthouse was on the market for a staggering $4.8 million, an amount proposed by the real estate agent, and more than ten times what Victor had paid for it in 1977.

She had also arranged for the wedding to take place three weeks hence, on Sunday, October 9, at the small Swedenborgian Church in Presidio Heights, which had the distinction of being nonsectarian as well as close to the family home. Edna would give a reception afterward in the chapel garden—with or without her husband.

Ever since the day Peter walked out of his office, Victor had pointedly refused to discuss the wedding and forbidden his wife to attend or have anything to do with it. As usual, Edna kept silent and did as she pleased. Sixty couples were already on her guest list. The invitations would come from Lauren Angelina Wilde and Peter Frederik Marsten, M.D.;

thus the absence of Victor's name would not be conspicuous, and Edna could still hope for his presence.

Trina was thrilled to hear they had set a date and immediately rescheduled an interview with *60 Minutes* in order to be matron of honor. Missy Edwards, Zelda Wilde, and Margit Marsten Banks would be Lauren's bridesmaids; Christopher Wilde, Scott Bellamy, and Margit's husband, George Banks, would be ushers. Peter's roommate in medical school was flying out to be best man.

That night, Lauren took Peter to meet her brother and sister-in-law for the first time. Zelda cooked her typical vegetarian dinner and was unusually warm to Lauren, Mallory felt ignored and peed in the flower pot, two cocker spaniels chased a Siamese cat around the table, and Peter relaxed and enjoyed the family feeling.

It disturbed him, however, to learn that Victor had threatened to disown his son if he attended the wedding. "That'd be okay with me." Chris laughed. "I'd just sell my interest in the hotel, buy a big yacht, and Zel and Mallory and I could sail around the world and be bums." Chris assured Peter that no living being, including his formidable father, could keep him from his sister's wedding. Their mutual love for her made them immediate friends.

The next day Lauren and Peter visited the pastor to discuss details of the wedding, and on Sunday they looked at several homes in San Mateo and Hillsborough, then crossed the Golden Gate Bridge and found one in Sausalito they liked immediately. Repairs and painting were needed, but the house had a fireplace in the bedroom, his and her bathrooms, a large sunken living room, and a spacious terrace with a panoramic view of the bay. Their bid was accepted, and to their delight, the sale was confirmed.

Toward the end of the week, Lauren looked up from her work one morning to find Ken Ferriday standing by her desk. It was the first time she had seen him since the night he attacked her; the sight of him gave her a cold chill.

"Got a minute?" he asked cheerfully.

"No!"

He ignored her hostility. "I guess I screwed up my chance

to get you to put in a good word to Trina about me. I hear she's looking for a new press secretary."

The man was incredible. "Go away."

"I hear you're getting married. Will I be invited to the festivities?"

"Go away!"

"You still owe me a lunch, you know."

Her voice lowered. "What I owe you, Ken Ferriday, are charges of mail harassment, attempted rape, and brutality. I called the police after you left that night and made a report. If you ever come near me again, so help me, I'll press those charges and I'll make them stick." She turned her back to him angrily and began typing on her VDT.

The words "attempted rape and brutality" seemed to have a quieting effect on him. They would not look good in his dossier, nor would a police record help his long-term political goals. "So I had a few drinks—big deal." He shrugged and walked quickly down the hall. Something in his voice told her she had gotten to him—that she would not be bothered again.

Later that morning, a call from Amelia Martin summoned her to Walter Belloc's office. The publisher was wearing his "old family friend" persona when she entered.

"Well, well," he chortled, coming out from behind his desk and taking her hands. "Here comes the beaming bride. Felicitations, my dear. I hear your lucky Lothario is quite a prize. When's the happy day?"

"Two weeks from Sunday," she said, feeling no urge to kiss his cheek. It pleased her to realize they were on professional terms, now. Her column was popular and her work consistent; she had earned the right to be confident. "Did you get your invitation?"

"Yes, I believe I did, thank you. Have a seat, my lamb. How does my oldest and dearest friend Victor feel about this rather sudden twist of events?"

She perched on a chair and tilted her head. "Guess."

"Knowing your father as I have for some thirty-odd years, I'd say he's spitting bullets. First Uncle Walter comes along to tempt his darling daughter into a life of sin and depravity. Poppa sends her sailing across the globe to spirit her away from this evil, and she returns with something far worse—a husband! Oh, Victor, Victor, if only I had a heart, it would bleed for you. . . ."

"Daddy's really suffering," she said, unamused. "And so are Mom and Peter and Chris—he's making all of us miserable. He's my one big heartache at a time when everything else is so wonderful."

"Can I expect to see his happy face at the wedding?"

"Not even his unhappy face. He's forbidden Mom to go, but she's not paying any attention to him. He says he's disowning me and Chris—that's okay, too. It's just all so unnecessary. If Peter were a dope addict or a murderer or something, I could understand his attitude—"

"Don't you understand his attitude?"

"Yes, I'm afraid I do." She stared down at the floor. "I think my getting married—his losing control of me, so to speak—is the one thing he's feared practically since I was born. He's always scared off any man who was interested in me. I know about a lot of the things he's done—I shudder to think of the things I don't know about."

Walter looked thoughtful, clasped his hands together, then unclasped them. "Well, my chicken, I see no reason to let that unreasonable rooster of a father ruin a perfectly glorious wedding day. Or a career. You've brought femininity, wit, humor, and the fresh scent of orchids to the fourth estate— that is, if orchids have a scent, which is irrelevant. You won't deprive us of your remarkable gifts, will you?"

"I love my work. I wouldn't give it up for anything." Except Peter, she thought, remembering her offer to move south. "I'm grateful to you for giving me a start."

"Tosh." He scowled. "Gratitude is for politicians and other no-talent wretches. You, my dear, are a delicate blossom with many years to bloom. And I shall be honored to watch you glide down the aisle. By the way, on whose strong arm will you be gliding? Might I have that honor?"

Her face fell. "That's one of the things we've been worried about. Why . . . . yes—why not? That would be fine—" She stopped with a sudden realization. "Oh, dear. Poor Daddy—"

"Yes, Daddy dearest will undoubtedly be the first man in space without a rocket when he hears that the dean of debauchery is taking over his filial duties." The publisher cackled. "Can't say I feel too sorry about that."

"It's his own doing," she murmured to herself, trying to sort out her feelings. "I guess I can't worry about what's going to upset him and what isn't." She hoisted her shoulder bag and headed toward the door. "The wedding's at four, so be there about three-thirty, okay?"

"Okay it is, my sweet. I shall be decked out in full regalia for this gala event, and assuming no objection, I shall be accompanied by a photographer."

She read his mind. The old goat wanted Victor to see a picture of him giving her away. The man was heartless—a sadist—a fiend. Still, the chapel would be awash in photographers and possibly a TV crew or two. One more camera would make little difference.

"That's fine." She nodded resignedly. "I'll see you in church."

The days flew by in a haze of work and wedding plans. A businessman from Hong Kong and a sheikh from Kuwait had both made offers on the penthouse. It was only a matter of who would come up with the asking price first. Peter was also looking at properties. Lauren wanted to invest the profits of the apartment sale in real estate, and what better investment than an office building with space for a skin clinic?

As the nuptials drew closer, Victor grew more and more irascible. Edna reported that he refused to go out. Wherever they went, people offered congratulations and asked about the wedding, and it was more than he could handle. Or wanted to. She feared it was affecting his health. He had no appetite for his favorite foods and even stopped smoking cigars. They had separate bedrooms, but she could hear him mumbling to himself and pacing back and forth throughout the night.

Lauren was troubled, too. She wrote her father an impassioned letter, explaining that they were all worried about him, begging him to relent and bring the family together again. Dora told her he tore it up without reading it. Knowing Lauren's unhappiness, Peter phoned on his own and asked if could see and talk with Victor. Dora had to convey her employer's refusal.

The day before the wedding, Lauren called his private number at the office. "Daddy?" was all she could say before he hung up. That night, Peter talked to her.

"You mustn't let Victor spoil tomorrow for us," he said firmly. "You've done everything possible to try to change his mind. If you ask me, you've done more than he deserves. We've both crawled on our knees to him—your mother, too. I tried to understand him at first, and I was sympathetic. But his selfishness—his stubbornness—is making a lot of people miserable, and I'm sick of it. I refuse to let him hurt you anymore."

"He doesn't realize what he's doing—"

"That's the dumbest thing I've ever heard you say! Love him all you want, but don't underestimate him. I warn you, he's a very scheming man. Even right now, wherever he is, he's making us argue, and we shouldn't be."

"You're right, darling. I'm sorry." She walked over to him. "Hold me?"

"My greatest pleasure," he said, drawing her to his chest. "Now, stop worrying about something you can't change and get your beauty sleep. I don't want a bride with bags under her eyes."

The early afternoon was warm and mild as the October sun broke through an overcast sky. Victor and Edna had eaten lunch in silence, and she had returned to her bedroom. A sharp knock made her turn around; her husband was approaching the dressing table.

"Why are you putting on makeup?" he demanded. "You're not going anywhere."

Edna stared at his face in the mirror. It was sad and broken, and she almost felt pity. "I'm going to my daughter's wedding."

"You're not going anywhere. I forbid it!"

Wheeling around on her stool, she glared at him. "I've lived with your tyranny for thirty-five years, Victor B. Wilde, and for reasons I often wondered about, I've loved you with all my heart. I still love you. But right now, I don't give a damn what you forbid. I'm going to my daughter's wedding."

It was the first time she had openly defied him; the idea

that he was powerless over the one person who had always stood by him, right or wrong, was shattering. He knew it was useless to argue. It was even useless to try to intimidate her. He only had one play left.

"I'll . . . leave you, Edna," he stammered, his voice barely above a whisper. "I swear I'll leave you if you go. You'll never see me again as long as you live."

She continued to powder her cheek. This was the moment she had spent hours preparing for and dreading. Over and over in her mind, she had rehearsed how to react, how to pretend unconcern for everything he might possibly do or threaten—including divorce.

Again she turned to face him. Her voice was calm and controlled. "I'll miss you, dear. I really will miss you."

Shock and disbelief followed her announcement. His wife and his daughter, the two women he had loved and would gladly have given his life for all those years, were willing to hurt him this way—to ignore his pleas and exhortations, when all he was doing was looking out for their happiness. His stunned realization turned into the fury of a man betrayed, and he spun around and stormed out of the room. Edna bit her lip and reached for the mascara.

"I'll miss you, dear," she said softly, "I really will."

The clock struck three-thirty as Victor sat solemnly in his leather armchair, staring out the bay window at the city—his city, his family's city—with its blue-green water sparkling beneath the Golden Gate Bridge. The combination of man and nature was unbeatable, he reflected, when one so gracefully enhanced the other. He had been staring at that view for over an hour, trying to forget the heaviness in his heart, the deep sadness that engulfed him.

He could easily imagine what a spectacular bride his daughter would be, all in white, with a lacy veil flowing behind her as she walked. That Peter was a handsome man, he had to admit. But a fool. Anyone who couldn't wait a year for a million dollars wasn't a fit husband for his daughter. You didn't get ahead in this world by being a reckless romantic or refusing to take the advice of those who knew better.

They would be sorry someday. They would all be sorry.

Or would they? He could almost hear their cries of joy and merriment about to start, while he sat home desperately unhappy. The only one suffering at the moment, it seemed, was he.

He had heard Edna leave the house over an hour ago, taking the car and driver. She would look radiant and beautiful, he thought. She had always been an elegant lady. His mother had been right to push him to marry her. What would Edna answer—what would the rest of his family answer when friends asked for him at the church? What excuse could possibly keep him from his beloved daughter's wedding? Well, that was their problem; let them worry about it.

The wind was coming up, beginning to rustle the trees in the garden. Edna would have to talk to the gardener—wait a minute, what gardener? What Edna? He had promised to leave his wife if she disregarded his wishes, and he never made idle threats. The walls in his study were heavy with plaques and trophies, medals, honors, awards—all for promises he had made and promises he had kept. He wasn't a man to go back on his word. But had he given his word? And if so, was it unbreakable? What good were all those pieces of paper on his wall without his family? What did honors mean when you had no one to be proud of you? What would life be without Edna? Without Thanksgiving and Christmas and anniversaries and birthdays? Without his squealing grandson running trains around the living room? Without Lauren to call him Daddy and brush off his coat and scold him about his cigars?

Brooding over his thoughts, he became aware of the ticking of the mantel clock. Three forty-five, only fifteen minutes before the wedding—his wedding. His little girl was getting married, about to start a new life—have her own home and children and grandchildren that he would never know. And why? Because he was stubborn. And unforgiving. And tyrannical. And stupid! His family was the only goddamn thing in the world he really cared about. He still had time; the church was only five minutes away. He could grab his suit and make it. . . .

No. That would be giving in. Yes, that would be giving in. It would make them all happy. It would make him happy. He wouldn't lose his wife or his children. Or his friends, or his standing in the community. They wouldn't have to ask for him or gossip about why he stayed away. They wouldn't be able to say the Wildes were a divided family. There had never been a divorce in six generations, and by God, there never would be.

"Call me a cab!" he bellowed into the intercom. The resounding silence told him Edna had taken all the help to the wedding. Grabbing the phone, he dialed 911. "This is an emergency, operator. Get me a police car as fast as you can— and I mean *fast*!" He rattled off his address, hung up, and dashed into the bedroom. He had barely tied his tie when the car arrived. Two policemen jumped out and pounded on the door.

He ran downstairs and opened it. "My daughter's getting married in three minutes," he cried. "You've got to get me to the church!"

The officers recognized him and asked no questions. "Climb in, Mr. Wilde. We'll do our best."

Policemen, chauffeurs, photographers, TV crews, and crowds of curious onlookers were gathered outside the iron gates of the small stone chapel on Lyon Street when the sound of a siren made everyone turn. The police car zoomed up to the entrance, and its occupant leaped out.

One of the guards barred his way. "Where's your invitation?"

"I don't need a goddamn invitation—I'm the father of the bride!" Several of the spectators hooted and cheered as the guard quickly stepped aside.

"Yessir, Mr. Wilde. Sorry, sir."

The choir was just finishing its refrain as Victor rushed into the lobby, where the bridal party was waiting. The maids and ushers were already halfway down the aisle, and Lauren stood nervously—looking prettier than he could have imagined—the most exquisite bride he had ever seen.

The sight of Walter holding on to her filled him with rage. "What the hell are *you* doing here?" he thundered, shoving him aside.

Walter brushed off his tuxedo indignantly. "I must say, Victor, your timing is despicable."

Lauren stared at her father, unable to believe. He grasped

her arm as the organ broke into the familiar strains. "D-daddy," she whispered, "you'll never know—"

"You didn't think I'd let you get married without me, did you, baby?"

Peter stood at the altar, hypnotized with pride and happiness, unable to take his eyes off his future wife as she walked slowly toward him. Moments later, he looked up to see Victor handing her to him, tears streaming down his face. "Take—good care of her, son," he choked.

As if Victor's presence were exactly what he had been expecting, Peter nodded silently and turned his attention to his bride as they waited for the wedding march to end. Victor found Edna in the first row.

"Isn't she the loveliest thing you've ever seen?" he whispered, sitting beside her. "Do you think he'll make her as happy as I make you?"

Edna turned to him with a smile in her eyes. "I don't know, dear," she said, taking his hand. "That's an awfully big order."

# The
# Best Modern Fiction
## from
# BALLANTINE